KILL ME ONCE, KILL ME TWICE

CLARA KENSIE

Kill Me Once, Kill Me Twice by Clara Kensie

First edition.

Published by Snowy Wings Publishing, PO Box 1035, Turner, OR 97392

Cover designed by RebecaCovers.

ISBN: 978-1-948661-49-2

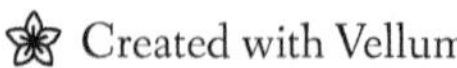

MORE YA BOOKS BY CLARA KENSIE

Deception So Series:

Deception So Deadly

Deception So Dark

~

Aftermath

For M:
I.D.I.M.W.

CHAPTER ONE

EVER ~ PRESENT DAY

Seventy-three percent: that's my probability of dying today.

As a healthy American seventeen-year-old female who makes a point of avoiding risky and dangerous behavior, my chance of dying on any other day is only 0.02 percent. But today, as I sit in my high school's overheated conference room for an interview with the scholarship committee, I estimate that my racing heart has a seventy-three percent chance of exploding.

My fingers tremble as they fiddle with the plastic daisy charm on my necklace, so I drop my hands to my lap. I have no reason to be nervous. The Lily Summerhays Memorial Scholarship is mine. It has to be.

With solemn faces, the committee sits in a row behind the long, glossy table at the front of the room. Propped on a sturdy wooden easel is an oversized framed poster of Lily Summerhays's senior yearbook portrait, taken eighteen years ago, a few weeks before she died.

With her demure smile, shy blue-eyed gaze, and copper hair falling straight down her back, it feels like she's here too.

In a way, Lily really *is* here. But I'm the only one who knows that.

A tapping noise echoes around the room. I've gained control of my hands, but my nerves have made their way down my body all the way to my feet, making me jitter-tap the heels of my black ballet flats on the tile floor. I force my legs to remain still.

I smile with what I hope is confidence at the committee. One by one, I meet the gazes of the five people who will determine my future:

1. Mrs. Summerhays: Head of the Ryland Beautification Committee, a former Miss Teen Indiana, co-founder of the Lily Summerhays Memorial Scholarship, and Lily's mother. She smiles back, polite but detached, and runs her manicured fingertips over her auburn French twist.

2. Mr. Summerhays: Lily's father and founder and CEO of Agri-So, Ryland's largest employer. His hair and suit are the color of a storm cloud. He's busy reading my scholarship application and doesn't look up at me at all.

3. Principal Duston: the no-nonsense principal of Ryland High, hair so blond it's almost white. In his mid-thirties, he replaced the previous principal when she retired two years ago. My former principal loved me and would have definitely voted for me to get the scholarship, but I don't think Principal Duston even knows who I am. We've spoken only once, when he congratulated me at last year's National Honor Society induction ceremony. He doesn't look up at me now. Instead, he gives Mr. Summerhays the side-eye and chomps the toothpick in his mouth.

4. Diana Buckley: The principal's administrative assistant, the other co-founder of the Lily Summerhays Memorial Scholarship, and Lily's best friend. Miss Buckley's glossy pink lipstick sparkles under the florescent lights, but her smile is strained, and she meets my gaze for only a moment before turning away.

5. Coach Nolan: Beloved, legendary baseball coach of the Ryland High Warriors, human teddy bear, and the father of Courtney

Nolan, who is *my* best friend. He usually wears a Warriors baseball jersey and hat, but today he's wearing a sport jacket and tie, and nothing on his balding head. He gives me an encouraging wink.

"Hi, I'm—" I say, then clear my throat and start again. "Hi, I'm Ever Abrams. Thank you so much for this opportunity. It's an honor to be a finalist for the Lily Summerhays Scholarship. I promise you if I win the scholarship, I'll make you proud." I rehearsed this opening a dozen times last night and this morning, but my voice is still shaky.

"It says here you applied to only one college." Mr. Summerhays looks at me over his glasses. "Griffin University. Do you think that was a wise decision?"

"Griffin is the only college I can go to," I say. "I've already been accepted."

"Why is it the only one?" Coach Nolan prompts. He's a big guy, massive actually, but his tone is gentle, encouraging.

"It's only a half hour away," I say. "I need to stay here in Ryland so I can take care of my little brother." I point through the open door. Joey's kneeling in the hallway, playing with his Matchbox cars. Our dad's old Warriors baseball cap hangs sideways on his head.

As if on cue, he lifts his head and smiles, showing his missing front teeth. He shouts, "I'm being very quiet, Ever!"

The committee bursts into laughter. Mrs. Summerhays goes, "*Awww.*" Thank goodness.

"Yes, you are, buddy," I say. "Just a few more minutes, okay?" I hold my finger up to my lips.

"Okay!" he shouts, even louder than before.

The committee is still chuckling when I turn back to them. "I promised I'd buy him a new Matchbox if he's quiet during the interview. Sorry. He's trying."

"He's adorable," Mrs. Summerhays coos. "Why are *you* taking care of him?"

I bring my fingers back to the daisy charm. "Our mom died three years ago. Ovarian cancer. I was fourteen. Joey was two." Mrs. Summerhays clucks sympathetically.

"And your father?" Mr. Summerhays asks.

"He's a truck driver for Siegel Freight and Transport," I say. "He's gone a lot."

Coach Nolan gives the committee a pitying, confirming nod. "Despite her hardships, Ever is one of the school's brightest and most responsible students."

My cheeks heat at the compliment, and I send him a silent *thank-you* for his support. Even without my other, secret reason for wanting this scholarship, my excellent grades and poor financial status should be enough to win it. But it's not a guarantee. Coach told me that the other finalist is Michael Granz. Michael's family has more money than mine does, but he's founder of the environmental club, president of the 4-H club, and a two-time finalist in the Science Olympiads. The scholarship decision all comes down to this interview. That's why I need to be perfect.

"What do you plan to major in?" Miss Buckley asks me, tossing back her chestnut hair and crossing her thin ankles under the table. Her red high heels make the bows on my ballet flats look silly and childish.

"Business," I say. "Accounting, specifically." A safe career, a career I can have in Ryland, rated one of the safest towns in Indiana and maybe the entire country. With friendly neighbors, an old-fashioned Main Street, and acres of lush farmland, we haven't had a single major crime here since Lily Summerhays was murdered in a home invasion almost eighteen years ago. Her killer, a drug-dealing thief named Vinnie Morrison, was apprehended immediately after. He's now on death row at Indiana State Prison, scheduled for execution in April, exactly five weeks from today.

Yes, Ryland is safe. And no one has ever died doing accounting. Once I get my degree, I'm going to be the accountant for my boyfriend's family's diner, The Batter's Box.

Mrs. Summerhays turns her wrinkle-free face to stare longingly at Lily's poster. "That's exactly what Lily was going to do," she says wistfully. "Major in business at Griffin University." Her gaze ping-pongs between Lily and me. A thin crease appears between her eyebrows.

I touch my daisy charm again. Does she... Does she see something? I look nothing like Lily did—she was tall and slender with porcelain skin, blue eyes, and long, copper hair, and I'm short and curvy with a light olive complexion, brown eyes, and dark blonde hair to my shoulders. But does Mrs. Summerhays recognize something in me? A hint of Lily? Did Lily play with her necklace when she was nervous too? I drop my hands back to my lap.

"Jacquelyn." Mr. Summerhays slides my application to her and gives it two rapid taps with his index finger. "Look at her birthday."

Mrs. Summerhays gasps. "Oh! Oh my. April 5th, eighteen years ago. You were born on the day Lily died."

Now everyone's gaze shoots up at me. Principal Duston stops chewing his toothpick. I swallow, shuffle my feet. Resist the urge to touch my daisy charm again.

The scholarship application didn't ask for my time of birth, but if it did, it would have shown that I was born at 9:48 p.m. on April 5th, almost exactly eighteen years ago. A few moments after Lily took her last breath, I took my first.

I don't remember anything about being Lily Summerhays, just the last few moments of her life as she lay sprawled on the floor of her living room, hurt and bloody and terrified. The last thing she saw was a tattoo of two crossed hatchets on Vinnie Morrison's wrist as he raised a sparkly pink paperweight high above her. "You left me no choice," he growled, just before slamming the paperweight into her skull.

Red hot terror shoots through my veins as sharp pain explodes in my head above my right eyebrow. I bite my lips to keep from crying out and fight the urge to check for blood—there is no blood, it's just a memory, a death-memory—and I breathe the pain away.

One...

Two...

Three.

When the deathpain clears, Miss Buckley is smoothing her already smooth hair with her slender, pale fingers. "Every year in Lily's memory, we give one Ryland High senior a full, four-year scholarship to the college of their choice. Previous winners of the scholarship have gone on to become leaders in business, technology, journalism, medicine, and politics. We work all year long to raise funds, and we have the financial support of Brandon Lennox, star of the New York Yankees and graduate of Ryland High. What can you say that will convince us to give the scholarship to *you* this year?"

What should I say? What *could* I say? I can't tell them that I was Lily Summerhays in my most recent past life. I can't tell them that I've lived hundreds of times before, in different countries and as different races and ethnicities, and that moments after one death, I'm reborn into the nearest new body. I can't tell them that I remember nothing of my past lives, that I remember only my deaths. I've died both male and female, young and old, by accident and injury, by illness and old age. I can't tell them that with every memory of a past death, I re-experience the terror, the loss, the pain.

I can't tell them that by giving the Lily Summerhays Memorial Scholarship to me, they'll be giving it to Lily as well.

CHAPTER TWO

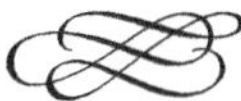

LILY ~ EIGHTEEN YEARS AGO

Four weeks. That's when I'd know if I would live or if I would die.

My decision letter from Carroll-Freywood Global University was supposed to come in four weeks. If I got in, I would live. If I didn't, I would die. Simple as that. Just

keel

over

and

die.

I flipped open the hollowed-out wooden globe that I kept in the corner of my bedroom and pulled out the course catalog from CFGU. The multi-ethnic students on the cover smiled brightly in the foreground with the Parthenon and the Sahara and the Great Wall of China in the background. Every semester in a different country. I wanted it so bad it hurt.

With a sigh, I hid the catalog back inside the globe and closed it again, then dug through the jumble of clothes on my floor to find my black lace-up boots.

"Lily. You're late." My mother appeared in my doorway. It wasn't even 8 a.m. yet, and she was already dressed in a skirt and heels, her hair up in a perfect twist. And her look wouldn't be complete without her crossed arms and her lips in an angry frown, directed at me.

Nope, eight hours of sleep hadn't done a thing to lessen her anger at me for driving my car into Mr. Kammer's tree last night. It was more of a tap than a crash, and my car was hardly dented, but now I had four weeks to prove to my parents that I was not, as they said, irresponsible and reckless. They'd never let me go to college overseas if they still thought I was irresponsible.

Of course, even if I were accepted to CFGU, my parents would probably kill me when they found out I'd applied against their wishes. They wanted me to go to Griffin University, a small, snobby, private college that was only a half hour away from Ryland. I'd already been accepted to Griffin, along with my best friend, Diana. We were going to room together in the dorms. But if I got into CFGU, she'd understand why I had to go there instead of Griffin. Diana wanted me to be happy, unlike my parents, who only wanted me to behave.

"Almost done," I told Mom. "I'm just looking for my boots." There they were—easy to spot under my pile of purses because yesterday during math class I used Diana's nail polish to paint pink hieroglyphics all over them.

"You didn't do your hair," Mom said.

"Ran out of time." *Doing my hair* meant blow-drying it straight, something that would take me the better part of an hour. I inherited my wild red hair from her. Well, she could waste every day of her life straightening *her* hair, but I didn't have the patience for that, or the desire. My curls would bounce back by noon anyway.

I checked the clock. 7:46. Already? I really *was* late. As punishment for my little car accident last night, my parents had taken away my car for a month. They were also making me work at my dad's enriched-soil manufacturing plant until I paid for my reckless driving ticket, the repairs to my car, and the damage I'd done to Mr. Kammer's lawn. And to his mailbox.

Everyone thought I hadn't been paying attention to the road or that I'd been lost in another daydream. I would tell them the *real* reason I'd lost control of the car, but they'd never believe me.

Mom's frown deepened as she surveyed my room. Drawers open, desk cluttered, globe littered with yellow circle stickers. She probably wished I had a pink floral bedspread, frilly white curtains, and shelves lined with more shiny pageant trophies. Instead, I stitched international flags together to hang over my windows, and I covered the cotton-candy pink paint on my walls with travel posters.

Instead of telling me to clean my room, she found something else to criticize. "Stop playing with your necklace. You'll break the chain."

I dropped my diamond pendant. I didn't realize I'd been playing with it. "I'll straighten my hair when I get home from work, okay?" I tell Mom. "And I'll clean my room. Promise." I gave her cheek a good-bye kiss like good, well-behaved daughters do, and rushed out of the house.

The early-March air was unseasonably warm, but the sky was gray and the trees were bare as I hurried four blocks over to the movie theater on Main Street. I made a mental note to stop by the theater on my way home today to see if Neal Mallick was there. I needed to tell him what had really happened when I crashed my car last night. He was the only person I trusted with my secret, and even though he was a total brainiac science nerd, he believed me.

I slipped into the alley behind the movie theater. Vinnie Morrison usually hung out by the dumpster back there, but he didn't scare me. Nothing scared me—except being stuck in Ryland for the rest of my life, and especially dying here.

But today, I was the only person in the alley. Vinnie Morrison wasn't loitering by the dumpster. Eight in the morning must be too early to make drug deals.

At the end of the alley I slid though the chain-link fence behind

Smiley's Used Cars and followed the train tracks through the patch of woods that surrounded Old Sutton Farm, all the way to Deep Creek. As I crossed Railroad Bridge over the creek, a little silvery fish swimming in the murky water below caught my eye. I stopped on the tracks and watched it flutter back and forth. That fish was so lucky. If it wanted, it could swim to the river, all the way north until it fed into Lake Michigan. Then it could swim through the rest of the Great Lakes, then eventually into the Atlantic Ocean. It could wind up in Europe, or Africa, or Asia, or Australia. Where *I* should be. Where I'd lived once, twice, a hundred times. Where I had adventures and died in exciting ways doing exciting things.

All I wanted to do was visit those places I'd once lived in, to explore the different countries and cultures of this world. To dig

and climb

and discover

and *experience*.

That little fish could go anywhere it wanted in the world, while I was stuck here in Ryland.

CHAPTER THREE

EVER ~ PRESENT DAY

Instead of telling the scholarship committee that I was Lily in my most recent past life, I tell them a much simpler reason why I should win the money, but a reason just as true. "My mother never went to college, and before she died, she made me promise her that I would. This scholarship is the only way I can afford it."

"What about student loans?" Miss Buckley says flatly.

"I do qualify for a Stafford loan," I say. "But that's just a few thousand. My dad would need to take out a Parent-Plus loan for the rest, but he doesn't qualify. His credit is too bad."

"Grants?" Miss Buckley says. "Other scholarships?"

"I've won other scholarships, small ones," I say, "and I have a grant from the state. But it's not enough. Not for Griffin."

"Savings?" asks Miss Buckley.

"My parents started a college savings account for me. But my mom was sick for so long. They didn't have good insurance, and the bills kept coming. They're still coming..." My voice is all high and pitchy. I'm ruining it, and I don't want to alarm Joey, so I calm myself. "There are no savings left."

"You could go to the community college in Eastfield," she says.

I shake my head. "I've taken so many AP courses that I've tested out of most gen eds, and the community college doesn't offer the advanced courses I'd need for a degree in accounting."

"What will you do if we choose the other candidate, Ever?" Mrs. Summerhays asks, not unkindly.

I can only shrug. I have no backup plan. I *have* to win that scholarship. I can't let down my mom, and I can't let down Lily.

Miss Buckley stacks my application and pushes it aside. "That's all we have time for today. Thank you, Miss Abrams."

It's over? Already? "But wait. Let me show you my spreadsheet." I open the file folder next to me and pull out a paper that shows exactly how I'll spend the scholarship money. I've calculated it down to the penny. "Tuition at Griffin is expensive, but I'll be living at home so I won't need room and board. I'll commute by bus to save money on gas and car insurance. And see this column? It's for books. I can order used textbooks, or even digital textbooks when I can, and save a lot of money—"

Miss Buckley holds up her palm. "I can see that you'd be an excellent accountant, Miss Abrams, but it's time for our next interview."

Mr. Summerhays picks up his phone and scrolls with his thumb. Principal Duston moves his toothpick from one side of his mouth to the other.

"That's it, then?" I ask.

"I guess so," Coach Nolan says. He beams at me and mouths, "Good job."

"It was wonderful to meet you, Ever," Mrs. Summerhays says. "We'll announce the winner at the ceremony next month." She pulls out the other application and scans it.

"Okay, well, then, thank you so much." I stand, smooth my skirt, and tuck my hair behind my ears. I survived the interview. My heart did not explode. My probability of dying today has returned to 0.02 percent. But did I blow it? Have I spent too much time focusing on grades? Should I have joined more clubs and activities, entered beauty pageants? Was I too different from Lily? Too similar?

I can't help touching my daisy charm again as I head for the door. I look over my shoulder to give the committee one last smile laced with fake confidence and slam into something hard enough to knock me to the floor.

Enormous scuffed black boots. Tree-trunk legs in black jeans that are faded at the knees. Black leather jacket over a white button-down shirt. Loose black tie. Hard onyx eyes. Long, tousled black hair.

Ash Morrison. What is *he* doing here?

"Morrison!" Principal Duston jumps out of his chair. "Why are you in this building today? Get out."

Ash Morrison is a senior like me, but he can't be here to interview for the scholarship. He wouldn't dare even *apply* for the scholarship. Not him.

"Miss Buckley said my interview is at 10:30," he says, crossing the room in three big strides and taking a seat, knees spread wide, in the chair I'd just vacated. He nods at the committee, gives a rehearsed smile. "Hello, I'm—"

"We know who you are," Mr. Summerhays rumbles.

"Diana?" Mrs. Summerhays stammers, looking at Miss Buckley. "You *told* him to come?" She double-checks the application in her hands. "The other candidate is a boy named Michael Granz. We all agreed. How could you make such a mistake?"

"It wasn't a mistake," Miss Buckley says evenly, her chin thrust out in defiance. "I replaced Ash's name with Michael's because I knew the committee would reject Ash on the first round without even reading his application. I only changed his name and a few other identifying details. The grades and financial information are his. You all kept passing the application on to the final round."

"Does Michael know you used his name?" Coach Nolan asks.

"No. But this was the only way the committee would be impartial. You know I'm right."

Principal Duston moves his toothpick from the right side of his mouth to his left. "Diana. I appreciate that you always look out for the troubled kids at this school. But *him*?" He looks at Ash with undisguised hatred. "I don't care how many A's he gets. Do you know how many problems he causes? How many times he's been suspended? Arrested?" He counts on his fingers. "Truancy. Drinking. Drugs. Shoplifting. Vandalism. Assault."

Ash shoots up straight and opens his mouth. "Ash," Diana says sharply, giving her head one quick shake. He closes his mouth and sits back, exhaling hard. His hands are clenched.

"This—This is unacceptable, Diana." Mrs. Summerhays says. "I started this scholarship in memory of my daughter. You can't give it to anyone without my approval. I simply can't approve..." She throws her hands up, unable to even say his name. "This candidate is disqualified." The issue is settled.

But Miss Buckley shakes her head. "I'm co-founder of the scholarship, Jacquelyn, and I'm the one who secured Brandon Lennox's financial support. I have as much say on this committee as you do, maybe more. You can't disqualify him without *my* approval."

Mrs. Summerhays is openly crying. Mr. Summerhays is about to detonate. Stunned beyond movement, I remain sprawled on the floor.

My competitor is Ash Morrison. Not Michael Granz.

This is... This is good.

Ash skips school most days, and when he is there, he antagonizes both students and teachers. He's always getting arrested for shoplifting and underage drinking. When my classmates want to buy pot, they go to Ash. He was only an infant when his father killed Lily, but he is destined to end up in prison too.

Besides, even if Ash were a model citizen—president of student council, homecoming King, captain of the baseball team—there's no way the committee would award the Lily Summerhays Memorial Scholarship to the son of the man who killed her.

Miss Buckley's sympathy for troubled kids is well-known, but she went too far by sneaking Ash through to the final round of the Lily Scholarship. I should thank her. The scholarship is mine. One hundred percent mine.

Principal Duston shoves the sleeves of his sport coat up his arms and stomps over to me. "You could have at least helped her up," he barks to Ash. He holds out his hand, the hatchet tattoo on his wrist clear and crisp.

No. That can't be right.

I slam my eyelids shut, then look again.

The tattoo is still there. Two hatchets crossed at the handles to form an X. One handle red, the other yellow. Two blades, sharp and gray.

I know every detail of that tattoo. I've seen it before, hundreds of times, every time I remember Lily's death. My head explodes with deathpain again, so severe that my eyes tear up.

Only one thought is able to cut through the pain. One horrible, horrible thought: That hatchet tattoo on my principal's wrist means Ash's father didn't kill Lily Summerhays.

Principal Duston did.

CHAPTER FOUR

LILY ~ EIGHTEEN YEARS AGO

Low laughter and heavy footsteps on Railroad Bridge interrupted the Lily Summerhays Pity Party I was having with the silver fish. Javier Soto and Will Duston, both in their maroon Warriors jerseys and baseball pants, heading to practice. It was baseball season at Ryland High. Hooray.

"Hey, Lily!" Javier waved and gave me one of his sweet, goofy grins. Will, with his hard blue eyes and white-blond hair,

God

I

hated

him

so

much

chewing one of those stupid toothpicks he always had in his mouth, said nothing, so I only said *hi* back to Javier.

It was no secret in Ryland that the Summerhayses and the

Dustons despised each other. Deep Creek bordered the eastern borders of my dad's plant and his family's farm, and the railroad tracks ran between them. The Dustons used to own the land that Agri-So now sat on, but now they were always trying to sue us over border disputes, or water rights, or proper land usage. Fighting the lawsuits was driving Agri-So out of business.

"Whatcha doing later?" Javier asked, hoisting up his pants. He was short, and his clothes were always too big on him. "I'm thinking of going for a ride. Wanna come?"

Of course I wanted to come. Javier's family owned Soto Agricultural Aerial Applications, and sometimes, just for fun, he took me up in one of their single-engine planes when they weren't using it for crop dusting. Sometimes he even let me fly the plane myself. "I can't," I said. "Sorry." My mother had forbidden me to fly in those "rickety tin death traps." Usually I would have ignored her, but I couldn't risk disobeying my parents anymore. Not if I wanted to go to CFGU. Besides, after work today, I wanted to stop by the theater and see if Neal Mallick was there. I needed to tell him what happened last night. He'd love it.

"I heard you crashed your car into a tree last night," Will said. He blinked innocently. "Were you drunk? Or were you just being typical Lily?"

"Shut up," was my brilliant retort. But I'd rather Will, and everyone, believe I was drunk or daydreaming than tell them that while I was driving home last night, I had a memory of dying in a barn fire, trying to rescue my horses. France, sometime in the 1700s. I'd been a man in that life. It wasn't the fire that had gotten me; it was smoke inhalation. The death-memory had hit as I drove home after spending the evening at Diana's house, assaulting me with

wheezing
breaths
spotty
vision
burning

skin

and I'd run my Firebird off Harrison Street, grazing Mr. Kammer's mailbox and hitting his oak tree. *Tapping* his oak tree.

I was pretty sure I'd saved those horses, though.

When I was a kid, I told my parents about my death-memories. They believed me, I'd thought, but eventually it became clear they were just humoring me. By second grade, they said it was time to give up those ridiculous, morbid stories. "What will people think?" my mother had said.

Even Diana told me to stop being so weird or I would lose all my friends. The only person who hadn't made fun of me was Neal Mallick. He believed me when we were little kids, and he still believed me now, even though he was an honors student and took a million AP science classes. Whenever I'd have a new death-memory, he was the only one I told. He was also the only one I told about my application to CFGU. He hardly ever said anything in return—he never spoke to anybody—but he'd nod and blink at me with his big eyes behind his big glasses. I couldn't prove any of my death-memories, but he didn't need science to believe me. He just did.

"You're not out here to jump, are you?" Javier asked me, throwing a stone into the creek.

"What makes you think that?"

"When we got here you were staring at the water like you want to jump in."

It was illegal to walk across Railroad Bridge, but we all did it anyway. Besides being the best shortcut—saving us a mile-long walk down Taft Avenue and another mile up Garfield Road—jumping from the bridge into the creek was the only fun thing to do in this town.

Will snorted. "It's only March. It may be warm today, but the water's still cold. Even Lily's not that stupid."

The clouds parted, and a ray of sun made the water glisten below me. Jumping into the creek *would* be fun. Besides, I was the first one of our friends to do it every year. And no one had ever jumped as early as March before.

"That wasn't a dare, Lily," Will said. "I mean it. Don't jump."

God, I hated that
condescending
toothpick-chewing
white-haired
farm boy.

How dare he call me stupid? How dare he tell me not to jump?

A little cold water wouldn't kill me. I would remember if it had.

Glaring at Will, I tucked my hair behind my ears. Took a deep breath.

"Lily! Don't!"

Too late. I was already plummeting through the air, into the—

cold.

Cold!

The sudden shock of frigid water made my heart seize. I forced myself calm, then opened my eyes to get a peek at the underwater world. Murky green water, weeds, rocks. A few little fish darted to and fro.

Ryland seemed so far away.

It really was cold, though. My waterlogged sweater weighed me down, and the glacial temperature weakened me, making my muscles heavy. I'd made my point and showed Will Duston that he couldn't tell me what to do. Time to go up before I lost all my strength. I pushed up toward the surface.

But I didn't go anywhere. Something was tangled around my ankle.

I wiggled my leg, trying to shake off the weed or branch or whatever it was. But it was hooked to my ankle, or my ankle was hooked to it.

My heart
squeezing,
my lungs

aching,

I twisted around to get my hands on the stupid thing.

But it wasn't a stupid thing.

It was a body.

Jaw hanging weightlessly, arms floating up, fingers dangling down. Eyes wide and black and hollowed, glasses broken and hanging askew from one ear, skin bloated and a strange shade of brownish-green. More ghoul than human. And my foot was caught in the torn collar of its Ryland High School jacket.

With every ounce of strength I had left, I tugged my foot from the collar. But it only got tangled more tightly. Without meaning to, I screamed, swallowing a mouthful of water.

Panic

coursed through my limbs, but the arctic water had paralyzed them into heavy worthless stumps. My boots—why had I jumped in my boots?—became anchors. My fingers were numb, but my lungs burned hot, so painfully hot—surely hot enough to warm me up and burn through the collar.

But no. Time was

slowing,

and everything was going

silent,

and I was about to die.

I didn't want to die. Not here. Not in Ryland. Please, no. I didn't want to be reborn in Ryland again.

But I didn't have the strength to fight anymore, and the water was so cold. So heavy. It was getting dark down here. And I was

tired

so

tired, and it was getting

dark

so

dark.

There was a pulling, a yanking ascent, and then a pressure on my chest, squeezing in mighty thrusts, forcing a huge amount of water from my lungs. That's when I realized sunlight filtered through my closed eyelids, and I was surrounded by air, not water. Lying on the hard ground. I gasped deep, deep raspy breaths. It took a few seconds for the shakes to begin.

"Jesus, Lily. I thought you were dead."

I blinked the water from my eyes. When the spots cleared from my vision, I saw my hero was none other than Will Duston. Soaked, shivering, and *pissed off.* The heat from the anger in his eyes could have warmed me up faster than the thickest blanket. "I *knew* it," he hissed through clenched teeth. "I *knew* you'd jump. Damn it, Lily, you are so..." With a frustrated roar, he punched the ground, the tattoo of two crossed hatchets on his wrist landing just inches from my head.

Javier ran over, perfectly dry. "Holy crap, Lily, you okay? I can't believe you did that!"

I spit more foul creek water from my mouth. "C-C-Call the p-p-police."

"No way," Will said. "Do you *want* everyone to know how stupid you were?"

"Th-Th-There's a body down there," I said through chattering teeth. "In the creek. I think... I think it's Neal Mallick."

CHAPTER FIVE

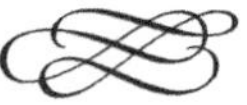

EVER ~ PRESENT DAY

Joey tugs my hand at the crosswalk outside the high school as I breathe away the deathpain in my head, trying to focus on the street in front of us. But the image of the crossed-hatchet tattoo is burned into my memory as permanently as it's inked on Principal Duston's wrist.

"Come on, Ever!" Joey says, excited to get to the drug store and pick out the new Matchbox car I promised him.

"Look both ways before you cross the street," I say automatically. As anxious as I am to get away from Principal Duston, I wait until there are no approaching vehicles before stepping off the curb. Four thousand pedestrians are killed while crossing the street each year in this country alone. And globally, 1.3 million people are killed in car accidents annually. Since cars were invented, they've killed me *twice*. Four deaths ago, I was an old man in Japan chasing a pickpocket across the street when I was hit by one of those fancy new passenger cars. Two deaths ago, I was a woman fleeing her wedding ceremony, driving from Oregon to New York City. My car skidded on the icy winter highway into a UPS truck, right outside of Ryland, Indiana, a few moments before Lily Summerhays was born.

I stifle a cringe at the memory of my yellow Puma, packed with Hefty bag luggage and a discarded poufy wedding dress, careening into the brown delivery truck. I close my eyes to breathe through the pain.

One...

Two...

Three.

I am not scared of death. I know that when I die, I'll be immediately reborn into the nearest, newest body. What I am scared of is leaving Joey all alone. I need to do everything it takes to stay alive for him. I need to stay alive, as Ever Abrams, and the only way to do that is to be vigilant. Organized. Meticulous. Follow the rules. Wear sunscreen. Look both ways before crossing the street.

At Kammer's Pharmacy and Gifts, Joey goes straight to the toy aisle and chooses a shiny Matchbox police car. I check for loose parts and choking hazards. Five thousand people choke to death every year. Food is the worst culprit, but toys are ranked second. But this police car is safe, so I approve. He skips happily beside me as we get the rest of the items on my mental list:

1. A new blue notebook for AP Lit and a new red notebook for Trig because the old ones are filled already.

2. A box of *SpongeBob* Band-Aids for Joey and a box of plain ones for Dad and me, in case we need them.

3. A historical romance novel from the magazine stand. Mom loved books, historical romances especially. I'm too busy studying to read as voraciously as she did, but I do read a lot in the summertime. I've had my eye on this book because the woman on the cover kind of looks like Mom—small and sweet; long, golden hair; and a twinkle in her eye. She's wearing a yellow ball gown, and yellow was Mom's favorite color.

Mom loved books so much that she and Dad owned a little bookstore on Main Street across from the movie theater. The Secret Garden, it was called, named after the novel by Frances Hodgson Burnett. I loved it there. It looked like a garden inside, with flowers and trees painted on the walls. If you looked closely at the bark on the trees, you could find etchings of classic literary characters. But when Mom got sick and we started getting all those medical bills, Dad couldn't afford to keep the business running. Now The Secret Garden Bookstore is the Twinkle Toes Nail Salon. The new owners painted over my mother's beautiful garden in a single afternoon, making the place a garish bright pink.

I know there's something else I need at Kammer's, number four on my mental list. But I can't focus. I can't get the image of Principal Duston's hatchet tattoo out of my head. Could he really have killed Lily Summerhays? I don't know much about him, other than he grew up here in Ryland and taught agriculture classes before becoming dean, then principal. He yells a lot. He seemed to dislike the Summerhayses today at the interview. Probably because he doesn't want them to find out that he killed their daughter.

Batteries. That's it. The last item on my mental list: Nine-volt batteries for our smoke alarms and carbon monoxide detectors. Almost three thousand people die in fires every year. I myself died in a fire in the 1700s when I was a man living in France. The barn was on fire, and I'd run in there to rescue the horses.

My lungs tighten like they're filling with smoke, my skin burns hot, and I slowly sip in air until the death-memory fades.

That pain is why, in my current life as Ever Abrams, I replace the batteries in our smoke alarms and carbon monoxide detectors every three months.

Joey and I go to the front of the store to buy our items. The gum-smacking cashier starts ringing them up. Someone grabs me around my waist and I freeze—Principal Duston, oh God, he knows I saw his tattoo, he knows I know he killed Lily—until cool lips nuzzle my neck.

"Keith!" I say, turning around in his arms. "You scared me."

Still in his maroon practice uniform, dusty from the baseball field, my boyfriend chuckles. This close to him, I can see the scar under his right eye from when he fell off his bicycle in third grade. "You didn't come get me after your interview," he says. "I was waiting for you. Glad I saw you come in here."

"Sorry, I forgot. I had to get away from the school."

"The interview went that bad, huh?" He brings me in tighter. "But you don't need college anyway. Now you can come work with me," he says with a smile.

Keith is going to work at his family's diner after we graduate high school in May. The Batter's Box has been a Ryland institution since his grandfather opened it sixty years ago, and Keith is going to own it one day. His parents offered me a job there too, as hostess, but I told them I'll hold off until after I get my degree so I can be the accountant.

"$18.57," the cashier says.

Keith hands her a twenty before I can reach into my purse. "You don't have to pay for my stuff," I say. "My dad left me cash."

"I like to pay for you." He grabs his change, the bag, and me, and we leave the store.

Outside, I give Joey his Matchbox car. He rips open the package immediately, and as I've taught him, tosses the package in a recycle bin that's been hand-painted with flowers and grass. Then we head for home. That's another nice thing about Ryland: it's small enough that I can walk everywhere. My house on Pierce Avenue is only a few blocks away from Main Street, and Joey's daycare is right next door at his best friend Hayden's house. The high school is on Jackson Boulevard, and the park and library are on Madison Avenue. My best friend Courtney lives a block away on Adams Road, and my boyfriend Keith lives directly across the street from me. Everything I need is within a six block radius. I have no reason, or desire, to ever move away.

Keith takes my hand as we head down Main Street. His hand is cool to the touch, and he's been biting his nails again. As we approach

The Batter's Box, he says, "Let's go tell my parents that you can start right after graduation."

"I can't," I say. "The interview wasn't great, but I still got the scholarship."

"You did? For real?" He stops in his tracks and lifts his hat, runs his hand through his floppy brown hair, then pulls the hat back on his head. It's a newer, brighter maroon than the old, faded one that Joey's wearing. "How do you know?"

"I don't know, not officially, not yet. But guess who had the other interview?"

"The 4-H kid. Michael Granz. Did he drop out or something?"

"No. The other finalist is Ash Morrison."

"What the hell? Ash Morrison?" Keith asks. "That asshole used to beat me up all the time."

"I know. Miss Buckley snuck him through. She said the committee needs to be impartial. The other judges were furious."

He brings his fourth finger between his front teeth and bites the nail. "But wait. Ash Morrison's father is the one who killed Lily Summerhays."

"Right," I say. "Which means they *have* to give the scholarship to me."

An image of the crossed hatchets tattooed on Principal Duston's wrist slices through my vision, and my skull feels like it's splitting open.

"Unless," I say, rubbing my head and breathing through the pain, "unless it turns out that Vinnie Morrison didn't kill Lily Summerhays after all."

CHAPTER SIX

LILY ~ EIGHTEEN YEARS AGO

Trying not to let my parents see me shiver, I kept my head down in the backseat of my dad's car as we drove home. Every time I glanced up, they were glaring at me through the rearview mirror. Their initial hugs and cries of relief that my plunge into the creek hadn't killed me had quickly turned into tight-lipped scoldings. Now the air inside the car was cold and fragile, like a thin sheet of ice that would

shatter

with one breath.

"Neal was my friend," I mumbled, "and he's dead. Why are you so mad at me?"

"It's tragic," Dad said, "and we're very sorry you lost your friend. But you almost died right along with him, Lily. I'm so tired of you doing things like this. You *know* it's illegal to be on that bridge. And jumping from it? What were you thinking?"

"She *wasn't* thinking." Mom shook her head, an apology to my dad for giving him such a disobedient, disappointing daughter. "She never does."

"I'm sorry," I said. The truth was, she was right. My impulsive jump into the creek this morning had also been a huge jump backward from proving to my parents that I was mature and responsible. All because I'd wanted to show that jerk Will Duston that he couldn't tell me what to do. What should have been my first day at Agri-So had been spent by the creek on the edge of Duston Farm. Will and I were both examined by EMTs and then questioned by Officer Paladino. Our parents came, Mr. and Mrs. Duston running down from their farmhouse and Dad sprinting out of his office, the two buildings just a few hundred feet away. Mom left her Ryland Beautification Committee meeting. The four parents had barely acknowledged each other, not even after Javier told them that Will had saved my life.

Neal's family had come too. His father stood stoically, frozen in denial and disbelief. His mother had wailed. I'd struggled to hold back my tears, but when his little sister started crying, I lost it. Neal was sweet. Trustworthy. So, so smart. He had never hurt anybody. Had never said an unkind word. And now he was

gone.

It wasn't fair.

Officer Paladino had decided that almost drowning wasn't punishment enough for me, so he issued me a citation. "Do you finally understand why it's illegal to be on Railroad Bridge?" he'd admonished me as emergency crews pulled Neal's body from the creek, zipped it up in a body bag, and drove it away. No need for the siren.

As impulsive as I was, I'd stopped myself from reminding Officer Paladino that he used to jump from the bridge too. When he and his friends were seniors and my friends and I were middle-schoolers, we'd watch them play chicken on the bridge. They'd dodge the oncoming trains at the very last second by jumping into the creek, much to my friends' horror and my delight. Back then he was Ricky, the boy with the whitest teeth and brown eyes so delicious and deep they were like bottomless mugs of hot chocolate. But his dazzling smile had faded and the warmth in his eyes had cooled when he became a cop.

I'd discovered the dead body of my friend, and instead of sympathy and hugs, I got a citation from the cops and anger from my parents.

Dad turned the car onto Adams Road. Our house was visible on the incline at the end of the street, stately and majestic with its red brick and two stories and dormer windows. Compared to most of the shoe-box houses in Ryland, our house was a mansion. But who needs marble countertops and hardwood floors? In West Africa in the 1300s, I had died a peaceful, uneventful death as an old woman, inside my home, which had been built from clay and straw.

But I couldn't tell my parents I thought our big house was unnecessary and pretentious, nor could I tell them I still had death-memories. When I was six, my mother brought me to a therapist in Eastfield, so concerned was she by the morbid, macabre "little stories" I'd told of my own deaths. Car accidents, burned in a fire, drowned in the ocean, shot in a war. She thought I was obsessed with death, or suicidal, or a future serial killer. But her biggest concern was that everyone in Ryland would think I was weird or delusional. I'd learned to shut up about my death-memories and people stopped thinking I was a weirdo. But I never gained back my mother's approval.

Throughout that entire ordeal, Dad had worked. Long hours, then longer, until he never stopped.

From the front seat of Dad's Lexus, Mom continued to scold me for jumping off the bridge, using the same words she always did when I disappointed her:

irresponsible
reckless
impulsive
uncontrollable

thoughtless

stubborn.

When she paused her word-assault, I said, "It was a stupid thing to do. I'm sorry. But at least I'm alive. Neal Mallick is dead. Imagine what his parents are going through right now."

"Of course I feel horrible for the Mallicks," she said. "But it doesn't change the fact that you wouldn't have had to walk to Agri-So in the first place if you hadn't crashed your car last night, you wouldn't have had to take the shortcut across the bridge if you weren't running late this morning, and you wouldn't have almost drowned if you hadn't jumped. Honestly, Lily. I don't know what to do with you."

"I know. I'm sorry." I was ruining everything for myself. "I promise I'll be better."

Dad let out a frustrated sigh, and Mom placed a consoling hand on his arm. He shifted away, the movement a bit too brusque to be casual. She turned to stare out the window, blinking rapidly.

"I'm sorry," I said, for the millionth time. "I'm really, really sorry."

CHAPTER SEVEN

EVER ~ PRESENT DAY

I tuck Joey into bed that night, his little teeth brushed, his little hand clutching his new Matchbox police car. On his dresser, Cheeks the hamster runs on her wheel. I worry the squeaking noises will keep him up, but they don't. He falls asleep quickly.

I go back down the hall to join my friends. My dad called earlier that afternoon to say he was stuck in Dubuque and wasn't going to make it home until tomorrow, so I asked Courtney to come here instead of me going to her house so I could stay home with Joey. Keith came over too, with a pizza from The Batter's Box. None of us were surprised my father didn't come home. If he had, he'd be too tired to help me anyway. But my best friend and my boyfriend will help me figure out what to do.

"So. Guys," I start, crossing my legs on the couch next to Keith. "I've been thinking."

"You're always thinking," Court says with a laugh, tossing her black braids behind her shoulders. "That's why you get straight A's."

Kind, supportive Courtney, with her warm green eyes and her easy, full smile. We've been best friends since second grade, when she pitched a softball to me during PE and it smashed my fingers. Nothing was broken, just swollen, but she felt so bad and cried so hard that when the school nurse gave me a lollipop, I let Court have it instead. She doesn't have a mom either. Her mother is still alive, but she lives in Cleveland with her second husband. For the past five years, it's been just Courtney and her dad, the Coach. But as sweet as she is, she's a killer on the softball field. She's ranked the number one high school pitcher in the state, and next year she's going to University of Illinois on a full softball scholarship.

"I'm serious, Court," I say. "I need to talk to you guys about something."

She immediately puts down her pizza slice. "What's wrong?"

I take a breath, suddenly unsure how I'm going to tell them about the hatchet tattoo without telling them about my death-memories. "I've been thinking about Lily Summerhays."

"The scholarship?" Court asks. "You said you got it. There's no way the Summerhayses will give it to Ash Morrison."

"But what if we don't know everything about how she was killed? What if they got some of the facts wrong?"

"They solved it the same night she died," Keith says, his mouth full of pizza. "We've heard about it our entire lives. Vinnie Morrison. Burglary. Smash. Dead." He mimes smashing his fist into his own head, which makes *my* head ache.

One...

Two...

Three.

He must see something in my expression because he says, "You don't have to be scared, babe. He's in prison. Death row." He puts his arm around me protectively. "Are you worried about Ash? I won't let him near you."

My sweet Keith. Our families have lived across the street from each other our entire lives. His parents got married right after high school, and they're still ridiculously in love. A couple days after my mom's funeral, Mr. and Mrs. Stout sent Keith over with burgers and fries from The Batter's Box. He came back the next day with hot dogs and peanut butter pie. That weekend, when my dad was still too heartsick to get off the couch, Keith mowed our lawn and trimmed the bushes in our front yard. And that was that. He's been around ever since, my gentle, lumbering, candy-coated boyfriend.

"Vinnie Morrison is going to be executed next month," I say. "But what if..." I pause for emphasis. "What if he didn't kill Lily? What if he's innocent?"

"Why would you think that?" Courtney asks.

"Over 19,000 people are murdered in the U.S every year. All those murders can't be solved correctly. What if they got the wrong guy for Lily's murder? What if the real killer is still here in Ryland?"

"Like who?" Keith stuffs another square of pizza in his mouth. Sausage, pepperoni, and bacon. The half with mushroom and onion is for Courtney and me.

"I don't know. It could be anyone." I pretend to think. "Even, like, Principal Duston." I gauge their reactions, and when they give me dubious looks, I add, "He's from Ryland. He knew Lily. I think they were the same age."

Keith nods. "He *is* a hardass. I could see him killing someone."

"I know, right?" I knew I could count on him.

"No way. It was Vinnie Morrison," Court says. "He confessed, remember? And they found Lily's diamond necklace in his apartment."

I drop the daisy charm on the necklace I've been fiddling with. Of course. They had a confession—and evidence. Convicted and sentenced to death. The average death row inmate spends fifteen years between sentencing and execution. Vinnie Morrison has been on death row for almost eighteen years, and not once has he claimed to be innocent. He admitted he killed her.

"You're just worried about the scholarship," Court continues. "You always doubt yourself about tests and stuff, and you get yourself all stressed out. That's why you still won't take your driver's test. But you deserve this scholarship, Ever. It's all you've ever wanted. You've been working for it your whole life. All that studying. All those AP classes. Just for this. Don't blow it now."

Court's right. Not completely right—I won't take my driver's test because I don't want to die in a car accident for a third time—but I do get stressed out about everything. And I *do* deserve the scholarship, much more than that bullying, cheating, drug-dealing vandal Ash Morrison.

Now I understand what happened at the interview. I was nervous, stressed out, and I'd just had the death-memory of Lily's murder. I must have projected my memory of the crossed-hatchet tattoo onto Principal Duston's wrist when he extended his hand to help me up from the floor.

Yes. A projection. That's all it was.

"You're right," I say. "I'm just worried I won't get the scholarship."

"You'll get it. Especially now that your competition is Ash Morrison," Courtney says. "Hey, have I shown you guys the banners for the Training Camp? They turned out really good. Look." She whips out her phone to show us the design.

Courtney and I are Batgirls, the pep squad for the baseball team. In addition to supporting the players, our big project every year is running the Little Warriors Training Camp. It started about twenty years ago when the Warriors baseball team hosted the elementary school kids after school one afternoon for skills practice and a fun game. Since then, the Training Camp has grown into a day-long, community-wide event. Courtney is the head Batgirl this year and is therefore in charge of the camp, and she takes her job very seriously.

I want to discuss the Lily Summerhays murder some more, but Courtney and Keith continue chatting about the Training Camp, and spring break, and graduation. Courtney asks me if I've asked my dad yet if I can go up to Chicago with her for her birthday on the Fourth of July. She wants to see the fireworks at Navy Pier.

"No, not yet," I say, and then she's off chatting again, this time about how much she hates one of the girls on her travel softball team. I don't bring up Lily Summerhays, Vinnie Morrison, or Principal Duston again, and neither do my friends. They've forgotten all about it, and I should too.

But still, after they leave that night, I can't sleep. Dad's not home, but that's not why. The hamster wheel is squeaking in Joey's room, but that's not why, either. I get up and open my chemistry textbook and try to study, but nothing sinks in. I straighten my room, even though it's already clean. I stack my Griffin University brochures by size, big to small. I separate my blue pens from my black pens. I remake my bed, making sure the sheets are perfectly smooth, then get back under the covers. I recite death stats in my head and assure myself that I'm doing nothing that jeopardizes my health and safety.

I still can't sleep.

Finally, I grab my phone and open the browser. But the screen is too small, so I pull my laptop into bed with me. It used to be my mother's, and even then it was old. Now it's ancient.

I turn it on. There's one image I need to find, and then I'll be able to sleep. But I don't even know if such an image exists.

I find it, finally, after an hour of browsing. An old newspaper photograph of Vinnie Morrison from behind as he was led out of the courtroom in an orange jumpsuit after his conviction, hands cuffed behind his back. Something was on his wrist. A tattoo.

Vinnie Morrison has a tattoo on his wrist. Good. All that worry for nothing. I can sleep now.

But—wait.

No. *Stop. Do not look again.* I need to stop and put the laptop away and go to sleep and forget about this whole thing. *Now.*

My fingers ignore my brain. They click the magnifying glass icon to enlarge the image and zoom in on the tattoo.

No dual gray blades. No red handle crossing over a yellow handle. Morrison's tattoo is solid black. Three capital letters in a fancy script: *ASH.*

I sit back with a huff. That is most definitely, one hundred percent, absolutely *not* the hand that gripped a pink paperweight in its fist, growled, *"You left me no choice,"* and slammed the paperweight into Lily Summerhays's skull.

Vinnie Morrison did not kill Lily Summerhays.

I don't want to know this. I hate that I know this.

But I do know it.

I could just say nothing. Do nothing, keep my mouth shut, win the scholarship. Go to Griffin University. Give my mom what she wanted. Give Lily what she wanted. Give *myself* what I've always wanted.

Vinnie Morrison didn't kill Lily, but he was still a criminal. He probably would have ended up killing someone anyway. And Ash must have cheated his way to the final round of the scholarship selection, tricked Miss Buckley somehow, lied to her, maybe even seduced her. He certainly didn't get there through years of hard work like I did.

The Lily Summerhays Memorial Scholarship belongs to Lily, and Lily is me. The scholarship is mine.

That's it. Decision made. Over. Done. I feel good about this. I close my laptop, pull up the covers, and close my eyes. Sleep.

I dream of hatchets and sparkly pink paperweights. Electric chairs and lethal injections.

When the early morning sun shines through my bedroom window, I wake up knowing four things.

1. I cannot let Vinnie Morrison be executed for a crime he did not commit.

2. Principal Duston is a killer, and he's walking around free. Ryland is not the safe town I've always thought it was.

3. Lily Summerhays deserves justice. Lily is me, so I deserve justice too.

4. Once I prove Principal Duston is the real killer, I am probably going to lose the scholarship.

CHAPTER EIGHT

LILY ~ EIGHTEEN YEARS AGO

The crowd at The Batter's Box was subdued that night, and although I usually liked the diner's baseball theme, tonight it seemed too cheery and victorious. My friends and I sat in our usual booth in the back. Neal Mallick never had a lot of friends, and he'd never hung out at The Batter's Box, but now that he was dead, his absence felt almost tangible.

He was the first member of our class to die. No one I knew personally had ever died before. Other than myself, but that didn't count. All four of my grandparents were still alive, even. My mom's parents lived in a condo over in Eastfield, and my dad's parents lived in a retirement community in Tennessee.

Diana sat across the booth from me with her boyfriend, Brandon Lennox. Her eyes were red and puffy and he was missing his usual lopsided grin, but otherwise, they looked like they'd stepped off the cover of *Teen Vogue*. They always looked like supermodels even when they were fighting, which was most of the time. But tonight Brandon kept his arm tight over her shoulders. Back together apparently, when they'd just broken up again last week.

I was squeezed between Javier Soto and Seth Siegel. The only reason my parents let me leave the house tonight was because Seth picked me up. My mother loooooved Seth Siegel. Partly because he was a lot taller than me and had an adorable dimple on his chin, but mostly because his father was the mayor of Ryland and his mother co-chaired the Miss Teen Ryland committee with her. I actually liked Seth. He always made silly faces from his position in right field to make me laugh because he knew how bored I was watching the games. I went to a couple of homecoming dances with him, and we had casual plans to go to prom together in May. But even though he—and my mother—wanted more, I drew a solid line at friendship. I didn't want any commitments that would tie me to anyone, not if I was going to travel the world.

Will Duston dragged over a chair to sit at the end of the booth. Usually, I'd make fun of his stupid toothpick and he'd make fun of my hair. But Will saved my life this morning—saved me from being reborn in Ryland—so this time I greeted him with a small nod. "Hey."

"Hey, Red." His gaze caught mine and held it. "You doing all right?"

I nodded, surprised at his concern.

"Dude, you were a rock star this morning," Javier said, giving Will a fist bump. "I still can't believe any of that happened."

"*I* can't believe we just saw Neal at school yesterday and now he's dead." Diana sniffled and laid her head on Brandon's shoulder.

Seth snorted from the far end of the table. "I'm gonna miss that little turtle." I shot him a glare. People always teased Neal because he looked like a turtle, with his big eyes and big glasses and wide mouth, shuffling down the hall and slouching under the weight of his big green backpack.

"Don't be an asshole, Seth." Will punched him in the arm. "Neal tutored a bunch of our team in school. Without him, they wouldn't have a GPA high enough to be eligible to play. You're one of those guys. We kind of owe everything to Neal."

Flushing, Seth gave a guilty nod. In the past twelve years, the Ryland Warriors baseball team won the state championship seven times. Coach Nolan, forever a Warrior, had turned down an offer to coach at Indiana State University. Some of the players got baseball scholarships to college. And Brandon Lennox was legendary in Indiana. His unbeatable batting skills had led the Warriors to the Indiana state championship the past three years, and he was expected to do it again this year. He was being scouted by both the New York Yankees and the Houston Astros. They wanted to sign him right out of high school.

"It'll be weird going to the movies now," Diana said, dabbing her eyes. "He always put extra butter on our popcorn."

Will popped a toothpick in his mouth, then concentrated on tearing a napkin into shreds.

I wished I could tell them that Neal was okay, that his soul, or spirit or essence or whatever, had already found a home in the nearest new body. But really, I had no idea if what happened to me happened to anyone else. Maybe everyone else became angels in heaven. Maybe they became nothing. I could only say for sure what happened to me.

"What'd he look like, Lily?" Tilting his head, Seth hung his tongue from his mouth and rolled his eyes back in a pathetic attempt to look like a dead body.

"Was he all bashed in from the train?" Diana whispered.

"It didn't look like a train hit him," I said. "He wasn't that banged up or anything. He looked... like Neal." I didn't want to describe how

bloated
his body was,
how hollow
and haunted

his eyes were.

"I just wish we knew what happened to him," I said. "Why he was on the bridge."

The waitress, a short, red-cheeked woman named Bubbles who was married to the owner's son, came over to refill our drinks. "I heard he was wasted," she said in her squeaky voice. "After work he met up with Vinnie Morrison behind the theater and bought a bunch of stuff from him. Coke or pills or something."

"Neal Mallick? Drugs?" I said. "No way."

"I'm just telling you what I heard," Bubbles said. She shook her head, her brown curly hair swaying, and put a protective hand on her belly. "All I know is, the cops really need to do something about that Vinnie Morrison before my baby is born." She sauntered off.

"Well, I heard it was suicide," Brandon said.

"He was going to MIT next year," Javier said, shrugging in his too-big shirt. "Why would he kill himself now?"

"Maybe he couldn't handle the pressure," Brandon said.

"Nah," said Seth. "They officially declared it an accidental death."

"How do you know?" I asked.

"My dad's the mayor," he said with a shrug. "The cops told him. Neal finished his shift at the movie theater, and on his way home he slipped off the bridge, hit his head on a rock or something, and drowned. His parents didn't know he never made it home until the cops called them this morning from the creek. They assumed he was in bed sleeping."

The others nodded, satisfied. I asked, "But why was he on the bridge in the first place?"

"Seth just told us," Javier said. "He was going home. He lives on the south side of town, so he took the shortcut across the bridge instead of walking the extra mile down Taft Avenue."

"Not Neal," I said. "He always took the long way around. Even during the day. He'd never take the bridge—alone—in the middle of the night."

"How do *you* know so much about him?" Will asked. "I don't remember you being friends with him."

"We talked sometimes." I couldn't tell him that Neal was the only one I talked to about my past deaths. "He was a nice guy. A good listener." A good secret-keeper too.

A sudden pang hit my heart. I never dated anyone because I didn't want any commitments to hold me back from traveling around the world, but now I wished I'd gone on a date with Neal. I wished I had asked him out—he would have been too shy to ask me—and we'd go out to dinner and then for a long, long walk under the stars, just talking and talking and talking. I wished, at the end of the night, that we parted with a sweet, slow, tender kiss. And now we'd never get that chance.

"Well, Neal *did* take the bridge last night," Brandon said, "so you didn't know him as well as you thought you did."

"I guess not." I plucked a stubby fry from the basket and dipped it in Javier's ketchup as my friends' conversation drifted from Neal Mallick to their college plans. Diana described the matching comforters she wanted for our dorm room at Griffin University: white with blue and purple paisleys.

Diana would have to find a new roommate if I went to CFGU. I hoped that new roommate liked blue and purple paisleys.

I could only half-listen as everyone discussed their after-graduation plans. My mind kept returning to Neal Mallick. His death had been declared an accident, but the more I thought about it, the more I couldn't believe it. He wouldn't have taken that bridge to get home. Never.

I ate the fry, and it was

cold.

My parents said I was irresponsible and reckless, and they always accused me of looking for trouble when there was none and making their lives miserable. That was probably true. And if I wanted them to trust me enough to let me go to Carroll-Freywood Global University, I needed to stay out of trouble.

But I owed it to Neal to find out what really happened to him. Why had he been on Railroad Bridge in the middle of the night?

I reached for another fry, only to see Will Duston watching me, his icy blue eyes narrowed.

CHAPTER NINE

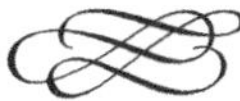

EVER ~ PRESENT DAY

"Hello, kids," Keith's dad greets Joey and me Sunday morning from his corner table at The Batter's Box, where he's flipping through a pile of check stubs and holding a stubby pencil in his stubby fingers, making stubby check marks on his bank statement. "You looking for Keith? He should still be home, sleeping."

"Morning, Mr. Stout," I say. I know Keith is still sleeping. He usually sleeps past noon on days he doesn't have school or baseball practice. "Joey and I are here for breakfast. I didn't feel like cooking."

"Sit wherever you want," he says, waving absently. "Bubbles will take your order in a sec."

Almost half the tables and booths are occupied. Joey scrambles over to an empty booth and climbs in, excited for a pancake breakfast at The Batter's Box. A rare treat. The Stouts never charge me—I'll be a member of the family one day, they say—but it makes me uncomfortable to accept their service and food for free, so I rarely come without Keith. But I'm on a mission today.

"Hey, Mr. Stout," I say casually, "you knew Lily Summerhays, didn't you?"

He grunts a little, then strokes his thick mustache. He's doughy and soft, like a banana nut muffin fresh out of the oven, and Keith is already starting to look like him. "Not well. She was seven or eight years younger than me. She came here a lot with her friends. My dad ran the place back then. I was assistant manager. Nice girl. Shame what happened to her."

"Yeah," I say, bracing myself against the deathpain in my skull. When I recover, I ask, "Did you know Principal Duston back then too?"

"Will Duston," he says with a nod. "Yep. Nice guy. Still is."

"Do you remember anything specific about them? Other than they were both nice?"

Mr. Stout takes a slurp from his coffee mug. "She was a generous tipper. Always appreciated that about her. Nice girl." Specks of light brown coffee cling to the bottom of his thick mustache.

"What about Principal Duston?" I ask.

"Will? He tipped the standard fifteen percent, sometimes ten. That's okay. Nice fella. Very polite. Respectful."

Mr. Stout probably isn't the right person to ask about this. He's never said a negative thing about anybody. "What do you remember about Vinnie Morrison?"

That got him. He stiffens a little. "Now that guy was nothing but a troublemaker. He came in one night and swiped the tip a patron left for Bubbles right off the table. Just pocketed it and left. She saw him, and he didn't care. He knew she was scared of him. She was pregnant too." He shakes his head a little, as if clearing it of any bad thoughts, and smiles at me. "Keith said your interview went well yesterday. We could really use your help around here with the accounting. You hurry up and get that college education you want so bad."

"I will, Mr. Stout," I say, then add, "I hope."

I join Joey at the booth. The Batter's Box is decorated with local baseball paraphernalia, mostly from back when Ryland High won a bunch of state championships. Framed and faded newspaper clippings adorn the walls, displaying photos of the players in action, receiving their trophies, celebrating their victories. A younger Coach Nolan is in many of the photos, slim and muscular. He had hair back then, and he didn't have a belly, but his eyes were just as kind as they are now. Hanging over the counter is an autographed poster of Brandon Lennox in his New York Yankees uniform, smiling with one side of his lips rising higher than the other. *To The Batter's Box,* he'd scrawled. *Couldn't have done it without you. Keep batting 1000, Brandon Lennox.*

Mrs. Stout comes over in her green uniform. "Ever, Joey, hello!" she squeaks. Always happy to see us.

"Pancakes, please!" Joey shouts before I can reply.

She ruffles his hair and gives him a little packet of crayons and a baseball-themed placemat to color. Her white waitress shoes have soles so thick, they make her almost five feet tall. I'm short, but I'm a giant compared to her.

I order an egg white omelet with mushrooms and broccoli and add a small fruit plate to Joey's order. I consider asking her what she remembers about Lily Summerhays and Will Duston, but I don't want to do it in front of Joey or with so many people around us.

I have a fleeting thought that Lily may have sat in this exact booth many times. My head hurts.

"Joey, let's go wash our hands," I say, then bring him to the restrooms in the back. He goes into the men's room—he's five now, he boasts, old enough to wash his hands by himself—and this time I don't argue. Instead of going to the women's room, I stop at the payphone that's stationed between the two doors. The only payphone left in Ryland.

I'm nervous suddenly. Heavy with a sense of dread and doom. Making this anonymous call will set things in motion, and once Vinnie Morrison is found innocent, the scholarship could go to Ash. But if I don't call, then an innocent man will be executed, and the real killer will still be free, living in Ryland, working at my school. I can't let that happen.

With a shaking hand, I slip two quarters into the slot. The Ryland police station doesn't have an anonymous tip line, only 911 and a non-emergency number. I dial the non-emergency number because I don't want cops to come running over here from the station across the street.

"Ryland police," a chipper lady answers.

"Um, I have—" I start, then stop when an elderly woman shuffles out of the restroom.

"Do you need help, miss?" the woman on the phone asks.

My heart is beating so fast it hurts. This is worse than the interview yesterday. "No, not me personally, not really." I cup my hand around the receiver and lower my voice. "I'm calling because I have new information about the Lily Summerhays murder."

Silence. Then, "Okay, what is it?"

I peek around the corner into the diner. People are eating, chatting, clinking utensils. Mr. Stout is frowning at his bank statement, Mrs. Stout is taking an order. No one is watching, no one is listening. Still, I make my voice even softer. "Vinnie Morrison didn't kill her."

The lady sighs into the phone. "Honey, if you're with another one of those anti-death penalty groups, you'll need to contact the district attorney, not the police."

"I'm not with a group like that," I say. My knuckles hurt from gripping the phone so tightly. "I just know he didn't kill her."

"How do you know that?"

If I tell her about my death-memory and the tattoo, she'll hang up on me. "Because I know who the real killer is."

"And who would that be?"

She's humoring me, I know. An anonymous caller with no proof is not the most credible of informants. But once the cops investigate my tip, they'll discover the truth.

In almost a whisper, I say, "Will Duston." When she doesn't respond, I add, "He's the principal at Ryland High School."

"Mm-hmm." She clickety-clacks on a keyboard.

"I know you don't believe me, but you need to question him," I say. "Investigate. You'll see."

"Okay," she says, then clickety-clacks some more. "Thank you for this information. I'll pass along your tip to the proper authorities. Can I have your name and contact information so we can foll—?"

I hang up before she can finish.

When Mrs. Stout delivers our breakfasts, I eat my egg white omelet while keeping an eye on the front picture window, watching the police station across the street, half expecting a cop to come out and head down Main Street to go question Will Duston.

None do.

CHAPTER TEN

LILY ~ EIGHTEEN YEARS AGO

Neal Mallick's death weighed down on Ryland High that week, the solemn atmosphere making it easier to be on my best behavior. Getting another detention would not help my quest to change my parents' minds about me. I wasn't tardy to a single class, and I refrained from talking to my friends during the teacher's lectures. But ever since The Batter's Box, all I could think about was Neal and why he was on that bridge.

Thursday after school I hustled down the hallway with Diana, dodging the other students who were also rushing off to home or clubs or practice. Diana somehow ran gracefully in her skirt and high heels while I clomped along in my jeans and flowered boots. The baseball team had an away game that afternoon over in Eastfield, and I was hitching a ride with Diana because my parents still wouldn't let me drive my car. I didn't care about the game at all. The Ryland Warriors had won seven state championships in the last twelve years, but that didn't change the fact that baseball is

the
most
boring
thing
to
ever
happen
in
the
history
of
the
universe.

Diana used to feel the same way until she started dating Brandon Lennox last year. He said what made him so good at the game were the kisses she blew to him whenever he was at bat. Gross. Now not only was she a huge fan of the game, she was president of the Batgirls, the pep squad that cheered on the players and made them homemade treats. Double gross.

I sped up to catch her, but just before we reached the exit, I screeched to a halt. One of the maroon lockers lining the hallway caught my eye—Neal Mallick's locker. Carnations and cards stuck out of the ventilation slots in a makeshift memorial.

"Lily!" Diana said, already halfway out the door. "You know I can't be late."

"You go on without me."

"What? Why?"

"I forgot that I have something to do."

"Come on, Lily. I know you hate the game, but your friends are on the team. They need your support."

"They'll do great whether I'm there or not."

With a roll of her eyes, she gave an impatient sigh. The door swung shut behind her as she rushed away.

I ran my fingers over the gigantic *R.I.P. Neal* that someone had written on his locker with a black Sharpie.

What had he been doing on that bridge?

Wasted on drugs, suicide... those rumors, which had spread like weeds and wrapped themselves around my throat like a prickly vine, were ridiculous. An accident was the official cause of death, and the most believable. Even so, if his death was an accident, someone must have been with him. I couldn't believe Neal would cross Railroad Bridge all by himself. Someone out there knew what had really happened that night on the bridge. And that person hadn't come forward, which made me suspicious.

One by one, I pulled the cards from the slots and read them. Maybe Neal had had a secret lover. Maybe they'd gone for a walk that night and he'd slipped off the bridge to his death.

None of the cards seemed overly sappy or heartsick. Everyone had signed their cards with impersonal sentiments like *You were so smart* or *Thanks for tutoring me.* The flowers were mostly cheap carnations—nothing romantic like roses or baby's breath. Almost all of the carnations were red and yellow, our school colors. No one even knew his favorite color. Not even me.

Something fluttered out from one of the cards to the floor. A photograph! Maybe it was a picture of Neal with his secret lover.

Oh. No. Just a page torn from the yearbook. The Mathletes. Neal was on the left end of the short row of Mathletes, slouched in his usual pose, eyes half-shut and clearly not ready for the camera. Someone had scrawled *Rest in Peice Turtle* on the photo. They hadn't even spelled *peace* right. Or *piece*, for that matter.

Frustrated, I returned the flowers and cards to the ventilation slots. They'd told me nothing except that no one had known anything about Neal at all, other than he'd been smart.

Hmm. If the cards hadn't told me anything, maybe something inside his locker would.

I jiggled the chrome handle. It wiggled but didn't open. The lockers at Ryland High were old, at least forty years or more, and they were never secure. I gave it a few staccato beats with my fist, right over the handle, which was how I got my own locker open whenever it jammed. It usually flew right open.

Nothing.

I took a few steps back, then rammed the locker with my shoulder.

Nothing, except now my shoulder was sore.

"Miss Summerhays," someone called in a wheezy voice. "May I help you?"

Principal Kimball came waddling down the hall, her brown, frizzy hair bouncing with each step. I'd spent many afternoons in detention with Principal Kimball.

I plastered an innocent smile on my lips as my mind scrambled to think of an excuse for why I was breaking into Neal's locker. "I thought someone should bring Neal's things to his parents," I said. "And, you know, the flowers and cards."

To my surprise, Principal Kimball smiled. "That's a lovely idea, Lily. I'm sure his parents will be touched to see how many of his classmates left flowers for him." She unlocked the locker with her master key and stood by while I opened it.

Neat and organized. Several notebooks, arranged by color, and a zippered pencil case marked "EXTRA PENS" in small, precise block letters. Only one textbook, AP Physics. Apparently, Neal brought his books home to study on the weekends, even this late in his senior year. A gray jacket hanging on the hook. A Spanish-English dictionary. A mini dry-erase board attached by magnets to the inside door, a blue marker hanging next to it and an eraser next to that. All three were lined up perfectly straight. On the board he'd written "FRI MID" in his block letters and circled it.

"*Fri mid*? What does that mean?" I asked aloud.

"I don't know, dear," Principal Kimball said. I'd forgotten that she was there. She'd never called me *dear* before.

I swept everything from the locker into my bookbag, hung his jacket over my arm, and carefully pulled the flowers and cards from the slots. "I'll bring everything to the Mallicks right now."

She thanked me. "You're a kind young woman, Lily. Neal was fortunate to have you as a friend."

CHAPTER ELEVEN

EVER ~ PRESENT DAY

My dad has been gone since Wednesday on his truck haul, and now, finally, he's due home any minute. I've spent the time after my anonymous call to the police at home, making sure it's spotless and welcoming. I open all the curtains, give everything an extra dusting, and put lemons in a bowl on the kitchen counter the way Mom used to.

Everything is clean, but something is missing. Something is always missing. When Mom was alive, our little house was alive too. I keep all of her craft fair finds exactly as she'd left them, and I display the historical romance I bought yesterday with the woman in the yellow dress who looks like her on the bookcase in the family room. But the house still feels hollow and lifeless.

While Joey and I wait for Dad, I do my chemistry homework. Joey would normally want to go next door to play with his friend Hayden, whose mom runs the home daycare I send him to while I'm at school, but today he stays home and builds a racetrack for his

Matchbox cars all around the family room. He lines up all of his vehicles, setting aside the new police car, reserving it for Dad to play with as soon as he gets home.

The motor on the garage door whirs. "Daddy!" Joey dashes to the door, jumping up and down until our dad walks in. Joey leaps onto him like a monkey onto a tree.

"Hey there, little guy," he says. "Take it easy. I'm tired. I've been driving all night."

"Dad, that's dangerous," I said. "Over fifteen hundred people die every year because they fall asleep behind the wheel."

"I know, Ever. You've told me before." He puts Joey down and kisses the top of my head. Whereas Joey takes after our mom—golden hair, a smattering of freckles across the nose, pale skin, and green eyes, I inherited Dad's dark blond hair, olive complexion, and brown eyes. But today his hair is disheveled. He's grown a beard in the years since Mom died, and it needs a trim. His clothes are wrinkled from driving the truck for so long. "How'd your scholarship interview go?" he asks as he walks past me.

"I don't know. It's complicated."

"I'm sure you did great. I'm proud of you, hon. I couldn't do this without you."

I cross my arms. "Yeah, I know."

Should I tell him about Principal Duston, how I know he killed Lily Summerhays? How I once *was* Lily Summerhays, and the last thing she saw was the hatchet tattoo on his wrist as he slammed a paperweight into her skull?

"You left me no choice."

The killer's words echo in my head as I rub the deathpain away.

One...

Two...

Three.

When I was little and spoke of my death-memories, my parents brought me to the pediatrician, who diagnosed me with an overactive imagination and non-clinical anxiety. The doctor gave me breathing exercises and told my parents to keep me away from the news. I learned two things:

1. How to breathe away the deathpain, and

2. Not to talk about my death-memories anymore.

And I haven't, until three years ago, when my mother was in agony and it was clear that the end was near. "Don't be scared, Mom," I whispered to her. "You'll be reborn within seconds." I reminded her of my death-memories. Even if it doesn't happen for everybody, I told her, it happens for me, so it must happen for her too.

"That's comforting," she said, her voice weak and whispery, her skin pale and paper-thin as she reached with a trembling hand to touch my cheek. "But I don't want to become someone else yet. I don't want to leave you and Daddy and Joey alone."

One day later, she did.

The first thing I did after her death, even before her funeral, was look up the birth announcements from the hospital in Eastfield. There were no babies born at that hospital the day my mother died. She was reborn somewhere else, and I would never be able to find her. But she was reborn and starting a new life. It was those she left behind who had a hard time moving on.

Death is hardest on the living. My father is proof of that.

He rubs his eyes as Joey drags him into the family room to show him the racetrack he built, chattering away about what happened at daycare that week and how Cheeks's running wheel is getting squeaky.

Dad pulls his hand from Joey's and collapses onto his armchair. "I'll fix the wheel later, okay? I need a nap."

"He wants to spend some time with you," I say. "He missed you. And I need to talk to you."

"Ever. I said later."

"If you're going to sleep, at least go to bed," I say, knowing he won't. He hasn't slept in the bedroom he shared with Mom since she died.

"I'm fine here."

Joey brings him the yellow afghan we keep on the couch, the one my mother crocheted herself. "No thanks, Joey," Dad says. He pushes the chair back, then closes his eyes. He didn't even take off his shoes. Probably so he can run out of here the second Seth Siegel calls him to go on another cross-country haul.

Joey stands there, dejected, the afghan limp in his arms.

"Come on, Joey," I say with a sigh. "Let's let him sleep. I'll read you a story." I take him to his bedroom, then give him kisses and cuddles and tickle him until he's breathless from laughing so hard. He may not have a mother, and he may have a father who can't stand to even look at him, but he will *never* feel unloved. I love him enough for two parents. It might be all he'll ever get, but it'll be all he'll ever need.

And I'll be damned if I ever let him find out that our father blames him for our mother's death.

I put him on my lap and open a Dr. Seuss book to read to him. One Fish, Two Fish. Three brisk, hard knocks at the front door interrupt me before I get to Red Fish. The knocking immediately turns into pounding.

I rush to open the door before my dad wakes up. Ash Morrison is on my porch, clad in his black boots and leather jacket, his fist raised and ready to pound again. His dark eyes burn into me. "Why did you tell the police I was messing with you?"

CHAPTER TWELVE

LILY ~ EIGHTEEN YEARS AGO

I paused, my hand raised to knock on the Mallick family's front door. Should I be doing this? Maybe my parents were right—again—that I was looking for trouble where there was none. No one else in this town was questioning why Neal was crossing Railroad Bridge in the middle of the night. Everyone else accepted that his death was an accident. No one was suspicious. Not even his family.

I should just place the things from Neal's locker on the porch and leave his poor family to mourn in peace. They didn't know me. They wouldn't believe he was my friend.

But Neal *was* my friend. Ever since the last week of summer before we started high school. That week had been blisteringly hot, and my friends had spent it as we usually did: running around, crossing Railroad Bridge back and forth at full speed, playing tag and capture the flag. To escape being tagged, if anyone got too hot, or if a train came along, they'd cannonball from the bridge into the creek.

I'd watched woefully from the bank of the creek with a cast on my arm, having shattered my elbow a few weeks before. At the time I'd thought it would be awesome to jump down from our giant oak tree onto my trampoline. And it *was* awesome. I just hadn't planned on ricocheting from the trampoline onto our brick patio.

A few feet away, I'd spotted someone in the trees, watching everyone playing. I recognized Neal Mallick right away by his glasses and his slouch. I was hot, and bored, and lonely, so I went over to talk to him.

He'd worn a white t-shirt and yellow shorts that were too wide around his scrawny brown legs. "You should go play with them," I'd told him. "The teams are uneven."

He'd stared at my friends as they ran across the bridge.

"You don't have to be scared," I'd said. "If a train comes, you just jump."

"It's illegal to be on the bridge," he'd said.

We'd spent that entire week in the shade of the trees, watching my friends play. I'd scratch under my cast with a twig and babble about everything and anything that came into my head. He'd pluck blades of grass from the ground and listen.

Late Sunday evening, as the sun had set on our last day of summer vacation and everyone was taking their last leaps into the creek, I blurted out the only thing I hadn't told him about myself yet. "I drowned once, you know. Sometime in the 1600s. In the Mediterranean Sea. I was thirty-seven. I was a fisherman, and my buddy fell off the boat. I jumped in to save him, but..." I'd shrugged. My lungs had

burned

and squeezed

at the memory. Then I'd remembered how everyone else had made fun of me or rolled their eyes when I used to talk about my past lives, and realized I'd just done it again with Neal.

But Neal had just stared at me and blinked. "Did it hurt? Drowning, I mean?"

My surprise at his reaction had been greater than the burning in my lungs. As soon as I'd recovered my breath, I said, "Yeah. A lot."

He'd blinked again, and his wide eyes had held no judgment, only curiosity. So I'd continued. "I've died in a fire, been trampled by horses, shot by bullets in World War II. I died of the Black Plague and the flu. Before I was me, I was a woman from Oregon on my way to New York City. But I never made it. I was killed in a car crash right outside of Ryland. Slid on the icy highway into a UPS truck." I'd cringed as the memories brought the deathpain back,

exploding

inside my head one by one like

fireworks,

then disappearing just as quickly.

"Did you save him?" Neal had asked.

"Who?"

"Your friend. The one who fell off the fishing boat in the 1600s."

"Oh. I don't think so. I feel... sad... when I remember that death."

He'd said nothing for maybe five minutes. As the sun had finally set and everyone had left for home, dripping and laughing, he nodded at the bridge. "It's illegal to be on the bridge," he'd said. "It's too dangerous. You should stay off it."

That had been the last time I'd really hung out with Neal like that. He'd been in all the advanced classes at school, and I'd been busy with my friends and clubs and those dreadful beauty pageants. And even though most of us had spent every summer after that out there by the bridge, Neal had never come back. After school I'd see him walking home the long way, taking Main to Taft, which would take him to Garfield and all the way to Adams Street. But every time I had a new death-memory, I'd seek him out and tell him. He'd never laughed at me. He'd taken me seriously. He'd believed me. And when I'd decided to defy my parents and apply to CFGU, he'd supported me.

Neal was my friend. And now, he needed my help. So I knocked on his family's front door.

A half-minute later, the door opened slowly. Neal's little sister blinked up at me with wide, brown eyes that were identical to his. Her complexion was creamy brown, bringing to mind my memory of Neal in the creek, and the way his brown skin had turned a deathly tint of green.

Devi's long, black hair melded into her black sweater and black pants. Mourning clothes. I was wearing a white button-down shirt, jeans, and my floral boots. Maybe I should have worn something more somber to visit the Mallicks.

No. I was fine. The color of deepest mourning among medieval queens was white, and white had been the official color of royal funerals in Spain until the fifteenth century. Although I personally hadn't been a member of Spain's royal family—just a soldier who'd been killed during the Castilian Succession in 1476.

I swiped away the pain from the bullet in my chest. "Hi. Devi, right?" I said, catching my breath.

When she nodded, I noticed the deep shadows under her eyes. Poor thing. I wanted to hug her.

"I'm Lily. I was friends with your brother." At her curious look, I showed her my bookbag. "I brought his things from his locker. I thought you'd like to have them."

She opened the door wider to let me in. "My mom's sleeping," she said. "Dad's watching TV." She gestured into the next room, where Mr. Mallick slouched on a bright red sofa, staring blankly at an infomercial for a home exercise machine. The top of his head was bald. He didn't seem to notice I was there.

I gave Devi the carnations first, and as I handed her Neal's jacket, something sprinkled from the pocket onto the tile floor. Little red pills.

Pills?

My heart

sank.

The rumors were

true.

Neal had been on drugs the night he died.

A second later, a box, thin and bright red, fell from the pocket. It landed with a soft plop. Splashed across the box in thick white letters were the words *Hot Tamales*.

Those weren't pills in his jacket; they were cinnamon candies. They sold them at the movie theater where Neal worked.

Ha! I *knew* he hadn't been on drugs.

With Devi's arms full with the flowers and Neal's jacket, I saw an opportunity. "I'll put the rest of his stuff in his bedroom for you," I said, dashing up the stairs before she could stop me.

One door was closed; probably where Mrs. Mallick was sleeping. The yellow and white room next to it was definitely Devi's. Across the hall was a room painted blue. It had to be Neal's. Yep—a felt MIT flag hung on the wall over the bed.

I opened my book bag and dumped the items from his locker onto his bed, which was made with tight corners. Had he done that himself the day he'd died, I wondered, or had his mother straightened it for him? Judging from how neat his locker had been and how everything on his desk and bookshelves sat at perfect right angles, he'd probably made his bed himself.

Now I felt guilty for making a mess on his bed. I took his notebooks and stacked them on his desk at right angles, then looked around the room. I didn't know what I was looking for, but I had to hurry. I could hear Devi coming up the stairs. Was it possible for footsteps to have feelings? Because her footsteps sounded heavy and sad.

I opened and shut his desk drawers as quickly and as quietly as I could. Even the contents of his drawers were neatly arranged. If my mother knew that, she'd probably have tried to set me up with sweet, smart Neal instead of Seth Siegel and his chin-dimple. But no—the Mallicks weren't "important" in Ryland.

Devi's footsteps were coming down the hallway now.

A quick peek in Neal's closet. Everything hung nicely, his shoes lined up in rows. His bulletin board even had everything at right angles with red push pins stuck through every paper at the top border, exactly at their centers. Even his—

Wait. There. On the bulletin board. A calendar. March, this month. Last Friday night was circled, with the word MIDNIGHT written in Neal's perfect block letters. Friday at midnight: FRI MID.

And written underneath that:

WILL DUSTON.

Neal had plans to meet Will Duston last Friday at midnight. And now Neal was dead, drowned in the creek that bordered Duston Farm.

I needed to tell Officer Paladino about this.

CHAPTER THIRTEEN

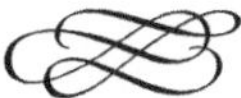

EVER ~ PRESENT DAY

Ash Morrison stands in my doorway, so angry he's practically breathing fire. "You called the cops and told them I was threatening you."

"What are you talking about?" I ask. Ash is huge and angry and irrational, but my dad is inside the house and my boyfriend is right across the street. I go outside to face Ash. "I didn't tell the cops you were threatening me."

"Oh yeah? That's not what Paladino told me a few minutes ago."

"Who's that?"

"Rick Paladino? The chief of police?" he says, his black hair falling in waves down to the collar of his black leather jacket. He's got the kind of golden beige skin that tans easily without burning. "He told me to stop harassing you."

"I've never talked to the chief of police."

His black-eyed gaze bores down on me. "This is about the scholarship, isn't it? I'm the only one standing in your way, so you told the police that I threatened you." He leans in close. "Listen, Ever," he rumbles. "I get enough trouble from them. I don't need you making more."

Ash and I have never spoken before. He's in my AP World History class, but I didn't think he even knew my name. But now he's at my house, trying to intimidate me, and suddenly my blood is boiling. How dare this guy, this cheating, thieving, drug-dealing vandal, come pounding on my door and accuse me of something I didn't do? I draw myself up as tall as I can. He's trying to scare me, but I'm not afraid of him. Well, I am, but I can't let him know it. "I've never said a word about you to the police, but you're kind of proving them right. You are threatening me. Right now."

That seems to scare *him* a bit, ha, and he steps back. "I'm not giving up that scholarship, Ever. You think I don't deserve it because of who my father is, but I'm nothing like that loser. I didn't kill anyone."

"Yeah, well, neither did—" I was about to say *neither did your father* but stop myself. Ash doesn't need to know that. Not yet. "Neither did I," I say instead.

"My GPA is two-tenths of a point higher than yours. I have less money than you do, too. Your house is a palace compared to the dump I live in. That scholarship is mine."

My blood boils. How did Ash know my GPA? Did Miss Buckley tell him? And he has *no* idea how much the Lily Summerhays Memorial Scholarship is mine. "You're not even at school half the time," I say, "and when you bother to come at all, you come in late and you sleep through every class. I study every single day just to get this scholarship. Late nights, weekends, holidays. My GPA didn't come easy. I worked for it. I earned it."

"You don't think I work for anything?" He steps closer, dwarfing me. His hair sweeps off his stubbled jaw, and his eyes are deep and black and furious. He smells like leather and wood. "I work for *everything*. I'm not at school half the time because Ryland High doesn't offer the classes I need so I have independent study. I get A's in all my classes, but everyone assumes I cheat. I can't walk down any street of this town without everyone looking at me, on guard. I can't go into a store without the owner following me up and down the aisles, just waiting for me to steal something."

"You *do* steal. You've been arrested for it."

He cocks his brow and rumbles, "I've been arrested for shoplifting, but never convicted. Ask your friend Paladino. He circles my block all night long, watching me, waiting for me to do something illegal. You don't think it's hard work, every day, for me to live here?"

"Then why do you live here?" I ask. "Just leave."

"That's what I need the scholarship for!" he roars. Then his voice quiets. "Listen. I've been accepted to Hidding University in Maryland. It's the top college in the country for astrophysics. They gave me some money, but not enough. I need the Lily scholarship to pay for the rest, and to get out of this town. And don't worry, once I leave, I will *never* come back."

The quick *whoop* of a siren interrupts him. A police cruiser is rolling down my street. Ash turns on his booted heel and storms to his motorcycle on my driveway.

I storm right after him. "Hey. Hey!"

"What?"

"There are other scholarships out there. You can take out a loan. What's so important to you about the Lily scholarship?"

He swings his leg over the seat and thrusts his heel onto the pedal. The engine roars to life. "I could ask you the same thing," he shouts over the engine, then he shoots past the police car, bolting down the street.

Motorcycle accidents cause over five thousand fatalities every year, and he's not even wearing a helmet.

The police cruiser pulls up to my curb, and the officer leans out his window. His eyes are intense and chocolate brown. "You okay, Miss Abrams? I warned him to stay away from you."

This must be Chief Paladino. As with Ash, I wasn't aware that the police know who I am. I've never been in trouble. Not at home, not at school, and certainly not with the law. I start to tell him that I'm not okay, that Ash was harassing me, but that's not quite true. "I'm fine."

"You can tell me the truth," the chief says. "He made you call the station this morning, didn't he? What did he do, threaten you?"

"No, sir. We've never even spoken to each other until just now." How does the chief know it was me who called? I used a public payphone, I made sure no one saw me, and I didn't leave my name.

He smiles patiently, paternally. His teeth are very white. "I know it was you, Miss Abrams. A call came in at 8:07 this morning. The caller, a young female, said that Vinnie Morrison is innocent, and that Will Duston, the principal at Ryland High School, is Lily Summerhays's real killer. The call came from the payphone at The Batter's Box. All I had to do was go across the street to ask Floyd Stout if anyone used the phone this morning. He didn't think anyone had, but when I asked if any young females came in this morning, he said there was only one. You."

"Oh." Betrayed by Mr. Stout, the nicest guy in the world.

"Did Ash Morrison force you to make that call?" Chief Paladino asks. "It's okay, sweetheart. You can tell me. I won't let him hurt you."

"He had nothing to do with it," I say.

The chief drums his clean, trimmed fingernails on the car door. His genuine concern has quickly turned into impatience and irritation. "Okay, fine. Then tell me, why did you say Will Duston killed Lily Summerhays? What happened, did he give you detention at school, and now you want revenge by accusing him of murder? I can see Ash Morrison pulling a stunt like that, but a good girl like you?"

"No, it's nothing like that. I've never even really spoken to Principal Duston before. Or Ash Morrison, except for a few minutes ago."

"Well, someone must have put that ridiculous idea in your head. If it wasn't Morrison, who was it? Who have you been talking to?"

I'm like a bug pinned under a microscope, so closely does he scrutinize me. "No one. It was my own idea." I dig my toe into the grass. "When you look into it, you'll see that I'm right."

"The case is closed, Miss Abrams. It's been closed for almost eighteen years. Lily Summerhays walked in on Vinnie Morrison burglarizing her house, and he killed her." He pulls a business card from his shirt pocket and holds it out between his fingers. "This is my direct number at the station. When you're ready to tell me what's really going on, give me a call."

"But—"

"*But,*" he says, "if you accuse Will Duston of murder again, I will arrest you for harassment and slander. Understood?"

Arrest me? Can he do that?

The chief is scowling, his nostrils flaring. Keeping me pinned with his eyes, he slowly, deliberately, removes his hand from the steering wheel and lowers it to the gun at his side, lightly stroking it. "Understood, Ever?" he rumbles again.

I nod because "*Yes, sir*" gets stuck in my throat.

"That's my good girl." He hands me his card and drives off.

CHAPTER FOURTEEN

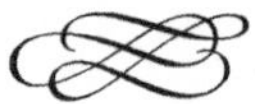

LILY ~ EIGHTEEN YEARS AGO

"Do you know the exact time Neal Mallick died?" I asked Officer Paladino. With the incriminating calendar page in my hand, I'd gone from Neal's house straight to The Batter's Box. I knew I'd find my favorite cop there. The owners always gave Ryland cops free coffee and pie.

"Hello, Lily. Nice to see you too." He raised his mug and took a loud slurp of his coffee. Black, I noticed. He should have been drinking hot chocolate, so it would match his eyes. "No, I do not know the exact time Neal Mallick died. Why are you asking?"

"I bet Will Duston knows." I slid into the booth across from him and slapped the calendar page onto the table. "Neal and Will had plans to meet at midnight."

Paladino froze for a moment, then put a forkful of cherry pie in his mouth. "So?"

"So, Will was there when Neal drowned."

Frowning, he tapped his fingers on the Formica, waiting until

Bubbles refilled his coffee to speak again. "You're saying that Will *might* have witnessed Neal falling off the bridge."

"I'm saying if Neal *accidentally* slipped off the bridge, Will should have called 911 right away. But he didn't report it. Don't you think that's suspicious? Will jumped in the creek to save me. Why didn't he jump in the creek to save Neal?"

"You sure like to jump, Lily. First you jumped off the bridge, and now you're jumping to conclusions."

"Ha ha. Will *warned* me not to jump off the bridge," I said. "Probably because he didn't want me to find Neal down there."

"Or because he knew it was a stupid, dangerous thing to do." Paladino drummed his fingers on the table. Even his fingernails were good-looking. Perfectly shaped and nicely trimmed. "Where'd you get this calendar page?"

"I found it in Neal's bedroom."

His right brow shot up. "You're quite the detective."

"I just want to know what really happened to him."

"Want to know what I think?" He took another bite of his pie and took forever to chew and swallow it. He wiped his mouth before speaking. "I think you're trying to find something that isn't there. There are almost two decades of bad blood between your family and the Dustons. And let's face it, Lily, you aren't exactly known for your calm, rational decisions."

I pushed my curls behind my ears. Even though my parents hated the Dustons, they'd probably tell me the same thing and accuse me of creating trouble where there was none.

"But something doesn't add up," I said. "Shouldn't you at least ask Will *why* he was meeting Neal at midnight?"

"Fine. On the off-chance that you're right, I'll look into it." I nodded with satisfaction as he folded the calendar page into quarters and slid it in the pocket behind his badge. "Now I need you to do something for me."

"What's that?"

"Leave this matter to the police." His chocolate-brown eyes seemed to bore into me through his thick lashes. "You stole that calendar page from Neal's bedroom. It was illegally obtained. If it turns out that you're correct about Will, I won't be able to use it as evidence."

"Oh. I hadn't thought of it that way. Sorry."

"If anything, it's proof that *you* broke the law, not Will. I don't think your parents would be very happy with you."

"You're not going to tell them, are you?"

"No, but you need to let the police handle things before you get yourself into more trouble. Do we have a deal, Lily?" Paladino said. "You'll stay out of it from now on?"

"Yes."

He gave me a dubious look.

"Yes, yes, *yes*. I promise. Just don't tell my parents, okay?"

"I won't." He raised his mug to take a sip of coffee, and I could see he was trying to hide an amused smile. The panic I'd felt just moments ago faded. Ha, he tried to act all stern and serious, but I knew he was on my side.

He slid out of the booth and stood to leave. "No more crashing your car or jumping off bridges either, got it?" He chuckled. "When I became a cop, I never thought Lily Summerhays would be my main source of trouble."

I shrugged and batted my eyelashes angelically. "Just trying to keep you on your toes, Officer."

CHAPTER FIFTEEN

EVER ~ PRESENT DAY

In a failed attempt to shield me from the rain, Keith keeps me tucked under his arm as we hustle across the school's parking lot on Monday morning.

"The ball field will be soaked by this afternoon," Keith says as we navigate around a puddle. "I hope they don't cancel the game." He raises his free arm in a greeting to a fellow Warrior.

I try to smile in reply, but I haven't been able to shake off yesterday's events. The visit from Ash Morrison, and then the chief of police. I haven't told Keith about it, or Courtney. Or my dad, who'd slept through everything that happened just a few feet away in our driveway. They'd all tell me I'm being ridiculous. I don't know what to do.

Keith pulls me back to let a school bus pass, its tires kicking up a spray of rainwater. As we near the school, thunder rumbles above us, threatening to rip open the sky. Holding up the hood of her pink raincoat, Miss Buckley rushes past, amazingly fast in her matching pink heels. Doesn't she know how dangerous it is to run in heels on this wet concrete? Keith tightens his arm around me and we pick up the pace, joining the stream of students rushing toward the crumbling building.

Then I stop short. Fifty feet away, just outside the front entrance under the awning, stand two men. One in a gray suit and tie, the other in a navy uniform and flat cap.

Principal Duston and Chief Paladino. Together.

"Ever, hurry up. We're getting soaked," Keith says, prodding me forward.

But I barely hear him. Barely feel the chilly rain. A serious Chief Paladino is speaking to Principal Duston, who's shaking his head, legs wide with his arms folded across his chest, as they watch the students rush through the parking lot.

I suddenly have the impulse to run and hide.

As I watch, Principal Duston visibly stiffens, and his gaze narrows in on someone. Ash Morrison strides through the rain, hunched over with his hands deep in the pockets of his leather jacket.

Paladino says something to him, an angry expression on his face, but Ash stalks into the building without looking up from his boots.

"Ever, come on." Keith pulls me forward. "What's wrong? Did you forget a book at home or something? I can go back for it if you want."

Shaking my head, I let him guide me to the building. I try to hide behind Keith as we approach the entrance, but it's too late. Chief Paladino sees me.

I glance at Principal Duston. His gaze flickers to Paladino, then his head turns slowly, following Paladino's line of sight until he's focused on me too.

The mouths of both men curve down into accusatory frowns—frowns aimed directly at me.

~

Courtney's desk is next to mine in our sixth period class, AP World History. My least favorite subject. I took AP U.S. History last year, and that wasn't so bad. I've only lived in this country since the late 1930s, so learning about its history doesn't trigger too many death-memories, or the deathpain that comes along with them. But in AP World History, sometimes the death-memories hit me like I'm a punching bag.

We have a quiz today about the Napoleonic Wars, a time period I struggle with. Not because I was a soldier killed in battle, but because my father was a soldier killed in battle, and two days later I, his only son, died at home of influenza at age nine. My last memory was of trying to draw a feverish breath, and my mother sobbing my name. *Philippe, Philippe!*

Mrs. Ricciardelli distributes the quizzes. This morning in Health and Wellness, Courtney drew an intricate design of dots and swirls the back of her left hand with an orange Sharpie, something she likes to do when she's bored in class. Now she takes out a blue Sharpie and adds even more dots and swirls to the design. She doesn't look up when Mrs. Ricciardelli puts the quiz on her desk. Tests always make her nervous.

In the back of the classroom, lounging at his desk with his long legs in the aisle, is Ash Morrison. I try not to look at him, but I feel his eyes on me.

In my periphery, I see a figure rush past the doorway. Principal Duston. Chief Paladino must have told him that I accused him of Lily's murder. There's no other reason he'd be walking past my classroom. He's watching me. He has to be.

No. Stop. I'm being paranoid.

Duston rushes past again, going the other way. My eyes automatically focus on his wrist, but he's too far away and he's walking too fast.

Mrs. Ricciardelli places the quiz on my desk, snapping me out of my reverie. The first question is, 'What political event started the

Napoleonic Wars?' I take a deep breath and brace myself. *No deathpain.*

But in my mind I hear my mother sobbing—*Philippe, Philippe!*—and my muscles ache and weaken, and I start hacking and gasping for breath.

"Sick again, Ever?" asks Mrs. Ricciardelli.

Wheezing, I shake my head. "I'll be okay in a sec." I try to breathe the deathpain away.

One...

Two...

Thr—

Mrs. Ricciardelli points to the doorway. "Nurse. Now."

"I'm not sick," I insist. "I'll be fine in a second."

"You look like you have a fever. Go. Do not come back without a note from the nurse."

Court watches me as I slowly, weakly stand. "Should I take you?" she asks out of habit. She's used to my sudden bouts of sickness that disappear as quickly as they come on. I shake my head. I'll just go to the nurse's office to get my strength back, get my note, and return to take the quiz. I cough again and almost trip over Ash's leg on my way out. Jerk.

Halfway down the hallway, I stop short. Principal Duston is standing there. It could be the fever, but I swear I see a flash of his tattoo as he crosses his arms. "Go back to your classroom, Miss Abrams, and stay there."

"Nurse," I say weakly, then rush past him to the nearest doorway. It leads to the back stairwell.

"Ever! Stop! Do *not* go down those stairs!"

That's exactly what I do, and he's right behind me. I clutch the railing as I descend, anxious to get away from him, but scared of falling even more. Thirteen hundred people die every year by falling down the stairs, and I'm weak and dizzy as it is.

"Ever! Stop right now!" the principal demands.

I step on something on one of the stairs—a pen. Whoa, that was close. I could have slipped on it. I grip the railing, then see that scattered on the steps below me are papers and books. A shoe—a pink high heel—lies on its side, like it was discarded by its wearer.

With a sinking heart, I know what I'm going to see before I actually see it.

At the bottom of the stairs is Miss Buckley, her skirt ripped and her blouse half-untucked, sprawled on her stomach with one arm crushed under her and the other twisted over her. Her chestnut hair fans out, not hiding the fact that her head is turned the wrong way on her body.

CHAPTER SIXTEEN

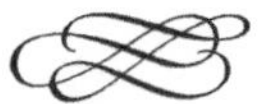

LILY ~ EIGHTEEN YEARS AGO

For four whole days, I watched and waited for Officer Paladino to arrest Will Duston for his involvement in Neal Mallick's death, but Will kept showing up to school like nothing had happened. He walked past me on his way to class, he went to practice on Monday and Tuesday, he played in the game against Forest Grove on Wednesday, he hung out with us at The Batter's Box afterward like he hadn't just been questioned by the police.

Like a well-behaved, responsible student, I did my homework every night, but nothing was really sinking in. How was I supposed to concentrate on classwork when

nothing

was

happening?

Everyone at school, everyone in this whole town, had moved on from Neal's death already. It wasn't fair.

Just after midnight, my phone rang. *Yes.* It had to be Seth, calling with news he'd heard from his father that Will Duston had been arrested.

Oh. It was Diana's number on caller ID. "Hey, Di."

A sniffle.

"Oh no, what's wrong?" I asked, although I could bet it was more Brandon drama.

She blubbered about how Brandon was supposed to come over for dinner with her family that night. "We waited an hour for him and he never came, so I called him, but he never answered his phone!" she cried. "I called Seth, and Seth said that Brandon was meeting with some recruiter from the Yankees. I mean, that's fine, that's great for him, but he didn't even call me to tell me! So I went to his house and waited in his driveway until he got home. When he got there, he said he forgot that he was supposed to come over for dinner. He *forgot*. He forgot about me. Again. So... " She took a hitchy breath. "I broke up with him. For real."

"You sound serious about it this time," I said.

"I mean, he'll be playing baseball for New York or Texas or wherever, and I'll be going to school here at Griffin. He'll be practicing all the time and traveling around the country for games. He'll forget about me again. There's no way it could last." She released a mournful sob. "I did the right thing, right?"

"You did, Diana." I said. "I know it's hard, but you need to look out for yourself."

Seriously, relationships weren't worth the hassle, especially in high school. I loved Diana and I loved Brandon, but she had cried at least once a month for two years over him. And now they had broken up for good. All that drama for nothing. And look at my parents. They'd started dating in high school and gotten married just weeks after graduation because she was pregnant with me. I couldn't remember a time when they weren't both miserable. Mom was desperate to please my father, who never even noticed. Or if he did notice, he didn't care. Diana would be much better off without Brandon.

"Hang tight," I told my friend. "I'll be there in ten minutes." My parents were sleeping. They'd never know.

She sniffled again. "Thanks, but it's late. I just want to go to bed. I'll see you tomorrow, okay?"

"Okay, if you're sure. Call me if you need me."

"I will. Love you."

"Love you too."

I was late to school the next morning because I stopped along the way to get Diana a box of her favorite doughnuts from The Batter's Box, something I did every time she and Brandon had a bad breakup. Hopefully, this was the last time.

As I rushed to school, I saw Officer Paladino's patrol car driving down the street. I waved at him to stop. He slowly pulled over and rolled down his window.

He looked at me over his sunglasses. Holding my books to my chest, I leaned into his window. "Hey, Ricky. Want a doughnut? Double chocolate with sprinkles, still warm."

"It's 'Officer Paladino,' Lily. I'm in uniform."

I smiled sweetly and handed him a doughnut. "In that case, I swear this isn't a bribe, Officer Paladino."

"A bribe for what?" He grumbled, but he still took the doughnut.

"Information," I said. "What happened with Will Duston? You were going to question him about the calendar?"

"That's right," he said, eating a quarter of the doughnut in one bite. "I talked to him on Monday."

Good. "And?"

"And nothing. Just like I thought."

"But Neal was supposed to meet with him at midnight on the night he died."

He sighed. "We had a deal, Lily. I'd follow up on Will, and you'd drop the issue. I followed up and it was nothing; and now you need to drop it."

"But—"

"I'm on duty, Lily. Please let me do my job." I followed his gaze to the movie theater. Vinnie Morrison's olive Mazda was pulling around to the back alley. "I have to go. Aren't you late for school?"

Of course I was. I stepped back as he rolled his car down the street toward the theater.

Except at lunch, I didn't run into Will often at school. We didn't have any classes together. He took lots of agriculture-type classes, which to me would be even worse than all the math and business classes my parents made me take. But I needed to find out what Will told Officer Paladino, so that afternoon I waited casually by his locker. As he approached, he narrowed his eyes at me. I was never in this area of the school, in the Ag wing. "What do you want, Red?" he rumbled.

I smiled innocently at him. "I heard Officer Paladino had a little talk with you."

That surprised him a little, and he almost stumbled. "Where'd you hear that?"

I shrugged. "What'd you talk about?"

He turned the lock on his locker. "None of your business."

"Was it about why Neal was meeting you at midnight on the night he died?"

He froze then. "How do you know about that?"

I shrugged again. "I just think it looks suspicious. He met you at midnight, and then he drowned in the creek on the border of your farm."

"You think I killed him?"

I decided to come out with it. "I don't know. Maybe. Yeah."

Will wasn't a bad-looking guy, now that I actually looked at him. It was only March and he hadn't been tanned in the sun yet, but his hair and eyebrows were light, like they were permanently sun-kissed. He was an inch or two taller than me, and I was taller than most girls and some boys. Working on the farm his whole life and working out with the Warriors made him lean and strong. But his eyes were icy with anger and annoyance, so I took away some points for that.

"If I'm such a cold-blooded killer, you should be afraid of me." He made a shooing motion with his hand, flashing his crossed-hatchet tattoo. "Go. Run away screaming. Save yourself."

I probably should have been afraid of him, but I wasn't. "I didn't say you were cold-blooded."

"I did not kill Neal Mallick," he said, grinding his teeth on his toothpick, "in cold blood or otherwise."

"Then you should be willing to tell me what happened." I took his arm. "Will, please.

I just want to know the truth. Why were you meeting him at midnight? Why was he on the bridge? If it truly was an accident, why didn't you call 911? Why didn't you jump in to save him like you saved me?"

The bell rang and he slammed his locker shut and stepped close to me. He removed the toothpick from his mouth and slowly, gently, tucked my hair behind my ear. He leaned in, his breath minty and cool on my cheek.

Breathless,

my heart

stopping,

I waited to finally hear the truth.

He leaned in even closer. "I would tell you," he whisper-growled, "but then I'd have to kill you. In cold blood." He walked off without another glance at me.

Who the hell did that boy think he was? No one in the world was more irritating and self-righteous than Will Duston.

I couldn't wait to get out of Ryland.

CHAPTER SEVENTEEN

EVER ~ PRESENT DAY

After the EMTs retrieve Miss Buckley's body and pack it away like luggage in the ambulance, school is canceled for the rest of the day. My classmates chatter in hushed, shocked voices as they slowly shuffle out. Some of the girls are crying. The boys stand around stoically. Courtney sags against the lockers, her eyes glazed and wet, pressing one hand against her mouth. The swirls and dots of her Sharpie design look too celebratory now.

"It's okay, Court," I coo, like I do when I comfort Joey from a nightmare. "It'll be okay." I was the one who actually saw Miss Buckley's broken body; Court should be the one comforting *me*. But I have experience with death—lots of experience. Miss Buckley, if she's like me, really is okay. She's probably already been reborn, or would be any second, into a new baby at the hospital in Eastfield.

"What did she look like?" Court asks me from behind her decorated hand. "Was it horrible? Was there blood?"

"None that I could see." Her head was backward on her body. But I can't bring myself to tell Courtney that.

"It was her shoes, wasn't it?" she says. "Those high heels she wears all the time. She tripped going down the stairs in them." She looks down at her feet. She's wearing heels too. Black ones. Not as high as the kind Miss Buckley liked to wear, but she kicks them off anyway and stands in her bare feet. Her sparkly blue nail polish is chipped a little on her big toe.

Like the giant bear that he is, Coach Nolan pushes through the throng of students and hugs both Courtney and me. "The principal told me you saw her body, Ever. He said you were really scared."

"I'm okay now, I think." It was Principal Duston who scared me, way more than Miss Buckley's body. He grabbed my arm and dragged me back up the stairs to my classroom and told Mrs. Ricciardelli to not let me, or anyone, leave.

"Is your father on the road?" Coach asks. "You can sleep at our house tonight if you don't want to be alone. Joey too, of course."

"Thanks. Our dad's home. I'll be fine."

"Call us if you need anything," he says, then takes Courtney home.

I push my way toward my locker, but my arm is grabbed for the second time that day.

But it's not Principal Duston. It's Ash Morrison. He drags me around the corner. Huffing heavily like he's holding back tears, he still manages to shoot daggers at me with his eyes. "I suppose I should say *congratulations* now. So congrats."

"For what?"

"The scholarship. It's yours."

Instead of hating him at that moment, instead of being afraid of him, I feel sorry for him. "Ash, we don't know that. The committee still has a few weeks to decide. A lot can change by then."

He grunts, working his jaw. "Miss Buckley *promised* she'd get me that scholarship. She got me to the final round, and she said she would do whatever it took to get the committee to vote for me. She said she knew how to get the committee to change their minds."

"How?"

He shrugs. "I don't know, and now I never will. Without her, I'm done." He slams his fist into a maroon locker, denting it. "So congratulations, you win. Have a great life."

He storms off, his hands clenched. He knocks into a freshman but doesn't stop.

"Ash, wait," I call after him. If he hears me, he doesn't turn back.

I go home in a daze. My mind won't stop churning. I make dinner for Dad and Joey, but I can't eat. I can't focus on my homework. I don't even try to sleep.

Ash is right: without Miss Buckley to advocate for him, the scholarship is mine. I should be happy, but I'm not. I know I'm probably slightly traumatized by the sight of Miss Buckley's body, but it's more than that. I feel betrayed by her too. She always had a soft spot for troubled kids like Ash, so sneaking his application through to the final round was understandable. Forgivable, even. But she promised the scholarship to him, told him she'd do whatever it took to get the committee to vote for him, said she knew how to get the committee to change their minds. Which means I never had a chance.

I worked so hard my entire life for that scholarship, and I never had a chance.

Miss Buckley was Lily's best friend. How could she promise the scholarship to the son of the man who killed her?

But Ash's father *didn't* kill Lily. *I* knew that. Maybe...

Maybe...

Maybe... somehow... Miss Buckley knew it too.

Maybe Miss Buckley knew who really killed Lily.

Maybe, to get the committee to give the scholarship to Ash, Miss Buckley was finally going to spill her secret after all these years and expose the real killer.

Only now she can't tell her secret because she fell down the stairs and died.

But maybe...

Maybe...

The end of that *maybe* rumbles around in my mind, getting louder and louder until it drowns out the sound of the TV show my dad's watching in the family room, drowns out the sound of the squeaky hamster wheel in Joey's room, drowns out every other thought.

Maybe she didn't fall.

Maybe she was pushed.

CHAPTER EIGHTEEN

LILY ~ EIGHTEEN YEARS AGO

"Need anything else, Dad?" I peeked into his office at Agri-So. "I finished the filing and restocked the coffee supplies." I'd also alphabetized the invoices, updated the customer database, and folded over two hundred advertisements, stuffed them into envelopes, and sealed them. I had several paper cuts on my fingers, and my tongue was heavy and sticky with envelope glue. I'd never realized that office work was such a hazardous job.

Dad glanced up from a letter he was reading. "You can run those envelopes through the stamp machine and drop them off at the post office. But take a break first, Lily. You worked hard today. See how much you can accomplish when you don't daydream all day long?"

Wow. Not the best of compliments, but I'd take what I could get from him. I curled up in the cushioned chair across his desk and opened my book. The plant was quiet; he didn't run production over the weekends. It was just Dad, me, and the permanent stench of Agri-So: chemicals and manure.

Dad broke the silence with a disgruntled sigh. He rubbed his eyes, then folded the letter.

"Bad news?" I asked.

"Another lawsuit," he mumbled.

"From the Dustons?" I asked.

"Yep. Trying to get a percentage of my profits. I bought them out fair and square over fifteen years ago. It's not my fault they don't know how to manage their money."

"You bought them out?" I asked. "What do you mean?"

"Fred and I started Agri-So together," Dad said.

"I didn't know that."

"Oh, yeah. I was the chemistry and business expert. He was the agriculture expert. The land this building is on was once part of his farm. But Agri-So didn't take off quickly enough. He got spooked and wanted to go back to farming, so I bought him out and bought the land from him too. For more than it was worth, I might add. Soon, Agri-So was turning a profit and I was able to expand the business and build a bigger plant, and his farm was struggling. He's been trying to sue me out of business ever since."

From the window over Dad's desk, I could see the railroad tracks dividing Agri-So's land from Duston's soybean field, and their crumbling white farmhouse and faded red barn beyond that. I looked for Will but didn't see him.

Should I tell Dad about Will, how I thought he might have had something to do with Neal's death?

"Is that a textbook you're reading?" Dad asked.

I showed him the cover.

"'*The Essentials of Human Anthropology*,'" he read. "I don't recall you taking that class."

That's because I wasn't; Ryland High didn't offer it. "It's a college textbook," I told him. "I ordered it from the bookstore. You know, the one on Main Street? The Secret Garden? I ordered another one too, a more advanced one. It's coming in a couple of weeks."

"College textbooks," he murmured, nodding. Good. He was impressed.

"I really like it, Dad. It's really interesting. I..." I should just tell him. We had a good day together. "I want to major in cultural anthropology in college."

"I know you love that kind of stuff, Lily, but as a career?" He looked at me over his glasses. "It's impractical."

"Not to me."

"You won't make any money being a cultural anthropologist."

"I don't care about money."

"You would care about money if you didn't have any," he said. "You can take a few classes in anthropology, but you need to major in business. It can be finance, or marketing, or business management. You have lots of choices. You'll find something you like. But it needs to be something you can use at Agri-So."

I looked around his office. A metal desk, a set of dusty bookshelves, thin blue industrial carpeting. The only things decorating the white drywall were a few photographs of me, a map of the U.S., the periodic table of elements, and a few awards from the Chamber of Commerce in cheap wooden frames. "What if I don't want to work at Agri-So?"

"Don't be ridiculous, Lily. You have a job—a good job—waiting for you when you graduate college. And one day you'll run this place. You'll own it. You know how many kids would kill for this opportunity?"

"But, Dad," I said. "I don't want to spend my life making *dirt*."

He laughed. "I didn't grow up dreaming of manufacturing enriched soil either. But I knew I wanted to own a business. Running my own business and making it grow is what I love. It's not necessarily the product."

I held back a sigh and returned to my book. I'd never convince him.

"It's not all about soil," Dad said. "I'm going to a convention for small business owners next week. Why don't you come with? You can miss a couple days of school."

Missing school sounded good, but not to go to a business convention. "No thanks."

"It's in New York City."

With a gasp, I jumped up. "New York? *City*?"

"I'll have my secretary buy you a plane ticket. I'm sure you'll enjoy flying too."

I'd already flown lots of times in Javier's single-engine, but Dad didn't know that. And this time I'd be flying in a jet. "We can go to Chinatown," I said. "And Little Italy. And Little Greece!" I'd died in each of those countries. Carroll-Freywood Global University was based in New York City too. Maybe a visit to the admissions office would help me get accepted, and as a bonus, convince my dad to let me go.

"What about Mom? She'd love to see a show on Broadway," I said, then instantly regretted it when he leaned back in his chair, rubbing his eyes again.

"This isn't a vacation, Lily. It's a business trip. I doubt your mother would be interested." He turned back to his computer. "Why don't you take care of those envelopes and then you can go home. I have a few more hours of work to do."

CHAPTER NINETEEN

EVER ~ PRESENT DAY

Maybe she was pushed. Maybe Miss Buckley was pushed.

I still can't get the idea out of my head the next day after school as I walk the three blocks down Main Street and turn into the alley behind the movie theater.

Earlier that day I slipped a note into Ash's locker, asking him to meet me here. I can't ask him to meet me at school, where Principal Duston could see us. And I can't ask him to meet me at any place along Main Street, where the police station is and Chief Paladino could see us. I can't ask him to go to my house. The only place I could think where no one would see us was here, in the alley.

Ash probably won't even come. He probably read my note and crumpled it up.

I'm about to leave when Ash's motorcycle roars into the alley. So much for subterfuge.

"Your engine is so loud," I hiss when he shuts it off. "This is supposed to be a secret meeting."

"Don't worry," he says, shaking his head and making his black hair brush his jaw. "I didn't tell anyone who I was meeting here."

"But if the cops followed you..."

"What's with the cloak and dagger? You need to buy some pot?" He chuckles. "Prudish little Ever Abrams, a pothead. Never would've guessed."

I'm too stunned to speak, but I feel my jaw fall open.

"I hate to break it to you, Ever, but despite what everyone thinks, I don't use illegal substances anymore. I don't sell them either. My mother's current boyfriend does, though. You need me to set you up?"

"I don't do drugs either."

At the end of the alley, a police cruiser rolls by quietly, slowly. Ash must see fear on my face because he suddenly becomes solemn. "Shit, you're serious about this, aren't you?"

"Yes." I hate the way my voice cracks.

"And the cops can't see us?"

"No one can."

"Then this isn't a great place. I hate it here anyway. Come with me."

He tucks his bike behind the dumpster. I follow him down the alley and around to the weed-ridden used-car dealership that went bankrupt two years ago. Ash doesn't appear to be rushing, but his legs are longer than mine, and I have to hustle to stay a few steps behind. He never looks back to see if I'm following.

He pushes open a loose section of the fence surrounding the car dealership and we slip through. We follow the train tracks as they disappear into the patch of trees that line Deep Creek. The only sound is the rush of the creek and Ash's booted footfalls as he plods along.

The tracks cross over Deep Creek by means of an old crumbling bridge. Ash gets halfway across before he realizes I'm not behind him. "You coming?" he calls.

A memory strikes—not a death-memory, but a memory from when I was little. A warning from my mother. "Didn't some kid slip off this bridge once and drown in the creek?"

"Yep. Kids used to jump from the bridge all the time. That's why they stopped. But come on. You'll be fine."

I lick my lips. "What if a train comes? Five hundred people a year die getting hit by a train."

"You just happen to know that statistic?"

"It's an important statistic to know."

"If a train comes," he says, "you'll hear it. Plenty of time to run to safety. But it'd be more fun if you jump in the creek."

Both options are way too risky. "Just come back," I say. "No one can see us here."

In an exaggerated, mocking manner, Ash peers up and down the tracks. "You're in luck. No train coming."

I look up and down the tracks too. No train in sight. No whistle. No rumbling. But I can't make my feet move. The rails are rusty and the wood is warped and rotting in places. What if I slip and fall like that kid did? My lungs squeeze at the death-memory of drowning when I was a fisherman in the early 1600s.

"Jesus." Ash stomps back to me, his black boots making the crumbling structure vibrate. He grabs my hand and yanks.

I stumble and have to grip him tight to keep from slipping as he tugs me across the bridge. His hand dwarfs mine and feels warm and rough. Odd. Unexpected. Keith's hands are big too, but they're soft. Holding Keith's hand always reminds me of when I was six and my dad took me fishing in his rowboat and made me take the fish off the hook.

Ash pulls me across the bridge. It's terrifying, but we reach the other side without tripping. That was literally the most dangerous thing I've done in my entire life. I stifle a relieved exhale, and it comes out sounding like a gleeful, triumphant giggle.

I follow him along the creek bed. The ground is dry, and the grass and weeds are plush. Soon we come upon a massive oak tree budding with leaves. Ash sinks against the trunk. From the other side he drags an old duffel bag covered with dirt. He pulls a flask from it and offers it to me. "Vodka?"

"Oh. No thanks."

He take a swig, then wipes his mouth with his forearm. The corner of his mouth turns up into a smirk. "I'm kidding. It's water. Thirsty?"

I am, thirsty enough to take a tiny sip, just enough to make sure he's not tricking me. Yes, it's water. I take a bigger sip and hand it back to him. "Thanks." I sit next to him and look around. Sprawled on the other side of the tracks is the squat, red-brick Agri-So plant, and on this side, there's an open weedy field and a few trees. It feels like we're in a different world, a world with just the two of us. "It's kind of nice here," I say. "Quiet."

"The field behind us," Ash says, slipping the flask back into his bag, "used to be Duston Farm."

"Duston, as in Principal Duston?"

"The very same. Agri-So bought the land a long time ago but never developed it beyond putting in an extra parking lot at the far end. No one ever comes back this way but me. In the summers sometimes I'll stay out here until dawn, looking at the stars through my telescope."

"Doesn't your mom worry about where you are?"

He gives a resentful huff and leans against the trunk. "Yeah, it's great out here. I just have to be on the lookout for snakes."

I scramble up with a shriek. "Snakes?"

With a chuckle, he takes my wrist and pulls me back down. "This is too easy. The only snakes I've seen around here are garter snakes. I swear."

"But Indiana has cottonmouths and copperheads. And two kinds of rattlesnakes. One hundred thousand people die from snakebites every year worldwide. And there are field mice, and squirrels, and raccoons out here. What if you get rabies?"

He gives me a grin. "Okay, tell me. How many people die from rabies every year?"

He still has his hand on my wrist. "Fifty-five thousand. Worldwide."

"You worry too much," he says.

"You don't worry enough." I slip my hand away and wrap my arms around my knees.

"You're probably right. But did you really go through all this espionage just so you could lecture me about death stats?"

That's right. I'm here for a reason. May as well come out with it. "Do you really believe your father killed Lily Summerhays?"

He stares at me, his black irises endlessly deep, angry yet vulnerable. "I don't like to talk about my father."

"So you do believe he killed her," I say.

"Why do you care? You trying to trick me or something? You got the scholarship, Ever. It's over. You won."

"I'm not trying to trick you, and this isn't about the scholarship."

"Then what *is* this all about?"

"I just really need to know."

With a disgusted grunt, he stands. "Whatever it is you're trying to do, it won't work. I'm out of here."

I grab his hand before he can walk away. "Ash. Please. I'll tell you what's going on. I'm just trying to figure out how." I'm literally on my knees, begging him. "Please."

He looks down at me. "You're serious."

"Yes."

"Well, I still don't trust you, but you got me curious at least." He sits back down and reclines against the trunk, resting his elbows on his knees. "Fine. I'll hear you out."

CHAPTER TWENTY

LILY ~ EIGHTEEN YEARS AGO

Dad was wrong. Mom was ecstatic when I told her about the business trip to New York City. She immediately called to make reservations for dinner one night at The Plaza. I told her to make it for two. She and Dad could use a romantic evening together. And while they were busy being romantic, maybe I would sneak away to explore the largest city in the world on my own.

Our upcoming trip kept us all buoyed that week, but I didn't forget about Neal. I'd been keeping my eye on Will, even making special trips across the school to find him. He went to his classes, went to baseball practice and games, attended the student council meeting and the FFA meeting. He slapped his buddies on the back, laughed, goofed around. Helped a freshman pick up the lunch tray he dropped. So far he'd been perfect.

He was bound to slip up sometime.

Diana, though, was a mess, although you'd never know it to look at her. Despite breaking up with Brandon last week, she still wore her Batgirl gear that Friday, her perfectly-styled chestnut head held high. The Warriors and the Batgirls were holding a clinic, like a mini training camp, for the little kids of Ryland after school, and Diana wasn't going to let Brandon stop her from fulfilling her duties as president of the Batgirls. I was the only one who noticed how her gaze always returned to Brandon when he wasn't looking, and the tiny tremble in her smile.

I knew that trembly smile well. I'd seen it a million times on my mother.

"Want to come over tonight after the training camp?" Diana asked me.

I was only half-listening to Diana as we walked down the hallway. I was busy concentrating on watching Will a few feet ahead of us. He strode quickly, with purpose, and when he passed by Neal's locker, now empty and repainted, his steps lost their rhythm for just a moment. His head turned toward the locker, just a millimeter.

When he saw me behind him, he rushed through the exit. The look on his face was clear: That boy felt

guilty

about something.

He was going to that training camp. I couldn't let him get away.

"Diana," I said, coming to a stop. "I want to be a Batgirl."

Joy lit her face for the first time in days. "You do? For real?"

I shrugged innocently. "I'm friends with all the guys on the team. I should do something, you know, to support them. I can help with the training camp today. Right now."

"Yay! We don't have a lot of time. I have an extra shirt in my locker. Hurry!" She dragged me back upstairs to her locker and tossed a T-shirt at me. Like all the Batgirls' shirts, it was yellow and featured the maroon silhouette of a curvy girl holding a baseball bat. So

so

so

gross. I was about to protest but clamped my lips shut. I had a mission, and I needed to be a Batgirl to do it.

I slid it over my blue tank top and slipped my diamond pendant under the neckline to keep it safe. Diana used a hair elastic to knot the shirt tightly around my waist. "You can wear one of my ribbons too." She pulled one of the twisty maroon-and-gold ribbons from her hair and clipped it into mine, on top of my ponytail. "You look so cute!" She rushed me back downstairs before I had time to feel like an idiot.

The ball field was already filling up with grade-school and middle-school kids, and the Warriors and Batgirls were taking their places at their stations, showing kids how to pitch, bat, catch, or slide. Batgirls passed out Gatorade. Diana pretended not to notice Brandon and Coach Nolan on the bleachers, talking to a newspaper reporter and photographer. At the photographer's request, Brandon smiled, flashing his lopsided grin.

One of the Batgirls called Diana over. "Just pick a station," she said to me. "Where do you want to go?"

I spotted Will by the dugout, teaching a group of kids how to hold the bat. "Um, there area lot of kids over by the dugout," I said. "I'll guess I'll go over there."

Diana hustled away and I went to the dugout. Will was slouched behind a little girl of about seven, showing her how to grip the bat. He straightened when he saw me. "What are you doing here, Red?"

I modeled my new shirt. "I'm a Batgirl now," I said. "Diana sent me to help you."

With a cocked eyebrow, he turned to the kids. "Say *hello* to Lily. She knows nothing about baseball."

I grinned. "Don't listen to anything this guy tells you. I know everything about baseball. If you want to be a good baseball player, just do what I do." I held the bat upside down and swung it like a golf club.

The kids laughed, and surprisingly, so did Will.

We spent the next hour showing each group of kids how to grip the bat and swing, with Will using me as an example of what not to do. I was horrible at batting and didn't hit a single one of his pitches, but the kids were having a blast, and I was laughing so hard that I didn't care.

Diana came by with some cookies for the kids, clearly ignoring Brandon, who was trailing behind her. "Diana," he begged. "I'm sorry! Just talk to me! Please!"

When they left, Will rolled his eyes at me. "Are you as sick of those two as I am?"

"More."

We instructed the kids to sit in a circle to eat their cookies. I served them Gatorade while Will told them about winning the state championship last year.

"Are you going into the pros?" a little boy asked.

"Me? No." Will took a deep, satisfied breath and lifted his face to the sun. "I'm staying right here on my farm."

Diana blew the whistle: time to rotate again. That girl kept a tight schedule. Still chewing their cookies, the kids moved to the next station while Will and I met the next group at home plate. These were the seventh-graders, and Devi Mallick was among them, with her long, black hair and wide, sad brown eyes. I gave her a wave. Did she know I took that calendar page from Neal's bulletin board?

When it was her turn, Will was extra patient with her as he positioned her hands the right way on the bat.

"Hey, Devi." I pulled the ribbons from my hair. "You want these?"

Her face lit up a bit, warming my heart. "Wow, yeah. Thanks!"

"Maybe you'll be a Batgirl when you get in high school."

The light extinguished. "We're moving," she said. "My mom doesn't want to live in Ryland anymore."

"I don't blame her."

There was that look again, just for a moment, but I saw the way Will

froze
averted his gaze
swallowed hard.
He tried to hide it, but I saw it:
Guilt.

CHAPTER TWENTY-ONE

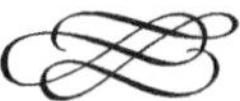

EVER ~ PRESENT DAY

Still on my knees under the giant oak tree by the creek, I repeat my question. "Do you really think your father killed Lily Summerhays?"

Ash dips his head so I can't see his face behind his long, black hair and doesn't speak. I'm going to have to ask him a third time if he believes his father is guilty.

But then he answers me. "I used to believe he was innocent," he says, "until I was about thirteen."

"What changed your mind?"

"I was at Kammer's Pharmacy. Just buying a Red Bull, but of course Kammer assumed I was shoplifting. So he called Paladino. He was furious when he couldn't find any stolen merch on me. But he said I was a loser and I would wind up on death row with my father anyway. I got pissed and said my dad was innocent. So he hauled me to the station and showed me the proof."

"The diamond pendant."

Starting with his thumb, he numbered with his fingers. "The diamond pendant. And the police reports. And the court transcriptions. And the tape of his confession."

"You watched the tape?"

"He doesn't remember killing her, but he had a history of getting violent when he was black-out wasted. After they showed him that they found Lily's diamond necklace in his apartment, he confessed that yeah, he probably did do it."

"And that's proof enough for you?"

"He confessed. Should be proof enough for anyone."

"But what if he didn't do it?" I asked, fiddling with my daisy charm.

"He killed her, Ever. I know it, the judge knows it, even my father knows it. Why do you care so much anyway?"

"Because," I say, whispering, "*I* know he didn't kill her."

"How could you possibly know something like that? Were you even alive yet?"

No, I wasn't. I was born a few seconds later. But Ash's curiosity has turned back to anger, and I still can't tell him how I know his father is innocent. I can't tell him about my intimate knowledge of Lily's last moments, how the last words she heard were her killer rumbling, *"You left me no choice,"* how the last thing she saw was the tattoo of two crossed hatchets on his wrist as he slammed a pink sparkly paperweight into her skull.

The deathpain hits, and I cry out, holding my head over my eyebrow.

"Jesus, you okay?" Ash asks.

"Headache," I croak, then I breathe the pain away.

One...

Two...

Three.

When I recover, I say, "You said that Miss Buckley promised you the scholarship. Did you ever wonder why?"

"I know why. Everyone in this town treats me like shit, and she knows how unfair that is. If it weren't for her, I'd probably be in prison by now, just like Paladino said. But freshman year she called me into her office. She said that she knew I was smart, that I had potential. She said if I stopped getting into fights, stopped doing drugs, and started going to class, that she would help me get into college and figure out how to pay for it."

"That's when she promised you the Lily scholarship?"

"Not at first. She said there were lots of scholarships out there I had a better chance at. Scholarships for people like me, who *overcome the odds*." He snaps a twig in half, then chucks both pieces far into the creek. "They even have scholarships specifically for kids with parents in prison. But I wanted the Lily scholarship. I wouldn't back down. So she finally agreed. She said if that was what I really wanted, she would do whatever it took to get it for me."

"So she pushed your application through to the final round," I say. "But how was she going to convince the committee once they found out it was *your* application? Especially Mr. and Mrs. Summerhays. Did you ever think about that?"

"All the time. I asked her once what she was going to do."

"What did she say?"

"She wouldn't tell me. She just got all quiet and told me not to worry about it."

"Ash. There's only one thing she could say that would convince Mr. and Mrs. Summerhays to give you that scholarship."

"What, that my father *didn't* kill their daughter?"

He says it sarcastically, but I'm serious. "Yes."

He sputters, and his sarcasm turns back to anger. "If my father didn't kill Lily, then who did?"

"Principal Duston," I say in a whisper.

That earns me a solid, barking laugh. "Nobody on Earth hates that guy more than I do, but why would you think he killed Lily Summerhays?"

"I overheard them talking about it. Principal Duston and Miss

Buckley. At... Kammer's Pharmacy. They were in the next aisle over." It's a lie, but there's no other way to get him to believe me.

"Do you have proof?"

"No." *That* is the truth. I have no way of proving the last thing Lily saw was the hatchet tattoo on Principal Duston's wrist.

"Why are you telling me this?" Ash asks. "Why don't you just tell the cops what you overheard?"

"I did," I say. "Chief Paladino didn't believe me."

"Ah." Ash nods. "That's why he accused me of threatening you. He thought I forced you to blame Duston. Asshole."

Slowly he stands, then paces around the tree. "Okay. I'm going to pretend for one second that you're not totally delusional, that you're not lying, and that you're not doing something to sabotage me. If what you're saying is correct, then my father has been rotting in prison for almost eighteen years and Miss Buckley knew the entire time that he was innocent."

"Maybe not the entire time," I say.

"Why didn't she say anything?"

"She was about to. That's what she was telling the principal at Kammer's."

"No. *No.* You must have misunderstood them. You can't be right about this."

"But what if I am?"

"Because that would mean..." A low rumbling fills the air and the ground vibrates as a train approaches, and Ash's steps become faster, fiercer around the tree. "*That's* why she was nice to me?" He rakes his fingers through his hair. He doesn't look angry; he looks like he's been stabbed in the heart by the one person he trusted.

The train rushes past, close enough to shake the tree, but not loud enough to disguise Ash's anguish. "She felt *guilty?*"

I stop him forcibly when he rounds the tree again. "She was going to do the right thing in the end, though. Whatever her reason, Ash, she turned your life around."

Defeated, he sinks to the ground again. "But then she had to go fall down the stairs. My dad's being executed next month, and she could have stopped it."

"That's the other thing. Falling down the stairs? I don't think it was an accident. Principal Duston was rushing back and forth in the hall right before I found her body."

"Yeah, I remember seeing him out there. I thought he was watching me." Through his tangled hair, he gives me a sideways glance, putting the pieces together. "She told him that she was going to expose him so I would get the scholarship, so he *pushed* her down those stairs to shut her up."

"I think so. He tried to stop me from going down the stairwell."

It takes Ash a long time to speak again. A long time to look at me. "Tell me, Ever," he says finally. "Why should I believe you? You have no proof, you said so yourself. How do I know you're not making this whole thing up?"

"Why would I? I'm the one who stands to lose the scholarship."

Another long look. Judgmental, suspicious. Lips twisted in doubt. Then his features relax, and he nods. "If you're right about this, Ever... everything will change. Everything."

That's what I'm afraid of.

CHAPTER TWENTY-TWO

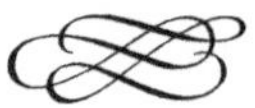

LILY ~ EIGHTEEN YEARS AGO

It was almost midnight, and I was still awake, packing my suitcases for New York. We weren't leaving until Monday, but I was trying to distract myself from thinking about Will Duston. I'd watched him closely this week. I'd really *watched* him instead of shooting insults at him or ignoring him. Surprisingly enough, most of the time he seemed like a

nice

kind-hearted

caring

guy. I'd actually had fun with him at the baseball training camp, and if he weren't a Duston, I could even be friends with him. The more time I spent with him, the harder it was to believe he killed Neal. But he couldn't hide that occasional look of guilt on his face. Not from me. I saw it every time. And just following him around and catching his guilty glances wasn't helping me prove anything.

My room suddenly became stifling and airless. I slammed my

suitcase shut. I'd never prove Will killed Neal unless I took some action.

I slid into a pair of jeans and tossed my denim jacket over my tank top, threw on my red Converse low-tops, then snuck past my parents' bedroom and down the stairs. As I passed through the family room, I noticed a lump on the couch. My father, asleep under a blanket.

Huh. That was new. Maybe.

I made my footsteps even quieter and, instead of heading for the side door in the kitchen, I navigated around the squeaky floorboards of the foyer. Making sure to leave the front door open just enough so the lock didn't catch, I slipped out into the clear, cool March night.

Now I was out, but where should I go?

Railroad Bridge. The place Neal died. Maybe I'd find... *something*.

Avoiding the flickering street lights by ducking into yards, I hustled to Main Street. Ryland was deathly quiet at midnight. Not even a car passed down the roads. I slipped behind the movie theater, toward the railroad tracks that would lead me to the bridge.

A shadow spoke, illuminated by a single orange ember. "There's only one reason a pretty thing like you would be out here this late."

There was only one person who hung out behind the movie theater: Vinnie Morrison.

There was only one reason *he* would be out here this late too.

Well, I might as well question him. I lifted my chin and prepared for my first conversation with Ryland's infamous drug dealer. "What's up, Vinnie?"

He held his cigarette between his lips and dug into the pockets of his camouflage jacket. "Siegel send you?"

"Mayor Siegel?"

He snickered. "His kid. Seth. The tall one with the chin. He usually comes himself, but I see you hanging out with him sometimes. Hard to forget that red hair of yours, princess." His gaze traveled from my hair, down to my boobs, and stopped. Gross.

"Seth didn't send me," I said, crossing my arms over my chest. "No one *sends* me anywhere. I came on my own. I need to ask you some questions."

He smirked, like I was amusing him. "Shoot."

"What do you know about Neal Mallick?"

Vinnie took a drag of his cigarette. "This again? Fine. I'll tell you what I know," he said. "For a price."

"I don't have any money on me." The truth. I would've thrown a few bucks at him for information, but I'd left my purse at home.

"Hurry up, Vinnie," someone called in a tired, impatient voice from his olive Mazda. The voice belonged to a woman in the front passenger seat. I recognized her by her overprocessed jet black hair and the way she held a cigarette dangling from her lips. Lydia, maybe. That was right–Lydia Romanski. She was a senior when I was a freshman. She was a burnout back then, too. I didn't know she and Vinnie were a couple now, though it didn't surprise me. She held a squirming infant, one tiny, bare foot sticking out from a blue blanket. "He's starting to cry," she said. "I want to get him home."

I'd cry too, if Vinnie Morrison and Lydia Romanski were my parents. Poor little thing.

Vinnie didn't even glance at Lydia, or the baby. His gaze remained glued to my chest. He took a step closer, cornering me between the theater's brick wall and the dumpster. "You don't need money," he said, reaching out his hand. On his wrist was a tattoo, so fresh it was still swollen and red around the edges. Three fancy letters in black ink: A S H. "I'll take that diamond."

"My pendant?" That's what he wanted? I clutched it tightly in my palm. "No way." My diamond was an inheritance from my great-grandmother, who'd worn it when she emigrated from Ireland. This diamond had traveled more than I had. More than I'd traveled in this lifetime, anyway.

A single, high-pitched *whoop* filled the air. A police siren.

Oh crap. No one would believe I wasn't buying drugs from Vinnie Morrison. My parents would never let me go to CFGU now.

Pure panic had never killed me before, but there was a first time for everything.

From the car, Lydia cursed. Vinnie, not panicking at all, flicked his cigarette to the ground as the patrol car rolled into the back alley. Rick Paladino was behind the wheel.

"What are you doing, Morrison?" he asked.

"Absolutely nothing, Officer." He saluted him. "Just on our way home."

Paladino's gaze landed on me. "Lily Summerhays. Why am I not completely surprised to see you here?"

Hey! Sure, sometimes I caused trouble, but not *this* kind of trouble. "I was cutting through on my way to Diana's," I said. "I forgot my physics book at school and she's letting me use hers."

"At midnight?"

Why was he questioning *me* when I was not the one with the criminal record here? "I forgot that I forgot it."

"Whatcha got there?" he asked. "In your hand?"

My fingers were still clutched around my diamond. "Nothing. Just my necklace."

He gestured toward Vinnie. "Anything happen that I need to know about?"

"Nope." I just wanted to get out of here. I couldn't risk a police report. I had the Diana-textbook excuse, but my parents would still flip that I'd snuck out of the house.

The baby cried from the front seat.

"Get out of here, Morrison," Paladino growled. "Go home."

Vinnie slid into his Mazda. "Absolutely, Officer. Have a pleasant evening." He winked at me. "You too, Lily Summerhays." He backed out in reverse, accidentally-on-purpose almost hitting the cruiser, then drove off.

"Come on, Lily," Paladino said wearily. "I'll drive you home."

"No thanks. I'm fine. Nothing happened," I said. "My parents—I don't want them to find out I forgot my book. Please. They'll be so pissed."

He opened the back door for me anyway. "I'll drive you to Diana's house so you can get it, then."

Out of options, I climbed into the back. "I hope you're not arresting me," I half-joked.

"No. I don't want you running around town in the middle of the night."

I scoffed as he pulled out onto the street. "Ryland's one of the safest towns in Indiana."

"Not with Vinnie Morrison here." He met my eyes in the rearview mirror. "He was going to take that necklace of yours."

"I wasn't going to *let* him."

"Trust me, Lily. When that guy gets violent, no one can stop him." He drove me to Diana's house. Her light was still on in her bedroom, thank goodness. Hopefully, she'd play along.

He opened the back door for me. "Thanks," I said, climbing out. "You don't have to stay. Diana will drive me home. Go on. Keep the streets of Ryland safe. Serve and protect."

As I passed him, he called out. "Hey. Lily."

"Yeah?"

"Stay away from Vinnie Morrison. I mean it. You don't want to get caught up with him."

The streetlight illuminated his chocolate eyes. He was being sincere. "Okay. Thanks, Officer Paladino." I walked up Diana's driveway, hoping she would hear me knocking before I woke up her parents.

Oh, wait—Paladino drove away before I reached the door. Whew. That was close.

As soon as he was out of sight, I pivoted and ran. Officer Paladino had done me a favor and he didn't even realize it. He'd driven me closer to Railroad Bridge.

CHAPTER TWENTY-THREE

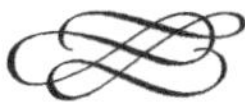

EVER ~ PRESENT DAY

The Summerhays house is the biggest and grandest in Ryland. It comes nowhere close to the majestic mansions I've seen on television, but it has a wraparound porch, dormer windows, and an attached three-car garage. Freshly painted a cheery yellow, it presides over a professionally manicured lawn and a garden of blossoming daffodils. In comparison, my house is a battered, dusty shoe box. But I love my home just as much as Lily had loved hers, I'm sure.

Beside me, Joey holds a platter of cupcakes while I ring the doorbell. Earlier that morning I let him decorate the cupcakes with chocolate frosting, then I helped him pipe T-H-A-N-K-Y-O-U with blue icing, one letter per cupcake.

This is Step One of the plan I made with Ash yesterday under the giant oak tree: talk to the Summerhayses and find out more about the night Lily was killed.

We do not have a Step Two yet.

Ash waits for me at the park across the street. He wants to question the Summerhayses too, but we both know they would never let him into their house. His job is to keep a lookout for Chief Paladino and text me if he sees him coming. As nervous as I am to talk to the Summerhayses—I don't know what to say, and I don't know what to look for—I'm glad Ash can't accompany me on this mission. If we get his father released from prison, the only advantage I'll have over him to win the scholarship is the fact that I'm... nice.

Shifting foot to foot with the occasional glance over my shoulder, I wait on the porch. Half-hoping no one's home, I ring the bell again.

Finally, Mrs. Summerhays opens the door. "Oh! Ever Abrams, from the scholarship," she says. "What can I do for you?" She tucks a loose strand of hair up into her French twist. It's a sunny Saturday afternoon, and she's wearing a dress and heels. I hope I'm not making her late for a party.

"I wanted to thank you for considering me for the scholarship," I say. "I'm sure it's a lot of work raising the money each year."

"You're welcome, but I don't think it's appropriate for you to—"

"We made you cupcakes and I helped!" Joey shouts up at her. His Warriors baseball cap is too big on his head. "They're really yummy, I promise!"

Eyes twinkling, Mrs. Summerhays bends down, hands to knees. "Well, now. Aren't you the most adorable thing? We will have to eat these delicious cupcakes right now, don't you think?"

"Yes!" Joey shouts, running inside.

She laughs with delight. "You're not trying to bribe me, are you, Ever?" She smiles as she says it, but it still surprises me.

"Oh, no, of course not!" I didn't think that my gesture would look like a bribe. "I just wanted to say thanks. Even if I don't win."

She opens her mouth, then snaps it shut. Finally she speaks, slowly, like she's choosing her words carefully. "While I was shocked and disappointed that Diana deceived us about Ash Morrison's application, her impartiality with the candidates was one of the reasons I always trusted her with the scholarship vote. I know that her heart was in the right place. Diana was Lily's best friend and I loved her like a daughter. I'm incredibly sad that she died so tragically herself. As far as the scholarship winner, we will have to wait and see how the committee votes."

She releases an almost imperceptible sigh of relief, like she finished a rehearsed speech without mistake. "Go have a seat in the living room, Ever. I'll get some plates. Where did that little boy run off to?"

Amusement returning to her voice, she calls for Joey and takes the cupcakes into the kitchen. Even though we're both lifelong residents of Ryland, this is my first time speaking to Mrs. Summerhays except for at the scholarship interview. We've attended many of the same community events—the Memorial Day parades, the farmers markets, the Little Warriors Training Camps. But I've always avoided the Summerhayses. They were Lily's parents, and therefore *my* parents when I was Lily. But I'm Ever Abrams now, and I have my own parents. The thought of approaching the Summerhayses as Ever Abrams always made me feel as if I were betraying my mom and dad somehow, and Lily as well. It feels like a betrayal now.

I find the living room to the left of the foyer. Heavy mahogany shelves line two walls all the way up to the crown molding on the high ceiling. Displayed on the shelves are fancy hardcover books that look frequently dusted but never read, and a lot of formal family portraits in frames. Faded photos of Lily, from baby to girl to teen. The most recent photograph is Lily holding back her hair as she blows out the candles on her birthday cake. *Happy Eighteen, Lily!* the cake reads in red icing. The window behind her shows snowflakes falling from a night sky.

I will be eighteen in less than two weeks. April 5th. My birthday is Lily's death day.

I study each photo, trying to feel a connection with her, the girl who used to be me. We look nothing alike. The one physical similarity I thought we had—straight hair—isn't real. She must have straightened it for the portrait the committee uses for the scholarship information. In these photos, her hair bounces in playful red coils. It's beautiful. I wish my hair was curly like that. My dark blonde hair always falls straight and flat within an hour whenever I've attempted to curl it. In Lily's photos, her blue eyes sparkle with merriment and fun. If anyone were to describe my eyes, they'd say they were brown and serious.

I walk around the room, searching for some kind of proof that Will Duston was in their house the night Lily was killed. It's impossible, I know. If the cops didn't find anything then, there's no chance I'll find something eighteen years later. There won't be physical proof. But maybe, now that I'm in the room where she died, I'll have a better death-memory.

Finally, when I step in front of the fireplace, a sudden deathpain hits me over my eyebrow. This is it. Right here. On the floor in front of the fireplace. I—Lily—was killed on this very spot. Through the pain, I try to open myself up to the memory and see something new.

But no. Nothing. *Nothing*. Just the same memory I have every time. The pink paperweight. The hatchet tattoo. The confusion. The helplessness. The terror. The *"You left me no choice."*

I stumble to the sofa, biting my lips to keep from crying out. Please don't let Mrs. Summerhays walk in and see me like this. Please.

I hold my skull so it won't split open. Breathe.

One...

Two...

Three.

What was Lily doing the night she died, I wonder as the deathpain subsides. Why did Will Duston kill her? How did he frame Vinnie Morrison? How long had Diana Buckley known the truth? Being in this room, on the very spot where she died, isn't giving me any answers.

Lily died in this room, this fancy, formal, adult space. It doesn't *feel* like Lily in here. To connect with her, maybe I need to go to her bedroom.

Do I dare? Do I dare sneak up there?

That would be

1. Wrong.

2. Inappropriate.

3. Rude.

4. An invasion of privacy. Guests don't go off uninvited to rifle through their hosts' bedrooms.

But there's a tiny part of me—okay, a huge part of me—that wants to see what I was like when I was Lily Summerhays. Who did I used to be, besides a girl with curly, copper hair? We share a soul; what else do we share?

I can hear Joey chatting away in the kitchen and Mrs. Summerhays's delighted responses. This could be my only opportunity.

I creep to the stairs, my heart pounding a warning: *don't-do-this-don't-do-this-don't-do-this.*

But I have to do it.

Go go go go go! I sprint up the stairs as fast as I can.

The door at the end of the hall is half-open, showcasing a white, four-poster bed and a fluffy pink comforter. Lily's room.

This is so wrong. I can't do this.

I push the door open wider and step inside.

Though dust-free, the room is cluttered. Messy and disorganized. Drawers half-open. Stacks of hastily-folded sweaters on the floor. Shoes and purses, their styles popular over fifteen years ago, spill from her closet. She doesn't have curtains. Instead, international flags cover her windows. Posters—the Eiffel Tower, the Amazon rainforest, the city of Tokyo at night—cover almost every inch of her walls, as if she wanted to hide the pink paint.

Attached to bulletin boards with funky flower-shaped pins are lots of photographs. I recognize a teenage Miss Buckley in many of them, mugging for the camera with Lily or dressing up in costumes for Halloween and in elegant dresses for school dances. Miss Buckley wore her famous high heels even back then. Lily wore Converse sneakers or Doc Martens with her dresses.

Best friends, now both dead. Both murdered by the same man, eighteen years apart.

I swallow the lump in my throat and scan the photos for a younger Principal Duston. Easy to recognize by his white-blond hair and those toothpicks, he's in several of Lily's group photos at parties and school events, but they're never alone or even standing close to each other. Lily's in several photos goofing around with a dark-haired boy whose clothes are too big on him, and she's in a couple of posed school dance photos with another boy who has a dimple on his chin—he must be a young Seth Siegel, who is now the owner of Siegel Freight and Transport and my dad's boss. Lily doesn't look like she was in love with him, though. She looks bored more than anything. But Miss Buckley is in several photos kissing—no way. *Brandon Lennox*? The baseball star? It has to be. Miss Buckley was Brandon Lennox's girlfriend in high school. Wow. No wonder she was able to get him to finance the scholarship.

I need to hurry. I have no idea how long I've been up here, but I haven't found anything useful yet. I scan the room one last time.

A globe stands in the corner—a big, ornately-painted globe suspended in a big wooden stand, with little yellow stickers dotting many of the countries. Greece. Italy. Israel. Japan. Nigeria. Turkey. Czechoslovakia. Spain. France. China. India.

A sticker on each of the countries I died in. Countries *we* died in.

Oh my God. *Lily remembered.*

It had never occurred to me that Lily had death-memories too. But of course she did. We have the same soul.

Relief pours out of me with a laugh. It's not just me. Well, it *is* just me, but knowing my previous incarnations had the same death-memories as me somehow makes me feel less alone.

The globe is hinged, I notice, and it opens at the equator. Knowing I shouldn't, but too curious to stop myself, I pry the two halves apart. With an aching, screaming creak, it splits. The interior is lined with green velvet, and tossed inside are several items:

1. A catalog for a college named Carroll-Freywood Global University.

2. A crumpled envelope from the same school with a letter inside.

3. An old, dirty box of Hot Tamales, empty.

4. A small purple case, like a cosmetic bag, decorated with hand-drawn Asian symbols.

5. A faded maroon Ryland High baseball cap.

What an odd collection. What do they mean? Why did Lily hide them in this globe?

I reach for the envelope so I can read the letter inside.

"Ever? Are you up here, sweetheart?"

I drop the envelope, and in a panic I close the globe, cringing at the angry creaking noise it makes. I step away from it as Mrs. Summerhays appears in the doorway. Is she angry that I'm in Lily's room?

She doesn't appear angry. "It's been almost eighteen years," she says wistfully, "but I've never been able to pack up her things." She sits on the bed and smooths the comforter. "I like to come in here sometimes. It feels like her in here."

"I won't get rid of anything of my mom's," I say. "But my dad won't even go in their bedroom. He sleeps on the couch."

"That's too bad," she says. "Of course, I've had a lot longer to get used to it than he has."

"I'm sorry I came up here. I—" I shut my mouth. I can't think of an excuse.

"It's okay, dear. You're curious. You probably more than most. Not only are you a finalist for the scholarship, but you were born on the day she died. I'm touched that you want to know her."

Unable to speak, I can only nod.

"That's one of the reasons I started the scholarship. So no one would forget her. So she would be remembered as more than a victim." She twists her lips. "You know, I think I remember your mother. She had that cute little bookstore on Main Street, didn't she? Sweet little thing. Her name was... something with a flower."

My hand flutters to my necklace. "Daisy," I croak.

She gazes at me for a long time, as if she's searching for something inside me. Technically, we were mother and daughter once. Does she feel a connection? Do I?

Maybe so.

The fine, distinguished lines on her face deepen into trenches as she stands and brushes herself off. "We should get back downstairs and eat those cupcakes."

CHAPTER TWENTY-FOUR

LILY ~ EIGHTEEN YEARS AGO

As soon as Officer Paladino's headlights disappeared, I ran all the way from Diana's house to Railroad Bridge before stopping to catch my breath. It was probably 1 a.m. by now. If I'd taken the time to plan instead of impulsively dashing out of my house, I would have thought to bring a flashlight. All I had now was the moonlight. I padded onto the bridge, my footsteps echoing eerily into the foggy night air. This was the last place Neal was alive.

I made my way across the bridge, plank by plank. Usually I sprinted, sure-footed, but this time I forced myself to go slowly to look for clues. Clues of what—I didn't know. But I examined each plank, hoping to see something unusual.

I made it all the way across, all the way to where the bridge ended on the Dustons' property, and found not a single clue on the planks or on the train tracks. But I was kidding myself anyway. If anything had been here, the first train to come by would have obliterated it.

Still, the bridge ended on the Dustons' farm. If Will had something to do with Neal's death, then maybe there was something here. I carefully stepped off the bridge and examined the land near the tracks.

The Dustons' farmhouse and barn were far off across the empty soybean field, illuminated by the moon. But there was nothing else here. Nothing by the train tracks or the gravel and weeds surrounding them. I didn't know what I was looking for, so anything unusual would have caught my eye. But there was nothing.

"What the hell are you doing out here, Red?"

The voice surprised me so much that I stumbled and almost tripped over one of the railroad ties. Will leaned against his towering oak tree. "Couldn't sleep," I said. "What are *you* doing out here?" I tried to keep my tone casual. I was in the dark, with a murder suspect, at the same location of said murder, and no one else knew I was here.

"Does it matter? It's my land."

I ignored his question. "It's one in the morning. Don't you farmers do that cock-a-doodle-doo, wake-when-the-rooster-crows, ass-crack-of-dawn thing?"

"It's 1:25 in the morning. And my farm doesn't have roosters, just soybeans. What are you doing here, Lily." It wasn't a question so much as a demand.

"I... wanted to see you."

"Why?"

I shrugged. "I thought you were really good with those kids at the training camp last week. You should be a coach. Or a teacher."

"You came all the way out here in the middle of the night to tell me that?"

"I told you. I couldn't sleep."

One brow cocked, he chuckled. "Typical Lily. You could have called instead, you know."

"Would you have picked up if you saw it was me on the caller ID?"

He snorted. "Probably not."

"Seriously, Will. What are you doing out here at 1 a.m.? 1:25 a.m.?"

His gaze locked on the bridge, he mimicked my shrug.

He was about to spill. I had to keep him talking. "Why do we hate each other so much, anyway?"

"Your dad's company is ruining my dad's farm."

"Your dad's lawsuits are ruining my dad's company."

Even in the dark, I could see his face reddening. Time to switch tactics. "But *I* don't want to ruin your farm," I said. "I don't care about Agri-So. You and I have never done anything to each other. It's just our dads."

"True." He glanced sideways at me, his eyes glinting. "But you *are* a pain in the ass."

I play-punched him in the arm. "You're a hick cowboy wannabe."

He blinked sadly at me. The jokes were over before they'd even started, which was a good thing, because for a moment there I forgot that he was a murder suspect. "Sorry. I'll go now."

I felt him watching me as I walked away. "You know, Lily, I feel really sorry for you."

His words made me stop in my tracks and turn around. "Me? Why?"

"Because your whole life, all you've talked about is getting out of this town. You grew up hating your home. That's really sad."

I opened my mouth to speak, but nothing came out.

"You keep saying how awful and boring Ryland is and how much you can't wait to leave it. You have the biggest house in town and you don't have to lift a finger to get what you want. Yet you're miserable. I have to get up early and do chores for two hours before school. I will have to work hard every day of my life and I'll never be rich. But you know what? I'm happier than you. I always have been, and I always will be."

His words shocked me for a moment. "Is that what you think of me? That I'm a spoiled, entitled little rich girl?" Angry tears stung my eyes. "You have no idea what my life is like, and you have no idea how little I care about money. I don't want to leave Ryland so I can live some pampered life in a city penthouse or a mansion in the suburbs somewhere. I want to travel around the world, Will. As in, hike around it. I want to explore rainforests and dig in caves and climb mountains in countries most people around here have probably never even heard of. I want to actually *see* the world, Will. I don't want to fly around it in a private jet."

He eyed me for a moment in the moonlight. "I know you hate it here. But I love it. I can't imagine living anywhere else. All that money your dad makes running his company... money's not real. This." He knelt and picked up a handful of dirt, then let it dribble through his fingers. "This is real." He gestured to his farmhouse in the distance. "That is real. I love it. I love the smell of it. The fresh air, working hard, growing my own food. To me, this is true living."

I blinked at him. "But there's so much out there," I said, throwing my arms wide. "How can you stand the thought of not experiencing it all?"

He shrugged. "I'm not saying I never want to leave Ryland. Visiting places would be nice. But you need a place to return to. You need a home. That's Ryland for me."

"The world is my home." He didn't know how true that was.

Will kicked at the ground. "My brother Tommy just re-enlisted in the army for the third time. And Craig was just promoted to sales director at his firm in Chicago. They have no interest in farming and they never have. But running Duston Farm, that's what I'm going to do. I'm going to carry on the family business. My parents just need to keep this place going for a little bit longer, and then I'm going to take it over." He rubbed a soybean plant between his finger and thumb. "I'm going to turn Duston Farm into an organic farm. No pesticides. No chemicals. The organic market is going to be huge one day."

"You know about marketing and stuff like that?"

"I do for agriculture."

I chewed my lip. "So I guess even if we stop hating each other, you'll never be one of Agri-So's customers. An organic farmer has no need for chemically enhanced soil."

He chuckled. "Guess not."

Though I had known Will my whole life, and I'd been spending lots of time with him lately, I looked at him, truly *looked* at him, for the first time. Or maybe it was the first time I truly saw him.

What I saw was peace. His wide eyes, his easy breath, the casual way he leaned against the tree, his quick laughter. His face, even in the moonlight, was flushed with the health only fresh air and sunshine can give. He wanted more for his farm, but he didn't have a constant yearning for more out of life. He didn't feel stifled. Ryland didn't suffocate him. Ryland freed him.

I was suddenly aware of how close we were standing. I had walked toward him and didn't even realize it, and now we were just inches apart. He must have noticed it too, because he stepped away. "It's late. I need to get some sleep. You know us farmers. Cock-a-doodle-doo, crow-of-the-rooster, ass-crack-of-dawn and all that."

"Oh." Why was I disappointed? It was becoming harder and harder to believe it, but he was a killer. Probably. "I should get home too."

"Come on. I'll give you a ride."

"No, that's okay. The muffler in that old pickup of yours will wake up my parents."

He snorted. "Ol' Blue is out of commission. I'll take my parents' car."

"Better not risk it. I'll walk."

"Careful crossing that bridge," he called.

Was he warning me not to fall off the bridge, or was he warning me not to let him push me off? I rushed as fast as I dared to the other side of the creek. When I looked back, he was still under the tree, watching me. Then he turned and ambled through his field toward his house.

Now that the clouds had cleared, the moon gave me a bit more light so it was easier to pick my way through the woods along the train tracks.

That was why I saw it. At the end of the bridge. The moonlight reflected on something glossy lying in the dirt and weeds.

A box of Hot Tamales. Neal Mallick's favorite candy.

I plucked it from the ground. Something was on it, something the dew had made sticky. Something rusty-red.

It could only be blood.

CHAPTER TWENTY-FIVE

EVER ~ PRESENT DAY

Sunday morning, I leave Joey with Dad—who'll probably just send him next door to play with Hayden all day—and head down the street to meet Ash. My meeting with Mrs. Summerhays yesterday failed to help us prove Principal Duston killed Lily, but Ash said he has another idea.

"Hey! Ever! Hold up!" To my surprise, Keith is rushing across the street to me. His maroon Warriors cap is too big and it bounces up and down over his sleepy eyes.

I give him a kiss. "Why are you up so early? It's only nine o'clock. You usually sleep until at least noon on Sundays."

"My parents are making me help out at The Batter's Box more," he says, giving me another kiss. "Come with me."

"Can't," I say. "I have plans."

"Again? You've had a lot of plans lately." He pouts and nibbles on his fingernail. "I never see you anymore."

"I know." I place my palm on his chest. "I'm sorry."

"What have you been doing?"

I think quickly. "A group project for school. One of my AP classes." God, I hate lying to my boyfriend. The only thing I've ever had to lie about—to Keith, to Courtney, to everyone—are my death-memories. Meeting with Ash today is directly related to that.

"Well, bring the group to the diner." Keith grins and does a cute little wiggle. "I'll get you all free waffles."

I shake my head. "You're sweet, but I can't. I'll see you tonight, okay? Come over for dinner. We can study together after." I give him another kiss and rush away before he can protest.

I hustle to the corner of Jefferson and Van Buren, a quiet road that leads out of town. Ash is already there waiting for me, his motorcycle leaning against a tree. The day is warm enough for me to go out in just a sweater, but he's still wearing his leather jacket. I'm kind of glad—I like the way he smells when he wears it. Leather and spice and strength.

"We're going to go talk to a friend of mine today," he says, not even bothering to say *hello* or *good morning*. "He grew up with Will Duston and Miss Buckley and Lily Summerhays. He might be able to give us some history into their relationship."

"Sounds promising," I say.

Ash gestures to his bike. "Hop on."

I feel the blood drain from my face and my heart flutters with panic. "No way. Over five thousand people a year die in motorcycle accidents."

"I promise you won't die today. Look, you can wear my helmet."

"No." I cross my arms over my chest.

He rakes his hand through his hair. "We could walk there, cut through some fields, I guess, but it's pretty far. How much time do you have?"

"I have all day." I'd rather walk a hundred miles than get on that motorized bicycle of death.

He grumbles, and together we trudge down the road. I have no idea where he's taking me. Van Buren is poorly paved—dangerous for motorcycles, I note with satisfaction—and surrounded on both sides by cornfields and soy fields. It's used mostly by farmers on their big John Deeres. The sun, feeling more May than March, beats down on us.

"This would be so much faster if you had a car," Ash says crossly as he takes off his leather jacket.

"Yes it would," I say. "But I don't. And, I should point out, neither do you."

"Let me guess. Twenty thousand people die in car accidents each year."

"Actually, it's thirty-three thousand in the United States, one-and-a-quarter-million worldwide. Young people more than anyone else."

"You let your boyfriend drive you around."

"Keith's a very safe driver."

"So *that's* why you like him."

"Yes." Then I add, "Among other things."

"Yeah? Like what?"

"He's dependable, loyal—"

"You sure about that?"

"Yes," I say immediately. Then I stop walking. There was a ridiculous rumor last year about Keith and some Eastfield girl after a baseball tournament. I didn't believe it. "Whatever you heard, it isn't true."

"I haven't heard anything," Ash says. He doesn't stop walking, and I have to run a few steps to catch up to him.

"Keith is dependable and loyal and sweet!" I almost shout it.

Now Ash stops. "So he's like a dog." He pants and brings his hands up to his chest, bending them like paws. "Oh, Ever, please love me. Please spend every single second with me, Ever. I love you, Ever."

"Stop it. He's not like that."

"He's dumb as a dog too."

"Just because he's not in our AP classes doesn't mean he's dumb," I say, my blood boiling.

"Admit it, Ever. Keith Stout has no brains and no ambition."

"Keith Stout is a good boyfriend," I say. "He loves me and I love him."

At the rumble of a tractor behind us, Ash grabs me around the waist and yanks me to the side of the road. "If he's that amazing," he says into my ear, "why isn't he here with us? Why haven't you told *him* your theory that Duston killed Lily Summerhays and Miss Buckley?"

"I... He..." My thoughts are all flustered, like my brain is being scrambled with a whisk. It's the way his soft breath brushes my neck, the scent of leather from his jacket, his firm yet gentle grip around my waist, the way his hair falls over his eyes, the stubble on his jaw... together they sweep all ability to think from my head.

I shake him off me. Any girl would be lucky to have Keith as a boyfriend. How dare Ash bring up untrue rumors that died a year ago? How dare Ash say *anything* bad about Keith? "At least Keith is nice. *You* are a jerk. "

One corner of Ash's lip curls up into a smirk. "I've been called worse."

The tractor passes, and as we start down the road again, I make sure to leave lots of space between us. Van Buren ends, and instead of turning right toward the highway, Ash turns left onto a flat field. We don't speak again, until a long, narrow paved road appears. In the distance is a yellow domed structure.

I gasp. "You brought me to Soto Airfield?"

"Statistically, flying is the safest mode of transportation," Ash says. "It's ten times safer than walking, which, I might point out, we're doing right now. Only five hundred people a year die in plane crashes." He's grinning so hard and so triumphantly I think his cheeks are going to burst. "But I'm sure you already know that."

"I do know that, but I don't care. No way am I getting in a plane, especially not one of those dilapidated single-engines. And stop using my death statistics against me."

He chuckles. "But you make it so easy. Don't worry. We're not flying today."

The runway is a half-mile long, and by the time we reach the yellow domed hangar, I'm exhausted, dirty, and thirsty. Ash walks right in and goes behind the front counter. He opens a little fridge, then tosses me a bottle of water from it.

"You act like you own this place," I say after I chug half the bottle.

"I do janitorial stuff and maintenance on the planes in exchange for fly time. Miss Buckley arranged it for me." He takes a long swig of his own bottle, almost emptying it.

"You fly planes?"

"Since I was fourteen," he says. "And one day, I'll fly a space shuttle." He looks a little lost at those words. He clears his throat and heads deeper into the hangar, toward one of the planes.

The single-engine is huge up close, and though I expected it to be constructed out of popsicle sticks and Elmer's glue, it actually looks pretty sturdy. Standing high on wheeled scaffolding, a man in brown coveralls leans over the plane's engine. Ash calls to him. "Hey! Javier!"

The dark-haired man looks down at us. I remember a younger, thinner version of him from the photos on Lily's wall. The coveralls swallow him up, the same way his clothes swallowed him up back then.

"Hey there, Morrison. Shame what happened to Diana Buckley," he says. "Tragic. But you and me, we're cool, if that's why you came in today. I hired you as a favor to Diana, but you've proven yourself over the years. You're a hard worker and a good pilot. Your job here is safe."

"Thanks. Appreciate it." Ash reddens and looks at his boots, clearly not used to hearing compliments.

Javier turns back to the engine and gestures to a plane on the other side of the hangar. "I'm working on the Cessna, but you can take the Piper up today. Be back by two, though. I gotta take Amelia to a birthday party. My three-year-old has a busier social life than *I* do."

Ash grunts a laugh in response. "Actually, Javier, my friend Ever and I came in today to ask you some questions."

"All right then, shoot," he says into the engine.

Ash gets right to the point. "How well did you know Lily Summerhays?"

Javier stops fiddling with the plane and looks down again. "Why?"

Ash gives a casual shrug. "Ever and I are both finalists for the scholarship. We just want to know more about her."

"Yeah, I heard something about how Diana snuck you through to the final round," Javier says, then chuckles. "Her final act of kindness. She really looked out for you."

"Yes, she did," Ash says. His voice sounds tight, like his throat is closing up.

"I knew Lily really well. Lots of fun. Always getting into trouble."

"Really? What kind of trouble?" I ask.

"Oh, you know. Fun trouble. Stuff like going to parties, sneaking out of her house at night, breaking curfew. She once jumped out of a tree onto a trampoline, bounced out of it, and shattered her elbow. She was the first one of us to jump off the bridge into the creek every year. Sometimes I'd bring her up in a plane with me and let her fly, and she'd always beg me to let her do a loop-de-loop. That girl was fearless, I'll tell you that."

The more I learn about Lily, the more surprised I am. She was definitely not the quiet, well-behaved girl her scholarship poster made her out to be—the girl *I* am now. How could Lily, who remembered all of our deaths and knew how easy it was to die, be so fearless?

Would she be happy that she had been reborn as... *me*?

"We know Lily was friends with you and Miss Buckley," Ash says. "Who else was she friends with?" With a shrug, he casually suggests, "Will Duston, maybe?"

Above us, Javier snorts. "No way. We all hung out, but Lily and Will despised each other. But you know, their families had that feud."

"A feud?" I ask.

"Over the business. Agri-So. I don't know the details, but they started that business together, but then the Summerhayses screwed the Dustons out of a lot of money. They lost their farm."

"Motive," I mouth to Ash, who nods. Now we know why he killed her: revenge.

The sound of tires driving over gravel echoes through the massive open door to the hangar. A black-and-white patrol car stops, and Chief Paladino unfolds himself from the front seat.

"Shit," Ash mutters. "What's he doing here?"

"Looking for you, probably," Javier says. "You in trouble again?"

"No, but knowing him, he'll say that I am." He pulls me deeper into the hangar, toward an area cluttered with corrugated boxes, engine parts, and metal shelves stocked with tools. "We'll take the back way out. Do me a favor, Javier. Don't tell him we were here, okay?"

"No problem, Morrison. Get out of here."

As we sneak out the back door, I peek into the hangar one more time. Hands on his hips and speaking in a low voice, Chief Paladino stands where Ash and I were standing just moments before, looking up at Javier on the scaffolding. I have just enough time to see Javier shaking his head before Ash pulls me away.

CHAPTER TWENTY-SIX

LILY ~ EIGHTEEN YEARS AGO

When I snuck out two hours ago, my house had been dark. Now, as I returned, it was all lit up.

Oh

crap.

No point in sneaking back inside. I didn't bother to be quiet when opening the front door. And there he was, just as I knew he'd be. Dad, standing in the foyer, his face red and scowling.

He eyed the dirty, bloody Hot Tamales box in my hands. "What's that?" The vein on his forehead thumped an angry beat. "Don't tell me you left in the middle of the night to buy some candy."

I should tell him. I should tell him about the box, about the bridge, about Neal. But he was so angry, he wouldn't believe me. Not tonight. "It's just some garbage I found on our lawn."

Mom came stumbling down the stairs in her blue terrycloth robe and matching slippers, hair tucked neatly into a paisley silk scarf, eyes blurry with sleep. "What's going on?"

"I caught her sneaking back into the house, after doing who knows what," Dad said.

Mom looked at me with horror. "Lily Anastasia. What were you doing out in the middle of the night?"

"I had to see Diana about something." If they asked her, she would cover for me. I was almost positive.

"What was so important that it couldn't wait until morning?" Dad demanded.

He was right, of course. There was no reason I couldn't have waited to investigate the movie theater and the bridge until daylight. "I'm sorry. I didn't think about the time." Will's voice echoed in my head: *Typical Lily.*

"You didn't think about the time." Dad's mouth set in a hard line. "I've had enough of this. You crashed your car, you jumped into the creek, and now you're sneaking out of the house in the middle of the night. I don't know what to do with you anymore."

"I'm sorry," I said. "I'll be better. I promise."

But he just frowned and shook his head. "That's what you said last time."

"You're grounded, Lily," Mom said. "One week."

I nodded in defeat. It could have been worse. "Okay. I'm sorry."

"Which means," Dad added, "you're not going with me to New York."

I gasped. "No! Please! I have to go to New York! I have an—" I stopped myself before I told him about the appointment I made at CFGU's admissions office. "Dad, please. Ground me for a month, for three months, take away my car forever, but please, please let me go to New York. I'll be on my best behavior. I promise." I looked to my mom for support, but she was mirroring Dad's angry head-shake.

"You'd better stay home too, Jacquelyn," Dad said. "We obviously can't trust her to stay home alone."

The anger in Mom's eyes turned into devastation.

"Go to your room, Lily," Dad said.

Holding back tears, I ran up to my room, gripping the bloody Hot

Tamales box so tightly that it crumpled. Stupid box. It meant nothing. Neal Mallick slipped off the bridge on his way home and drowned. The bridge was slick with dew, it was dark, he slipped, he drowned. Simple as that. Everyone else accepted it. And now so would I.

The blood on the box? Probably from some forest animal.

I shoved the

stupid,

stupid,

stupid

box deep into my wastebasket.

I was going to be responsible from now on.

CHAPTER TWENTY-SEVEN

EVER ~ PRESENT DAY

His hand wrapped around my arm, Ash rushes us away from the hangar, practically dragging me across the back lot. We crouch behind a bright blue plane with *Soto Agricultural Aerial Applications* printed across it in white letters. I can't see inside the hangar from here, but I'm certain that any second Chief Paladino will come storming out after us.

"What if Javier tells him we're out here?" I ask.

"Even if he does, we didn't do anything wrong. We just asked him some questions about Lily. Nothing illegal about that." Ash peers through his hair at the direction of the hangar.

"No, but Paladino won't be happy that I'm asking about Principal Duston." It's warm today, but not hot enough for me to be sweating the way I am. "Talking to Javier was a bad idea, Ash. Miss Buckley knew the truth and now she's dead. We can't talk to anyone else about this. Not anyone in Ryland, anyway. It's too risky."

Ash stands to his full height and looks down at me. "We can talk to whoever we want and no one will take us seriously. You know why? You *say* you *overheard* Miss Buckley telling Duston that she knew he was Lily's real killer. You know how flimsy that sounds? No one is going to believe us based on something you overheard. I don't even know if *I* believe you."

Ash is right. On all points. I lied about overhearing a conversation between Principal Duston and Miss Buckley. "If you think I'm lying, why are you helping me?"

"Honestly, I don't know." He rubs his huge palm on the plane, the span of his outstretched fingers reaching wide. "Maybe because I *want* to believe you. Maybe because Duston is an asshole, and if there's even a chance that he killed Lily Summerhays and Miss Buckley, he needs to pay. Maybe because I need that scholarship and this is the only way I'll get it."

The scholarship. I wish I never saw that hatchet tattoo on Principal Duston's wrist. None of this would be happening, and the scholarship would be mine.

But that wouldn't be fair to Lily, or to Vinnie Morrison.

"You should ask your dad," I tell Ash. "He might know something."

"I told you, he doesn't remember anything about that night. He was black-out wasted."

"True, but Duston had to do something to frame your dad so he didn't get caught, right? He must have planted that diamond pendant in your dad's place. They must have had some kind of connection."

"I guess my father could have been Duston's dealer." Ash gives half a nod, then rapidly turns it into a shake. "No. Forget it."

"Why?"

"Because even if my father says he was Duston's dealer, we'd still have no way of proving anything. I'm not talking to him. I closed that door a long time ago and I'm not opening it again. We'll have to think of something else."

And with that, Ash gets up and stomps his massive form down

the runway, like he'd rather Chief Paladino catch him than talk to his own father.

~

Ash and I don't say a word as he walks me all the way back into town, occasionally watching over his shoulder for Chief Paladino.

"I'm sorry," I say when we arrive at his motorcycle, still parked under the tree where he left it that morning. "You don't have to talk to your dad. We shouldn't get his hopes up over something we can't prove."

"Thanks," he mumbles. He shakes his long hair from his eyes.

"So what now?" I ask, but neither of us have an answer. It's late afternoon, and we've walked miles and miles today. I'm tired and achy. I'd almost be willing to accept a ride home on Ash's motorcycle —if he goes slow—but he doesn't offer. He just wheels it along as we trudge slowly down Jefferson, back into town.

When we reach Main Street, I turn left toward my home, and he turns right toward his.

"Are you hungry? We could get something to eat." My ears hear the words before my brain registers that I'm the one saying them.

He grunts and gestures down the street to The Batter's Box. "Where, at your boyfriend's diner? I don't think so. See you tomorrow, Ever."

He swings his leg over his bike. He holds out his white helmet. "Safety first." He chuckles, and with a flourish, he places it over his head. I feel an immediate, sharp loss over the fact that I can no longer see his dark, intense, soulful eyes. He starts the bike and roars away. I watch until he disappears.

"Was that Ash Morrison? You okay?"

The question makes me jump. It's Keith, wearing his forest green Batter's Box polo, panting slightly. He's holding a couple of menus and his little apron is tied around his waist. He must have seen me from the diner talking to Ash and rushed over.

"Yeah, I'm fine," I say.

Keith pulls me in and plants a wet kiss on my lips. "Was he bothering you?"

"No." I resist the urge to wipe the slobber from my face and brush the airfield dirt from my jeans instead.

"He's not the one you're doing that group project with, is he?" he says warily.

"He is, actually," I say, and realize it's technically not a lie.

"How did that happen?"

"I didn't have a choice," I say. "The teacher just made us partners." *There's* the lie.

"Can't you do it without him?" He puts his arm around me protectively and guides me toward The Batter's Box.

"It's a *group* project." Back to the truth. "We're partners."

"Fine. I'll come with you from now on."

"What?" I huff and stop walking. "You want to come with me to my group project?"

He steps back. "I don't want you to be alone with that guy. Why are you getting so mad?"

"Because you don't like Ash for reasons that aren't true." When Keith raises a doubtful eyebrow, I elaborate. "He doesn't do drugs. He doesn't steal. He doesn't cheat. He's not violent. You don't know him and you have no right to judge him."

What am I doing? I'm snapping at my boyfriend for believing rumors that I myself believed until just recently. I sigh, then run my hand over his chest to make him feel better. "Keith, thank you for wanting to protect me. But I'll be fine." I stand on tiptoe and give him a quick kiss.

His body relaxing, he pulls me to him and presses his tongue into my mouth. I need to reassure him, so I kiss him back.

"I'm sorry, Ever," he says when we part. "You're right. I didn't mean to make you upset. I'm sorry. Don't be mad, okay?"

He may as well have bent his hands under his chin and panted like a dog. Damn Ash for putting that image in my head.

As we enter The Batter's Box, I stealthily wipe my mouth with the back of my hand. So what if Keith's kisses are slobbery? Who cares if he works just hard enough in school to pass? So what if he's not the smartest or most ambitious guy in the world? Keith is

1. Dependable
2. Loyal
3. Kind
4. Sweet
5. Protective

There. Five reasons why I love Keith. And here's one more:

6. He loves me.

In my head, I can hear Ash taunting me. *Dogs are all those things too.*

CHAPTER TWENTY-EIGHT

LILY ~ EIGHTEEN YEARS AGO

I was good all week. I was perfect.

Usually when I'm grounded, I pout and generally make such a nuisance of myself that my parents push me out of the house just to get some peace. But not this time. This time, I cleaned my room. I woke up early every day to straighten my hair. I did my homework right after school. I gave Dad a hug when he left for New York without me and wished him a good trip. I let my mother show me how to play bridge. I had

officially

learned

my

lesson,

and not once did I even glance at the crushed box of Hot Tamales in my wastebasket.

My good behavior seemed to be working. Mom smiled with approval at my hair and clothes, and she thanked me for clearing the dinner table each night. She was impressed with my bridge-playing skills. She must have told Dad, because when he got back from his trip, he brought me a snow globe of New York City.

The baseball team had a home game against our rival Eastfield High on Friday night, the last game before spring break, and Dad gave me permission to go to the game. Grounding: over.

Wearing my official Batgirl T-shirt and hair ribbons, I sat next to Diana in the stands. Usually Diana sat in the front row, ready to blow good-luck kisses to Brandon. The two had reconciled a few days ago but had broken up again last night. She did not blow any kisses to him today as he took his turn at bat. Instead, she glared at him, as well as at the New York Yankees recruiter standing next to Coach Nolan in the dugout.

When the Eastfield pitcher threw the ball, Brandon hit it easily with the bat and sent it far into the outfield. The crowd, with the exception of Diana, went nuts as he sailed around to third base.

Will Duston was up next. He hit the ball with a

smack!

As the crowd flew into a frenzy, Brandon crossed home plate and Will ran to second base before the shortstop caught the ball. Grinning, Will peered into the bleachers. His eyes met mine, and I realized I'd been clapping and cheering for him like I *didn't* despise him with every fiber of my being. Quickly, before he realized it too, I dropped my hands.

He was too far away to see clearly, all the way across the diamond on second base, but I could have sworn his pale cheeks flushed, and his grin grew even wider anyway.

I got home from the game as Mom was hanging up the phone, her brows knit with worry. "Dad's late for dinner and he's not answering his phone," she said.

I shrugged as I slid into my place at the table. "He had a meeting in Lafayette, remember?"

She frowned. "He's had meetings in Lafayette before. He's always been home for dinner. Now it's ruined."

She just sat there looking forlornly at his place setting, which she'd set perfectly. On our plates were rotisserie chicken, a green salad, and mashed potatoes. In the middle of the table she'd placed a tasteful bouquet of fresh spring flowers in a bright white vase.

"It's not ruined, Mom," I said, cutting off a big chuck of chicken. "It looks delicious."

Mom smiled at me weakly.

"Aren't you going to eat?" I asked.

She shook her head. "I'll wait until Dad gets home." She got up and put plastic wrap over their plates, then put them in the fridge.

To fill the silence as I ate, I said, "Isn't that show you like on tonight? I'll watch it with you."

She nodded absently as she wiped the counters. After I finished, she took my plate and cleaned the kitchen, glancing at the phone every few minutes, as if watching it would make it ring. I helped as much as she would let me.

Finally, the garage door rumbled open, and she rushed over to greet him with a hug that he returned with a perfunctory one of his own, then breezed past her to take off his coat.

"How was your meeting?" she asked.

"You're late," I said at the same time.

His stony face told me he did not appreciate my tone. Mom shot me a look too. "We were worried," I added.

"The meeting ran late," he said.

Mom reheated their dinner and served it while Dad complained about the business. Something about revenues and expenditures and the latest lawsuit from the Dustons. I stopped paying attention, but Mom listened dutifully. After he finished, he wiped his mouth on the cloth napkin and stood up. "Thanks for dinner. I've got more work to do. Don't wait up."

Blinking rapidly, Mom watched him as he started to leave the kitchen.

"Dad!" I cried. "That show you and Mom like is on tonight. I thought we'd all watch it together."

"I have work, Lily."

"Please, Daddy. You worked all day today, and Mom worked so hard making this nice dinner. It's Friday night. Shouldn't you both relax for a while? Go. You guys get started and I'll join you after I clean up in here."

His gaze traveled to me, then to Mom. "You're right," he said. "Good idea." And he actually

smiled.

When I peeked in on them, they were sitting on the couch together, under one blanket. She had her head on his shoulder and he was lazily stroking her arm with his thumb. They laughed at the same time.

I should leave them alone instead of joining them. I didn't want to ruin the moment. I tiptoed away, but not before my gaze landed on the TV screen. The characters in the show were in India to attend a wedding. I blinked at the bright colors, and a new death-memory flashed: In the 1800s I died there as a twenty-year-old woman while performing in a traveling circus. I'd been attempting a new trick on the trapeze.

The deathpain from falling fifty feet to the hard ground was nothing compared to the excitement I felt at this new memory. Wow. *India.* Another country for me to visit. Another adventure for me to have.

I ran up to my room as quietly as I could and pressed a yellow circle sticker over India on my globe.

I wanted to tell someone. I *needed* to tell someone. I wanted someone to share my excitement. The only person I could tell, who would have believed me and taken me seriously, was Neal Mallick.

But Neal was dead.

I couldn't tell my parents. They wouldn't believe me. Neither would Diana, or Brandon, or Seth, or Javier.

Will?

No. How did that ridiculous thought even form in my head? Will Duston was the enemy. I shouldn't want to tell him anything about myself, especially not a secret as big as my death-memories. He'd use it against me.

I ran my finger over the India sticker. My new death-memory was a secret I could never share, not with anyone, ever.

Ignoring my *Adventures in Anthropology* textbook, I chose a novel from the shelf—a sword-and-sorcery fantasy that took place in a fictional world, a place I could never have possibly lived, so a death-memory wouldn't come—and curled up in bed to read. See, I was being good. Good daughters stayed home and read books in their tidy bedrooms and did everything they could to prevent death-memories.

Two hours later, when my parents finally came upstairs, I was still reading the first chapter. Actually, I wasn't reading anything. My eyes were glued to the words on the page, but none of them had sunk in.

Instead I was thinking about the box of Hot Tamales I'd found by Railroad Bridge, and the blood I'd convinced myself had come from a forest animal.

Neal had kept my secret all these years. He hadn't laughed at me. He'd taken me seriously. And now I was ignoring him when he needed me most, just because I wanted to go away to college.

I had to make this right.

In a flash I was in my doorway, peeking down the dark hall. My parents' door was closed. I tiptoed into the hall—

No.

Stop.

I didn't have a plan. And I was breaking the rules again by sneaking out of the house. I would mess everything up if I did that. I needed to

slow

down. I needed to

think.

As much as it killed me, I returned to my room and shut the door. I would not go bolting out into the night again. I would stay. I would think.

Maybe there was a way I could help Neal and not get into trouble.

"I'll look tomorrow," I whispered to Neal as I dug the candy box from my wastebasket and hid it inside my globe. "In the daylight. I promise."

CHAPTER TWENTY-NINE

EVER ~ PRESENT DAY

2:48 Friday morning. The moon shines brightly through my curtains. Flashes from the TV light up the hallway because Dad fell asleep on the couch in the family room again. Joey is asleep in his room and the hamster wheel is squeaking quietly. I can usually sleep through all of that, but not this week. Ash hasn't spoken to me, or even made eye contact, since I suggested he talk to his father last weekend. Spring break is next week, and he's skipped school twice out of the past four days. Maybe he's no longer interested in proving that Principal Duston killed Lily Summerhays and Miss Buckley. He's probably forgotten all about it.

But I haven't. I can't think about anything else. Well, that's not true. I can't stop thinking about many things:

1. The scholarship.
2. Vinnie Morrison and his rapidly-approaching execution.
3. Chief Paladino and his unwillingness to help.
4. Keith and his devotion.

5. Ash and his... everything.

6. Lily Summerhays and the strange collection of items she had hidden in her globe.

7. Miss Buckley and her shoes.

8. Principal Duston and his crossed-hatchet tattoo, the sparkly pink paperweight, the *"You left me no choice."*

After I breathe away the deathpain that hits, I pick up my phone. It's too late—too early?—to call Ash, but I do it anyway.

"You avoid me all week, and then you call me in the middle of the night?" he growls.

"I thought *you* were avoiding *me*," I say, relieved he's acknowledging my existence after all. "Besides, you answered on the first ring. You weren't sleeping either."

"I was online researching."

"Researching what?"

"What do you think?"

Lily's murder, of course. "What'd you find?"

"Nothing new. Why are you calling me at almost three in the morning?"

"I have an idea. We've been going about this all wrong. We're trying to prove Principal Duston killed Lily, but that happened almost eighteen years ago in her living room. No witnesses. What we need to do is prove he killed Miss Buckley. That happened a couple weeks ago at school."

"Still no witnesses."

"But there was a witness. One with a perfect memory."

"Who?"

"Not who. What. The security camera, Ash. They have cameras all over school, including the back stairwell."

Ash lets out a low whistle. "Brilliant, Abrams. I'm impressed."

"So. I have a plan. Tomorrow morning, I'll ask the secretary in the front office where they store the security footage. I'll tell her I'm writing an article for the school website about the security guards. Then, we'll have to figure out a way—"

"Got it."

"But tomorrow's the last day of school before spring break. It's our only chance. We need to—"

"I know what to do. See you in the morning." And with that, he hangs up.

Three hours later, the sun has replaced the moon in the sky, I still haven't slept well, and Dad is leaving. I catch him on his way out. "I thought you had the day off."

"I did, but the boss called a few minutes ago. They need an emergency delivery and he asked if I'd like the extra money."

Seth Siegel. I know I should be grateful that he always gives my father extra jobs, but instead I feel resentful. "Doesn't he realize that you're a widower with two kids home alone?"

"Don't start, Ever." He slides into his jacket.

"Will you be back tonight?"

"Tuesday, maybe Wednesday. The delivery is in Arizona."

"At least say *goodbye* to Joey," I remind him.

He stiffens, just the tiniest bit. "I don't want to wake him up."

"He won't care. He just wants to know you'll miss him."

"I'll call him tonight," he says, then walks out the door.

He always says that but rarely follows through. Later that morning when I drop Joey off next door for daycare, I double my usual number of good-bye kisses on his chubby, freckled little face.

Keith had to be at school early for baseball conditioning, the last one before Spring break, so I'll have to walk to school today. That's fine, because Ash and I need to figure out how to get that security footage and I don't want Keith to see us together. But before I can leave for school, there's a knock at my door. Ash is leaning against the pillar, and his motorcycle is parked in my driveway.

"Hey, beautiful," he says with a smirk. "Come with me to The Batter's Box. I'll buy you breakfast."

I have a million reasons why that's a bad idea, the five most obvious being:

1. Just yesterday he refused my offer to go to that same exact restaurant.

2. He was right to refuse that offer.

3. He has even less money than I do, and I don't want him to spend what little money he has on me.

4. I'm not about to get on his bike.

5. I've already eaten breakfast.

But I settle for the sixth most obvious reason. "We don't have time. School starts in half an hour."

He shrugs innocently. "Guess we'll have to eat here then." He walks past me and through my front door. "Whatcha cooking?"

"Come on in," I say, trying to sound sarcastic as I follow him into the kitchen. I made scrambled eggs for Joey, but I refuse to cook anything for Ash. "Frozen waffles are all we have time for."

"Mmm. Scrumptious." He pulls a chair from the table, swivels it around on one leg, and straddles it.

I consider throwing the waffles at him, still frozen. Instead, I drop two in the toaster and place butter and syrup on the table. "Tell me, Ash," I say when the waffles are done. "Why is the Lily Scholarship the only one you applied for?"

He shrugs and reaches for the plate, but I hold it behind my back. "No answers, no waffles. Hurry up. Clock's ticking."

That infuriating smirk stretches across his face again. "Fine. I've wanted that scholarship since freshman year. Since Miss Buckley convinced me to clean up my act. At first it was because winning it would mean that everyone in Ryland acknowledged that I am *not* my father. But no matter how good my grades were, no matter what I did, everyone still saw me as a thug."

"It's not like you did anything to dispel the rumors," I say.

He shrugs again. "I tried. The more I defended myself, the less they believed me. Whatever. I gave up and stayed quiet and let everyone believe what they want to believe. Now I want the scholarship for a different reason."

"What's that?"

"If everyone wants me out of this town so bad, they're gonna have to pay me to leave. And it won't be just Ryland that I leave. I'll go as far away as anyone can get."

"Where, like Alaska?"

"Farther."

"China?"

He grunts. "Farther."

I grab my phone and Google it. There's a text from Courtney about meeting with the Batgirls over spring break to plan the Little Warriors Training Camp, but I ignore it. "Perth, Australia," I say. "It's the farthest city from Ryland. Almost nineteen thousand miles away."

"Nope. Australia is still too close. I'm getting off this planet."

I gasp a little. "Are you talking about—" Oh, God. "Ash, you're not thinking of—"

"No, I don't want to kill myself." He chuckles. "But thanks for your concern. It warms my heart to know you care. No. After I get my bachelors in astrophysics, I'll get my masters in aerospace engineering."

"You want to be an astronaut," I say, putting the pieces together. He mentioned flying a space shuttle when we were at Soto Airfield.

"Farther than the moon, too. NASA hopes to have people living on Mars by the 2030s, and I'm going to be one of them."

"You want to be an astronaut to escape not just Ryland, but the entire planet? Is life here really that horrible for you?"

Instead of answering, he slowly peels the label off the bottle of generic-brand syrup. He looks so sad, so vulnerable. I have an urge to hug him.

"What if you don't win the scholarship?" I ask.

There's a flash of pain in his expression, then he gives a stubborn thrust of his chin. "Then I'll stay here in Ryland and live down to everyone's expectations of me."

Any sympathy I had for him disappears and I drop his plate in front of him. "You know what, Ash? For such a smart guy, you're really stupid. There are other ways to get your degree without winning that scholarship."

He pours syrup on the top waffle and shoves a quarter of it in his mouth. "I can say the same thing for you. What are you going to do if you don't win?"

I collapse in the chair across from him. "I don't know. I've always assumed I would win it. I need that degree to be an accountant at The Batter's Box. Keith and his parents are counting on me."

"You sure about that?" he asks.

I don't have an answer.

Compared to Ash, my grand aspiration to be an accountant for my boyfriend's baseball-themed diner in Ryland, Indiana suddenly seems trivial and unimportant, and a waste of the scholarship money.

Even if Ash is thinking the same thing, he doesn't say so. Instead, he says, "I can't see you as an accountant. The boredom would kill you within a month."

I have to laugh. "Whatever kills me, it won't be boredom. Trust me."

His gaze locks on to mine. "I do."

My breath catches.

Slowly, he leans forward until his face is just inches from mine. His eyes are dark and bottomless, his jaw is rough with stubble. His breath is sweet and warm. He murmurs, "Are you ready?"

I feel myself licking my lips. "For what?"

"To break the rules for the first time in your life."

"What rules?"

"School started five minutes ago," he says. "We're tardy."

~

As if he expects trumpets to announce our arrival, Ash pushes open the school's front doors with both hands and strides victoriously inside. We've missed the first bell, the late bell, and the first ten minutes of first period. The front hall is empty except for a tall, very thin security guard leaning against the over-stuffed trophy case. Hanging over the trophy case, encased in glass, is the school's most treasured possession: Brandon Lennox's Warriors baseball jersey, the number 09 embroidered in large white numerals over the maroon fabric. They even left on the dirt from his last championship game.

The security guard, who would be swallowed up by Brandon's jersey, looks at Ash over his iPad.

"Hey, Garvin. We're late," Ash tells him, grinning as I pant beside him with my hands on my knees, catching my breath from running the whole way here. "No note, no excuse. Just late."

The guard points wearily over his shoulder with his thumb. "You know the drill, Morrison." He cuts his gaze down to me. "You too. Come on."

I do not, in fact, know the drill. I've never been late to school, or to anything for that matter, not even by a second. Now Ash made us tardy on purpose. I could punch him! How dare he do this to me? As I follow him and the guard to the back hallway, he winks at me over his shoulder. I return his wink by pinching him hard on the arm, but he doesn't even feel it through his leather jacket.

The security office, a place I've never been, is in the back of the building near the boiler room. Also a place I've never been. Cluttered and dusty, the utilitarian, L-shaped desk is dominated by one computer connected to four monitors, three of their screens split into multiple black-and-white live images from around the building. Ash sprawls onto a metal folding chair. I sit stiffly in the chair next to him as the guard enters our information into the computer. He knows Ash's information without asking, but I have to give him my name and student ID number.

"Unexcused tardy," he says, handing each of us a slip of paper. His Adam's apple bobs sharply as he speaks.

This can't be happening. "Will this go on my transcript?"

"Yep."

"But please—"

"Hey, Garvin," Ash says, interrupting. "If you're gonna make the girl cry, at least get her a Kleenex, would you?" He nudges me with his foot.

I'm not crying, but I'm so furious with Ash for getting me in trouble that I'm about to. I hide my face in my hands. The moment the guard leaves, Ash jumps into his chair and slides a flash drive into the computer.

"What are you doing?" I ask.

"Last year they accused me of stealing cash from the cafeteria. I made them show me the security cam footage, which proved I wasn't even at school that day." Rapidly, he taps the keyboard with his long fingers. "But now I know exactly where the files are. The idiot hasn't even changed his password."

He pulls out the flash drive and tosses it to me. "This is everything from the camera in the back stairwell the day Miss Buckley died. Hide it."

Heart pounding, I unzip my backpack and stuff the flash drive into a little case that holds my tampons. Ash returns to his chair behind the desk just as the guard comes back with a box of tissues.

I take one and wipe pretend tears from my eyes. "Is there anything I can do to get this off my transcript?" I ask the guard. "I've never had an unexcused absence before."

"Save it for someone who cares, Abrams," Ash says. "You'd better hurry or you'll be late for second period too." He pulls me away before the guard can respond.

"That unexcused tardy is going to affect my class rank," I say as he tugs me down the hall. "Thanks a lot."

"You're welcome." When we reach my locker, Ash stops and whispers into my ear. "I'll stop by later tonight to watch the footage. And don't worry about that tardy. When I was in the computer, I took it off your transcript."

CHAPTER THIRTY

LILY ~ EIGHTEEN YEARS AGO

Mom and Dad were still sleeping—and Dad wasn't on the couch, which meant they slept together last night, gross, but hooray!—when I left the house Saturday morning. I knew—I *knew*—Will Duston had something to do with Neal's death, and today I was going to figure out exactly what that *something* was.

And unlike last time, I had a plan.

Step One: leave a note for my parents so they wouldn't worry. In my neatest handwriting, I wrote, "*Meeting up with Diana. Have a great day! Hugs and kisses!*" on a sheet of notebook paper, decorated it with smiley faces and hearts, and propped it up against the vase of flowers on the kitchen table where they would see it.

Step Two: head to the movie theater. My car was all fixed from my little accident, but I was still not allowed to drive it. I had to walk again, but that was okay. Walking was part of my plan.

Step Three: trace Neal's path from the theater to Railroad Bridge.

The theater was closed, of course, this early in the morning. As I headed away from it, I walked slowly, letting every detail sink in. I was going to trace Neal's path from the theater to Railroad Bridge in daylight. On Main Street I noted the daffodils blooming in large terracotta pots next to the wrought-iron benches lining the street. The American flags swaying in the breeze. The fancy garbage cans on each corner decorated with painted flowers on green grass, a project sponsored by the Ryland Beautification Committee.

The smoky scent of bacon floated from The Batter's Box as I neared. Rick Paladino was inside, visible through the big picture window. Bubbles was pouring him coffee. I quelled my impulse to wave at them and scurried past. If Rick saw me out here this early on a Saturday morning, he might get suspicious.

At the corner of Main and Adams, the fancy garbage can was dented and scratched. Scrapes of bright blue paint covered some of the cheery flowers. A few feet beyond that, on the street lamp, were more scrapes of blue paint. And on the curb, something glinted. Plastic, yellow, and thick: pieces of a broken headlight.

I wouldn't have thought anything of it—a car accident; I'd had a minor one myself recently—except for one thing. Scattered among the pieces of broken headlight were red pill-shaped objects.

Hot Tamales.

Holy

wow.

Will's pickup truck was blue, like the scraped paint on the garbage can. And that night when we'd talked on his land, he'd told me it was out of commission. Now I knew why.

Instantly, I figured out what had happened. I saw it play out like a movie in my head. Neal had plans with Will after his shift the night he'd died. At some point that night, Will must have gotten into an accident that had injured Neal right here on the corner, then Will had driven him, either gravely injured or already dead, to Duston Farm and dumped him in the creek.

God. Poor Neal. I hoped he had died immediately upon impact so he hadn't spent the last few minutes of his life aching and terrified.

No. Scratch that. I hoped that Neal had stayed alive for a few seconds at least, and that he'd thought of me. I hoped that he'd remembered my secret as he died, and that the knowledge that he would soon be reborn had given him comfort in his last moments.

Despair made a hole in my heart, twice as big as it should have been. I felt like I'd lost two friends: Neal *and* Will. A small part of me had actually kind of almost thought that Will and I were becoming friends, and I'd been actually kind of almost hoping that my theory about him killing Neal was wrong. But that was stupid. I wasn't wrong about him, and he had never been my friend. I hated him. I shouldn't be surprised that he'd done something as callous as this.

Then why did I feel so

heartbroken?

I had a purple makeup case at the bottom of my purse. I'd drawn Asian symbols on it a couple years ago. I dumped the contents, including a hideous pink lipstick from my mom that I'd never worn and a brown eyeliner I'd once used as an emergency pencil during a math test, into the garbage can, then dropped the broken glass and candies inside the makeup case. Evidence.

Now I had to find Will's truck and match the broken glass to his headlights. Time to go to Duston Farm.

I ducked into the alley behind Main Street, slipped under the fence at Smiley's Used Cars, and followed the train tracks through the woods. As I stepped out of the trees onto the creek bed, Will was crossing Railroad Bridge, his Warriors cap pulled low over his eyes.

I slipped behind a tree. I heard his shoes clomping across the bridge, and then he was standing right in front of me. "What do you want this time, Red?"

That same small part of me that had thought we were becoming friends wanted to lie, wanted to tell him to forget it, that he'd be able to live his simple, peaceful farmer's life in Ryland. But I couldn't lie. I couldn't do that to Neal.

I stood tall, almost matching his height, and thrust out my chin. "I know you killed Neal, Will. I *know* it."

His blue eyes turned dark with anguish. "Well, Lily, you're right. I did."

CHAPTER THIRTY-ONE

EVER ~ PRESENT DAY

It's just a tiny flash drive, hidden at the bottom of my backpack in a tampon case under my textbooks, but I slink through the day feeling like a criminal holding a bag of explosives. Every time I see Keith, he asks about Ash. In AP World History, Courtney reminds me that the Little Warriors Training Camp is coming up and I'm supposed to be helping her and the rest of the Batgirls plan it, then she asks if I've asked my dad yet if I can go to Chicago with her for her birthday this summer. I've forgotten about both of those things completely. I've been a bad friend. I apologize to her and promise to do better, but with a disapproving frown, she raises her brows and slides a knowing, suspicious look to Ash.

After dinner that evening, I wave across the street at Keith, who's watching me from his front window. He was supposed to be out partying with the baseball team, celebrating the start of spring break, but he stayed home. When Ash rumbles up my driveway on his bike, I know why.

Keith holds up his phone and mouths, *"Text me if you need me."* I blow him a kiss, signaling, *Everything is fine. You have nothing to be worried about.* To prove it, I leave my front curtains wide open.

Without fanfare or even much conversation, Ash sprawls himself over a kitchen chair and slides the flash drive into my laptop. I'm a little worried the ancient processor wouldn't read the files, but after a few minutes of chugging and churning and some fancy programming by Ash, a grainy, black-and-white image of the school's back stairwell appears on my screen.

This is it. Within the next few minutes we'll have proof that Principal Duston killed Miss Buckley.

On the screen, students trickle into view, a few at first, then more and more as everyone goes to their lockers and then first period. Then the stairwell empties; class must have started.

"Ever?" Joey, in his yellow and blue SpongeBob pajamas, peeks into the kitchen.

"Come on over here, buddy," I say, closing the lid on the laptop. "Couldn't sleep?"

He shakes his head as he pads into the kitchen and climbs onto my lap.

"This is my friend Ash," I say. "We're doing a project together."

Joey gives Ash an appraising look. Ash returns it. "You play baseball?" Joey asks him.

"Nope."

"What do you do?"

"I fly planes."

Joey considers that for a moment. "I have a hamster," he says. "His name is Cheeks."

"I have a cat," Ash says. "His name is Valeri."

Joey wrinkles his nose. "That's a girl's name."

"Not in Russia," Ash says. "He's named after Valeri Polyakov, a cosmonaut who lived in outer space longer than any other person in history."

Joey breathes a slow, worshipful, "Wwwwooooooow."

Before Ash can give my baby brother the ludicrous idea that he should also fly planes or live on Mars himself, I smooth his hair and nudge him off my lap. "It's late, Joey. Go back to bed and I'll come in soon to tuck you in again."

After a glass of water, a hug, a kiss, and a sprinkling of magic fairy dust, Joey finally scampers off to his room. "He'll be asleep within five minutes," I tell Ash.

"You take care of him all the time, don't you?"

I shrug. "I'm all he has."

"What about your dad?"

I open the laptop. "We should get started again. We've got a lot of footage to watch."

From the corner of my eye, I can see Ash, one brow cocked, continuing to stare at me. When I refuse to meet his gaze, he finally turns back to the computer. He slides the mouse over the progress bar, fast-forwarding through the footage of students going up and down the stairs—there's Courtney, bobbing along with the crowd after second period; there's Michael Granz, the Science Olympiad finalist, talking animatedly with a teammate after third period; there's Ash, skulking his way through everyone after fourth period—alternating with long stretches of empty stillness while everyone's in class.

Finally, we see Miss Buckley. Alone. The time stamp in the corner shows 13:05:24, a little after one o'clock. I found her body a few minutes later. On the screen, Principal Duston should be appearing any second now.

In black-and-white silence, she walks up the stairs in her high heels and pencil skirt. Her arms filled with books and papers, she has one pen in her mouth and another holding up her hair in a twist. She's almost at the top when she falls back, her body arcing almost in slow motion as she scrambles for purchase, books and papers flying everywhere, arms flailing as she tumbles down the stairs. She comes to a stop on her stomach, limbs askew, hair loose, head backward, and becomes so still that if the time stamp in the corner hadn't been marking the seconds, I would have thought the computer had frozen.

But *I* am the one who's frozen. I just watched someone die. I remember dying, dozens of times, but this time it's different.

"So she did trip," Ash says. "No one pushed her." He sighs heavily.

That's it? She fell? She wasn't murdered? All that work for nothing? I was so sure, so positive, that Principal Duston pushed her.

I don't know if I'm relieved or disappointed. "Maybe we missed something. Rewind it. Go back to right before she fell."

Lips in a tight line, Ash rewinds the footage and plays it again. I lean close, watching each movement.

"There!" I say. "She stops right before the top step and looks up. Like someone's there, surprising her. Do it again. Maybe we can see who it is."

Both of us lean in, inches from the screen and each other, his breath cool and soft on my cheek. We watch the footage again, but Miss Buckley is alone. "No one else was there," I say. "She really did trip on her high heels." I swivel in my chair to face him. "Ash. I'm so sorry. I really thought—"

"Hold on," he says, frowning. "I'm running it again, frame by frame. This time watch the time stamp."

At 13:05:32, Mrs. Buckley reaches the second-to-top step. At 13:05:33, she pauses and glances up. At 13:05:34—

There is no 13:05:34. The next frame shows Miss Buckley falling, but the time stamp reads 13:05:39. "Did you see that?" Ash asks. He flips between the two frames again, back and forth. Thirty-three to thirty-nine. Thirty-three to thirty-nine.

An icy tremor runs up my spine. "Five seconds are missing."

"Gotta say, Ever," Ash says. "I didn't completely believe you before, but I do now. Duston tampered with the footage. Why would he do that if he weren't hiding something?"

Five seconds. In the grand scheme of things, five seconds don't amount to much. There are more than thirty-one million seconds in a year. Eighty-six thousand seconds in a day. Thirty-six hundred seconds in an hour.

We only need five of them. Five little seconds.

But those five little seconds, five seconds of evidence that could bring justice to Diana Buckley and Lily Summerhays, five seconds that could save Vinnie Morrison's life, five seconds that would make Ryland safe again, are gone.

CHAPTER THIRTY-TWO

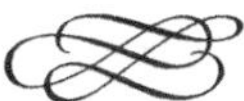

LILY ~ EIGHTEEN YEARS AGO

Will did it.

He admitted it, right here in the woods by Railroad Bridge. He killed Neal Mallick.

All the air left my lungs, all the strength left my muscles, and I sank against a tree trunk. I knew I should run away from him, a killer, but I couldn't. I knew I should feel hatred for him, and fear for myself, but all I felt was sorrow. "How did it happen?"

The temperature dropped ten degrees as he answered. "I forgot about him."

"Forgot?"

"I was going to have a party. That Friday night. My parents were going to visit my brother in Chicago, and I thought I'd have a party for the team."

"I was with Diana that night because she and Brandon broke up again. I don't remember hearing about a party."

He gave a sad laugh. "That's because the party never happened.

My parents ended up staying home and I had to cancel it. I told the team, but I forgot to tell Neal. He wasn't friends with any of us. I only told him about the party because he was standing there in the hallway and heard us talking about it. You know how he's always hovering a little too close. Seth was being an asshole and said something like, 'Girls and players only, no turtles allowed.' I felt bad for him, so I said, 'No, you can come too, Neal.' I never thought he'd actually come. And then when I had to cancel it, I didn't even think to tell him. I didn't think about him at all."

I sighed, my heart aching. "But what exactly happened?"

Will shrugged. "He was crossing the bridge on the way to the party he didn't know was canceled, slipped off, and drowned. You found his body the next morning."

Wait. No. Will still wasn't telling me the truth. "But when did you hit him with your truck?"

"*Hit* him? With my *truck*? Lily, what are you talking about?"

"Your truck is blue."

"Yeah. That's why I call it Ol' Blue."

"You told me it was out of commission."

"It is."

"It's out of commission because you hit him with it."

He gave me a strange look. "No, it's out of commission because it's old. It was old when my brother bought it ten years ago. The transmission blew out again last month. Why the hell would you think I hit Neal with my truck?"

"You haven't driven it in over a month?"

"That's correct."

"Show me the truck. I need to see it."

Looking at me curiously, he led me back across the bridge and through the field to the side of a large storage shed and pointed. Dusty and tired, the blue Toyota sat dejectedly in a patch of dirt and weeds. The headlights were dirty from being outside, but they were whole.

"These are old headlights," I said.

"The originals. Came with the truck."

"They've never been broken."

"Never." He rubbed the back of his neck. "Lily. Why do you think I hit Neal with my truck?"

"Because I found—" I gasped, and it was like the air was helium, because I suddenly felt lighter than a balloon. "Will! Do you know what this means?"

"No."

"It means it *wasn't* you." I threw my arms around him. "It wasn't your fault, Will!"

And then I was kissing him. We were two separate people one moment, and the next we were one.

My mouth
on his,
our bodies
pressed together,
limbs
intertwined,
leaning against his old, dirty, dented, undamaged, beautiful truck, and I was laughing and crying and kissing at the same time.

He pulled away, breathless, his blue eyes lit with surprise. "I—why—what—"

So happy. So relieved. I ran my palms down his face. I wanted to kiss his reddening cheeks. And then I turned somber. "Neal didn't slip off the bridge, Will. He didn't get that far. He was hit by a car outside the movie theater." I told him about the blue paint on the street lamp, the broken headlight and the candies on the curb, and the empty, bloody box of Hot Tamales in the woods. "I think whoever hit him took his body to the bridge and dumped it in the creek."

As he stared at me, his face paled from red to white. "So it wasn't my fault? You're sure?"

"I'm positive. It wasn't you." I swiped tears from my cheeks. "I was so upset when I saw that blue paint. I didn't want it to be you. And it's not."

He removed his hat and swiped his hand through his hair, his beautiful white-blond hair. As the enormity of the truth hit him, he sank against the truck. "It wasn't me."

Suddenly, he whooped and threw his hat on the ground. "It wasn't me!" He swooped me up and spun me around, crushing his lips to mine.

When he finally put me back on the ground, I was dizzy. And not because of the spinning.

CHAPTER THIRTY-THREE

EVER ~ PRESENT DAY

It's been three days since Ash and I watched the footage of Miss Buckley's death together, and a little over two weeks since I saw the crossed-hatchet tattoo on Principal Duston's wrist. I originally wanted to show the footage with the missing five seconds to the cops, but Ash talked me out of it. "Duston and Paladino hate me," he said, "and Duston and Paladino are buddies. Duston will say we edited the footage ourselves and Paladino will believe him. We need absolute proof that Duston killed Miss Buckley before we can tell anyone."

We have fewer than three weeks to find that proof, or Ash's father is going to be executed for a crime he didn't commit.

Principal Duston is on to us. He's always passing by my classrooms at school, always standing in the entrance, watching me come and go. Sometimes Chief Paladino is with him.

Keith is suspicious too. Not of Principal Duston, but of Ash.

Keith has been dominating any free time I have, demanding to come over every evening. He's determined to keep me away from Ash.

But now it's spring break and I don't have to worry about running into Principal Duston at school, and Keith's parents are making him work at The Batter's Box every day. First thing Monday morning, I call Ash. "Can you come over?"

"Not today," he says. "I'm busy."

"But we need to figure out what to do. We need to find proof."

"You'll have to come with me then. I'll be at the corner of Jefferson and Van Buren in sixty minutes. If you're not there, I'm going without you."

"Where?"

But he's hung up.

Fifty-nine minutes later, Joey is playing with Hayden next door, and I'm waiting for Ash at the intersection of Jefferson and Van Buren. A little buzz of anticipation sizzles up my spine.

My phone buzzes—a text from Courtney. *Batgirls meeting today at 10, my house.*

That's right. I keep forgetting about that. We're planning the training camp.

Before I can text a reply, Ash roars up on his motorcycle. He removes his helmet and smirks. "Didn't think you'd actually come."

I tuck my phone into my back pocket. "You wore a helmet."

"What can I say? You're a good influence on me." He pats the seat behind him. "Get on."

He can't be serious. "No way."

"I told you, I have plans today. If you want to talk, you'll have to come with."

"Can't we go talk at your place by the creek?"

He reaches into a leather bag on the back of the bike. "I brought you your own helmet. And here." He shrugs out of his leather jacket, revealing strong, taut biceps and pecs under a black T-shirt. "You can wear this too."

The black helmet is shiny and looks new, but I shake my head. "I can't wear your jacket. You'll be cold, and besides, you're probably not wearing sunscreen." I can't stop myself from adding, "Three thousand people die from skin cancer every year."

"Suit yourself," he says, slipping back into his jacket. "See you around." He pushes his heel to the pedal and the engine roars again.

"Wait!" I shout. Lily Summerhays, I've learned, was fearless. She wouldn't have been too scared to ride on the back of a motorcycle.

I yank the helmet from him and push it down hard over my head and slip into his jacket. "You'll go slow. The speed limit," I say to Ash. "No. Ten miles under the speed limit."

He salutes. "Aye aye, cap'n."

Awkwardly, I swing my leg over the seat behind him. My legs straddle outside of his, and I press against him, gripping my hands around his waist. His stomach is hard, and I want to hold it tighter, to run my fingertips over his ab muscles. What I really want to do is slide my hands under his shirt to feel his skin.

I try not to think of how much of my body is touching so much of his body. I've never touched Keith this way.

Ash slowly rolls down the street, so slowly I barely feel the wind. The engine purrs. "I can't believe I'm doing this," I say.

I feel more than hear him chuckle again. "Hold on tight."

And then we're off, flyyyyyying down the road. I scream, and he laughs.

"You said you'd go slow!"

"This is slow!" he shouts, then goes even faster.

We fly down Van Buren, but I don't see any of it. My head pressed to Ash's back, I squeeze my eyes shut. We turn left, and I open them just enough to see that we're nearing the airfield. "We could have walked here again!" I shout into the wind. Then I'm struck by a horrible thought. "There's no way I'm letting you fly me in a plane!"

"Sorry, I can't today, but I promise we'll do that next time!" he shouts, and instead of turning left onto the runway, he turns right, onto the highway.

I have no idea where he's taking me. I scream as we sail down the highway, leaving Ryland behind. My arms grip him so tightly, I'm sure I'm breaking his ribs. My legs squeeze his legs. His leather jacket, zipped up to my chin, intoxicates me with its leathery, Ash-y scent.

I should be terrified. I *try* to feel terrified.

But I'm not. I feel... free. Joyful. Exhilarated.

I throw my head back, loving the wind in my face, loving each cold, fresh breath. I want to throw off the helmet and let my hair fly free. To keep myself from throwing my hands in the air, I grip Ash even tighter.

"What was that?" Ash shouts. "Did you just say to go faster? Whatever you say, boss!" And we go even faster.

He thinks I'm sitting behind him freaking out, so he's just messing with me. He doesn't know how much I'm loving this. I scream, but out of joy rather than fear.

Much too quickly, although we've probably been on the road for at least an hour, Ash slows down. I open my eyes as he pulls into a parking lot of what looks like a castle, with stories-high walls of brown stone, surrounded by tall electric fences topped with coils of barbed wire along the perimeter. On the top floor of the brick towers at each corner of the property are guards with rifles. Ash has brought me to Indiana State Prison.

He shuts off the engine, and the sudden silence is filled with dread. "You said you didn't want to talk to your dad," I say.

"Changed my mind," he mumbles as he helps me off the bike. He holds my arm longer than necessary.

"When was the last time you saw him?" I ask.

"Five years ago."

I stare up at him as he looks up at the towers. A shadow of vulnerability crosses his face. Something makes me reach out and take his hand. He glances down in surprise but doesn't remove his hand from mine. He meets my eyes, his grief obvious.

"Does he know about you?" I ask. "How smart you are? That

you've been accepted to college? That you fly planes? Does he know you want to be an astronaut?"

He shakes his head. He looks again at the building but doesn't move.

"Do you want me to come in with you?" I ask.

He nods curtly and, tightening his grip on my hand, takes a step forward.

The death row building, a small, thick, dark structure, is separated from the rest of the prison. It takes over an hour to get through security. In the clean, tiled lobby, we place our belongings—my phone and ID, Ash's wallet and keys—in a plastic crate, where they're run through an X-ray machine and then examined inside and out by guards with dull eyes in drab, brown uniforms. One at a time, Ash and I walk slowly through a metal detector, then we're frisked head to toe by a warden with cold, calloused hands.

The warden grunts as he flips Ash's driver's license between his fingers. "You're Morrison's kid, huh? Guy's got less than three weeks left. Come to say good-bye?"

Ash swallows visibly and nods.

The guard instructs us to stand before an electric door made of steel and wire-laced glass. After standing in silence for a long minute with Ash's hand in both of mine, I jump at a sudden buzzer, then the door rolls opened with a motorized whir. Another officer escorts us deeper into the prison to another door, only to repeat the process twice more. It smells faintly of mold and vomit in here. The deeper we go, the darker and grimier the building becomes, and the tighter Ash grips my hand. To comfort me, or to comfort himself?

After the last set of doors, an armed guard leads us past a thick, intimidating metal door. The prison cells must be behind that door.

The inmates in those cells have all committed crimes so heinous that society has decided that death is the only punishment harsh enough for them. Every instinct I have screams at me to run, to flee from this horrid place, these detestable criminals, but there's no way I'll abandon Ash now.

A short guard with brown, slimy hair escorts us down the corridor and around a corner to a cell, three walls of concrete and one wall of thick wire-laced glass with ventilation holes. I focus on the ventilation holes because I don't know how I'll react when I see the man inside. In my peripheral vision, I see a figure: male, wearing slippers and a denim jumpsuit, hunched on a yellow plastic chair. This is the man whom, for my entire life up until a couple weeks ago, I believed had murdered Lily—had murdered me. My breath is caught in my throat. I can't look directly at him.

The guard knocks once with his knuckle on the bulletproof glass. "Your visitors are here," he announces to the prisoner, and with his foot, slides two upside-down milk crates to Ash and me to sit on. We remain standing. Stiff, unmoving. Ash grips my hand so tightly, I think he'll break it. I clutch his just as hard.

Finally, I force myself to look directly at Vinnie Morrison. At the same time, he lifts his head. Black eyes. Hard. Cold. Defensive. Identical to Ash's, before I got to know him. Panic flutters in my throat.

"They shoulda told you at the gate," Vinnie Morrison says, his voice a low growl. "I don't talk to reporters or lawyers."

"Vinnie. It's me. Ash."

Vinnie looks him up and down. "Well, fuck. It *is* you. Damn, you're big."

Vinnie is big himself. Large chest and arms, broad shoulders, enormous hands. Cropped, dark hair, chiseled jaw. He nods to me. "You his girl?"

I shake my head, then pull my hand from Ash's and fiddle with my daisy charm instead.

"This is Ever," Ash says. "She's the one who convinced me to come see you."

"Why, so you can tell me what a shitty father I was before I die?"

His eyes burrow into mine. "Shoulda saved yourself the trip. I already know."

"We're trying to find who really killed Lily Summerhays," Ash says.

Vinnie Morrison laughs hollowly. "I thought *I* killed Lily Summerhays." He leans back in his chair and hooks his fingers behind his head. Still clearly inked on his wrist are the letters ASH.

The fear that had rendered me mute melts away. "No," I say. I'm absolutely sure of it. "You didn't."

Vinnie doesn't move, doesn't even breathe. "Now why would you think that?"

"Do you remember Diana Buckley and Will Duston?" Ash asks, almost whispering their names. "They were Lily's friends. Well, Miss Buckley was."

"Diana Buckley," Vinnie says thoughtfully. "Yeah."

"You knew her?" Ash asks.

"Never talked to her personally. But she sends me stuff every once in a while. Books. Cash for the commissary. Keeps me up to date on what you're doing."

Ash and I glance at each other. Proof Miss Buckley knew he was innocent. She wouldn't have sent books, letters, and money to her best friend's killer.

"She said I should be real proud of you," Vinnie continues. "Says you're going to college. On a scholarship. That true?"

"Depends," Ash says. Ash's hair is long and Vinnie's head is shaved, but I'm struck by how similar these men are. Both are large, both have dark eyes and golden beige skin, and both have gruff, guttural voices and speak in clipped sentences. Vinnie has been in prison since Ash was an infant, but it's obvious they're father and son.

"Did Miss Buckley ever tell you if she knew what really happened to Lily?" I ask. "Did she say anything about Will Duston in her letters?"

"Will Duston." He scrunches his lips and narrows his eyes, thinking. "That pale farmer kid, right? The one with the toothpicks."

"He's the high school principal now," Ash says. "Total asshole."

"We need to prove that he framed you for Lily's murder," I say. "Is there anything you remember from that night, anything at all? Was he a, you know, a customer of yours? A client?"

Vinnie runs his tongue over his teeth. "You need to prove that he framed me for Lily's murder," he repeats in an amused murmur.

I nod, and Vinnie snorts. "Listen. Ash. My one and only piece of fatherly advice: Take that scholarship, get the hell out of Ryland, and make something of yourself. Don't fuck up your life just to get some petty revenge against an asshole principal you don't like."

"I won't get that scholarship if I can't prove he killed Lily," Ash says. "But even if the scholarship goes to someone else," he adds, sliding a glance at me, "we can't let you be executed for his crime. He should be in here, not you."

Vinnie shakes his head, a low growl in his throat. "You already saved my life once. You don't need to do it again."

"How'd I do that?"

"By being born. They accused me of killing some kid named Neal Mallick. Said I sold him drugs or something, got him wasted, and he slipped off the bridge and drowned in the creek. But I had an alibi."

"What was that?"

"I was with your mother in the hospital while you were being born. I didn't kill that kid, but I did kill Lily Summerhays. I don't have an alibi because I did it. I accepted it a long time ago. Now you should too."

I look again at Vinnie's wrist. Three letters. ASH. He did *not* kill Lily.

"Hey. Princess. What's so fascinating about my hands?" Vinnie snaps at me, holding them out. "You keep looking at them."

Startled, I mumble, "Oh. Um, the tattoo on your wrist caught my attention. Ash's name."

"Got it the day after he was born." He traces the letters with his finger. "Why, you expected a hatchet tattoo?"

I feel the blood drain from my face. "H—How—"

"Like all those guys have. Duston, the mayor's kid, all of 'em."

I swallow hard. "What?"

"The hatchet tattoo," Vinnie says. "Warrior baseball team tradition. Everyone on the baseball team gets one when they win a state championship. What, they don't do that no more?"

Ash says, "I don't think they've gotten past the playoffs lately."

"Good. Back when I was around, they won eight years out of ten, something like that. It was all Ryland cared about. Fucking asswipes, strutting around with their tattoos. Thinking they owned the town."

"And they *all* got that tattoo?" I squeak. I make a cross on my wrist. "Two hatchets crossed at the handles, one red handle and one yellow?"

"That's it," Vinnie says. "Every player on every winning team. Hell, there's probably over a hundred of those jerkoffs with that tattoo." He chuckles. "Cute of you to think that I'd have one. Trust me, princess, my extracurricular activities had nothing to do with baseball."

It's hard to hear him over the ringing in my ears. My vision narrows and the floor sways. Only one thing he says resonates over and over, like an echo. "Over a hundred?" I can barely hear myself either. All I can hear is *over a hundred. Over a hundred.*

I press the heel of my hand to my eyebrow, stopping the flow of invisible blood.

"Ah, shit. She's sick again," Ash says. "This happens a lot. Vinnie, I gotta get her out of here." His arm is around me, holding me up. Warm, strong, protective. He pauses, and from far away, I hear him say, "I'm...I don't know what else to say. I'm sorry, I guess."

Over a hundred. Over a hundred.

"Don't be. I'm glad you came," Vinnie says, then his tone grows cold, like he's trying not to choke on his emotions. "Thanks for visiting, nice to see you, have a good life, don't fuck it up like I did. Now get out of here and forget about me." He turns his back to us.

I allow Ash to lead me away, accompanied by the guard. I try to breathe the pain away.

One...

Two...

Three.

The pain is still there. Throbbing, bleeding invisible blood.

Four...

Five...

Six.

Still there. Pain, blood, fear.

Seven...

Eight...

Nine.

The pain isn't going away. I don't know if it'll ever go away.

My pool of suspects just went from one to one hundred.

CHAPTER THIRTY-FOUR

LILY ~ EIGHTEEN YEARS AGO

My pool of suspects just went from one to zero.

"Now that I know it's not you, Neal's killer could be anybody," I said to Will under his oak tree the next day. The Day After. The day after I realized Will did not kill Neal. The day after we kissed.

I wanted to kiss him again as he leaned against the tree trunk, all tall and lean and blond. I wanted to make up for the time we lost to unjustified hatred. I wanted to feel his lips on mine, to taste him.

But I didn't kiss him again. Yesterday's kiss had surprised me as much as it had him. It had been an impulse, and I was trying *not* to be impulsive. I wanted to kiss him, absolutely. But more than that, I wanted him to want to kiss me too.

"Neal's killer is someone who has a blue car with a broken headlight," Will said. "That narrows it down. The police will figure it out."

"We can't tell the police," I said. "Not yet."

"Why not?"

"I already told Rick Paladino a couple of times, but he didn't take me seriously."

"He thought you were making up drama because this town is so boring?" Will grinned. "Can't say I blame him for thinking that."

He was teasing me this time, not taunting me. I gave him a playful punch. "He told me to stop being a detective. He won't believe me until I have proof."

Will shifted, and his shoulder was almost touching mine, generating heat between us. "Maybe you're right. When he asked me about that calendar page you found, he did tell me not to say anything about my canceled party. He said Neal's death wasn't my fault, but any connection to it would lead to controversy for the baseball team, which could hurt our standing."

"All this town cares about is the stupid baseball team," I said.

"Hey," Will replied, feigning insult. "I'm on that *stupid* baseball team, and so are most of your friends."

"But it proves that before I can tell the cops, I need to find who hit Neal with their car, and I need evidence."

"We," Will said.

"Hmm?"

"*We* need to find who hit Neal with their car."

"You'll help me?"

"Of course."

Did he actually believe me, or did he just *want* to believe me so he wouldn't blame himself for Neal's death anymore?

Didn't matter. It felt good to tell someone and not have them laugh at me or accuse me of stirring up trouble when there was none. I wanted his help, and he was willing to give it. "Okay," I said. "*We a*re looking for the owner of a blue car with a broken headlight."

Ryland was a small town, sure, but there were probably a couple hundred blue cars. We didn't even know the make or model. "We could ask Brandon," Will said. "Whoever hit Neal probably brought their car in to Lennox Auto Body. It's the only car repair place around."

"We should go see if he's working there today."

But he didn't move, and neither did I. His gaze flickered from my eyes to my lips and back again.

Oh, screw it. Screw not being impulsive. I planted a kiss on him.

It was delicious. And even more delicious: he kissed me back.

"What are we doing?" he asked between kisses. "We hate each other."

I grabbed the collar of his Warriors T-shirt and pulled him closer. "Come here then so I can hate you some more."

Brandon Lennox may have been working at his family's auto body shop that day, but he wasn't working very hard. When Will and I got there, Brandon was in the parking lot, tossing a baseball with Seth and Javier. It was probably my imagination—their faces were shadowed by the brims of their Warriors hats—but all three looked surprised to see Will and me approaching together.

"You crash your Firebird into another tree?" Brandon asked me.

"Ha ha," I replied. "No. Has anyone come in recently who needed a headlight repaired? Like they'd been in an accident?"

Brandon lobbied the baseball to Seth, who caught it in his mitt. "Don't know. This is my first time in the shop since baseball season started."

"Can you check?"

He shrugged. Will took Brandon's place, tossing the ball to Javier as Brandon brought me inside the cluttered shop and stepped behind the counter. Seth wandered in after us, pulling off his mitt. He opened his mouth and squeezed his bottle of red Gatorade into it as he fiddled with the car deodorizers next to the cash register.

"Don't get that red shit on the merchandise," Brandon snapped at Seth, then asked me, overly casual, "You talk to Diana?"

"Not since last night." And when I had talked to her, I hadn't told her about kissing Will. I hadn't gotten a chance. All Diana had talked about was if she should get back together with Brandon or not.

"When you see her, tell her I need to talk to her, okay?" He turned on the computer. "She won't answer when I call and she won't answer her door."

Suppressing a sigh, I nodded.

"What's the make and model of that car you're looking for?"

"All I know is it's blue. It needed a new headlight and probably has a dent in it."

He slid his Warriors hat backward on his head, then with the mouse, scrolled through the records. "Nothing here," he said. "No headlight replacements, no dents, except for your Firebird three weeks ago."

"Has anyone ordered a new headlight? Maybe they wanted to install it themselves."

More scrolling and clicking. "Nope. Why are you asking?"

Seth, who was still guzzling Gatorade, choked on it. He coughed, spraying the car deodorizers on the counter with red liquid. "Damn it, Siegel," Brandon muttered, rushing to get a rag. Seth, cracking up with laughter, wiped his mouth with the back of his hand. Some of the Gatorade dribbled onto his hatchet tattoo. It looked like blood.

I used the distraction to escape to the parking lot. Will and Javier were still tossing the ball. "Any luck?" Will asked. He'd taken off his Warrior's hat, and the sun hit his eyes just right to make them deep and dark blue.

I shook my head. Lennox Auto Body was a dead end. The car that hit Neal was probably hidden in the owner's garage or something. How was I supposed to find it now?

We, I reminded myself. How were *we*—Will and I—supposed to find it now?

"Why are you looking for a car with a broken headlight?" Seth asked from behind me.

"Um, I—"

"Hey, Lily," Javier called from across the lot, rescuing me. "You want to come flying with me this afternoon?"

Normally, I would have jumped at the chance. But today Will and I needed to find that blue car. And maybe, probably, we would

hate

each other a little bit under his tree.

I met Will's eyes and bit back a smile.

Seth cleared his throat and glared at Will. Was Seth jealous? I'd always made it perfectly clear to Seth that he and I were just friends. But if he knew I was hanging out with Will, he would tell his parents, who would tell my parents that I was crushing on a Duston. And then I'd get in trouble again.

I couldn't risk it.

I stepped a few feet away from Will. "Yeah," I said to Javier. "Let's fly."

Javier's father was busy in the back storage room when we got there, so Javier distracted him while I slipped into the little single-engine Piper that they used for crop dusting. The desire to be with Will was surprisingly overwhelming, but the excitement of flying took the edge off a bit. Javier slid into the pilot's seat next to me, then clicked and pulled and flicked the buttons on the dashboard, the hatchet tattoo on his wrist swiping and slicing. Soon the Piper was kicking up dirt on the runway. We went faster and faster, the engine

sputtering

whirring

humming,

and I let out a *Whoo!* as we lifted off the ground.

Javier laughed as I watched Ryland get smaller and smaller. "You never get tired of this, do you?"

"Nope." This was freedom, flying like this. "Go higher!"

Javier, the little scaredy cat, never went as high as I wanted. "This is a low-altitude plane, Lily," he said.

But we were high enough in the air that I could see Ryland's farms spread out beneath us like a giant quilt of golds and greens. I couldn't help myself—I checked Duston Farm for Will, hoping he'd be in his soybean field.

And he was, halfway between the creek and his farmhouse, scattering seeds among the sprouting greens. He waved his Warriors hat up at the plane.

I laughed and waved back at him, although I knew he couldn't see me.

"Aren't you two supposed to hate each other?" Javier asked.

"We do," I said, unable to stop the grin from spreading. "We've hated each other a lot the past couple of days."

From up here, Ryland didn't look that bad. It wasn't so suffocating. The rusty train tracks bisected the land between Duston Farm and my dad's company, through the patch of trees along Deep Creek, running along Old Sutton Farm and its crumbling, abandoned barn, and finally running behind the buildings on Main Street and beyond. I could see only the roofs of the buildings along Main Street, but I knew the town well enough to recognize each building. The Batter's Box, the police station, the bookstore, the pharmacy, the movie theater. The corner of Main and Adams, where Neal had been hit.

Huh.

"Hey, Javier," I said. "Head back to the creek for a minute. To Railroad Bridge."

"Why?"

"I just want to see something."

Javier circled back over Main Street. I kept my eyes on the ground. Neal had been hit at the corner of Main and Adams. Whoever hit him must have driven his body to the creek—no way could someone carry a dead or unconscious body that far, so they must have driven him—but there was no road near the creek. The car must have driven through the fields and woods along the train tracks.

As we flew along the tracks, I kept my eyes on the ground, imagining someone—a shadow—driving his car from Adams Street, into the alley, then off-road, through the grassy, weedy fields of Old Sutton Farm. Getting as close as possible to the bridge. Putting it in park. Opening the doors. Then taking Neal's body, dragging it through the trees to the bridge. Pushing Neal into the creek.

Okay. Now what would the driver have done? Taking a deep breath, I closed my eyes.

Think.

The car had just hit someone. It was damaged, at least enough to break a headlight. Dented. The paint was scraped. Maybe, probably, the driver had a difficult time driving it through the field to the bridge. Regardless, I realized now, the shadow-driver most likely would not have taken the car back out onto the road and risked getting pulled over for a broken headlight. He certainly would not have taken it to Lennox Auto Body to be fixed, not after he'd killed someone with it.

He'd have to hide it. Quickly. Somewhere close.

I opened my eyes, and my gaze landed on the perfect place to hide a car that had just killed someone.

CHAPTER THIRTY-FIVE

EVER ~ PRESENT DAY

Over a hundred men with crossed-hatchet tattoos. I can't get the thought from my mind as Ash and I exit the penitentiary and speed away on his bike. Gone is the thrill, the freedom, of flying down the highway on a motorcycle. I hug Ash tightly from behind, partly for warmth, mostly for comfort.

Over a hundred.

Principal Duston could have killed Lily, but so could have a hundred other men. It may as well be a million.

Ash doesn't speak at all until he stops in my driveway. I take off his helmet and leather jacket and give them back. I'm shivering.

"You're still not feeling well," he says, rubbing my arms. "Your dad home?"

"He should be back tonight."

"I'll stay until he gets here."

God, I want him to. I want him to come inside and hold me until I stop shaking, until the fear inside me stops swirling, until Ryland is safe again, until the world makes sense again. I want to breathe in his scent—

I jump at the sound of a door slamming. Keith's front door, across the street. He steps out onto his porch, watching Ash and me. Frowning. I step away from Ash. "You should go. I'm sorry we're at another dead end."

"We can't give up, though."

I almost sag with relief. Ash is still in. He still believes me. He still wants to help.

"I'll never give up," I promise him. "But we can't trust anyone. Even if it wasn't Principal Duston who killed Lily, he might be covering for the person who did."

"You don't think it's Duston anymore?" Ash asks, clearly confused. "But you said you overheard him and Miss Buckley talking about it at Kammer's Pharmacy."

"I thought it was him, but..." I shrug. "I don't know. It could have been someone else."

His eyes narrow in suspicion. "Like who?"

My mind scurries to make up a believable lie. "When your father mentioned the baseball teams today," I say, "I remembered that Miss Buckley and the man she was talking to said something about state champions. Maybe the killer is someone from those old championship baseball teams." It's the closest I can come to telling him the truth. The *new* truth. One hundred tattoos. One hundred suspects.

The dubious look did not leave Ash's face. Across the street, Keith has left his porch and is on his way over. He doesn't look happy.

"I just think we need to broaden our focus," I say to Ash. *Please, please, please,* I beg him silently. *Just believe me.*

He sighs and rubs the back of his neck. "Well, we're not getting anywhere with Duston, so I guess we should cast a wider net." He slides a glance at the rapidly-approaching Keith, then back at me. "I'm outta here. Stay safe. Call me if you need me." He gets on his bike and roars away.

Keith takes Ash's place on my driveway, replacing Ash's suspicion with his own. "You were gone all day."

I replace the lies to Ash with a lie to Keith. "We had to go out of town to do some research."

"On his motorcycle?"

"I wore a helmet."

"I want you to find a new group for that project, Ever," he says, his voice low and threatening.

"I can't."

"Then do it without Ash."

"I can't."

After an impossibly long moment, his anger turns to despair as he whispers, "Did you kiss him?"

"*Kiss* him? That's a big leap, Keith. No, I did not kiss him. We're working on a project. That's all." But *is* that all? I put my hand on Keith's chest to reassure him, and myself. "I promise you. I've never kissed Ash."

"Do you want to?"

I can't answer him. I can't meet his eyes.

He nibbles on his fingernail. "What is it about him?" he asks. "Is it his motorcycle? Do you want me to get a motorcycle? I'll get a motorcycle if you want me to."

"No. It's not that."

"Are you trying to make me jealous?" he asks. "Is it because of that girl in Eastfield last year? I told you, that never happened. It was just a rumor and it's not true."

"I know," I tell him. "And no, I'm not trying to make you jealous."

"Then why are you doing this?" He exhales with frustration. "Is it because I don't want you to win that scholarship?"

"What?"

"That's it, isn't it?" he says. "Fine. I don't want you to go to college. What if you decide you don't want to stay in Ryland with me? What if college makes you think you're too good for me? You're going to meet other people, other guys—"

"Jesus, Keith." I pull away, but he grabs my arm.

"But I realize now that I was wrong to think that way," he says. "I *want* you to get that scholarship. I'm okay with you going to college. I was holding you back, and I'm sorry. I'm just scared of losing you."

His eyes are so large and pleading. He's my little devoted puppy dog, so, so, so in love with me.

"I was saving this as a surprise for after graduation," he says, "but you know that empty lot over there on Polk Lane? The one near the school? My dad's going to co-sign a loan for me to buy that lot and build a house on it. For you and me."

I sputter. "Keith, we're still in high school. I still have four years of college. And then—" And then what? Why am I having trouble breathing? "What about Joey? I can't leave him."

"It's just a plot of land for now," Keith says. "But when we get married, we'll already have a house. And if Joey wants to live with us, he can. I'll manage the diner, you'll do the accounting, and I'll spend every day making you happy."

My mind whirls. Am I hearing him correctly? "Joey can live with us?"

"I'll do anything for you, Ever. You're everything to me," he says, tucking my hair behind my ear. "I love you."

He waits for me to return his affections. Why am I hesitating? My stable, predictable, safe boyfriend has just offered me the stable, predictable, safe life I've always wanted. The life I *need*.

"Keith, I... thank you. I love you too." I reach up and kiss him.

He kisses me back, then pulls away and holds me at arm's length. "But none of that can happen if you keep hanging out with Ash Morrison."

Dad comes home in time for dinner that night, but he falls asleep in his armchair while his pasta is still warm on the TV tray at his side.

What would he say if I tell him that

1. I rode on Ash Morrison's motorcycle today?

2. I went to the prison to visit Vinnie Morrison on death row?

3. Keith basically proposed to me, with an ultimatum?

Would he care about any of that?

As if Dad knows I'm looking at him, he shifts, his arm snaking out from under the afghan.

He grew up in Ryland. He played on the Warriors baseball team, but before they were state-championship caliber. I've lived with him my entire life so I *know* he doesn't have a tattoo. But I have to check anyway. Slowly, so I don't disturb him, I flip his arm so his palm faces up.

No hatchet tattoo on his wrist. I knew he didn't have a tattoo, but I'm still relieved.

Joey is getting antsy, so I take him to his room and dump a giant tub of LEGO bricks onto his carpet and we build bridges and tunnels for his Matchbox cars. Cheeks the hamster runs on her squeaky wheel. Once Joey is engrossed in his cars and tunnels, I pick up my phone to call Ash. I have several notifications. Texts from earlier today, some from Keith but most from Courtney.

From Keith, 10:15 a.m.: *Just checking to make sure you're okay. What time will you be back?*

From Courtney, 10:20 a.m.: *Hey, where are you? The Batgirls are here to plan the Training Camp.*

From Courtney, 10:30 a.m.: *We can't wait any longer. I have an away softball game later.*

From Courtney, 10:47 a.m.: *Keith just told me you're with Ash Morrison. Seriously, wtf?*

From Keith, 11:11 a.m.: *Where are you? You OK?*

From Courtney, 11:31 a.m.: *What group project are you doing with Ash Morrison anyway? What class is it for? No one else has a group project.*

From Keith, 12:18 p.m.: *Why aren't you home yet?*

From Courtney, 12:49 p.m.: *Ash Morrison is trouble. You need to stay away from him.*

From Keith, 1:15 p.m.: *Why the hell aren't you texting me back?*

From Courtney, 1:20 p.m.: *Keith is really mad, Ev. Gotta say, I am too.*

From Courtney, 1:26 p.m.: *Whatever Ash Morrison is telling you, it's a lie. He's tricking you so he can win that scholarship.*

From Courtney, 1:27 p.m.: *You're ruining everything.*

I need to call her. This is too important for a text. We've never argued before. Never even disagreed on anything before.

She answers on the first ring but says nothing.

"Hi, Court," I say. "I'm so sorry for not texting you back today."

She still says nothing. Frenetic, heavy metal music comes through the phone, something she doesn't usually listen to. The low, angry bass clashes with the high-pitched squeaks of Cheeks's hamster wheel.

What would *Courtney* say if I told her that I rode on Ash Morrison's motorcycle and visited his father on death row, and that Keith told me he bought a plot of land for a house for us, but only if I stop hanging out with Ash?

I don't tell her the first part. But I've never fought with my best friend before, and I want to make things right. So I tell her the second part.

It works, because for the first time in weeks, she's not upset with me. "Oh my God! That's basically a marriage proposal. You said *yes*, right?"

I grin. Best friends once again. "We're not even out of high school yet, Court," I remind her. "It'll be a few years before anything happens." Then I add, "And a lot could change between now and then."

"You and Keith are the perfect couple. You're made for each other."

I'm ready to stop talking about Keith. "How was your softball game?"

She doesn't answer right away. "Horrible. We lost five to one."

"Yikes, what happened?"

"My pitches were off. I walked four players. The coach pulled me out in the fourth inning and benched me."

"You're allowed to have one bad day," I say.

"I'm having a lot of bad days lately," she whimpers, and she sounds like she's about to cry.

"Court, no! What's wrong?"

It takes her even longer to respond this time. "I don't know. Nothing. Everything. End-of-senior-year stuff. Lots of tests coming up and I suck at tests. Softball. College. The Training Camp. I really want it to be special this year."

It's a lot of work to plan the Little Warriors Training Camp, but it's worth it because it's such a fun event. This year, however, it seems so unimportant and frivolous. An innocent man is about to be executed. A killer is walking free. That killer could be any one of a hundred suspects.

And all of those suspects used to be on the baseball team.

My heart surges with adrenaline as I get an idea.

"You know what we should do," I say. "We should invite all of the former players to come to the Training Camp." I'm amped up, pacing Joey's room and sweeping errant LEGOs out of the way with my foot. "You know, the guys who used to be on the team. Especially the ones who played on the state championship teams. They can play an exhibition game. That would make this year really special." Death-pain surges over my eye at the thought of being on a baseball field with one hundred men who have that hatchet tattoo, but it might be a good opportunity to identify Lily's real killer.

"That's a good idea," Courtney says, a little enthusiasm returning to her tone. "Lots of them still live around here, and I bet my dad keeps in touch with most of them. I can get their contact info from him."

"Forward their info over to me," I say. "I'll send them an e-vite." One bird, two stones: I can help my overwhelmed friend, and Ash and I will be better able to investigate the players if we have a list of their names, email addresses, and other personal information.

Another idea strikes me, one that makes me stop in my tracks. "Hey, how long has your dad been the coach? Twenty-five years, right?"

"Twenty-six," says Courtney.

I've been to the Nolan house hundreds of times, slept overnight dozens of times. Eaten dinner at their kitchen table. I often feel that Coach Nolan is more of a father to me than my own dad. Yet I've never seen a tattoo on Coach's wrist either. Maybe Vinnie was wrong about the tradition. Maybe he was just messing with me.

"Your dad doesn't have a tattoo, does he?" I ask. "Two crossed hatchets on his wrist? One with a red handle, one with a yellow handle?"

"Are you talking about that old state championship thing?" Court asks. "That tattoo was something the players did. Not the coach."

I sit down hard on Joey's bed, feeling both relieved and disappointed. Relieved that Coach is not the killer. Disappointment that Vinnie had not lied.

"Why are you asking about that?" Courtney asks.

I don't want to completely lie to my best friend, so once again, I tell her only half the story. "I just heard about the tattoos for the first time today."

"Well, that's not surprising."

"Why?"

"Because all you do is study and take care of Joey. You don't do anything or go anywhere. The only places you go are your house, my house, The Batter's Box, and school. You've never even been to the pool at the YMCA. You probably would have seen that tattoo on some of the dads there at least."

I've never gone swimming because I drowned in the early 1600s. If I'd at least gone to the pool, I probably would have seen that tattoo on some shirtless man's wrist before. And not just at the pool—any man wearing a short-sleeved shirt anywhere around town. Why haven't I ever noticed? Because I'm always looking down at my feet to make sure I don't trip over anything, or looking at my food as I cut it into small bites so I don't choke, or looking up at the ceiling to check for smoke alarms so I don't burn in a fire. I never look at *people.*

How much life have I missed because I'm too busy trying not to die?

"I guess I've always been kind of out of it, haven't I?" I say. "I'm sorry."

"Well, I'm just glad you're done with Ash Morrison. Now things can finally get back to normal. Hey, did you ever ask your dad if you can come with me to Chicago for my birthday?"

"I'm not done with Ash," I say.

"Of course you are. Keith is building you a *house.*"

"That doesn't—Court, we're still working on that project. I can't be *done* with Ash just because Keith is building me a house."

"But that was the deal," she says. "No more Ash."

"Keith had no right to give me that ultimatum," I say. "I love him, but that was wrong. And besides, there's only a couple weeks left in the project. Once it's over, it's over. Regardless of the outcome, Ash will be out of my life." It does not hurt my heart to say that. It does *not.*

"Ash the astronaut," Joey murmurs from his place on the floor, flying one of his cars in the air like a rocket. "Three, two, one, liftoff!"

"What *is* this project?" Courtney snaps into the phone. "You spend hours on it, but no one else at school is doing one and you can't tell anyone what it is."

"It's, um..."

"Right. You don't have to tell me. I know what this *project* is," she says. "Ash convinced you that his father is innocent. But he's lying. He's just trying to get you to give up the scholarship."

"But what if his dad *is* innocent?"

"Have you found any evidence of that?" She sounds like she's trying very hard not to lose patience with me.

"Nothing solid," I admit. "But I'm trying to do the right thing."

"The right thing to do, Ever, is to forget about Vinnie Morrison, forget about Ash, get your scholarship, and be with Keith and live the life you've worked so hard for. *That's* the right thing."

"So we're just supposed to let his father be executed for a crime he didn't commit?"

"He *did* do it, Ever," she huffs. "They have *evidence.* He *confessed.* My God. You worked so hard your entire life to get that scholarship. How can you do this to Keith? How can you do this to your *mother*? You promised her on *her death bed* that you'd go to college. What would she think if she knew you were giving up your chance at that scholarship just to hang out with Ash Morrison?"

I blink away hot, sudden tears as grief grips my heart like a claw. My mother. I need my mother. She would know what to do.

I clutch the daisy charm on my necklace and I must make a noise because Joey looks up at me, alarmed. I swipe the tears from my eyes and force a smile. Cheeks stops running on her wheel. "Why do you care so much?" I ask Courtney.

"Because you're my best friend and I love you, and I'm trying to stop you from messing up your entire life," Court says. "Everything was perfect before you started hanging out with that guy. Promise me you'll stay away from him."

One hundred hatchet tattoos. One hundred murder suspects. I need my mother, but Vinnie needs me. Ash needs me. Lily needs me.

I know what my mother would want me to do.

"I'm not going to stay away from him," I tell Courtney.

She hangs up without saying goodbye.

CHAPTER THIRTY-SIX

LILY ~ EIGHTEEN YEARS AGO

The barn at Old Sutton Farm had been sitting there, crumbling and abandoned, for longer than I'd been alive. The grass surrounding it was higher than my waist. The paint had been rained off years ago, leaving the wood rotting and gray. As far as I knew, not even Vinnie Morrison and his buddies came here to do their drug deals, although it would have been the perfect spot. Ironically, the only people in Ryland who paid attention to Old Sutton Farm were my mother, who called it an eyesore, and my father, who wanted to buy the land one day to expand Agri-So.

The car that hit Neal Mallick was in that barn. I just knew it.

After my plane ride with Javier this afternoon, instead of going home, I came here, to Old Sutton Farm. I trampled through the weeds and grass toward the dilapidated barn. I was right—a car had been driven, or at least rolled, through this grass recently. The grass wasn't flattened, but there was a definite trail of broken blades.

I'd poked around this barn a few years ago when I was looking for a place to make a haunted house for Halloween, but I couldn't get inside because the doors were boarded up with six two-by-fours. Those same rotting two-by-fours were still nailed to the door frame, but hey, would you look at that: the nail heads were shiny. Not rusty.

Someone had been here recently. Someone had pried the two-by-fours off the barn doors, rolled the car in, then nailed the two-by-fours back on. With new nails.

Ha. I had it.

I started to pull on the boards.

No. Stop. *Think.* If Neal's killer came back, he'd see the boards had been pried off and know that someone had been here after he was. I had to find a different way in.

The sun was setting. My parents would be expecting me home soon.

Think.

Could I get in through a window? No, the windows were boarded up with sheets of plywood. No luck there.

A chirping bird flew by and landed on the roof.

The roof.

Ten minutes later, I crouched on a branch of the tall tree that was next to the barn. I'd died once while climbing the tallest tree in the Amazon rainforest. Climbing this dinky tree in Ryland was not a big deal at all. All I needed to do now was jump onto the roof. A micro-thought flitted through my brain that if I missed, I would fall to my death, just like in the Amazon. But this was one time when I couldn't afford to think. I had to act.

So I did.

I pushed with my legs, propelling myself from the branch onto the angled roof. I

slipped
slid
scrambled
sliced

my palms open on the ledge as I hauled myself up and over the edge. I lay flat on the roof, hiding myself, sucking in deep breaths.

When I could breathe again, I wiped my bloody palms on my jeans—shoot, these were Diana's, she'd kill me when she saw how I'd messed them up—carefully rolled onto my stomach and looked around. More wood, tar, and rotting shingles. In the corner, the roof looked soft, like it was caving in.

All I needed was a little hole in the roof. Something I could peek through. The sun was setting fast, making my shadow long, and I needed to see in there before it got too dark.

I should have brought a flashlight. But I hadn't thought to bring one. God, why did I always rush into things? Impulsive, irresponsible Lily. If I'd planned for this, I would have—

The roof gave way, and I fell.

It wasn't time to end my existence as Lily Summerhays yet because I landed in a pile of moldy grass and hay. I checked to make sure my diamond pendant survived the fall. It had. I was filthy, stinky, and a little sore, but alive. And best of all, I was inside the barn.

And sitting right in front of me, out in the open, well, as open as you could get inside a dim abandoned barn, was a car.

There was just enough light coming through the hole in the roof that I could see that the car was cobalt blue, with scraped paint and a broken headlight.

And a dent in the front bumper.

Oh, poor Neal. This was the car that hit him. I was right.

I rushed over to it. Whose car was it? Blue, shiny, sleek, with no back seat. A Dodge Viper. I didn't recognize it at all. As far as I knew, no one in Ryland drove a sports car like this. No license plates on it either.

I walked around the Viper, slowly, carefully, deliberately, looking at every detail. The trunk was down, but it wasn't latched shut. I lifted it open and looked inside. The tiny trunk was empty, just a box of emergency items and one of those metal things you use to unscrew the lug nuts on a tire when you had a flat.

And there was something else. A single red pill. Only I knew it wasn't a pill. It was a Hot Tamale.

Neal had been in this trunk.

Sudden hot tears burned my eyes as anger boiled up inside me. The driver had an emergency first aid kit in his trunk! He didn't even *try* to help Neal. Poor Neal. Had he still been alive when the driver shoved him in the trunk, probably folding his broken body so it would fit?

Damn him. Damn him! I was going to find out who did this if it was the last thing I did.

I shook my head as I swiped the tears away. I had the murder weapon, but I didn't know who owned it, and I couldn't ask anyone without drawing suspicion.

"Think, Lily." I actually said the words out loud to myself. "Think."

There might be something inside the car that would identify the owner. He or she had taken off the license plates, but maybe there was a forgotten insurance card inside. Or a credit card receipt. Or a bill. Something with the owner's name on it, or the spouse's.

Opening the car door made the overhead light turn on, and by now the barn was so dark that even that small bit of light illuminated the car and some of the barn around it. I slid into the driver's seat. This car was new—perfectly clean inside, and the strong leathery, clean new-car-scent was unmistakable.

I looked in the glove compartment. Nothing, except for the owner's manual. No clutter or garbage.

Except what was that under the driver's seat, peeking out just the tiniest bit?

Something dark red—no, more of a maroon.

I pulled it out.

A baseball hat. A Ryland Warriors baseball hat.

What was a Warrior's hat doing in the car that killed Neal?

There was only one explanation: someone from the baseball team had been in that car.

~

A sudden cracking sound coming from the door made me gasp. Someone was here! Prying off the two-by-fours from the barn door.

My heart in my throat, I dashed to the back of the barn to hide, then dashed back to the car. I shut the trunk, then the car door, as quietly as I could. I couldn't close them all the way without making noise, so I shut them just enough so the doors *looked* shut. But I couldn't click them into place. Please let it be good enough.

The barn door creaked open. I ran to the back of the barn and dove into the pile of dead grass and hay that I'd fallen onto earlier. The hay stunk, stinging my eyes and burning my nostrils. I blinked my eyes to cool them and breathed through my mouth. Slow breaths. Don't sneeze.

The old me would have stayed to confront him and probably gotten myself into a load of trouble. The new me, the thoughtful, cautious me, knew enough to stay put. Gather my evidence. Then go to the authorities.

Instead of confronting him, I peeked through the pile of hay to see who was entering the barn. The opened door let in some light from the outside, but it was almost dark now, and all I could see was a tall, featureless shadow. But he had a familiar gait as he strode into the barn with quick, purposeful steps. A strut.

I recognized that gait. My mind scrambled to match the shadow and the gait to the boys on the baseball team. Will? No, of course not. Seth? No. Brandon? No. Javier? No, no, no. None of them had that strut, and this guy was wider through the chest than any of the boys on the team.

A fumbling, then a beam of bright light. Unlike me, Mr. Killer had thought to bring a flashlight.

The beam of light aimed directly at the blue Viper, and I could no longer see the shadow holding the flashlight.

He opened the door, then stood up straight with a little intake of breath. The beam of light darted around the barn.

Did he notice the door was already open a little?

I held my breath. Didn't dare move farther behind the pile of hay.

The light swept past me, blinding me for a second. Then the light aimed at the ground around the car. Footprints! Had I left footprints in the dirt around the car? I was wearing my Doc Martens. I didn't have tiny feet, but they were too small to be a man's print. The killer would know, at least, that a woman had been here.

I let out my breath in a silent exhale as the flashlight aimed again inside the Viper, and the killer ducked to look inside.

I stifled a gasp. The overhead light gave me enough illumination to see who he was.

Oh

my

God.

Why was I so surprised? He'd told me, more than once, to stop investigating Neal's death. Now I knew why.

Officer Rick Paladino had played for the Ryland High baseball team when he was in high school. His team had won the state championship not just one year, but two. He had the hatchet tattoo to prove it.

He searched between the seats, under the seats, in the trunk. The only noise I heard was my heart pounding. I stayed still as a statue. Finally, he stood up. He pulled a cell phone from his pocket and dialed. After a few seconds, he said, "It's fine. Your hat's not here."

My heart jumped into my throat. I had the hat clutched in my hands.

"*Yes*, I looked everywhere," he continued. "Under and between the seats. Front and back. In the trunk. It's nowhere outside either."

After a moment, he said, "Hey, I *saved* your ass when I should've arrested you for vehicular manslaughter. You'd be sitting in jail right now instead of heading to the state championships if it weren't for me. So don't give me that shit."

I clamped my hands over my mouth. Don't move. Don't move.

"Just relax. It's not in the car. That's the important thing. Now don't contact me again."

Paladino pressed a button on his phone, then thrust it back into his jacket. In the silence, he swept the beam of his flashlight around the car again. He bent at the waist and plucked something from the front seat. When he stood, he shone the light on something he held pressed in his fingertips. Another Hot Tamale, probably.

Oh crap, what if he found a strand of my hair?

I squelched a yelp, then flinched as he slammed the car doors. "Damn it!" he shouted, and the word echoed angrily throughout the barn. He stormed out, then pounded the boards back onto the door, hammering so hard the entire barn shook.

I couldn't hear him retreat, so I stayed hidden in the haystack, breathing through my mouth. Then I slowly crawled out from my hiding place and tiptoed around the barn until I found some boards in the back wall that were rotted and loose enough that I could pull them off. I wiggled through the hole I'd created, a jagged edge scraping my side.

Then I dashed home and hid the Warriors baseball hat inside my globe.

CHAPTER THIRTY-SEVEN

EVER ~ PRESENT DAY

Pink tulips, unwatered for weeks now, sprawl limp, brittle, and dry in large terracotta pots on either side of Miss Buckley's red front door. "I can't believe we're doing this," I say to Ash, my heart thumping wildly. The sun is low on the horizon and the streetlights haven't turned on yet. It's the perfect time to commit a crime.

Courtney hasn't sent me the contact information of the former players. She hasn't even talked to me since she hung up on me last night. If she knew what I'm about to do with Ash right now, she'd never talk to me again.

"It's not like we're breaking in or anything." Ash pulls a leather string from the pocket of his jacket. Dangling from the string is a silver key. "Miss Buckley always gave me odd jobs to do for her. Fixing her garbage disposal, changing her air filters, things like that. She wanted me to have the extra money."

Suddenly, he pulls me off the porch and behind the bushes. I peek through the foliage. Chief Paladino rolls by in his cruiser, one elbow out his window, his head turning slowly side to side. "We're not breaking in," Ash reminds me in a whisper, "but if that asshole sees us here, he'll find a reason to arrest me anyway."

My heart stops beating completely as Paladino pauses for a moment too long in front of Miss Buckley's house, and resumes beating only when he continues down the street. I raise a shaky hand to my daisy charm in relief.

Ash slides the key into the lock and pushes the door open. I rush inside, breathing only after he closes the door behind us.

Shadowed. Still. Quiet. A wistful longing fills the air, as if the house itself knows its owner is dead.

As I wait for my eyes to adjust to the dimness, I jump at a tiny click: her DVR has kicked on, recording a show she will never watch.

"What are we looking for?" Ash asks in a whisper.

"I don't know," I say truthfully. "Something that'll prove who killed Lily Summerhays. Did Miss Buckley keep a journal or anything?"

Ash shrugs. "She never really talked about herself."

I point to a laptop on the coffee table. "Try her computer."

As Ash busies himself on the laptop, I investigate the room. Outdated wallpaper that was faded in some places. A chipped wooden coffee table. A couch and love seat that didn't quite match. Miss Buckley's love of fashion did not carry over into home decor. Either that, or she spent her salary as Principal Duston's administrative assistant on clothes rather than nice things for her house.

I pick up knickknacks and put them down, running my fingers over the things on her shelves. Mostly vases and books, but no yearbooks. No photographs either, which means no photos of Lily.

I follow the hallway down to her bedroom. More books, more knickknacks. My eyes land on something on her nightstand that makes my head pound, and Lily's death appears in a rush.

What is that doing here? I sink to the floor, holding my head to keep it from splitting open. *"You left me no choice."*

One...

Two...

Three.

"Ash?" I call when I recover, hoping my voice didn't sound too weak or shaky. "The murder weapon—do you know what it was?"

"Something solid and heavy. Like a rock or brick."

"Right. But did they identify it in the police report? Do they have it in evidence?"

"Nope. They never found it."

That's right. They couldn't have found the murder weapon.

Because *I* just found it.

A huge sparkly, pink, diamond-shaped paperweight.

Carefully, slowly, not knowing what to expect, I touch my finger to the paperweight, and when nothing happens, I pick it up. I now hold in my hands the thing that killed Lily—killed *me*. It's heavy. It makes my head hurt. It makes my heart hurt.

On the top is something new, something I can't see in my death-memory because it's covered by the killer's hand. An engraved inscription: *Gems are precious, friends are priceless.*

This is the murder weapon. Why does Miss Buckley have it on her nightstand? Did she *know* it's the murder weapon? If she did, it must have been agonizing, seeing it first thing every morning and last thing every night.

Will holding it make me remember more of my murder?

I close my eyes, hold my breath, and tighten my grip on the paperweight. Open myself up to the death-memory.

No. Only pain, and the hatchet tattoo, and the flash of the paperweight as it comes crashing down on me. Just as being in Lily's living room and standing in the very spot she was murdered didn't help me remember more of her death, neither does holding the murder weapon.

I stuff the paperweight into my bag to try again later at home. It probably weighs a couple of pounds, but it feels like twenty. I return to the tiny living room, where Ash is still plucking away at the laptop. "She's got a huge file in here about Lily's murder," he says. "The investigation, my dad's arrest and trial, things like that. I'm going through her browser history now. The last time she was on the computer, she was looking up defense lawyers."

"For your dad?"

"Maybe. But he fired his lawyers long ago and refused to get a new one." Then he exhales. "Here we go. A chat. From the night before she died."

I sit next to him to read the conversation.

dbuckley: I can't take it anymore. Vinnie Morrison is about to be executed. I can't let that happen. I'm going to a defense lawyer to tell him who really killed Lily. You should get one too.

warrior74: Diana. Don't be ridiculous. Meet me tomorrow. We need to talk about this.

dbuckley: There's nothing to discuss.

warrior74: You didn't kill Lily, but you're just as guilty as I am. You'll go to prison too.

dbuckley: I don't care. I can't live like this anymore.

warrior74: We can work something out.

warrior74: Please just meet me tomorrow.

warrior74: Diana, please. We need to talk.

"Ash, this is proof that your father didn't kill Lily!" I want to wrap my arms around the computer, bring it to my chest, and hug it tight.

"Technically it's hearsay, but yeah, this could be huge." He rakes his hands through his hair, letting out a shaky breath. "Okay. Now we just have to see who warrior74 is." He hovers the cursor over the name.

One click, and we'll have warrior74's profile page, and the killer's identity. Who is it, I wonder. Principal Duston, or one of the other hundred men with the hatchet tattoo?

Ash exhales. I hold my breath. He clicks.

Error code 0034P2. Account warrior74 has been deleted.

Ash sits back, crestfallen.

"I'm sorry," I say, putting my hand on his arm. He's warm.

"It was a long shot anyway."

We're only inches apart. It's getting dark in here, and we're alone. He smells like leather and spice and strength. My hand is still on his arm. He could lean in a tiny bit, and we'd be close enough to kiss.

He leans in.

I lean in even closer.

But then he licks his lips and draws away. "It's, um, it's getting late. We should get out of here."

"Yeah." I sigh. He did the right thing, pulling away like that. I can't kiss him. I'm with Keith. I love *Keith.* Keith is building me a house and giving me the peaceful, safe life I've always wanted.

"I'll bring the laptop with me so I can look through it some more," Ash says, tucking it into his jacket. The lights are off already, so all we have to do is shut the front door behind us and step out into the night. But before we can, Ash grabs me and pulls me behind the bushes again, pulling me down to a crouch. The streetlights show a red sedan in the driveway now, and someone is getting out of it.

Miss Buckley's door is still open an inch. I stare at Ash in horror, covering my own mouth to keep from crying out. The tall, thin man walks up to the front door, reaches his hand to the doorknob, then freezes. He glances around—I swear he looks right at the bush we're hiding behind, thank God the porch lights are off—then over his shoulder at the street, then finally steps inside.

Ash and I slink away as quickly and quietly as we can, keeping to the shadows, the laptop under Ash's arm, the paperweight bouncing heavily in my purse.

I recognize that man. I've only met him a couple of times, but I recognize the dimple on his chin. Seth Siegel, my dad's boss.

What is he doing at Miss Buckley's? Is *he* warrior74?

CHAPTER THIRTY-EIGHT

LILY ~ EIGHTEEN YEARS AGO

I sat with Will under his giant oak tree, which had just begun to sprout its spring leaves. Old Sutton Farm and its dilapidated barn, hiding the car that killed Neal, was out of sight. In front of us was the creek. Sitting on the ground, our backs against the thick trunk, surrounded by high grass, we were hidden. A long freight train rumbled slowly down the tracks, over Railroad Bridge, and into the trees. Soon, except for the occasional bird chirping and the rush of the warm wind through the grass, the world around us was silent.

Silent, but changed. One of my friends was a killer. Another friend had betrayed his duty as a police officer to help him cover it up.

With legs out straight, one cowboy-booted heel crossed over the other, his face tilted to the sun, Will lounged close to me. So close that the edge of his little finger was almost touching the edge of *my* little finger. Did he realize how close our hands were? Did he feel the heat that radiated between our fingers too?

I did not move my hand. I didn't want to ruin the peaceful ease between us. But I needed to tell him what happened in the barn last night.

"I'm pretty close to figuring out who killed Neal," I said.

He stiffened the tiniest bit. "Who?"

I took a breath. "Someone on the baseball team."

He stiffened even more, his body going tight with alarm. "*My* baseball team?"

I told him about the car in the barn, the hat, and Rick Paladino's cell phone call.

"But our friends would never do something like that," Will said, almost angrily. "And Rick is a cop. A police officer."

"I know," I said. "I can't believe it either."

"You must have misunderstood him."

"I understood him perfectly," I said. "I just don't know whom he was talking to. Which one of the players has a Viper? Or, more likely, their parents have one. Maybe they took their dad's Viper out that night."

"You know the guys as well as I do, Red. None of them has a Viper."

That was true. Seth's family was the only one in this town that could even afford a Viper. Well, mine too, probably. "So, no one on the team has a Viper," I said. "Maybe it was stolen?"

Will shook his head. "I can't think of anyone on the team who would steal a car."

"If someone is ruthless enough to kill Neal and dump his body in the creek, they're ruthless enough to steal a car. I don't want to believe it either, but someone on the baseball team did it."

He huffed angrily. "Where around here would someone even steal a Viper from, anyway?"

"You're right," I said gently. I didn't want to fight with him. He was hurting, he was feeling betrayed, and I didn't want to make things worse. "Forget about the Viper. It's a dead end. We need to find out which player is missing their hat. Did anyone come to practice without theirs?"

"Not that I know of."

Will wasn't going to help. He didn't want to help because he didn't want to believe one of his teammates—one of his friends—was a killer.

But then Will closed his eyes and sighed, like he'd been fighting an internal battle and had lost. "But it's our only lead," he said, defeated. "I'll keep my eyes peeled. Ask around. See what I can find."

He was going to help after all. My heart swelled so big, it was threatening to burst. "Thank you, Will. I know it's hard. Thank you."

"Just, from now on, be careful, okay? If what you say is true, we can't trust Rick Paladino anymore. You need to stay away from him."

"It *is* true," I said. "But Rick Paladino wouldn't hurt me." At Will's demanding look, I added, "But fine, I'll stay away from him."

We sat together for a few minutes more. The side of my pinky finger grew warm, and when I looked down, I saw that Will's pinky was now touching mine.

When you think about it, a pinky is so small, comparatively, to the rest of a body. Just a tiny part of it. A person doesn't even need it most of the time. A person could certainly get along without it. But Will's pinky touching mine—well, that was the biggest thing in the world.

I realized that I had moved, just the slightest bit, and our arms, all the way to our shoulders, were touching each other's.

"Near Constantinople in the 1500s," I said, "I was stoned to death for touching a boy I wasn't married to, just like this. My name was Fatima and I was fifteen."

Crap.

What

did

I

just

do?

I hadn't meant to tell Will about my past lives. The words had just tumbled out of my mouth. It was too late to take them back now. The words were out there.

I held my breath and watched Will. Emotions crossed his face too quickly to interpret. Did he think I was lying? Making up stories? If he didn't believe me about my death-memories, he wouldn't believe me about Neal Mallick or the hat or Rick Paladino, either.

He said nothing for a long time. Then: "Stoned to death. In the year 1500."

Encouraged, I continued. "*Sometime* in the 1500s. I don't know the exact year, probably because Fatima didn't know. But I do know the boy's name was Yusuf or Yunus."

"What are you talking about, Red?" He sounded suspicious, almost angry. But there was no turning back now.

"My father had arranged for me to marry a different boy," I said, "but I ran away because I was in love with Yusuf. They found me and stoned me to death."

My breath turned shallow and my lungs grew heavy as they bore the weight of the heavy stones. I sucked in a raspy breath and it sounded wheezy, like I was breathing through a straw.

"Jesus, you okay?" Will asked.

I nodded and breathed out slowly, willing the deathpain away. "I'm fine," I said. "The memories, sometimes they feel like they're happening now." One ...two ...three. I took a clear, full deep breath and let it out again. "But I'm fine now. I know how to breathe through them."

"You remember living in the 1500s."

"No. I remember *dying* in 1500s. And in the 1400s, and the 1600s, and every time before and since then. I remember the last few seconds of all of my past lives. Who I was. Where I was. How I died. When a memory hits, I feel like I'm dying again."

"You used to tell people that when we were kids," he said. "I thought you were making it up to cause drama and get attention."

"I wasn't making it up. I stopped because everyone made fun of me. Neal Mallick was the only one who didn't."

Will watched me closely, but he didn't move his pinky. "That's why you want to help him now."

If I had told Will a year ago, a week ago even, that I was still having death-memories, he would have taunted me with a cruel sneer. But not anymore. Now he just looked at me, almost the same way Neal had looked at me: with curiosity and fascination. So I told him everything I knew. How I was always reborn to the nearest empty body. How I always died doing adventurous or heroic things.

He asked questions: Does it happen to everyone or just to you? How does it work with twins and triplets—same soul divided or multiple souls? What about animals? Plants? Does this mean there is no heaven and hell? What about population growth—how do new souls get created? Or what if a shipwrecked couple is living on a deserted island and they have a baby, how does that baby get a soul if there's no one else around?

"That last one is original." I laughed. "Neal asked me a lot of the same questions. We did some research into religions and philosophy, but we didn't find anything conclusive. Lots of conflicting information. Neal said that even if we found the one correct answer and were able to prove it, people of different faiths wouldn't accept it. They wouldn't want to change their beliefs."

"You're right about that," he said, then asked, "but without proof, how do I know you're not making all this up just to cause drama?" There was no mistaking the suspicion in his tone. "The past lives thing *and* the Neal thing?"

Slightly hurt, I shook my head. "I'm not making up anything. It's all true. Every word."

He stared at me again, and he must have decided to take a leap of faith because he whispered, "I believe you."

And then he kissed me. A quick kiss, just one, before pulling away. Then, cheeks flushed, pupils large, breath heavy, he kissed me again, this time for longer. Much, much longer.

~

That night I couldn't sleep. Not because I was impatient to get my acceptance or rejection letter from CFGU, or because I was consoling Diana over another breakup with Brandon, or because my dad was sleeping on the couch again, or because I was trying to figure out who was driving the car that had killed Neal and what the heck I was going to do about Rick Paladino covering it up.

No, I couldn't sleep because Will Duston had kissed me, and I'd kissed him back. A lot. A *lot* a lot. And then we more than kissed.

Hours later, as I lay in bed, I could still feel his lips on mine,

on my neck,

on my stomach...

His fingers roaming,

caressing.

His body warm,

and lean,

and strong.

I was alone in my bedroom, but I hid my face in my pillow. I was grinning so hard that my cheeks ached.

Forget leaping from bridges or jumping from trees. Forget flying in Javier's plane. Kissing Will was the biggest adrenaline rush I'd ever experienced. Was it because I'd kissed a boy I knew my parents would disapprove of? No, it was because I'd kissed a boy I really,

really

really

really

liked. Will Duston, Will Duston, Will Duston!

I woke in the morning without realizing I'd fallen asleep, and after a quick shower, breakfast, and a wave good-bye to Mom, I ran out the door. It was still spring break, and I had to spend the morning working for Dad. But after that, Will and I had the rest of the day to spend together. We'd figure out which member of the baseball team had killed Neal, and then we'd reward each other with kisses.

I didn't want to risk running into Rick Paladino on my way to Agri-So, so I purposely avoided the police station and The Batter's

Box by taking the long way around to the back alley behind the theater. Vinnie Morrison was there, leaning against the brick wall by the dumpster in his oversized camouflage jacket. His dark hair was long enough to cover his eyes, but I could see that he looked tired. His new baby was probably keeping him up all night.

"Lookin' good, princess," he said, exhaling cigarette smoke from the corner of his mouth.

Gross. I walked past without acknowledging him. He had nothing to do with Neal's death, I knew that now, so I had no reason to talk to him. I could feel him leering at me from behind, and I tucked my diamond pendant under my top, just to keep it safe.

I slipped under the chain-link fence behind Smiley's and followed the train tracks through the woods. Birds chirped and the sun shone through the lattice of leaves. The last thing I wanted was to spend the morning stuffing envelopes inside a factory. I should take another look at that Viper, maybe find another clue. Just a quick look, then I'd go to work. Old Sutton Farm was practically on my way anyway.

I detoured from the tracks through Old Sutton Farm's weedy fields and approached the abandoned barn. No climbing trees and jumping onto roofs this time—I was much more responsible now. I sensibly crawled through the hole I'd made at the back of the barn, taking care not to scrape my side against that jagged piece of wood again.

I stood and wiped the dirt from my knees and palms. It was full daylight, and there were enough holes in the structure that the barn was only semi-dark. Finding additional clues, if there were any, should be easy. That was why, when I went to look, I was so surprised that I stopped. Blinked. Because there was something wrong. Something was missing.

The car was missing.

There was

nothing

there. Except for the piles of old hay and crumbling horse stalls, the barn was completely empty. There weren't even tire tracks in the dirt on the floor. My footprints, and Paladino's, were gone too.

There had been a Viper here two days ago. A brand new, shiny blue Viper. I saw it. I *touched* it. I rubbed my side, where I'd scraped myself leaving the barn. It hurt a little, confirming that I hadn't imagined it.

I exited the barn through the hole in the back and went around to the front. The doors were still boarded up. Someone—Rick Paladino, or the killer, or both—had removed the car yesterday, then swept the dirt clean of tracks and prints, and boarded up the doors again. It was the only explanation.

There was a noise behind me, a twig snapping, and I jumped and whirled around. I couldn't see anyone, but there was a toothpick in the trampled dirt at my feet. "Will?"

He stepped out from the other side of the barn, the sun behind him, shadowing his face. "Red? What are you doing here?"

"What are *you* doing here?"

He came over to me, rubbing the back of his neck. "I wanted to check out that Viper," he said. "I looked through one of the holes in the wall, but it's not in there." He looked at me suspiciously.

A panicked thought flew through my brain—Will didn't believe me anymore. He thought I'd lied, that I had made everything up to cause trouble and get attention.

That thought was quickly followed by another—my original suspicions were correct, Will *did* kill Neal and throw his body in the creek.

Then a third—Will had removed the car from the barn after I told him about it yesterday, literally covering his tracks.

"Paladino must have taken it out of here," he said, then drew me into his arms. "You okay?" He kissed my forehead so tenderly, and when he moved down to my lips, all those panicked thoughts disappeared.

CHAPTER THIRTY-NINE

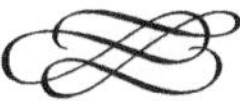

EVER ~ PRESENT DAY

I lean against Ash's tree the next day, listening to the babble of the creek below. The spring leaves are beginning to bud. It's cooler today, with gray clouds in the sky. Joey frolics in the field nearby, chasing a frog or maybe a grasshopper.

Ash is at his house, digging through Miss Buckley's computer. I'm doing my own detective work by trying to figure out who warrior74 is. My best guess is he was a baseball player, a former state champion, and 74 was his uniform number. I texted Courtney last night, reminding her to send me the players' contact information so I can send them an e-vite to the Training Camp. That contact info could help me identify warrior74, but my texts to Courtney have so far gone unread. Hopefully she'll read my texts when she gets back from her softball tournament later today. But a small part of me is afraid those texts will go unread until Ash is no longer part of my life.

Until I get that info, I'm on my own. I researched on my laptop for hours last night, and I'm scrolling on my phone now. But I can't find a list of the players from back then. The high school's website doesn't list them, and the official Ryland website is no help. The Wikipedia page about the town has a paragraph about Agri-So with a link to the Agri-So website, a sentence about Lily Summerhays with a link to a separate Wikipedia page about her murder, and two paragraphs about the Warriors in their glory days of winning eight state championships. One of those paragraphs is dedicated to Brandon Lennox, with a link to his own Wikipedia page. But his high school uniform number was number 09. His jersey is hanging over the trophy case in the front hallway. I see it every time I enter the building.

There are a few photos of the players from back then, mostly the same images that are hanging on the walls at The Batter's Box. I'm able to make out a few uniform numbers, but none of them are 74. Javier Soto, Ash's boss at the airfield, is in one of the photos, but it's only of his face, not his number.

Maybe the 74 isn't a uniform number after all. It could be a birth year or a lucky number. That number could mean anything. It could mean nothing. Maybe there were seventy-three other accounts that started with "Warrior," and 74 was the next one available.

A shadow falls over me. I look up at the tall, broad shape, features darkened by shadow, the sun glowing like a halo around him.

"So my secret place is public property now?" There's amusement behind Ash's rumbled tone as he settles next to me.

"Joey needed to get out of the house and run around, but with all those murder suspects out there, I couldn't think of anywhere else to go."

At that moment, Joey rushes over and jumps on Ash with a whoop, climbing onto his back like a little monkey. "Caught a frog," he says proudly, reaching over Ash's shoulder and showing him the frog in his tiny hand, then scampering away again.

"I thought for sure you'd freak out over how dirty he is," Ash says. "Or give me some statistic about how many people are killed by frogs every year."

I didn't even notice that Joey was dirty. A first for me. "The poison dart frog is one of the deadliest animals in the world," I say. "But they're native to South America. Joey is fine."

"You took Joey and walked all the way across Railroad Bridge," he says. "You didn't slip off into the creek and you didn't get hit by a train. You're becoming quite the little badass."

"What can I say?" I chuckle. "You're a bad influence on me."

We sit comfortably in silence, his long legs splayed casually as he digs a stick into the dirt.

Ash is scary, and big, and rough and growly and kind of mean. He breaks all kinds of rules. He's intimidating and he hates everybody. He does things on purpose to scare me and he teases me endlessly. He's dangerous.

Then they spill from my mouth, words I've never spoken aloud before, not even to Court or Keith. "It was always my mom, my dad, and me. We had our little house and our little family. And then... surprise. When I was twelve, my mom got pregnant."

Ash doesn't move. Just continues digging in the dirt with the twig.

"She was only four months along when she found out she had ovarian cancer. She refused treatment. My dad begged her, *begged* her, but she wouldn't do it. She didn't want it to hurt the baby. The doctors said it was safe, that there was a ninety percent chance the baby would be fine. But my mom didn't want to take even the small risk. She was so positive it would be okay. She thought she could wait until after he was born to get treatment. But she was wrong. She waited too long."

I blink, and Ash becomes blurry, my tears making it look like rays of sun are reflecting off him.

"Joey is healthy," I say. "That's what she wanted. She never regretted it, not for one moment. But my dad... he works long hours. He says it's to pay the medical bills and the default on the loan for the bookstore. He didn't have to take a trucking job. He could have gotten a job at Agri-So or anywhere else in town. I tell myself that he took the trucking job because he misses my mom so much that it hurts to be home. Or that Joey looks so much like my mom that it hurts too much to look at him. Something romantic like that. But I know that's not true."

Keith, if he were here, would tell me that I'm wrong and that I need to stop being so upset and then change the subject. But Ash says nothing. He just sits, digging at the ground with his stick, listening, waiting for me to tell him more.

I exhale with a huge, squeaky breath. "My dad has never played with Joey. When Joey comes into a room, within five minutes my dad finds an excuse to leave. He can't even look at him. If it weren't for Joey, my mom would have started treatment right away and she would probably still be alive today."

I confess the last, horrible truth. "My dad blames Joey for my mom's death."

Ash purses his lips, and for the longest time, I think he's never going to speak. "He doesn't blame Joey," he finally says, his voice low. "He blames himself."

"What do you mean?"

"He begged your mom to get treatment and she refused. He couldn't save her. He failed. Your mother took a risk. She lost, but Joey won. Your father was willing to sacrifice Joey's health, so in addition to grief, he feels guilt. He thinks he's a bad husband and a bad father. He loves Joey, but he hates himself more."

It's the most Ash has ever spoken to me at once, and it takes a while for the lump in my throat to dissipate. I see my father differently now, though. Instead of resentment for him, I feel pity.

Forcefully, Ash digs the heel of his boot into the dirt. "What your mom did for Joey? My mother would *never* have done that for me. She told me once that she didn't know she was pregnant with me until she was six months along and it was too late to get an abortion. She wasn't even drunk when she told me that, so I know she meant it."

I run the back of my finger down his jaw, feeling the stubble. "It must have been awful growing up like that." Father in prison, mother resentful of her own son's existence, misunderstood, feared, and hated by his own hometown. "For what it's worth, I'm really, really happy you're here."

We stare at each other, his eyes warm and inky black, the anger in them fading into desire as his breath becomes heavier, matching mine. I swallow hard, lick my lips. He tucks a lock of hair behind my ear, and his fingers linger.

"Go away," Joey shouts from a few feet away. "This is *our* secret place!"

I glance up. Keith is on Railroad Bridge, frozen, eyes wide, mouth hanging open.

He clamps his mouth shut, pivots on his heel, and storms back down the tracks.

"Go," Ash says. "Go talk to him."

"Keith!" I chase after him, running across the bridge. "Keith, stop! Wait!" I catch up to him on the other side and grab his arm. "I didn't kiss him."

"You were about to," he says.

I try to disagree, but I can't.

"I knew it. I *knew* I'd find you with him." He's panting, his face red, his hands in fists at his sides. "The chief said Ash hangs out by Railroad Bridge, so when you weren't home, I decided to see if you were here with him. And yep, here you were, under the tree, about to kiss him."

"The chief told you that?" I ask. "Paladino? When did you talk to him?"

"I was good to you, Ever." His chin is trembling.

"Yes. You were. You *are* good to me."

"I gave you everything you've ever wanted."

"I—" I stop. I can't agree with that. Not anymore.

"We were supposed to have one of those magical stories like my parents." His gaze cuts across the creek to Ash, who's standing guard by the tree, watching intently. "I was going to build a house for you. We were going to run the diner together. But no, instead of letting me give you the perfect life, you'd rather be with a drug dealer whose father is a killer."

"I can explain if you'd just listen." I put my hand on his arm, but he jerks away, biting on his lip the way he did when his dog died and he was trying not to cry.

But *can* I explain? I've already tried several times to tell him that Ash is *not* a drug dealer, and that his father is *not* a killer. I can't tell him that someone murdered Miss Buckley. And I can't tell him about remembering my past deaths. He wouldn't understand.

But none of that matters anyway. I *was* about to kiss Ash. There's no coming back from that. It's over between Keith and me. I want it to be over. I'm relieved it's over.

"I thought you loved me, Ever." His voice cracks.

"I do love you," I say, and it's the truth. "You were there for me after my mom died. I will always love for you being there when I needed you."

"But you don't need me anymore."

"I'm so sorry." I put my hand on his chest to make him feel better, so we can part as friends, but he slaps it away.

"Hey!" Ash shouts a warning and starts over to us, but I wave him off.

"I had sex with that girl, you know," Keith says, practically spitting the words. "That chick from Eastfield at that tournament last year. You stayed home to study and she was there, watching me play every inning, and it happened. I felt really guilty about it, but now I'm glad. So yeah. Go ahead and fuck Ash Morrison, you slut. You fucking bitch."

As I blink the stinging tears from my eyes, he turns and marches down the railroad tracks, through the trees, and never looks back.

CHAPTER FORTY

LILY ~ EIGHTEEN YEARS AGO

"Door's open!" a tired female voice called from inside the Dustons' farmhouse a second after I rang the doorbell.

I opened the creaky screen door and stepped inside. I'd never been in Will's house before. The Summerhayses and the Dustons did not invite each other to birthday parties or dinner parties or any other kind of gathering. The weathered farmhouse was over a hundred years old, and it showed. The rooms were small and the ceilings were low. The flowered wallpaper was faded and curling at the edges in some places. But the house was clean and bright. In thin wooden frames hanging unevenly on the walls were photos of Will and his brothers, mixed in with photos of past generations of the extended Duston clan. The windows were open, and the curtains waved gently in the breeze. I was sure Mrs. Duston cleaned this place herself instead of having a cleaning crew come in twice a week to do it. Instead of smelling like lemon cleanser, the Duston house smelled like a mix of fresh air and grass and sunshine. It smelled like Will.

Mrs. Duston came into the foyer wearing pleated jeans and carrying a stack of loose papers. "Oh! Lily!"

"Hi, Mrs. Duston," I said sheepishly. I felt like I should apologize for being in her house. "I came to see Will. Is he here?"

"He's out back helping his dad fix the tractor," she said. "He'll be back in a minute." Her tone wasn't unfriendly. She sounded curious, and maybe tired. "Come on in. I'll get you some lemonade."

I followed her into the kitchen. "Have a seat," she said, nodding at the table. She dumped the stack of papers on the counter, turning over the top page before going to the fridge. She poured two glasses of lemonade into jelly jars, then sat across from me.

She was the same age as my mother, yet she looked at least ten years older. She did nothing to hide the gray in her hair, and her skin was dry, as if the dirt from decades of working on the farm had been embedded in all the tiny cracks in her skin. She was not a woman to treat herself to expensive moisturizers. But there was a beauty behind those tired eyes. Warmth and love. Contentment.

The Dustons' kitchen was outdated, like the rest of the house I'd seen so far. Mrs. Duston, or maybe some past relative, had decorated the kitchen in a rooster theme. Roosters on the oven mitts, a rooster clock on the wall, rooster magnets on the fridge. The appliances were old, a faded avocado color. The cabinets didn't shine with the blinding gloss like mine did. Instead, they were covered with crayon drawings and art projects. A childish "WILL" was scrawled at the bottom of several of them, mixed in with his brothers'.

I had been in the same kindergarten class as Will. I must have made the same projects that he had. Where were *my* kindergarten drawings? I wasn't sure if my mother had even kept any of them, and Will's mom still kept his displayed on the cabinets after all these years.

For once in my life, I couldn't think of anything to say. I took a sip of the lemonade.

"So," Mrs. Duston said. She drummed her short nails on her jelly jar.

"So," I agreed.

She drummed. I sipped.

"You and Will doing a school project together or something?" she asked.

"Kind of," I said. Not a complete lie. I took yet another sip. "This lemonade is good. You made it from real lemons, didn't you? With real sugar. It's so much better than the powder mix with Splenda that my mom makes."

"It's real." She chuckled a little. "How is your mom?"

I blinked, surprised that Mrs. Duston would ask about her. "She's fine. She's good."

"We used to be friends, you know. Your dad and Mr. Duston were friends too."

"Best friends. I know."

The phone rang in the other room.

"I'd better get that." She dashed out, probably as relieved to end that awkward conversation as I was.

I sat alone, drinking my lemonade and waiting for Will. The wooden kitchen table was marred with decades of scratches and dents and water stains, and eight mismatched chairs were shoved around it. The table had probably been here since the house was built. How many generations of Dustons had sat at this table? My kitchen table was only five years old, small, round, and glass. The houses my parents grew up were in the older part of town. I'd been to each of them many times before my mom's parents moved to a condo in Eastfield and my dad bought his parents a place in a retirement village in Tennessee. Now those houses were occupied by other families with their own kitchen tables.

It was kind of nice, the Duston farmhouse being passed from generation to generation. I could understand why Will liked it here, why he wanted to stay on his farm his entire life.

But just the idea of staying in one place *my* entire life made me want to run. I couldn't sit at this table anymore. I stood and walked over to the cabinets to get a better look at some of the artwork. Report cards, flyers, yellowed recipes torn from magazines were taped to the cabinet doors. Will's latest report card was taped on the cabinet over the toaster. Straight A's. Nicely done, Duston.

On the counter in front of the toaster was the stack of papers that Mrs. Duston had placed there earlier. My hand, seemingly of its own accord, turned over the top paper. A utility bill, with "SECOND NOTICE" stamped on it in angry red letters. The paper underneath was from a collection agency. Another was from the bank. I didn't know exactly what *foreclose* meant, but I knew it had to do with property and money, and I knew it wasn't good.

Heavy footfalls at the back door alerted me to Will's imminent presence. I quickly stacked the papers again, turned the top one over, and rushed back to my seat at the table.

He stood tall and lean in the back doorway, so surprised to see me sitting in his kitchen that he stopped chewing his toothpick for a moment. I couldn't help myself; I grinned. "The enemy has infiltrated your headquarters."

He grinned back. "What are you doing here, Red?"

"Thought today would be a good day to look for a certain cobalt blue Viper with a broken headlight. Wanna help?"

"Let me change. Be right back." He strode through the kitchen, glanced past me into the hall, and when he saw the coast was clear, gave my forehead a quick kiss as he walked by. My whole body flushed with happiness.

Will and I looked around town for the Viper until well after dark. We didn't find the car, but we didn't see Rick Paladino either. Will didn't mention anything about the late notices and bank papers, so neither did I. Maybe he didn't know about them.

Around dinner time, we met the gang at The Batter's Box for pizza. Seth, Javier, Brandon, and Diana. Will and I watched each of the boys closely. I was one hundred percent certain that whoever killed Neal was not sitting at our table that night. They'd be acting differently. But everyone was their usual goofing-around selves. Brandon and Diana were their usual make-up-and-break-up selves.

Will and I purposely didn't sit next to each other, and to keep up appearances, I said *yes* when Seth offered to drive me home that night. Will got a ride with Javier. There would be no goodnight kisses from Will tonight, and I felt cheated.

Seth pulled into my driveway, but before I could get out of his Mitsubishi, he asked, "What's up with you and Duston?"

"What? Nothing. I don't know what you're talking about."

"You were both weird tonight. You kept looking at each other and grinning."

"Ugh, gross," I said. But apparently, the only ones acting differently tonight had been Will and me. Thinking back, I realized that we hadn't bickered at all. We hadn't slung a single insult at each other the whole time. "I hate that guy." It hurt to say that.

"It's like you were flirting," Seth said, rubbing the dimple on his chin with the tip of his index finger. "You're like that at school too. And at the games. Even at Lennox Auto Body the other day. You're always staring and smiling at him." His tone was bitter and accusatory.

"You watch me that closely?" I shot back. Seth Siegel had no right to be jealous. I'd always made it perfectly clear that I only wanted to be friends with him.

"So what if I do?"

"So, who I look and smile at is none of your business."

"I think I've been pretty patient with you."

"Patient with me? What do you mean?"

"When you needed a date to the homecoming dance, I took you. I took you to prom last year. We hang out all the time."

Was this guy serious? My cheeks burned with flames of anger. "First of all, I've never *needed* a date to the dance, or to anywhere.

You and I went as *friends*. Second of all, I hang out with all of you guys, as *friends*."

I opened the car door, but he grabbed my arm, stopping me from leaving. "That was more than friendship between you and Will tonight," he said. "Seriously, Lily. You play hard to get with me, but you drop your panties for Will, just like that?"

I wrestled away from him and climbed out. "Screw you, Seth." I slammed the car door shut and stomped away.

He called after me, shouting out the window, "That's what I've been waiting patiently for!"

I slammed my front door shut too, and stifled a scream.

"What's wrong?" my dad asked from the study, peeking over his newspaper.

Great. Just great. I made myself unclench my fists and smile at him. "Nothing."

"You look upset."

"I'm fine." I smoothed my hair and willed the angry red in my cheeks to fade.

He folded his paper and put it aside. "Anything I can do to help?"

"No."

"Lily, you are clearly upset about something. I want to help. Tell me."

Wow, he really did look concerned. He *cared,* for once. I had to tell him something, but I didn't need his help dealing with that jerk Seth Siegel. And I couldn't ask him to help Will and me investigate Neal's murder, not if I wanted him to keep thinking I was responsible and well-behaved so I could go to CFGU.

So what should I tell him?

I *did* have a third problem. "It's not me," I said. "I have a ... friend... who's in trouble."

"What kind of trouble?"

"Financial."

He pursed his lips. "It's not Seth, is it? I thought the Siegels were doing fine."

"No, Dad. It's not Seth." I took a deep breath. "It's Will. Duston."

Dad's face turned a bit red at the name Duston.

"His parents are about to lose their farm," I said. "That's what foreclosure means, right?"

"How did you find out this information?"

"I saw the foreclosure notice and late notices."

"And you read them, obviously."

I squirmed uncomfortably. "Yeah."

He sighed. "Where did you see them?"

"In their kitchen."

His lips thinned into a straight line. "Why were you in the Dustons' kitchen?"

"Will and I are working on a project together." Not a lie.

"Duston Farm hasn't been profitable in years, Lily. It's no surprise that they're facing foreclosure."

"But you and Mr. Duston used to be friends. Best friends. Can you let that happen to him?"

"Don and I haven't been friends in a long time."

"I know, but what if..." I took a deep breath. "What if you gave him the money they need to keep the farm?"

Dad's eyebrows raised. "*Give* him money? Why should I do that? I've already spent a lot of money on him fighting his lawsuits."

"Yeah, and you win every time. But aren't you tired of being sued all the time? It's bad for the reputation of your business. Make a deal with him. He takes a loan from you, and you promise not to take any more of his land. The Dustons would keep their farm, and they would stop the lawsuits against Agri-So."

He picked up a pen from the coffee table and started clicking it, exposing and retracting the nib over and over. "It wouldn't be as simple as that, but no more lawsuits would be nice."

"Everyone wins." Especially Will.

Click-click-click. "Let me think about it. I'll see what I can do." He clicked some more as he considered my idea, then he gave me a smile. "See, sweetheart, you have an acumen for business after all."

I nodded and went upstairs, satisfied. I had just saved Duston Farm, *and* I'd made my dad proud of me. I might be going to CFGU after all.

CHAPTER FORTY-ONE

EVER ~ PRESENT DAY

When Keith passes me in the school hallway on Monday, he doesn't even glance my way.

And why would he? I'm no longer his girlfriend.

Keith and I were supposed to get married and live the rest of our lives in Ryland, Indiana. I always pictured us in a little white house with white shutters and an American flag hanging from our porch. We were supposed to work at The Batter's Box together, he as the manager and I as the accountant, and then one day we would own it together. That was the plan. That was the *only* plan. I was so sure it would happen—and that I wanted it to happen—that I'd never considered anything else, not even when I first heard the rumor that he'd cheated on me, not even after he admitted he didn't want me to win the Lily Scholarship so I couldn't go to college.

Whether I win the scholarship or not, the life I'd always dreamed of having with Keith is not going to happen. For the first time in my life, I have no idea what's going to happen next.

So why do I feel like I can breathe for the first time in three years? Why do I feel so light? So free?

I scold myself for feeling so happy as I walk to AP World History. I shouldn't feel so happy. Vinnie Morrison is days away from execution for a crime he didn't commit. Ash and I still haven't identified warrior74. If we do find him and set Vinnie free, there's a very good chance I'll lose the Lily Scholarship to Ash.

What do I want from him after this? Friendship?

No, I want more than that.

I shake the thought from my head. It doesn't matter anyway because

1. If he wins the scholarship, he's leaving. First for college, then outer space. Mars. The farthest place he can possibly get. I'll never see him again.

2. If *I* win the scholarship, then Ash will stay in Ryland. I'll be here too, living at home with Joey while I commute to Griffin. But if we can't find the killer and his father is executed, he'll never forgive me for giving him hope and then taking it away.

3. So no matter what happens, we're doomed. Ash and I have no chance.

But I can't help looking for him as I enter AP World History. There he is, slouching with his knees sprawled wide at his desk in the back row. Our eyes meet and the coldness in his expression thaws, the corner of his mouth turning up just the tiniest bit, and my entire body floods with warmth and happiness.

I wonder if my mother would have liked him, or if she would have preferred me to stay with Keith.

Ash. She'd approve of him. I know it.

I walk right up to him now. No need to be sneaky anymore. If people want to think we're together, I'm not going to stop them. But reminding myself that we have no chance, I ignore the scent of his leather jacket and get down to business. "Find anything in Miss Buckley's computer last night?" I murmur.

"I looked all over it," he rumbles back. "Recovered her deleted files, looked in her deactivated email accounts. Nothing new. You have any luck with warrior74?"

"Nope."

"Hey." He slides his hand close to mine. "Want me to come over tonight? We can, I don't know. Order a pizza. Do some more investigating."

There's something in the way he asks, something in the way he shifts his body. A vulnerability, a hope. He loops his pinky over mine.

He wants more, too.

"Yes," I say softly. "I'd like that."

Mrs. Ricciardelli snaps her fingers to start the class. The gaze between Ash and me lasts a millisecond longer than it should before I tear away and go to my seat next to Courtney.

She shakes her head in disapproval. "Keith told me what happened. I don't understand why you'd dump him for that guy." She's not even trying to be quiet. Ash can hear everything.

"Keith broke up with *me*. And he cheated on me." Anger bubbles in my blood. "What *I* don't understand is why you're so upset about this. We're best friends, Court. You should be supporting me, not Keith."

The classroom door bursts open and Chief Paladino marches inside, followed by Principal Duston. The chief is swinging handcuffs from one finger, and his other hand is resting on the butt of the gun at his waist.

"Ash Morrison," he announces triumphantly, "I have a warrant for your arrest."

I freeze. "For what?" Ash and I say at the same time.

"Trespassing and burglary, for starters." His white teeth gleam through the vengeful smirk on his lips as he opens the handcuffs. "We have a witness who saw you breaking into Diana Buckley's house."

I feel the blood drain from my cheeks. Mr. Siegel, my dad's boss, must have seen us at Miss Buckley's house after all.

"I wasn't trespassing," Ash says coolly. "She gave me a key."

"Maybe so, but I'm sure she didn't give you a key so you could steal her laptop. I found it in your bedroom."

"You can't go in his house," I cry, surprising myself, and probably everyone else in the room. "Not without a warrant."

He tilts his head and squints at me. "My source says he saw *two* kids running from the house. The other kid wasn't you, was it?" He gives me a knowing look, daring me to confess.

"Fine," Ash says. "I did it. But I was alone. She wasn't there." He stands and holds out his wrists.

"Ash, no!" I dash over to him, trying to block the chief.

"Miss Abrams," Principal Duston says, his blue eyes like ice. "Sit down."

"Do what he says, Ever." Ash says. "Stay out of this."

"But—"

"I've been through this a million times. I'll call a public defender and be home by tonight."

"Yeah, maybe a few weeks ago," the chief says, "but you're eighteen now. A legal adult. No juvenile court for you."

"Doesn't matter," Ash says, tossing his hair. "Theft is just a misdemeanor."

"It would be," the chief says, "if I also didn't find two bags of cocaine in your locker just now. Coke on school property is a Class A felony. That's three years in prison. Too bad you can't spend that time with dear ol' dad."

"You planted that!" Ash roars.

"I'm also charging you with possession with intent to sell. That's an additional two years in prison." He shoves Ash against the wall, then pulls his hands behind his back and cuffs him as he gleefully recites his Miranda rights.

"No! Wait!" I run after them as Paladino yanks Ash to the doorway, but Principal Duston grabs my arm.

"Go back to your seat," he warns. "Now."

From the hallway, Ash yells, "Save my dad, Ever!"

There are a few seconds of stunned silence before my classmates burst into excited chatter. Principal Duston still has me by the arm. He pulls me closer and mutters, "Stay out of this. I mean it. You don't want to get mixed up in this."

His teeth are clenched, his gaze intense and urgent and angry. He's *threatening* me. I try to pull my arm away, but he grips it tighter, hurting me. His hatchet tattoo is hidden under his suit jacket, but I know it's there. I can feel it. I feel faint. Deathpain erupts over my eye. Fear makes my knees weak, but I won't let him know it. Not this time.

"Let go of me," I demand. "Do *not* touch me."

He releases me like my skin is burning him, and I shuffle back to my seat. The class is still chattering with excitement, and Mrs. Ricciardelli is yelling at everyone to calm down. I turn to Court, expecting help or sympathy or *something*, but the only thing she gives me is a desperate, teary glare. "You broke into Miss Buckley's house with him?" she whimpers. "*Now* do you see how bad he is for you?"

Principal Duston blocks the doorway as Mrs. Ricciardelli shakily begins her lesson. I can't pay attention. I can't look at Court. I don't dare lift my head.

Apparently satisfied that I'm staying put, Principal Duston leaves. I count to one hundred, then run from the classroom.

The mousy receptionist behind the desk at the police station jumps when I run inside, breathless and frantic. "Ash Morrison," I pant. "Where is he? I need to see him."

She licks her lips and squeaks. "Um..." Her fingers fumble over her keyboard. "Ash Morr... I don't see..."

"He's not here?" I ask, hoping that she doesn't hear the crack of panic in my voice. Ash isn't here yet. There's no way I could have gotten to the police station first, not when I was on foot. Where did Paladino take him? Visions race through my mind: the chief dragging a handcuffed Ash to a remote cornfield. The chief forcing him to his knees. The chief shooting him. I almost throw up.

"Don't worry. He's here," says a deep voice from behind me. I whirl around to face Chief Paladino. "Just not in the system yet. Who knows when I'll get around to processing him. I'm very busy, you know." He leans against the wall and holds up his hand, fingers bent, and examines his nails.

I march up to him. "Let me see him." Entering this small town jail is nothing after I visited Indiana State Prison's death row. Ash is probably the only one back there anyway.

"Can't do that, sorry." He reaches up to adjust his cap, and—

Deathpain pummels me, and I have to steady myself against the wall until I can breathe it away.

On his wrist. A tattoo. A crossed-hatchet tattoo.

"No visitors allowed," he's saying when I can focus again.

"That can't be true. He has a right to visitors."

"Are you his lawyer?" he says. "Only lawyers are allowed to see him at this stage of processing."

I don't know the law well enough to know if he's lying or not. "He shouldn't be back there anyway," I say. "You planted that cocaine in his locker. You set him up."

He raises one eyebrow.

"You set up his father too, didn't you? Maybe *you* killed Lily Summerhays. That's why you're doing this to Ash."

He throws back his head and laughs, once, sharply, like a dog bark: "Ha!" Then he leans close. His teeth are perfectly straight and sparkling white, but his breath smells like coffee. "You'd better watch what you say, little lady, or someone might find drugs in your locker too. And then I'd have to stop what I was doing and go all the way to the high school to arrest you. And I really don't want to do that. But I would, if I had to."

A flash of panic—how could I get Ash out of jail if I was in jail too? Who would take care of Joey?—but I can't let the chief see that.

Instead, I force myself to scoff. "No one would believe that *I'd* have drugs in my locker. They'd know someone planted it."

"You're right," he says. "Someone like Ash Morrison. Forcing you to hold drugs for him. That would probably be another charge against him."

That wasn't what I meant at all. He's turning my own threat against me.

"Tell you what, Nancy Drew," he says. "I'll make you a deal. Put your little detective kit away, and I won't bring charges against your drug dealer boyfriend. I'll let him walk out of here like it never happened."

Paladino wouldn't need to make a deal if Ash and I weren't getting close to figuring out who killed Lily Summerhays. *Save my dad, Ever,* was the last thing Ash said to me before Paladino hauled him away.

"I can't let Vinnie Morrison be executed for a murder he didn't commit," I tell the chief. I stand as tall as I can and declare, "No deal."

CHAPTER FORTY-TWO

LILY ~ EIGHTEEN YEARS AGO

It had been a few days, and Will and I still hadn't found the missing Viper or figured out which of his teammates was missing his hat. My father still hadn't offered to help the Dustons save their farm. Worst of all, I still hadn't heard from CFGU.

On the bright side, Dad was sleeping in the master bedroom with Mom again instead of on the couch in his study. On the even brighter side, Will and I were spending every free moment together, mostly kissing. He was the best kisser in the world. He was the best kisser in history, probably. I should know.

What I *didn't* know was what the future held for Will and me if I went to CGFU. Would we try to make it work long-distance—him here in Ryland and me in a different country every few months—or would we break up because it would be too hard to be separated?

I didn't need to worry about that unless I was accepted to CFGU. Until then, I was going to spend as much time as possible with him and have fun.

He had baseball practice after class today, so I headed for home after school. Maybe a letter from CFGU was waiting for me in my mailbox.

As I walked down Main Street, Rick Paladino was standing with another cop outside the police station. He was wearing his uniform, tanned and muscular and so handsome that I almost forgot that he was helping the bad guy cover up Neal's murder and I was supposed to stay away from him.

I slipped into the nearest store before he saw me. The Secret Garden bookstore. The advanced anthropology textbook I'd ordered should be in by now anyway. The store was bright and cheery, with walls painted floor to ceiling with flowers and leafy trees, and etched into the bark of the trees were images of characters from famous books. Pretty cool.

The woman who owned the place, Mrs. Abrams, stood by a bookcase, taking new novels from a box and arranging them on the shelves. Her gold hair was in two long, messy braids down her back.

Mr. Abrams came up and took the box from her. He gently caressed her belly, which was now huge. I don't remember my dad ever, even once, looking at my mom with such love and devotion.

"You're working too hard, Daisy," Mr. Abrams said. "These books are heavy."

She grinned at him. "I think I can handle a couple of books at a time." Even so, she huffed a little as she squatted to place a book on the bottom shelf.

"Let me help you," I said, rushing over.

"Oh, Lily, I didn't see you. Thank you."

"How long do you have left?" I asked when Mr. Abrams returned to the back.

"About a week," she said. "Ben put a crib in the back room so she can come to work with us."

"She? It's a girl?"

"We haven't found out officially. Ben wants to be surprised. But I feel that she's a girl." She nodded toward the counter. "Your book came in."

"Yay! Thanks!" I went to the counter, and there it was: *Anthropology: A Study of Culture* by Dr. Thomas Moore, a professor at CFGU. Even for a college textbook, it was thicker and heavier than I'd expected.

Mrs. Abrams wiped her hands on her maternity dress. "I really admire you, Lily."

I blinked, shocked at her words. No one had ever admired me before. "Why?"

"Because the high school doesn't offer anthropology, but you didn't let that stop you from learning about it. You ordered your own college textbooks. You set your goals high and you settle for nothing less. You're determined and fearless. I hope my baby is like you."

Determined and fearless. Not impulsive and irresponsible. I wished Daisy Abrams was my mother. "What are you going to name the baby?"

She patted her belly and sighed. "We can't decide."

"Whatever you do, don't name her after a flower."

"Why not? Flowers are pretty."

"I'm Lily, you're Daisy. Isn't that enough flowers in this town? And pretty is nice, but there are more important things than being pretty."

"True." She laughed. "Well, what would you suggest? I want a name that's meaningful. Something that shows I'll love her forever."

"Hmm. Are there any names that mean forever?"

"Oo, I like that idea. I'll go look it up in one of the baby name books. Hang on."

"Wait," I said. "Forever. Ever. You should name her Ever."

"Ever... Ever..." she said, trying it out. She looked down at her belly. "Ever Abrams. Do you like that name, little baby?"

"It's perfect," I said. It was perfect on so many levels.

"I think you're right," she said, grinning. "Ever. I love it. I'm sure Ben will too."

I peeked outside to the street as she rang up my textbook. Rick Paladino was gone. Time to get out of here.

"$74.87," Mrs. Abrams said. "Sorry. College textbooks are expensive."

"That's okay." I pulled a hundred-dollar bill from my handbag and placed it on the counter. When she started to give me change, I stopped her. "Keep it. For Ever's college fund."

I raced away before Rick Paladino showed up again.

First thing when I got home, panting a little because I'd rushed, I checked the mailbox. Still nothing from CFGU, darn it.

I ran upstairs to drop off my backpack and my new anthropology textbook. I'd been keeping my bedroom neat to show my parents how responsible I was, but I must have forgotten to straighten it this morning. Especially my closet. My purses and tote bags, which I kept stuffed on a low shelf next to my pile of shoes, had all

tumbled

to the floor. Some of the contents had spilled out,

cluttering

the area with coins, socks, receipts, and old notes.

I must have knocked the bags over this morning and hadn't noticed. Thank goodness my mother didn't see this. I scooped them up and shoved them back, then swept the clutter under the bottom shelf.

The little drawer in my vanity, where I kept my scrunchies and other hair things, was open. The bottom drawer of my dresser was open too. My socks were spilling out. Did I leave it like that? Did I leave my vanity drawer open?

Now that I looked, it seemed that lots of things weren't as I remembered leaving them this morning. Everything looked just a bit out of place. A couple of the old stuffed animals that I kept piled on a chair had fallen

to the floor. My pageant trophies, which I hadn't looked at in years, were

crooked

on the top shelf of my bookcase. The things on my desk were moved, just so slightly—my CDs, my pictures, my makeup case. My snow globe of New York was on its side, a

horizontal

Statue of Liberty in a horizontal skyline.

My mother must have been in here looking for something. Maybe she wanted to borrow one of my handbags, or a pair of earrings or a lipstick.

A noise came from downstairs. A little tap.

"Mom, is that you?" I called out. "Hey, were you going through my stuff?"

She didn't answer.

I fingered my diamond pendant and slid it back and forth on the chain. If Mom had gone through my things, she would have closed the drawers after. If she'd knocked over my snow globe, she would have righted it. She certainly wouldn't have left my pageant trophies out of place.

Another little echoey tap. Like a shoe tiptoeing on our hardwood floor.

I went to the top of the stairs. "Mom?"

Silence.

No answers from Mom, no more little echoey taps.

But then: *Tap.*

"Hello?" I shouted downstairs over the railing. "Is someone here?"

Tap.

Yes.

Someone

was

in

our

house.

Slowly, I walked down each step, listening for the sound.

Tap. Tap. Tap.

The kitchen—that was where the taps were coming from. I had to catch whoever it was before they left through the patio door. Go, go, *go!* I flew down the hall and into the kitchen—

But it was

empty.

The patio door was closed, and when I checked, it was locked from the inside.

Tap.

The tapping sound came from the window over the sink. A branch from a tree, waving in the wind.

That was all it was? A branch and the wind?

I checked again that the patio door was locked, then I looked in every room of our house. Nothing else was out of place. As pristine as always. Our electronics—our computer, our TVs, sound system—were all still there. My dad's little fireproof safe was still in his study, under a stack of papers in his desk drawer. Upstairs, my mom's jewelry cabinet, white and tall with spindly legs and painted with Japanese flowers, was untouched in her closet. Each piece of her jewelry was still perfectly displayed. The ceramic ash tray I made for my dad at summer camp when I six was on his nightstand, still filled with coins.

Which meant that whoever had been in our house, if there even *was* someone in our house, had only been in my room. Going through *my* stuff. There was only one thing they could have been looking for.

I went to my room again. My wooden globe seemed to be untouched. Europe was still facing out. My little yellow stickers were still in place. I opened the top and checked, just in case.

The Ryland High baseball cap was still tucked inside.

I was just being paranoid. My room was messy, that was all. I was always digging through my closet and drawers and pulling things out and not putting them back. And this morning I had been running late, as usual. My pageant trophies had probably been out of place for months and I'd just never noticed.

I tucked my socks back into the drawer, straightened the trophies, righted my snow globe, tossed the stuffed animals back onto the chair.

No one had broken into my house. I was sure of it.

CHAPTER FORTY-THREE

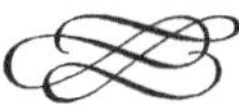

EVER ~ PRESENT DAY

No police cars are waiting for me in my driveway when I get home from the police station. I half-expected Chief Paladino to send someone to follow me, watch me, but the only vehicle on my street is a red sedan, and it's driving away.

I fetch Joey from Hayden's, unlock our front door and usher him inside, then lock it again. Once he's settled with a snack and his Matchbox cars, I open my laptop. I have to find a lawyer for Ash.

From the corner of my eye, I see the blinking light on our answering machine. I press *play*, knowing it's be a message from Dad. He's the only one who calls our landline anymore. I also know his message will say that he won't be home tomorrow, as he promised. He always calls the landline when he knows I won't be home to answer.

Hey, Ev. I'm going to be on the road for a few more days. I was heading home, but Seth Siegel called a few minutes ago. I have to turn around and pick up something in the Vegas warehouse and bring it to Seattle. Big job. Bonus pay. Thanks.

Come on, Dad. I really needed you this time. Just this once.

I press the *erase* button. The house screams with sudden silence.

Pulling the front curtains back the tiniest bit, I peek out to make sure Paladino's cop car isn't there. There's no movement outside at all, except for the branches swaying in the breeze. Keith's house is across the street, the lights off, the driveway empty.

My doors and windows are locked. I double-, then triple-check.

There's an old phone book in one of our cupboards. The front cover is an advertisement for Siegel Freight and Transport, with Seth Siegel himself smiling over his dimpled chin and waving from behind the wheel of one of his cobalt-blue eighteen-wheelers. I open the phone book and try looking up the number for Ash's mom, but the only listing I can find is for *Morrison, Vincent*. When I call the number, a tinny robotic voice informs me it's been disconnected.

Was Ash's mom ever married to Ash's dad? If not, maybe she's still going by her maiden name, and I don't know what that is. I don't even know her first name.

Dinner is elbow macaroni and jarred pasta sauce, cucumbers and dip, and strawberries. But I can't eat it. Anxiety, worry, fear, and heartache are building up inside of me, making me almost dizzy and nauseated. I don't know what to do. I need help, and there's no one who *can* help.

Joey's not hungry either. He's tired and fussy, so I send him to change into his pajamas while I Google lawyers for Ash. I don't trust that Paladino will let him call one for himself.

There are a handful of defense attorneys to choose from. That's a good thing, but I get exhausted just thinking about calling all of them. What if I pick the wrong one? How will either of us afford it? What I really want to do is go to sleep. A dull headache throbs behind my eyes. Today was exhausting. These last few weeks have been exhausting. They were overwhelming, really, and now my muscles feel heavy. I just want to go to sleep.

But I can't go to bed yet. I need to help Ash. I pick the top attorney on the list. But before I can gather the strength to dial, Joey comes back into the kitchen. "Ever, I think Cheeks is sick." He cups his hamster in his little hands. "She's not moving."

Only now I realize that the house has been strangely quiet. The hamster wheel hasn't squeaked all evening. Cheeks lies stiff and still in Joey's hands.

"Oh, no. Oh, buddy." I sink down next to Joey and put my arm around him.

His little chin quivers. "Is she dead?"

"Yeah, she is, sweetie. She was very old." *Was* she old? How long do hamsters live? I don't know anything about the lifespan of hamsters. Joey's only had her for about a year, but I don't know how old she was when we got her.

"Is she in heaven with Mommy?"

"I—" I don't know what to tell him. I can't tell him that our mom was reborn into someone else moments after she died. He's not ready to hear that yet, and besides, I don't know if that happens to anyone but me. Maybe Mom and Cheeks really are in heaven. "Yeah," I tell my grieving baby brother. "Cheeks loved you, and she knows that you loved her. You gave her a really good life. She loved being your pet. Now Mommy will take good care of her in heaven."

Joey cries while I rub his back, comforting him.

I wish Ash were here, comforting me.

We place Cheeks in a shoe box and tuck her in with a soft dishrag. We'll bury her tomorrow in the back yard.

I tuck Joey into bed and give him a hundred extra kisses. He falls asleep quickly, his cheeks bright red and warm.

My heart is hurting, and my head is throbbing. So tired. *So* tired. I take my laptop into bed with me to resume my search for a lawyer. I just want to sleep, but how can I sleep when Paladino has Ash locked up? He needs me. His father needs me. I have to keep going.

But my head hurts so much, and I'm just so, so tired...

~

A weak whimper, invading my sleep, comes from down the hall. So weak it barely registers. But it's Joey, so my ears prick up. My head is throbbing, splitting in two, and I'm nauseated. I run my hand over my forehead, willing the death-memory of pain away. But this ache can't be from a death-memory or a dream. This pain is real because it's not fading. I wasn't feeling well after dinner either. Maybe I'm getting sick.

Is this the flu? Do I have the flu? Eighty thousand people died of the flu last year. But it's not flu season, and I had my flu shot. I always get my flu shot.

It's almost impossible, but I force my eyelids open and check the clock. Just after midnight.

Joey whimpers again.

My head is a constant ache, like my brain is pushing against my skull. Joey's whimper turns into a faint moan.

I need to check on him. I'll just go back to sleep for five more minutes, then I'll get up.

Another whimper. "Ever..."

Oh, God. Is he sick too? That thought is enough to force me out of bed despite my aching skull.

But I'm so weak. Every movement brings waves of nausea. Sitting up makes my head burst. But I need to get to Joey. I pull myself to standing, but my knees buckle and I collapse back to the bed. My head. My *head*.

Headache, weakness, nausea. But we can't have the flu. Food poisoning? No, we'd both be vomiting regularly by now if we had food poisoning.

An image of Joey's dead hamster flashes in my mind.

It's not food poisoning.

With a gasp, I fling myself from the bed before the thought fully forms. Carbon monoxide. It's carbon monoxide!

Get Joey. Get Joey. Get out. "Joey!" I cry, adrenaline forcing a scream from my lungs. I stumble to my door, grasp the doorframe, pull myself along the wall. "Joey, get up," I croak, hoping he can hear me. "I'm coming for you." Dizzy, weak. The floor is warped, topsy-turvy. I dry heave as I crawl. We have to get out, we have to get out, we have to get out!

The air is clear, clean, no scent, yet it's poisoning us. The CO detector is plugged into the outlet in the hallway, between Joey's bedroom and the bathroom. Why isn't the alarm ringing? I have three carbon monoxide detectors in this little house and none of them are ringing.

I need to get us out of here. I pull myself down the hall to Joey's room. He lays in his bed, moaning. He's so small, so little, so young. If I'm this weak and dizzy and nauseated, he must be overpowered.

"Come on, Joey. We need to get outside."

I unlock his window to let in from fresh air, but I can't get it open. I can't lift it. My arms are like jelly. Every movement makes me dizzy.

If I can't even open Joey's window, there's no way I can lift him. I can't. I don't have the strength.

But I find it. My head is splitting open and the world is spinning and I'm about to puke up everything I've ever eaten in my entire life, but I grab my baby brother under his shoulders and pull him out of bed and drag him backward, whimpering and moaning.

The air feels fine; it's easy to breathe, it's clear, but it's poisoning us. "Hold your breath, Joey. Try not to breathe." Out his doorway, all the way down the hall. All the way through the family room. All the way to the front door. Every breath we take forces more poison into our bodies.

With my last ounce of strength, I drag him through the doorway. And drag. Onto the porch.

Cold fresh spring air hits us, but not enough. I drag again, screaming with effort, down the three concrete steps, his little bare heels scraping on the concrete. Drag again, past the bushes. And finally. Finally. To the grass.

I collapse. "Breathe, Joey," I gasp. "Breathe deep." I suck in great lungfuls of air. It doesn't smell or taste any different from the air in my house, but it's cold, and fresh, and clean.

Already I'm feeling better. My headache and dizziness are starting to fade. Finally, I have the strength to sit up. Joey is still lying on the ground. I pull him into my lap and rub his forehead. "Breathe," I say over and over again. "Breathe."

Cheeks the hamster didn't die of old age. She died of carbon monoxide poisoning. Joey and I were breathing in that poison all evening.

A red car rolls silently down the street, its headlights off.

A fire truck comes after we ask the neighbors to call 911, along with an ambulance. Inside the ambulance, the EMTs treat Joey and me with oxygen. I feel fine, but I can't stop shaking as I give them our information. Joey perks up quickly. His excitement about all the cool things in the ambulance extinguish any fear he may have had, and soon he's chatting away with one of the EMTs through his oxygen mask.

A little white car with the Citizens Gas Company logo on the door comes next and parks in our driveway. A round-faced man in a mask and a blue work shirt goes inside to find the CO leak, holding a flashlight and a bag. On the sidewalk, a group of neighbors has gathered. Keith is among them, but I can't see his expression from the ambulance.

At the EMT's request, I give him my father's phone number. He has to call three times before Dad wakes up and answers. He tells Dad what happened, and that Joey and I are fine but he's taking us to get checked out at the emergency room as a precaution. The gas company is fixing the leak and everything is safe for now, but he should still get the furnace checked out so it doesn't happen again. I get on the phone with him next.

He's frantic, almost crying. "Ever, my God, are you okay? Is Joey okay?"

"We're fine now," I say. He asked about Joey. He *does* love Joey—Ash was right. Now *I'm* choking back tears.

"I'm coming straight home," he says. "I'm in Seattle, so... day after tomorrow. You'll be okay until then?"

"Uh-huh." I sigh, knowing that he'll come home for one night and then leave again. I remember my conversation with Ash under his tree and draw strength from it. "But, Dad, we need you home every night," I say. "Things need to change. Joey needs a father, not just a big sister."

"I know," he whispers, and I can hear the guilt in his voice.

"You need to talk to Seth Siegel and tell him you won't accept any more overnight hauls. We need you more than we need the money."

He's silent for a moment, then says, "Okay."

"You promise?"

"I promise. I'll be home every night. Put Joey on. I need to hear his voice."

I give the phone to my brother. Our father is coming home. Joey and I had to almost die before he realized that he should be home every night. The gas leak was good for something at least. Cheeks the hamster did not die in vain.

The round-faced man from the gas company is waiting to speak to me next. He climbs into the ambulance and sits next to me on the gurney. He's wearing a laminated badge pinned to his shirt pocket with his name on it: Jonah Caplan.

"I counted three CO detectors in your house," he says, making notes on his clip board. He sounds like his nose is stuffed up. "That's great, but they won't work if you don't put batteries in them." He sniffs, or tries to.

I'm about to tell him that there *are* batteries in my carbon monoxide detectors, that I put fresh batteries in them myself, just a couple weeks ago. The day of the scholarship interview. I bought them at Kammer's Pharmacy. There's no reason why the alarms wouldn't have gone off.

Unless—

I snap my mouth shut.

Jonah Caplan looks at me then, locks his gaze to mine. "Carbon monoxide is a silent killer."

He clicks his pen closed. And that's when I see it: a crossed-hatchet tattoo on his wrist.

Someone else climbs into the ambulance and clamps his hand on the gas man's shoulder. Just below it, on the wrist, is another hatchet tattoo.

"You can leave, Jonah," Chief Paladino says. He gives me a patronizing smile. "I'll take it from here."

CHAPTER FORTY-FOUR

LILY ~ EIGHTEEN YEARS AGO

I chanted and cheered with the rest of the Batgirls as the Warriors stepped off the school bus the next day, returning to Ryland High victorious after their latest win. I clapped too, but I didn't mean any of it. One of these guys killed Neal.

As Brandon paraded past, Diana whirled around so fast that her hair hit him in the face, showing him exactly how much she didn't love him anymore.

Will walked by and our eyes met. "Congratulations, hotshot," I said, grinning.

He grinned back. "I only hit a single, and the next time I was at bat, I got an out." He swiped at the dirt on his uniform pants.

"Who cares? We won. You helped."

I wanted to touch him somehow, so I wiggled the Warriors cap on his head. This whole secret relationship thing was a pain in the butt. The second my dad loaned his dad that money and saved their farm, their feud would be over and I would be free to kiss Will in front of the entire team. The entire school. The entire town.

Seth Siegel shouldered past Will, knocking into him. "Watch it, asswipe," he muttered.

"What's his problem?" Will asked me. "He's been like that with me for days now."

"Who cares? He's a jerk. Ignore him."

We marched into the building behind a round-faced freshman named Jonah Caplan, who always had a stuffy nose and was dragging a bag of mitts, balls, and bases behind him. The bag was almost as big as he was. He turned left into the equipment room.

Hmm.

"Wanna meet me tonight?" I asked Will.

"Sure. Where?"

"Under your oak tree. 8:00? But I can't stay too late. My curfew's at 10."

"You care about curfews now?"

"More than ever. I'm on my best behavior."

"I hope you won't be on your best behavior under my tree tonight," Will said, wiggling his brows.

I gave him a playful shove. "Go on and change, dirty boy. I'll see you later." Will went to the locker room, and I went to the equipment room.

Jonah was kneeling on the floor over the open mesh bag, taking out baseball equipment and wiping them clean with a rag. "Hey, Jonah," I called cheerfully, breathing through my mouth to avoid the smell of sweat. "Need any help?"

That night, on the edge of Duston Farm under the big oak tree by Railroad Bridge, Will kept me warm under his arm. He smelled like soap, and his white-blond hair brushed the collar of his Ryland

Warriors sweatshirt. "I talked to the equipment manager today," I told him. "You know, Jonah?"

"Caplan? That freshman with all those allergies? How that guy can stand to be outside on the baseball field is beyond me. He's allergic to grass."

"I asked him if anyone asked for a new Warriors cap in the past two weeks."

"And?"

"He said *no*."

"Anyone who loses their uniform has to pay to get it replaced," Will said. "That includes the hat. But Jonah isn't the only one who issues the equipment. It could have been someone else."

"I figured. So I made him show me the records."

"And?"

"Still no. They ordered twenty-one hats at the beginning of the season and gave out sixteen to the team and one to the coach. There were four left in inventory. I counted them myself. No one's bought a new hat this season. And there are too many hats that've been distributed over the years to account for all of them. It's another dead end."

"It was a good idea, anyway." He pulled me closer to him and kissed my forehead. "Maybe you were a detective in one of your past lives."

I chuckled. "Maybe." Snuggling back into him, I said, "Thanks."

"For what?"

"The way you said that, about my past lives. Casual, you know? You aren't making fun of me, and you don't think I'm lying or crazy."

He stroked my arm with his index finger. "I think it's cool."

"I think so too." I turned my head to kiss him in that soft spot under his jaw where his pulse beat. "Have your parents said anything to you?"

"About what?" His voice was getting softer.

"Your farm. My dad. Did they talk?"

"My dad said something about your dad calling him to set up a meeting. I don't want to hear about it. Not anymore. You know what I *do* want to do?"

"What?"

"This." He slid his hand behind my head, then kissed my lips.

I lay back, pulling him with me, our legs tangling. A part of me wanted to ravish him, to grab him and rip off his sweatshirt and crush my lips to his, but he was so slow, so gentle, his breath so soft on my neck, his hand so warm as it slid under my sweater. I relaxed into it

and kissed him back,
slowly,
gently,
softly.
I could no longer deny it.
I was
in love
with Will Duston.

At 9:40, Will and I reluctantly parted. I had to get home before ten. The old me would have stayed under the oak tree with Will, and told my parents an obvious lie when they would inevitably catch me sneaking back into the house past curfew. But I was mature and responsible now. I didn't get into trouble anymore.

Will had offered to drive me home, but with the time it would take us to cross his field to get to his parents' car and drive around town to my house, it would be faster to walk. The moon was covered by clouds, but I knew my way around Ryland blindfolded. I darted across Railroad Bridge and down the dirt path through the woods, shuffled through the pebbles and weeds behind the used car lot, squeezed through the hole in the chain link fence, and rushed down the alley behind Main Street.

I paused when I got to the dumpster behind the movie theater. Two guys stood in the shadows, having a low, urgent discussion. Vinnie Morrison and—it was too dark to see the dimple on this chin, but I recognized his height and shape—Seth Siegel. He was trembling and sniveling. What was Vinnie doing to him?

No. Wait. That was definitely Seth, but the other guy, the one confronting him, wasn't Vinnie Morrison. He was wearing a police uniform. His badge flashed under the dim light over the movie theater's exit. Rick Paladino.

I crouched low behind the dumpster, then leaned closer to listen.

"Christ on a cracker, are you *crying*?" Paladino hissed. "If you keep this up, people will get suspicious."

Seth sniveled and wiped his eyes. "S-Sorry."

"I'm sick of constantly having to save your ass. Your daddy better make good on his promise to get me a promotion. If anyone finds out about all the shit I've covered up for you, I won't just lose my badge. I could go to prison."

Seth sniveled again, and then he squealed when Paladino grabbed him by the collar and shoved him against the dumpster. "But remember, if I go down, I'm bringing you down too," he said. "You'll go to prison right along with me. So go home and don't speak a word about any of this to anyone, ever. Keep your mouth shut."

I slipped back into the shadows just before Seth rushed past me, terrified.

I stayed crouched in the dark between the dumpster and the wall,

heart pounding

not moving

not breathing.

Paladino stepped into the alley, watching Seth run, then

finally

finally

he marched away.

I waited until his booted footsteps faded completely, then I stood, so slowly my muscles ached, and slowly, silently, tiptoed from my hiding spot, staying in the shadows. I quickened my pace, and soon I was running home. I needed to call Will. He needed to know about this.

CHAPTER FORTY-FIVE

EVER ~ PRESENT DAY

There should be no reason for Ryland's chief of police to come to my house for a carbon monoxide leak. But here he is, standing at the back door to the ambulance. Jonah Caplan gives him a nervous, curt nod, then slips past him. He escapes to his white Citizens Gas Company car and drives away.

I have no such escape. Paladino says to the EMTs, "I need to talk to the girl before you take them to the ER." To Joey he says, "I need to borrow your sister for a sec, big guy. We'll be right outside. You stay here in the ambulance and I'll bring her right back." To me, he says, "Let's go."

With no choice, I climb out of the ambulance. The neighbors are still mingling on the sidewalk under the streetlight, some drifting home now that the excitement is over. Others stay and watch, Keith among them.

I'm in my pajamas, a maroon Ryland High T-shirt and gray shorts. "Poor thing, you're shivering," Paladino says. His cruiser is parked nearby, and he goes to his trunk and takes out a royal blue blanket embroidered with the Ryland Police Department logo.

He holds it open for me. When I don't step into it, he places it around my shoulders himself. He smooths the blanket over my arms, rubbing them to warm me up. For the second time today, someone with a hatchet tattoo is touching me. Fear and dread curdle in my stomach, bringing back the nausea.

"A month ago, Miss Abrams, you were just a quiet, studious, well-behaved girl on track to win the Lily Summerhays Memorial Scholarship and attend Griffin University," he says, practically cooing. "But now look at all the trouble you've had lately, ever since you hooked up with Ash Morrison. And tonight you had a carbon monoxide leak. I wonder how that happened?"

"It wasn't an accident," I say. "I know you did it."

"Don't be silly, sweetheart. I'm a police officer. My job is to protect you. Besides, you know I was at the police station with your drug dealer boyfriend, charging him with possession." His gaze bores into me, telling me that he may not have made the leak happen himself, but he made it happen.

"I'm just saying, Miss Abrams, that you could've died tonight." The chief gives a pointed look to Joey in the ambulance. "And so could've your little brother. I'd hate for something else to happen to him. Something worse."

My blood stops running through my veins. I feel faint. "Don't. Not Joey. Please."

"I think you should reconsider my offer from before," he says. "I'll let Ash out of jail, and I'll make sure that you and your brother are safe. You'll win that scholarship, and everything will go back to the way it's supposed to be." His voice is soft, gentle, almost like a lullaby, but his gaze is as hard and cold as ice. "But in order for that to happen, you need to *stop* this silly investigation of yours. Now."

I watch Joey in the ambulance, gleefully chatting with the EMTs. A half hour ago he was lying on the grass, eyes half-closed, skin cold, face pale as death.

"Joey will be safe?" I have to bite my lips to keep myself from vomiting. "You promise?"

Paladino nods, sincerity in his brown eyes. "You have my solemn vow, Miss Abrams. Nothing will happen to Joey. He'll be the safest citizen of Ryland there ever was."

"And Ash," I say. "I want the same deal for him. No jail, no charges, no harassment, no *accidental* carbon monoxide poisoning. Nothing. He stays safe too."

"As long as you two uphold your end of the deal, so will I," Paladino says. "Are we in agreement?"

That red car I saw earlier, driving down the street. Did the driver of that car break into my house, remove the batteries from my CO detectors, and cause the gas leak? Was it Jonah Caplan, the gas company guy? Or maybe Paladino had someone else do it. How many people does the chief have in his pocket? How many people is he bribing, blackmailing, and threatening to do his bidding?

Whatever the number, I am now one of them. I don't have a choice. "Yes, sir. We have a deal."

"That's my good girl."

Paladino points at Keith and emits a quick, high-pitched whistle, calling him over. Keith hesitantly lumbers to us. "Our girl here has gotten herself into quite a bit of trouble lately," Paladino tells him. "She promised me she's done with all that. But just to be sure, you'll watch her for me, won't you, son?"

Keith, eyes wide with shock, nods. "Um, yeah. Sure."

"Good. Make sure you keep her out of trouble. Pick her up for school, bring her home, spend every spare second with her, just like you used to. She wants things to go back the way they used to be. She just needs your supervision to stay in line."

Keith looks at me, and, feeling faint, I nod. "Yep," I manage to squeak.

"I'll be checking in with you, son. I need to you stick to her like glue. Why don't you follow her to the ER, make sure she and her brother are okay, and then you can take them back home." Paladino squeezes Keith's shoulder, then retreats to his police cruiser. He watches us from the window.

"Do you mean it?" Keith asks me. "You want things to go back the way they were? You and me?"

I don't answer. I can't. All I can do is nod.

"I can forgive you for kissing Ash Morrison. It only happened a few times, right?"

"I never kissed him." Regret, on so many levels. I wish we *had* kissed. It would have been our one and only.

"Just don't do it again," Keith says.

"I didn't—"

"Stay away from him, and I'll forgive you."

"Okay." I don't even bother to bring up the fact that he had *sex* with that girl from Eastfield.

"So... we're back together?"

I nod again. Keith puts his arm around me. I want to vomit, but I don't shake him off.

Ash will understand why I'm doing this, why I have to do this. I had to make this deal with the chief. I have to do whatever it takes to keep Joey safe. He'll understand that.

Ash will understand, but will he forgive me?

The engine rumbling in his cruiser, Paladino watches. It's not until I stand on tiptoe and give Keith a kiss that he drives away.

CHAPTER FORTY-SIX

LILY ~ EIGHTEEN YEARS AGO

I made it home at 9:59, one minute to spare before curfew. My house was dim, quiet. My parents were in bed already, which meant I'd rushed home for nothing. I could have stayed in the field with Will, wrapped in his arms, for at least a little while longer. But if I hadn't left when I did, I wouldn't have overheard Paladino and Seth in the alley behind the movie theater.

I needed to call Will about that right away.

In the wastebasket in the kitchen, an envelope, green and emblazoned with big, bold yellow letters, caught my eye. Green and gold: Carroll-Freywood Global University's school colors. My mother must have thought it was junk mail and tossed it without a second glance.

But this was so much more than junk mail. I slid my finger under the envelope's seal, my heart

skipping

then I reminded myself not to get too excited—this could be a rejection letter.

What would I do if this *was* a rejection letter? I'd go to Griffin, room with Diana, get a degree in business, then work at Agri-So and eventually own the company. That was what my parents wanted.

But it wasn't what *I* wanted. Even though Will would be here in Ryland. He would make things better, but I didn't want to go to Griffin, I didn't want to study business, and I didn't want to one day own Agri-So. No. I wouldn't do it.

No

matter

what.

If this letter from CFGU was a rejection letter, I could still leave Ryland. I didn't need a college degree to travel around the world. I didn't need my parents' approval either. I *wanted* it, but I didn't *need* it. I also didn't need their financial support. I would work for my dad for the summer—something I was going to do anyway—and save up some money. Then in the fall, instead of going to Griffin University, I would buy the cheapest ticket to... wherever I wanted. South America, Europe, Africa, Asia. I could do odd jobs, anything I could find, to support myself and my travels. I didn't mind doing menial tasks, working hard, and getting dirty. Even better, I could volunteer for organizations that built homes and schools and waterways in underdeveloped countries. That was a better way to discover the world anyway.

That was it. I was leaving Ryland in the fall to travel the world, even if this letter from CFGU was a rejection.

Decision

made.

Reminding myself that it didn't matter what the letter said, I pulled out the letter from the envelope, and read it.

Dear Miss Lily Summerhays,

We'd like to congratulate you on your acceptance to the global program of Carroll-Freywood University...

I read the letter again, then a third time. I blinked, then read it again. But it was the same each time: I was in! I did it! I was accepted to Carroll-Freywood Global University! For the next four years, I'd be attending classes in eight different countries on six different continents, and I'd graduate with a degree in cultural anthropology and I'd spend the rest of my life traveling the world and having adventures and oh my God, oh my God, oh my God, oh my God!

Something else to tell Will. He was going to be so happy for me. There was no question in my mind that if I stayed local, we'd continue our relationship. But now that I'd be traveling, did I still want to be committed to him while he stayed back in Indiana?

Yes. Absolutely yes. We'd figure it out. I'd see him when I came home for semester breaks.

And after college...

No. I wasn't going to think about that now. Will wanted to live on Duston Farm for the rest of his life, and I wanted to continue exploring the world for the rest of mine. That would be something we'd have to figure out together. Things were going too well for me right now to worry about something that wouldn't happen until after college. I was with Will, I finally had a suspect in Neal's murder—Seth Seigel, with the help of Rick Paladino—and I'd just been accepted to CFGU. Everything was

perfect.

And then—a sniffle. Coming from the living room. Followed by a sob.

"Mom?" I made my way to the living room. Mom was there, huddled on the floor by the fireplace, her French twist fallen, her makeup smeared. A panicked thought flew through my head—

Seth and Paladino

they did this

they saw me behind the dumpster

they hurt my mother

they came for me but they hurt my mom—

as I rushed over to her. "Mom, what happened?"

She looked up at me, completely broken. "It's over," she said simply.

"What's over?"

"He left. Your father left."

"Like on a business trip?" But even as I said it, I knew what she meant. "He left *you*?"

My lungs

deflated

and I sank to my knees. "But I thought you guys were getting along now," I said. "I thought things were better."

"I thought so too," she said. "He said he tried, for you, but he couldn't do it anymore." She sobbed fresh tears onto my shoulder.

I should be crying too, but anger was building and building and building inside me, turning my blood hot, turning my vision red. How could he do this? How could he?

"I'm all alone now," Mom sobbed. "What am I going to do? I don't know how to be alone."

"You're not alone, Mom," I said, swallowing the lump in my throat. "I'm here. I'm going to Griffin next year, remember? It's only a half hour away. I'll come see you all the time. I can even live at home, instead of in the dorms. I won't leave you." And finally, I let a tear fall.

"I can't ask you—" She sobbed again, then said, "Thank you, Lily. Thank you so much. I won't be able to get through this without you. I love you so much." She pulled back and sniffled, wiping her eyes with her fingertips. "It's you and me now," she said. She tried to smile but failed. She cried instead, grabbing me into her arms again.

"You and me," I repeated. Behind her back, I crumpled up the letter from CFGU.

Later that night, after I gave Mom a sleeping pill and put her to bed, I went to my room. It was a *good* thing that I was staying in Ryland. I was going to stay here with my mother, who needed me, and Will Duston, who loved me. I would stay here, in Ryland, and I would never speak to my father again. I'd pass him on the street and pretend I didn't know him.

It was a *good* thing I was staying in Ryland.

I tossed the crumpled-up letter from CFGU into my wastebasket.

No. It

hurt

too much to see that letter in the wastebasket.

I took it out, smoothed it, put it back inside the envelope, and hid it inside my globe. I was staying in Ryland. One day, far in the future, I might take the letter from the globe and look at it and think about what might have been.

CHAPTER FORTY-SEVEN

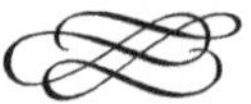

EVER ~ PRESENT DAY

Taking Paladino's instructions to heart, Keith has stuck to me like glue. Last night he followed Joey and me to the ER, he didn't leave my side as we breathed in oxygen for a few hours, then he drove us home and walked us inside.

Now it's a couple hours later and the sun is shining bright and low in the sky, and he's on my doorstep so he can escort me to school. He kisses me full on the mouth and walks with me to take Joey next door for daycare.

I'm exhausted and my eyes are heavy and puffy, but Joey isn't tired despite spending the night in the ER. Instead, he tells the other kids all about last night's adventure. "We had a gas leak!" he announces proudly. "My hamster died. And I got sick! But Ever took me outside in my PJs to feel better and it was after midnight! And a fire engine came! And a police car! And we got to ride in an ambulance and the hospital gave us special air!"

Joey runs off with Hayden and the other kids, and I stand there, watching him leave, until Keith pulls me away. I don't resist. Joey will be safe at daycare. Joey is the safest citizen in Ryland, according to Chief Paladino, because I am sticking to my end of the deal.

Keith drives me to Ryland High, where Principal Duston and Chief Paladino are standing by the front entrance, pretending they aren't watching me as I enter the building. I take Keith's hand. The chief, with an almost imperceptible smirk, gives him a nod as we pass.

As we walk down the hallways toward our lockers, I scan the crowd for Ash. We pass his locker, but he's not there. Is he still in jail? Did the chief break his part of our deal? Keith tucks me under his arm, chipper in his steps as we stop at his locker, then mine. As I turn the dial on my combination lock, he stands close behind me, running his fingertips up and down my arm, tucking my hair behind my ear, kissing my neck.

"What's this?" A voice, dubious yet hopeful, behind us. Courtney. I turn to see her watching us. "Are you—?" She gasps, her hand flying to her mouth. She hasn't drawn her swirls and dots on her hand lately.

A few feet away, pushing through the throng of students toward me, comes Ash. My knees almost give out in relief. Thank God. He's here. He needs to shave and he's wearing the same jeans and T-shirt as yesterday, but he doesn't look bruised or beaten. Paladino released him. He kept his end of the deal.

But now I have to keep mine.

"Keith and I made up last night," I tell Courtney, loud enough for Ash to hear. He stops in his tracks.

Court tilts her head, twists her lips. "What about Ash Morrison?"

With Ash watching, I step closer to Keith and pull his arms around me. "Ash is a thief and a druggie." In my peripheral vision, Ash goes rigid, his scowling eyes widening with shock. "He lied to me. He made me think his father is innocent."

I can't look at Ash. I hate myself for doing this to him. *Please understand, please understand.*

From behind me, Keith squeezes me tightly and rests his chin on my head. Courtney, however, is still not convinced. "Whatever you were doing with Ash, you're done? It's over?"

I nod, definitively. "It's over." *I'm sorry, Ash. I'm sorry, I'm sorry, I'm so, so sorry.*

"You swear?" She's pleading, begging, desperate for it to be true.

"She promised me last night," Keith adds.

"I'm sorry, Courtney," I say. "You're my best friend. I don't want to fight anymore." That part, at least, is the truth.

Slowly, her shoulders relax. "So, you're back to normal?"

I nod, and she takes me from Keith to envelop me in a hug. "I missed you," she says. "I kept picking up my phone to text you, but then I remembered we were fighting, and it was the worst time of my life. But everything's okay now."

The warning bell rings. I find the strength to look at Ash, but he's already gone.

In his place, watching and listening, is Principal Duston. "Courtney, Keith, you two get to class. I need to talk to Ever for a moment."

Keith draws me back into his arms. "Why, what'd she do?" he asks Principal Duston.

"She had nothing to do with those drugs in Ash Morrison's locker," Court says, defending me. "And anyway, she's done with him. She promised."

"I know. Go to class," Principal Duston orders.

Court gives me a shrug, mouths *text me,* and reluctantly shuffles away. Keith slowly releases me from his arms, leaving me alone with Principal Duston.

"I, um, I don't want to be late for first period," I say.

"This won't take long." He chews his toothpick, his eyes shadowed and suspicious under his white-blond hair. When he speaks next, his voice is low, conspiratorial. "How much do you know?"

How much has Paladino told him? Should I feign ignorance? Before I can decide what to say, he answers for me. "I know you think I killed Lily Summerhays."

My body turns cold. "I don't—how—There are others..." I want to run, but I can't make my legs work.

"Why do you think that? What do you remem—" He cuts himself off. He closes his eyes and lets out a breath. He opens his eyes again, light blue and penetrating. "Listen. Lily and I were friends. More than friends, for a while. While we were more than friends, she told me something about herself. A secret. I stopped believing it—maybe I never really did believe it—but I'm starting to believe it now. You know what I'm talking about, don't you." It's not a question.

Even if I knew how to reply, I can't. He keeps me frozen in his gaze. My lungs don't work.

He leans in close, muttering between clenched teeth. "You did the right thing, making that deal with Paladino. Keep doing what he says. I'll be watching."

His breath catches, like a hesitation. Then he exhales, and it sounds like a whispered word carried away in the wind: "Lily."

CHAPTER FORTY-EIGHT

LILY ~ EIGHTEEN YEARS AGO

My dad was gone, and my mom was sobbing in her sleep. There was only one person I wanted to talk to right now. Only one person who could make me feel better.

I called, but he didn't answer. "Call me, Will," I whispered into the phone. "I need to talk to you." I lay with my head on the phone for over an hour, but he didn't call back. I considered sneaking out of the house and running over there, but I didn't want to leave my mother alone. I'd see him tomorrow at school.

After a sleepless night, I called one of my mom's friends to come stay with her. Then I went to school and waited for Will. I leaned against his locker, hugging my books to my chest.

I saw his white-blond hair curled around the bottom of his maroon baseball cap first. As he came down the hall, he didn't appear to see me. He was staring straight ahead, not really seeing anything, like he was dazed. He bumped into a girl with a French braid and barely mumbled an apology as he walked to his locker.

"Will!" I called out. My voice sounded strangled, but I didn't care. I was tired of holding it together, and now that I saw him, all I wanted was for him to

hold me tight

in his arms.

He looked up, and the vacancy in his gaze became solid and dark. His lips tightened into a frown and his cheeks flamed. He strode over to me in four steps, then made a fist, flexing his hatchet tattoo, and pounded the locker right next to my head. I flinched. "What the hell did you do, Lily?"

"What are you talking about?" Why was he so angry?

"You told your dad that we were bankrupt?" He pounded the locker again. Heads turned and the hall grew silent at his outburst as the crowd looked over.

"So he could give you money—"

"He gave us money all right. A lot of money. More than enough to pay our debts. More than my parents have made in the past ten years combined."

"But that's—that's good, right?"

"It's *not* good!" His nostrils flared, his face was red. "He gave us the money in exchange for our land. *My* land. My *farm.*"

"But—But he told me—"

"That's what this whole thing was about, wasn't it?" He brought his face up close, his face sneering like he was something evil. "You made up that whole story about Neal being murdered, that whole ridiculous past lives thing. The things we did together"—he swiped his lips with his forearm, wiping away all the kisses I'd given him —"it was all just to get close to me, get in my house, and snoop around."

I gasped. "Will! No!"

He threw his fist back and hurled his fist into the locker just inches from my head. "You ruined my life, Lily! What the hell am I going to do now?"

"Your parents were going to lose the farm anyway," I said.

"They could have held on for a while longer!" he roared. "I had a plan! I was going to turn things around!"

"You don't know that," I said, but logic wasn't calming him. I put my hands on his chest, trying to draw him close. "Will, I'm sorry. I would never, ever do anything to hurt you."

He jerked away. "Don't touch me again," he hissed through gritted teeth. "Don't you ever speak to me again." He stalked off with wide strides.

"Will!" I chased after him, not caring that everyone was watching. "Will, wait!" I grabbed his shirt. "I love you! I *love* you."

He made a face like my words sickened him. "Stay away from me."

I stood frozen as he pulled away and stormed off. Only when someone jostled me did I move again. I passed the day in a daze. I

loved

Will, and he

hated

me. My heart literally

hurt

inside my chest.

At some point Diana asked me if it was true; did the Dustons really sell their land to my dad. "I guess so," I said, numb.

"Will's pissed. He says it's your fault."

I looked at my best friend. I wanted to tell her that Will broke up with me, and I needed her to comfort me the way I had comforted her the countless times she and Brandon had broken up. But Diana didn't even know that for a short time—a beautiful, wondrous, glorious time—Will and I had been together. She didn't know that I was in love with him. "Diana, Will and I—"

"Brandon, stop!" Diana shouted down the hall. "We'll talk later, okay?" she said to me, already rushing off. "I have to go talk to him. Brandon!" She pushed through the crowd toward him.

Instinctively, I looked for Will so we could roll our eyes and wonder if Diana and Brandon had just gotten back together or if they had just broken up again. But then I remembered that Will wasn't there. I loved him, and told him so, but he hated me. I ruined his life.

My dad's car was in the driveway when I got home from school on Friday. I found him in his office, packing some things in a white corrugated banker's box. "Hello, sweetheart."

He held out his arms for me and had a pitying look on his face, but I didn't move. "What are you doing here?" I asked.

"I came to see you. To explain."

"There's nothing to explain. You left us," I said, not even trying to hide the disgust in my voice.

"I left your mother, not you."

"You don't want me."

"Of course I do, Lily. I love you more than anything."

"If that's true, then don't leave Mom. Figure out how to make it work. Do it for me." The venom in my voice turned to pleading. "Daddy, please. How could you do this to her?"

My father sighed. "Your mother will be very well taken care of. I've instructed my lawyer to let her keep the house, her car, and the time share. I'm offering her a very generous settlement, plus monthly alimony. Enough that she won't have to get a job. Your mother can continue living as she did before."

"Except she'll be alone." I swiped away angry tears before they fell.

He looked like he was about to cry himself. "Your mom and I have been having trouble for a long time." Unable to look at me, he dumped more files into the box. "I tried to make it work. I even suggested counseling, but she wouldn't go. She thought it would look bad. Now we both have a chance to be happy. It's a relief. Your mom will realize that soon. And you'll be happier because your parents are happier."

I couldn't say anything to that. Of course my mother would think going to a marriage counselor would look bad. We'd all been pretty miserable. And right now, my father was so sad, so defeated. I almost felt sorry for him, but then I remembered. "You lied to me."

He looked startled. "I've never lied to you."

"You said you would give the Dustons money."

"I did give them money. A lot of money."

"Yeah, but the deal was that in return, you wouldn't take any more of their land. But you took *all* of it! Their entire farm!"

"I couldn't just *give* them all that money. I needed something in exchange. I need to expand the plant if Agri-So is going to remain competitive. Buying Duston Farm was cheaper than building a new plant outside of town. This way I can keep our employees in Ryland, and I can hire even more. This business deal is good for the whole town. Don and Sandra Duston know that. That farm was bleeding money for the past decade. Now Don is back at Agri-So and he has a steady income for the first time in fifteen years. Quite a good one at that. They can afford to send Will to college now." He blinked at me, hopeful. "They were pleased, Lily. They're happy about this."

"Will's not happy. He's never going to forgive me. You don't know what you did, Dad. You ruined everything for him. And for me," I added.

Dad put the final file in the bankers box and hoisted it into his arms. "I know it seems like it now," he said, "but I'm not a bad guy, Lily. One day you'll see this is all for the best."

I thought of my mother, collapsed on the floor, sobbing in despair. I thought of Will, betrayed and furious. I thought of my acceptance letter to CFGU, crumpled up in my globe.

"I'll die before that happens," I told him.

CHAPTER FORTY-NINE

EVER ~ PRESENT DAY

Keith comes over extra early on Friday morning to escort me to school and gives me a bouquet of red roses and a long, wet kiss. Then I remember: it's April 5th. My birthday. I'm eighteen years old today.

Before we leave, my father calls from the road to wish me a happy birthday.

"Are you almost home?" I ask him, hoping Keith doesn't hear the desperation and hopelessness in my voice.

Keith doesn't react, but Dad must hear something. He says yes, he's been driving straight home since the moment he got the call about the carbon monoxide leak, and he'll be here by lunchtime today. We'll celebrate my birthday tonight. He'll call someone to check the furnace. He won't accept overnight hauls anymore so he can be home with us from now on. Before he hangs up, he promises that everything will be better.

I don't know how he can keep that promise.

Since I made that deal with Chief Paladino, I've done what I'm supposed to do: I go to school, I go home. I take care of Joey. I'm devoted to Keith. I help Courtney with her plans for the Little Warriors Training Camp. I don't contact Ash, and he doesn't contact me. I don't try to find Lily's killer. I don't try to save Vinnie Morrison.

Principal Duston knows. He called me "*Lily.*" He knows I used to be her. He *must* have killed her. I was right about him all along. Chief Paladino probably knows too. His patrol car circles around my block every night.

Today is my birthday. I was born eighteen years ago on April 5th at 9:48 p.m. A few seconds before that, Lily Summerhays was murdered.

What else happened on this day eighteen years ago? What was Lily doing? Did she feel it, some sense of doom, that it would be her last day alive? Did Vinnie Morrison have a feeling that it would be his last day of freedom? What was Paladino doing? Principal Duston? What was Lily's *real* killer doing on this day?

I'm the age Lily was when she was murdered. Eighteen. A part of me hoped, on the anniversary of her death, that I'd remember more of her last moments, that some kind of portal would open up and allow me to remember more than the terror, the rumbled words "*You left me no choice,*" and the teary, blurred sight of the hatchet tattoo and the pink diamond paperweight. Even a few extra seconds. Even one extra second.

But no, try as I might, despite opening myself up to the deathpain and embracing it, I have no new memories.

Vinnie Morrison is going to be executed by lethal injection, just after the clock strikes midnight, exactly one week from today.

Guilt punches me in the gut when I see Ash in the hallway at school. I've been avoiding eye contact with him, but I can't help looking at him now. He glances at me expectantly, like he's hoping I'll talk to him, but when I don't, he slips into his physics classroom.

I try to squelch the guilt. Ash is smart. *Really* smart, when he isn't being a stubborn jerk. He'll figure out how to save his dad. He'll just have to do it without my help. He has to understand that I have to keep Joey safe.

Later, as I pretend to listen to my AP Lit teacher, my phone vibrates. Keith, probably, checking on me for the sixth time that day, or Courtney. But I'm relieved to see it's a call from an area code I don't recognize. Spam. A spam call is better than having to force cheerfulness and lies into my voice every time Keith calls me. I ignore the call.

During our lunch hour, Courtney presents me with a birthday cupcake and a promise of a girls-night-in next week, then drags me outside to the baseball field. Now that I'm back with Keith, it's like our fight never happened. The Little Warriors Training Camp is tomorrow and she wants to double-check that we have everything ready to go. "I took your idea and invited all of the former state champions to play in an exhibition game," she says. "A lot of them are coming. The ones who live close by, anyway. I didn't give the out-of-towners enough notice. Maybe next year. We'll be in college, but you'll be living at home, and I'll try to come back for it."

She's so excited, chatting away, but I'm dreading the training camp. I'll be surrounded by multiple state champions, all with a crossed-hatchet tattoo on their wrist, and any one of them could have killed Lily. And to keep Joey safe and Ash out of jail, I won't be able to do anything about it.

I'm helping Courtney straighten the banner on the right outfield fence when I see a man in a suit rushing over. As he gets closer, I see the dimple in his chin, and I immediately go rigid.

Seth Siegel, my dad's boss, and the one who told Paladino that he saw Ash and me break into Miss Buckley's house. What is he doing here, at the high school, in the middle of the day?

Instinctively, I look for a place to hide, but we're out in the middle of the baseball field, surrounded by a chain-link fence. He's heading straight for me. "Hey! Ever!" he shouts, waving and picking up his pace.

"What does he want?" Courtney asks, blowing the bangs from her eyes. "Why is he calling for *you*?"

He jogs over to us, breathless. "Found you," he says, putting his hands on his knees, panting. "Finally. Your father—I'm sorry to have to tell you—"

My heart drops to my feet. "My dad? Did something happen?"

He exhales. "Accident. Drove into a viaduct. Fell asleep behind the wheel, they think. The cops saw Siegel Freight on the truck and called me."

"An accident?" My voice is high and squeaky, and I can't possibly be hearing him right.

"Is he okay?" Court asks.

"He's alive," he says. "But unconscious. Lost a lot of blood. Broken bones. Internal injuries. They took him to a hospital in Quincy, Illinois. He's in surgery." He reaches out his hand for me. "You should be there. Come on, I'll take you."

And that's when I see it peeking out from the sleeve of his suit: a crossed-hatchet tattoo.

I back away, shaking my head. "I don't believe you." This is some kind of trap. It has to be. He turned Ash and me in to the chief. He's got a hatchet tattoo. Did *he* kill Lily Summerhays?

"Ever, what are you saying?" Court asks. "You need to get to the hospital."

Mr. Siegel comes closer, palms up in innocence. I step back until I hit the fence. Cornered. "I don't believe you," I say again.

"Why don't you try calling him?" Courtney says. "Maybe there was a mistake."

I nod. Yes. Good idea. My fingers are trembling a little, but I pull out my phone and dial Dad. It rings and goes to voice mail.

Then I remember that he said he'd be home by lunchtime today. It's lunchtime now. Maybe he got home a little early and turned off his phone so he could sleep. I call our landline, but it rings and rings until the answering machine picks up.

There's a little voice mail icon in the notification bar on my phone. From the call I got today from the unknown area code, the call I assumed was spam.

My vision tunnels. "No. No, no, no, no, no, no, no." I force my fingers to behave and play my voice mail.

"Ever Abrams, my name is Vonda Richards, and I'm calling from Mercy Hospital in Quincy, Illinois. You're listed as the emergency contact in the phone of a Mr. Benjamin Abrams. He was brought in this morning..." The bored, nasally lady repeats the same information that Seth Siegel just told me. Accident. Unconscious. Broken. Blood. Surgery.

Courtney takes the phone from me. "It's true," I tell her. "He was in an accident, a bad one, and he's in surgery. I have to go."

"Come on," Mr. Siegel says, reaching for me again. "My car is waiting. Let's go."

"I'm not going anywhere with you," I say. He was truthful about my dad, but that doesn't erase his hatchet tattoo. He could be Lily's killer.

"Ever, he's just trying to help." Courtney throws Mr. Siegel an apologetic look. "I think she's in shock. I should get my dad. He can take her. Or her boyfriend, Keith."

I nod. Anyone but Seth Siegel and his hatchet tattoo. Keith will take me to the hospital in Quincy. He has to. Keith is sticking to me like glue.

I try to make a mental list, but my thoughts are scrambled, tumbled, muddled. "How long will we be in Quincy, I wonder? How long is the drive? I have a test on Monday. Do you think I'll miss it? Oh no, the training camp is tomorrow! Should I..." What was I about to say? I don't remember. "I need to get Joey." My breath hitches. "He's only five. He can't lose both parents—"

"He won't. Your dad will be fine." Courtney grabs my arms. "Don't worry about the training camp, don't worry about your test.

Go get Keith. He'll take you to your dad. Everything will be fine, I promise. Now go."

I give her a hug, a tight one, and then I run.

It's fifth period. Keith has geometry fifth period. I race inside to the mathematics wing and find myself at the opposite side of the building, in the science wing. The AP Physics classroom.

I burst inside and immediately head to the only person I want. The only person I need. I ignore the teacher's shout and dash to the back of the room, to Ash, and sob.

"My dad," I blubber. "After the gas leak, he promised me that he wasn't going to accept any more overnight hauls—"

"*Gas* leak?" Ash says.

"He was supposed to be home tonight and every night from now on"—my breath hitches, and I sob—"and he drove all day and all night to get home, that's why he fell asleep behind the wheel"—another sob—"and now he's in surgery and it's bad, and I need to get to Quincy now, right now!"

I heave another sob, and through my tears, I see Ash stand, slowly, his expression grim. "Okay," he rumbles. "Let's go."

CHAPTER FIFTY

LILY ~ EIGHTEEN YEARS AGO

Dad left with his
stupid
boxes to go live in a
stupid
apartment across
stupid
town. I stayed home to be with my mom, but she was at a meeting with a
stupid
divorce lawyer. It was just me, alone in the house.

I drummed my fingers on the phone in my bedroom. I wanted to call Will. I wanted to call Diana. But all of the Warriors and the Batgirls were at a party at Jonah Caplan's house. I wasn't going to CFGU, so there was no reason why I needed to stay home and behave for my parents anymore, but I didn't feel like partying tonight. I had nothing to celebrate.

The doorbell rang, the singsong melody echoing through the empty house. I jogged downstairs and peeked through the peephole. Diana, grinning. I almost

melted

with relief. I needed my best friend tonight. I opened the door and let her in.

"Here you are, Lily!" She wore heels, tight jeans, a silk top, and a Warriors cap on her head, backward. "I've been looking all over for you. Why aren't you at the party?"

I shrugged. "Not in the mood. Did you walk here alone?"

"It's just a couple blocks. I need to talk to you. Here, I brought a present for you. Because I love you, Lily, so much. You're my best friend, my very best friend in the whole world, and I don't want you to be upset." She thrust a pink gift bag at me. Whatever was inside of it was heavy.

"You're drunk," I say. Jonah's party must have been fun. Good thing my mother wasn't home.

"Just a little," she whispered loudly, then giggled. "Open your present."

I brought her inside to the living room and sat her down. I reached into the pink bag, moved the tissue paper out of the way, and withdrew a huge, pink paperweight shaped like a diamond. Engraved on the flat part on top were the words *Gems are precious, friends are priceless.*

"This is so sweet, Diana, thanks," I said. I tossed it in my hand a few times before placing it on the coffee table. Heavy.

"It's true, what it says. You're priceless to me," she said. "We're going to be friends forever, right? No matter what. You could tell me anything and I wouldn't get mad at you. And you won't get mad at me, no matter what I'm about to tell you right now, right?"

"Of course not. What is it?"

She shook her head, her cheeks flushed by alcohol. "No, I can't do it. You're going to be so mad at me. You're going to hate me."

"Diana, stop. I could never be mad at you. I will never hate you. Tell me."

"Promise you won't be mad? Promise you won't hate me?"

"I promise." I pointed to the paperweight. "Friends are priceless. And we're best friends."

"Okay." She exhaled. "Well, you know how Brandon and I have been fighting a lot lately?"

"Did you break up again?" I didn't remember when or if they'd gotten back together. It was impossible to keep track.

She shook her head. "He was fielding offers from the pros, and I was staying here in Indiana to go to Griffin. We didn't want a long-distance relationship, and we didn't want to break up. So we were fighting because we didn't know what to do. But a few days ago..." She took another breath. "The Yankees made him an official offer. He can't announce it until the press conference, but he told me."

"That's great," I said. Great, but not unexpected. The Yankees and the Astros had been scouting him for months. The Yankees got him, apparently.

"The way it works is," Diana continued, "all new players have to start on their Triple-A team in Florida for a year or two, and then they move up to the majors."

"Okay..."

"But the thing is," Diana said, squeezing her eyes shut. "The thing is, he asked me to go to Florida with him and I said *yes*." It came out like one word.

"Diana, that's fantastic! Congratulations! Why would I be upset about that?"

She groaned and covered her face with her hands. "Because we were supposed to be roommates at Griffin! We were going to buy matching comforters and get one of those mini refrigerators and string twinkle lights on the ceiling. And now we can't, and you have to go to Griffin all alone, and you'll probably end up with some mean, weird girl as your roommate, and I would be so upset with you if *you* did that to *me*." She cried into her hands. "I'm sorry, Lily! You must hate me so much. Please don't hate me!"

"I don't hate you." I was disappointed, but I couldn't hate her. I couldn't be angry at her. Up until last night, I'd planned on abandoning *her* so I could travel the world with CFGU. If my father hadn't left my mother, Diana and I would be on opposite sides of this conversation.

"Do you promise? You're not mad at me?"

"Diana, the only way I'd be upset is if you stayed here because of me. And now, it actually frees me up to live at home instead of in the dorms."

"Why? Because I can't be your roommate?"

"No, because of my mom. My dad left—" And then I noticed something. "Di, that Warriors hat you're wearing. Is it new?"

CHAPTER FIFTY-ONE

EVER ~ PRESENT DAY

Ash keeps a tight hold of my hand as we rush to the school's back exit, burst through the doors, and dash to the parking lot. Principal Duston is probably watching us. Maybe even Paladino is watching us. But I don't care. I'm back with Ash, my hand in his. Safe. Strong. *Right.* But he still won't look me in the eye. His lips are turned down.

I stop. "Ash."

He tries to pull his hand away, but I hold tight.

"Ash," I say again. "I'm sorry." I explain everything that happened since he was arrested three days ago. Running after him to the police station, turning down Paladino's offer, Cheeks dying, Joey and me getting sick, the carbon monoxide poisoning. Accepting Paladino's second offer. "I didn't want to do it, but it was the only way to get you out of jail. The only way to keep Joey safe."

"I figured it was something like that," he says gently, and finally, when he raises his eyes, they are warm, earnest, kind. "You did the right thing. They're watching you, you know. Paladino mostly, but Duston drives by your place at least once a night."

I nod. Then it occurs to me that Ash can only know this because he's been watching me too.

I want to wrap my arms around him and kiss him, crush my lips to his, but he says, "We need to go." He glances at the building. The door could open any second, and Principal Duston could come running after us.

Ash zips me away on his motorcycle to my house, where I hurriedly pack overnight bags for myself and for Joey, then run next door to get him. He's playing happily with Hayden and the other daycare kids, and I quietly, hurriedly, explain to Mrs. Yost what's happening. She offers to keep Joey for the weekend. They're leaving tonight to go camping over in Forest Grove, and Hayden would love to have a friend along. At first I say *no*, then change my mind. Pulling Joey out of daycare unexpectedly and driving for hours, only to sit in a hospital for who-knows-how-long to wait for his only remaining parent to wake up—*if* he wakes up, oh God—will be traumatic for him. Ash and I can't take him on the bike anyway, so we'd have to take a Greyhound.

And most importantly, I broke the deal that I made with the chief. Once Keith finds out that I left Ryland with Ash, he'll tell Paladino. Paladino will assume Joey is with Ash and me, but Joey will really be camping with Hayden, happy and safe.

I take Mrs. Yost up on her offer and thank her profusely, then go talk to Joey. I tell him that Daddy got stuck a few hours away and I need to go get him, and he's going to stay with Hayden and go camping for the weekend. He's so excited that he dances through the big hug and million kisses I give him, then he squirms out of my arms and runs off to join his friend.

Finally, Ash and I are back on his bike, whipping down Van Buren Road. It's not long before I realize we're not headed west toward Illinois. We're going east, toward—

"The airfield?" I shout into his ear.

"Flying is the quickest way to get to Quincy," Ash shouts over his shoulder. "It would take almost five hours to get there on my bike. If we fly, we can be there in sixty minutes."

"What about a commercial plane? It's safer."

"It will take an hour just to drive to the airport in Indianapolis, another hour to get through security, at least one layover, and about $500 that neither of us have. Ever, trust me. I can fly you to your father quickly and safely."

He sounds so confident. I squeeze my arms tighter around him, not because I'm afraid of falling off the bike—I'm not—but to show him that I *do* trust him. I trust him completely.

Ash's boss, Javier, is surprised to see us in his hangar in the middle of a school day, but my tears must be enough to convince him that we don't need a plane to go on a little joy ride. He turns pale and tells Ash to take the Piper. Frowning and arms crossed, he watches from the hangar as Ash does a safety check and we climb aboard. Ash radios in his flight plan to the airfield in Quincy while I strap the seatbelt as tightly as it will go. I can't believe I'm about to fly in this thing. I remind myself that riding a motorcycle is the most dangerous mode of transportation, and I don't have a problem doing that anymore. I even enjoy it. I can easily fly in a plane.

Still, I can't help gripping the armrests as Ash steers us to the runway. The plane goes faster and faster, the engine roaring, and the plane inclines. The back wheels leave the ground. We're in the air. We're flying.

"Open your eyes," Ash says.

I didn't even realize they were closed.

I don't look out the windows; I don't want to see how high up we are. Instead, I watch Ash, sure and confident as he pulls the levers, even smiling a little. It's all so easy to him. He's at home up here in the air. I can easily imagine him flying a rocket ship into the stars.

I relax enough to release my fingers from the armrest and sneak a peek to the ground below. From up here, the world looks green and small and peaceful. The roads look like ribbons and the fields look like a patchwork quilt. This is why Ash loves flying. It's so easy to forget all the problems down there on the ground. It's just us and the sky.

The plane lurches. Ash chuckles, extinguishing my panic before it can fully ignite. "Just an air pocket," he says. "Nothing to worry about."

The engine sputters, and this time Ash's eyebrows knit. He speaks into his radio. "Javier? Acknowledge, Soto Airfield."

Now the panic flares full force. "What is it?" I ask, my chest tight, my throat closing up. "What's wrong?"

"It feels like we're running out of fuel, but it says the tank is full." He flicks the fuel gauge with his finger and it doesn't budge. "I'm sure everything's fine, but I'm turning around and going back. Sorry. Just a quick check on the ground and then we'll take off again."

Ash turns the plane, making a smooth U-turn. I release a shaky breath. Ash knows what he's doing. We're going to be o—

The plane dips, lurches, drops, and I scream. "Damn it," Ash mutters, his knuckles white as he grips the wheel. He takes to the radio again. "Mayday, mayday. Minimum fuel. Losing altitude. Soto Airfield, please acknowledge. Javier, acknowledge. Javier? Javier!"

Javier.

The engine sputters yet again, and in a burst of clarity I understand why the plane is going down. "Ash," I whisper, "does Javier have a tattoo on his wrist?"

He gives me a quick sideways glance, his jaw tight. "Yeah. Two crossed hatchets."

CHAPTER FIFTY-TWO

LILY ~ EIGHTEEN YEARS AGO

The maroon and gold colors on Diana's Warriors baseball hat were bright, not faded. It was clean, not dusted with dirt. "That's a brand new hat, isn't it?" I asked.

Diana took it off her head. "Yeah, Brandon lost his, so he's been wearing his old ratty one from last year. I bought him a new one today at school." She giggled again. "He gave it right back to me. Isn't he the sweetest?"

I blinked at her. "Brandon lost his hat."

"Yeah."

"*Brandon* lost his hat."

"Yeah, that's what I said." She cocked her head at me. "What's the big deal?"

The room
narrowed. I felt the
blood

drain from my cheeks. "When did he lose it? When was the last time he wore it?"

She pursed her lips and looked up at the ceiling, thinking. "I don't know. Four weeks ago, I guess? He's been going crazy looking for it."

"Four weeks ago was the night I hung out at your house and on the way home I drove my car into the mailbox. What was Brandon doing that night?"

"He had a meeting with the recruiter for the Yankees," Diana said.

"He lost his hat that night," I confirmed. "You're sure?"

"Yeah. He called me the next day and asked if I'd seen it."

"Because he lost it the night before."

"Yes," Diana said. "Lily, why are you being so weird?"

"Did he say anything to you about a car? A blue Viper?"

She let out an impatient huff. "I don't know if it's a Viper, but yeah, he's getting a car as part of his signing bonus with the Yankees. He said he drove one around that night, but he didn't like it so he gave it back. He hasn't had time to choose a new one."

"So he came back from his meeting with the Yankees, without his hat, and without a car?"

"He was more upset about losing his hat than not getting the car," she said. "He said he would just pick out a car when he gets to Florida."

"The night he had that meeting was the night Neal was killed," I said. "I found the car that hit him. A blue Viper. There was a Warriors hat inside it. I've been trying to find the owner of that hat."

Diana laughed again, but this time it had a shaky tone to it. "Neal wasn't hit by a car. He slipped off the bridge and drowned."

"No. Neal would never have been on that bridge, especially not alone and at night. I *knew* he was killed," I said, victorious. "I found tire skid marks and pieces of a broken headlight near the movie theater. And Hot Tamales, Neal's favorite candy."

"That doesn't prove—"

"Diana. Listen to me. I found the car with the broken headlight in that old barn at Sutton Farm, near the creek. It was a blue Viper, brand new. Inside that car were more Hot Tamales and Brandon's baseball hat."

I waited for Diana to understand, but she just shook her head. "What are you saying?"

"I'm saying Brandon hit Neal with that car, Diana. He killed him."

She went pale, deathly so. "No."

"It was an accident, I'm sure, but Brandon killed Neal. And then he dumped his body in the creek and hid the car in the barn until he could get rid of it." I sent Neal a silent message. *I figured it out, Neal. It was Brandon Lennox. I'll make sure he pays.*

"No," Diana said again. "You're wrong. Brandon would never do something like that."

"I'm not wrong, Di." She looked so distraught that I pulled her in for a hug. "I'm so sorry." I'd help her get through this final breakup. My heart ached for her, but hope bloomed there as well. I needed to tell Will. He'd know then that I wasn't lying to him. He'd have to believe me, at least about Neal. Maybe we'd get back together.

Everything was going to be okay. For me, anyway. But not for Neal, and not for Brandon.

And not for Diana either. She wasn't crying or hugging me back, and when I pulled away, she was frozen, clutching the hat with white knuckles, completely sober now. "You're just jealous."

"What?"

"You're jealous because you've never had a boyfriend and you're stuck here in this stupid boring town that you hate." She was calm, slow, deliberate. "And I'm leaving, going to Florida with my boyfriend, a future baseball star. That's what this is. You're making this up because you're jealous. You're so jealous of me that you're trying to ruin Brandon's career before it even starts."

"Diana, no. Just think about it. I'm sorry, I'm so sorry, but you know I'm right."

Slowly, her white face turned as red as the hat she clutched in her hands. "No. Shut up! You're lying! You have to be lying!"

I needed to show her the hat I had hidden in my room. Brandon's hat. She'd recognize it and know I was telling the truth. "Wait here, okay? I'll show you." I stood and took a step toward the staircase.

"No!" Diana howled as she grabbed my arm and yanked me back, swinging me around. I tumbled, fell, landed hard as my head slammed into the fireplace hearth. An immediate shot of pain burst in my skull, then it seeped through the rest of my body. Blood,

warm

sticky

thick

dribbled down my face, stinging my eyes,

it hurts it hurts

my head

hurts so much

Through a veil of red, I saw Diana kneeling next to me, wavy, fading, crying, screaming. "OhmyGodohmyGodohmyGod, Lily! I didn't mean... Lily? Lily, answer me. Lily?"

"Di..." I said, but my mouth was filled with

blood

like copper,

I was drowning in it, and everything went

gray

and

far

away.

CHAPTER FIFTY-THREE

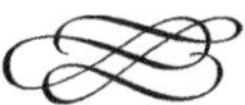

EVER ~ PRESENT DAY

Ash and I are falling, dropping, plummeting from the sky. The ground gets closer and closer. "Soto Airfield, acknowledge," he repeats into the radio. "Mayday. Minimum fuel. Losing altitude."

"He's not going to answer." I'm breathless as I grip the armrest. "Javier sabotaged the plane and waited for you to fly it. He's got the tattoo. He killed Lily."

Clenching his teeth with the effort, Ash pulls back on the steering yoke. We glide, slowly, gracefully, riding an air wave, and he whoops with victory.

We're going to be okay. He's going to land the plane, slowly, softly, safely. He can do it. Ash will save us.

The radio buzzes with static, and suddenly Javier's panicked voice fills the cabin, coming in and out. "Morrison—sorry—had to do it—said he'd destroy me—threatened my daughter—had to do it—so sorry—"

And then the plane rocks from side to side, the wings dipping sharply. My ears pop painfully. My stomach flips. Ash swears and pulls on the yoke again, yanking it, but we plummet.

This is it. I'm going to die, again.

I feel my jaw open wide, and I know I'm screaming, but I can't hear it. Slowly, Ash turns his head and yells something, but no sound comes from his mouth. My fingers ache from digging into the armrests. The intense rush of air pushes me back against my seat, crushing my ribs.

Five hundred people die in small plane crashes every year, and this year Ash and I will be two of them.

Please, please let my dad survive, Joey needs him, please, please, please.

We're gliding, falling, plummeting, screaming, slow and silent.

The wings of the plane brush over treetops, and Ash dives at me. I can't hear him, but I see him shout *Get down!* I see his terror as he grabs me, bends me, pushes my head between my knees and covers me with his body, and I can't see, can't hear, my lungs hurt, my head hurts, my ears hurt, my heart hurts, it's my eighteenth birthday and I don't want to die today, I don't want to die this way, and there's a tremendous, slow, silent crash as the plane hits the ground and then there's

nothing.

CHAPTER FIFTY-FOUR

LILY ~ EIGHTEEN YEARS AGO

Through a tunnel of muffled sound, I heard deep panting. I couldn't see much, and it hurt to move. Pain surrounded me, suffocated me. My head was bleeding, split open, I could feel it, and the pain radiated outward, encompassing everything. Diana was crying, panicking, pleading with someone who was standing over me, close, breathing hard. Did the ambulance come? I didn't remember hearing sirens. Why was the guy yelling at Diana? Why was she screaming *no, no, please no*?

"Di?" I tried to say, but it came out as a gurgled groan. I choked on blood. Using all my strength, I pried open my eyes. One opened a tiny bit. One wouldn't open at all.

A fist was hovering above me, trembling, clutching the pink diamond paperweight that Diana had given me a few minutes ago. *Gems are precious, friends are priceless.*

Under the fist was a tattoo of two crossed hatchets.

"Will?" I begged. "Is that you?" Blood soaked my face, stinging my eyes, blinding me, and my plea came out garbled. "I'm hurt. Help me. Please."

"I don't want to do this," the voice rumbled, "but you left me no choice." He panted furiously, once, twice, like he was gathering courage, summoning adrenaline, and he raised the paperweight.

Oh my God. He wanted to kill me, he was going to kill me, I needed to run, hide, protect myself, but my body wouldn't move. No, no, no, no, no, no, please, please—

He erupted in a primal, animalistic howl as he slammed the paperweight into my head, then he did it again

and

again

and

again.

As I slipped away, the hatchet moved slower, like it was moving through water. But the pain never receded, and though it slowed with each second, the hatchet never stopped. I heard the sickening crushing sounds as my skull caved in, I heard the blood as it spattered on the fireplace hearth, and then, as the blows rained down one after another, everything grew quieter, and darker.

I was dying, again. Lily Summerhays was dying.

I love you, Mom. I love you, Dad. When I come back, in my next life, I promise I'll do everything right.

"You left me no choice!" my killer roared again. He howled, and the pink diamond paperweight and the crossed-hatchet tattoo came at me with one last smash, and

everything

stopped

and became

nothing.

CHAPTER FIFTY-FIVE

EVER ~ PRESENT DAY

Crickets chirp.

This tells me three things:

1. It's night time.
2. I'm alive. I did not die.
3. I'm still me. Ever Abrams.

What about Ash? Is he alive? I survived, but did he?

What about my dad, in the hospital in Quincy? Is he in surgery? Is *he* alive?

I try to move, but I can't. "Ash?" I croak. It takes all of my strength to say that. All of my strength to open my eyelids. All of my strength to turn my head.

Dim moonlight illuminates the cockpit. I can only see Ash's silhouette, slumped over in his seat, chin to chest. The dashboard is dark. The windshield is cracked like a spider web. We're surrounded by tall trees and foliage—we landed in a forest. The plane's wing on my side is broken, angling us slightly to the right. Crickets chirp endlessly. The air smells like dirt and grass. It's cold.

No one has come for us. No wailing sirens, no one shouting our names. Did no one witness the plane fall from the sky? Or are Javier and Paladino covering up reports of the crash? Maybe they assume we're dead. Or maybe they're on their way to finish the job.

"Ash," I say again, then cough. It hurts. My chest, my head.

Ash doesn't move. Is he breathing? Slowly, painfully, I reach across to put my hand on his shoulder. I go statue-still, waiting, hoping, praying. Finally, I feel a small movement: he's breathing. Shallow, slow.

I put my hand on his neck to feel for his pulse. Like his breath, it's shallow and slow. His neck is sticky and wet, and my hand comes back bloody.

I twist, slowly, and find the lock for my seatbelt. I press it, but the belt won't retract. I'm stuck in my seat.

My head hurts. I feel for blood, but the only place I'm bleeding is from a cut on my cheek, which is swollen. The side of my head is tender. It must have slammed against the side of the plane when we crashed. My neck hurts too. Whiplash. My ribs are sore. Gently, I press on them. Nothing broken, I don't think, but definitely bruised.

I move my arms and legs, wiggle my fingers and toes. No broken bones, and my circulation is good.

I'm fine. If it weren't for the jammed seatbelt, I could walk away from this plane crash in one piece. Ash saved my life. But did he save his own? "Ash," I croak again. "Please wake up."

No answer.

I need to call 911. I need to call my dad. I need to call Mrs. Yost and check on Joey. Keith has probably called me a million times, and Courtney too, angry that I went off with Ash. The contents of my purse are scattered all over the floor of the plane, but where's my phone? Did it slide under my seat? I try again to unlock my seatbelt, but it won't click open. I feel around on the floor with my foot. It touches something flat and smooth, and carefully, slowly, I nudge it closer, closer... That's it. I can just reach it with my fingertips. I grab it and turn it on.

The screen is cracked. It won't even light up.

I reach for Ash again, ignoring the blood to feel his pulse. It's slower now, much slower than it was before. I put my hand on his chest. He's hardly breathing.

I shake him, as much as I can trapped in my seat, but still, he doesn't wake up. I emit a panicked whine as adrenaline seizes me and I pull at the seatbelt, howling and tugging, jabbing the lock, again and again and again, and finally, finally, it comes loose. I wiggle out of the seatbelt and scramble to Ash, feeling for his pulse again. "Ash."

It takes a long time, but finally, there's a tiny, weak pulse. Then nothing.

"Ash, breathe! Wake up!" The plane has us at a slight angle, and I can't get him out of his seat to do CPR. "Ash!" I hit his chest as hard as I can. His head wobbles upon impact, blood dripping from his mouth, but he doesn't wake up.

A great sob escapes from my throat as I beg him to please wake up, please, please, please don't die. I grab him, bury my head into his chest, and weep. He's dying. He's close, I can tell, and there's nothing I can do to save him.

And then I realize... it's okay. He'll be okay.

I lift my head. Gently, I kiss his cheek. "Don't be scared." I don't know if he can hear me, but I don't want him to be scared, because there's nothing to be scared of. "If you die, you're going to be reborn right away, into the next baby that's born closest to where we are, wherever that is. You'll have a new life, and a new family, a family that will love you so much. As much as I love you now."

He's breathing so slowly. Is he breathing at all? I move my fingers to his pulse. So slow.

I smooth his hair, caress his cheek. "You know how I know that you're going to be reborn right away?" I whisper. "Because it happens to me. Every time. I remember my past lives. My past deaths, really, just the last moments. I was Lily Summerhays before I was Ever Abrams. I was born a few seconds after she died. That's how I knew about Principal Duston. It wasn't a conversation I overheard between him and Miss Buckley. That was a lie. I saw his tattoo, during the scholarship interview, and the person who killed Lily had that same tattoo. That crossed-hatchet tattoo was the last thing I saw—the last thing Lily saw—before she died. Until I saw it at the interview, I didn't know that Principal Duston had that tattoo, and I didn't know that your father didn't. And now I don't know if it was Principal Duston who killed Lily, and I don't know who killed Miss Buckley, maybe it was Paladino, or Javier, or all three, but now they're trying to kill us and it looks like they've succeeded. Ash, I'm so sorry."

My voice cracks. I'm getting off track. Closing in on panic and despair. I want to soothe him, not make him feel worse. I calm myself, then kiss him again. I murmur, "Before I was Lily, I was someone else. And someone else before that. And on and on, for hundreds of years. When I die, I'll soon be someone else. You too, Ash. Your next life is going to be amazing. If we both die tonight, here, we'll be reborn close together. We'll be together in our next lives. I *promise.* I'll love you in our next lives as much as I love you in this one. So it's okay. Don't be scared. I love you."

I kiss him again, then watch him. No response. His eyes are closed and he doesn't move.

I place my hand on his chest, right over his heart. I put my lips on his neck, right over his pulse.

I wait for his lungs to expand and contract. I wait for his heart to beat. I wait for his pulse.

And I wait.

And I wait.

CHAPTER FIFTY-SIX

EVER ~ PRESENT DAY

There's wind in my hair. Crickets chirp. No light penetrates my closed eyelids. The wind is gentle, slow, soothing, warm. Like a caress. And then it whispers, "Ever."

A warm breeze on my neck. The wind touches the top of my head, the gentlest kiss. "Ever, wake up," it says.

Slowly, I open my eyes. My fingers hurt from gripping Ash's shirt over his heart.

"Ever," the wind says again, low.

I bolt upright in disbelief. "Ash?"

He's alive, he's alive. The moonlight illuminates him leaning back in his seat, hair tousled, dried blood on his chin. My sudden movement jostled him and he grimaces, but it turns into a small relieved smile. "Hey, beautiful."

I immediately start bawling. "You're alive?"

"Apparently," he says. "So are you."

"I thought you were dying. I thought *I* was dying. It felt the same."

"Same as what?" he asks.

He didn't hear my earlier confession, or if he did, he doesn't remember. I don't know if I'm relieved or disappointed. "Nothing."

He grimaces again as he shifts in his seat, trying to push himself straight. "You okay? Any injuries?"

"Um..." I wipe my eyes and take inventory. "Bruised ribs, I think, and I hit my head. Your mouth is bleeding."

"Yeah, I bit my lip. It was a hard landing."

"All that blood from a split lip? No internal bleeding?"

"Internal bleeding, I don't think so. Internal screaming, definitely yes. That was pretty scary, even for me." He cringes again. "I pulled my arm from its socket too. Can't move it." He looks away, out the window, and curses to himself. "I can't believe Javier sabotaged the plane."

"He was forced to do it," I say.

"He told me to take this specific plane. '*Take the Piper*,' he said. If it was just me, that's one thing. But you were with me! He told me to take the Piper and then he stood there and watched you get into the plane with me and let us fly off, knowing..." He punches the dashboard and flinches in pain. "I fucking trusted him."

Everyone Ash has ever trusted has eventually betrayed him. Even me, when I went back to Keith. Well, I will never betray him again. I put my hand on his leg to comfort him, and he doesn't move away.

"Someone made Javier do it," I say. "It had to be Paladino. Javier said the guy threatened his daughter. That's Paladino's M.O.—threatening little kids."

Ash closes his eyes and sighs heavily. "No one's come for us, which means Javier must have contacted the airfield in Quincy and canceled my flight plan. We were flying over the forest when we went down, so it's possible no one saw the crash. But more likely, Paladino is covering it up."

"That's what I'm thinking too. We need to get help." Except for the moonlight and stars in the black sky, all I can see out the window are the trees surrounding us. "Can we get out of this plane? Can you walk? What time is it? I wonder where we are."

He chuckles, then winces again. "Yes, we can get out of this plane, yes, I can walk, judging from the stars' position it's around 10 p.m. and we're not too far from Ryland. We were only in the air for a few minutes and were heading back when we went down."

He tries to open the door but falls back into his seat with a groan. "You'll have to do it."

I twist toward the door and pull the latch, gritting my teeth against the pain in my ribs. The door is too heavy to lift, though. It won't budge.

"The hydraulic cylinder must be busted," Ash says. "Damn it. We're stuck. Here, switch with me. I'll push it open with my good arm."

"No, I got it. Hold on." I swivel in my seat, place my feet flat on the door, and push. *Push.* It takes all my strength and I hurt my ribs even more, but the door finally lifts. I pull myself up and out, then carefully help Ash.

Standing next to the downed plane, surrounded by forest in the cool moonlit air, Ash and I evaluate each other, checking for injuries, making sure the other is okay. He uses his good arm to put his bad hand behind his head, then takes a deep breath and arches his back. He roars, his shoulder pops, and I scream.

"What are you doing?" I cry.

"Had to pop my arm back into its socket," he says, slowly lowering it. He rubs his shoulder, then grins. "It'll be sore for a while, but at least I can move it again."

"Come on. Let's get out of here. Paladino and Javier are probably looking for us."

Together, we trudge as fast as we can through the trees, leaving the plane behind us. It's dark, and cold, and we're in the middle of a forest somewhere in Indiana.

As we walk, I catch Ash looking up at the sky. "Wishing you were up there right now, living on Mars?"

"I don't know," he says. "Even with everything going on, I'm kind of happy here on Earth right now." His hand slides into mine, and it's warm.

He's beautiful and terrifying, fearless and vulnerable, invincible and wounded, powerful and gentle. My gaze locks into his inky black eyes. My heart is beating so fast, my breath comes in quick bursts from the exertion of trampling through the woods, and from something else. I grab him and kiss him. His cheek, then his forehead, then his neck, and damn that split lip, because I want to kiss him everywhere.

I finally stop and rest my forehead on his chest. We breathe together. "You saved my life," I say.

With his good hand, he lifts my chin, and with his thumb he caresses my cheek, then my lips. "And you changed mine."

CHAPTER FIFTY-SEVEN

EVER ~ PRESENT DAY

Using the stars as a map, Ash navigates us away from the downed plane. "Ryland is northwest of here," he says. "But the nearest highway is east. Route 21, I think." Keeping me under his good arm, he pushes onward through the woods toward a field. "Let's head east, but we should zigzag our path in case Paladino's looking for us."

The cropped jeans and black ballet flats I'm wearing are not meant for trudging through forests and fields in the middle of the night. Ash insists I wear his jacket, saying that our quick pace is enough to keep him warm. But when I start shivering uncontrollably despite his jacket, he decides I've had enough, overruling my objections. Across the field is a barn and a few sheds. We make our way over and find a shed that's unlocked, so we hide inside it. He puts his arms around me and kisses me with slow, gentle kisses until I fall asleep.

The sun wakes us up in the morning. We both feel better after the rest, and after a half hour walk, the sound of car engines and wheels whirring on pavement tells us that we're finally close to the highway. We approach a sign that informs us that Mabel's All U Can Eat Waffle Junction is a half mile away.

Soon Ash and I are sitting in a corner booth at Mabel's, cupping mugs of coffee to warm our hands. My head throbs where I hit it in the crash, and my ribs are sore. The dried blood itches from on my cheek and I wipe it off with a napkin. Under the florescent lights, I see that Ash's lip is bruised and cut, but not split. His black hair is wind-whipped, and I don't even want to think about what mine looks like.

The waitress doesn't bat an eye at our cuts and bruises as Ash orders two breakfast skillets and six Belgian waffles for the two of us to share. I'm not hungry, but we haven't eaten since lunch yesterday and Ash insists I eat something. "We survived a murder attempt via plane crash," he rumbles. "We deserve a waffle at least."

Besides the waitress, the cook, and a couple of truck drivers, Ash and I are the only ones in the place. The TV hanging over the counter behind me is turned to the local channel, which is showing the morning news. Ash holds a glass of ice water to his lip and closes his eyes. He's in more pain than he's letting on. "I'm sorry I couldn't get you to your dad."

"I'll call the hospital to check on him. We need to get back to Ryland."

Ash gestures at the TV with his chin. "Ryland is on the news right now."

The TV shows a young blonde reporter on the baseball field behind the high school, standing next to Brandon Lennox, who's wearing his Yankees jersey and a maroon Warriors cap. "In just a couple hours Ryland's annual Little Warriors Training Camp will begin," the reporter says to the camera, "the highlight of the year for the town's young baseball players who hope to follow Brandon Lennox's path from Ryland, Indiana to Major League Baseball's Hall of Fame. Brandon, what prompted your surprise appearance this year?"

"The Training Camp started as a simple after-school clinic when I was in high school and I always had fun showing the little kids how to play," Brandon says, all smiles and charm. "Last week I was invited to attend by the girl who planned the camp this year. The daughter of my old coach, as a matter of fact. The Yankees had a game in Chicago yesterday, so I decided to stop by Ryland on my way back to New York." He tosses a baseball over his head and catches it.

I'm not surprised to see a crossed-hatchet tattoo on his wrist. Brandon Lennox is the main reason the Warriors were state champions all those years ago.

The reporter asks, "Still planning to retire after this year?"

"I've been playing major league ball for seventeen years," Brandon says, tossing the ball. "I'm an old man compared to most of my teammates." He's all lopsided smiles and flirty charm. "I thought about retiring, but I think I still have a season or two left in me."

"I'm sure your fans will be happy to hear that," the reporter says. "Any plans for after retirement?"

"Maybe coaching, maybe on-air commentary," he says. "I also want to start a support group for players and their families who are going through tough times."

"Are you talking about players like your teammate, Rob Krabowski?" the reporter asks. "How's he doing? Was it a difficult decision to turn him in?"

He turns somber. "Robbie's one of my best buddies. I gave him a chance to stop, a few chances actually, even offered to take him to rehab personally. But he wouldn't stop using. He was a danger to himself and others, driving under the influence, becoming violent. So I said to him, 'I don't want to do this, but you left me no choice.' And I turned him in...."

"You left me no choice."

My vision narrows, zeroing in on Brandon Lennox tossing the

baseball and catching it. His hatchet tattoo goes up and down, up and down, slashing through the air.

The baseball in his hand shifts, waves, changes, turns pink and sparkly and diamond-shaped, and I'm no longer in Mable's Waffle Junction. I'm bloody, hurt, sprawled on the floor, begging for my life, and Brandon towers over me, gripping the paperweight in his fist and roars *"You left me no choice."* He raises the diamond high over his head, and with a furious howl, he slams it down—

The pain, the pain, oh, God, the pain—

"Ever?" Ash says from far away. "Ever, you okay? What's wrong?"

I come back to myself. I'm clutching my head with both hands, and Ash is now next to me in the booth, frantic.

"He did it," I say, blinking the pain and the tears away. "He killed Lily."

"Brandon Lennox? How do you know it's—" He sucks in a breath. "You remember."

CHAPTER FIFTY-EIGHT

EVER ~ PRESENT DAY

I freeze, then my voice comes out all high and squeaky. "You heard me last night?"

He nods, his expression unreadable, and I want to hide behind my stack of uneaten waffles.

"I thought maybe I was dreaming it," he says. "Then I thought you made it up because you thought I was about to die. But seeing your reaction just now—you were telling the truth."

He heard my confession, and he's still with me. Still on my side. Still supporting me. "Did you hear *everything*?" Even the *I love you* part?

"Everything." He tucks my hair behind my ear, lets his hand linger, brushes my cheek with his thumb. His lips are so close to mine. His eyelashes are so long. His eyes so dark, so deep. I suck in a breath, and suddenly his lips are on mine, and then—

"Ow!" He pulls back with a hiss and puts his hand to his lip. "Forgot it's cut." It's bleeding again.

"Are you okay?"

He grins as he presses a napkin to his lip. "I'm good, yeah. But we should probably hold off on that for a while. But not forever," he adds, grinning. "While we wait for my lip to heal, we should probably discuss the tiny little fact that you remember your past lives."

"My past *deaths*," I clarify. "It's okay if you don't believe me—"

He holds up a palm. "Just tell me."

I give him a brief history. It feels good, freeing, to tell him. No more lies. No need for it. He believes me.

"And you remember Brandon Lennox killing you."

"I remember being killed," I say. "But I didn't know it was Brandon Lennox who killed me. Lily couldn't see his face, so neither could I. *I* assumed all along that it was your dad who did it because that's what everyone believed, until I saw the tattoo on Principal Duston. Then I found out that it could have been anyone with that tattoo. Now I know it was Brandon Lennox. I remember lying on the floor, bloody and hurt, and I remember the hatchet tattoo on his wrist, and the pink diamond paperweight in his fist, and him saying *"You left me no choice."* And then he..." I mimic him slamming the paperweight into Lily's head. I cringe again as the memory shoots the pain through my own skull. "He did it," I confirm.

"Wait," Ash says. "A pink diamond paperweight. That's the murder weapon? I thought it was a rock or something. They never found it."

"Paladino lied on the police report," I say. "He set up your father to protect Brandon. He lied about the murder weapon too, probably to keep anyone from finding it. He's been protecting him all along."

"Why would he protect him? And why would Brandon Lennox kill Lily?" He leans back and checks his napkin. His lip has stopped bleeding. "He wasn't in Ryland when Miss Buckley died. That had to be Duston. He has to be involved too."

"We finally know who the killer is, but we have even more questions than before," I say. "And we still can't prove anything. No one will believe the memories of a dead girl."

"True, but we also know what the murder weapon is. I wonder what happened to it."

"Actually," I say, "I have it. I found it in Miss Buckley's bedroom and took it. I hid it in my closet."

"Wait." Ash breaks out into a broad grin. "You *stole* it?"

I smile back proudly. "What can I say? You're a bad influence on me."

CHAPTER FIFTY-NINE

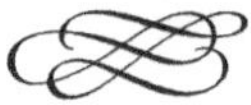

EVER ~ PRESENT DAY

My mind calculates, makes lists, makes plans. Ash goes over to the truck drivers at the counter to find us a ride, and I go to the payphone between the gumball machine and the rotating pie display case to call my father.

I call the directory for the number of the hospital in Quincy. A nurse tells me his surgery went well, thank God, thank God. He's sleeping, the nurse says, and I ask her to tell him when he wakes up that I had a little trouble on the way to the hospital, but I'm fine and I'll be there as soon as I can.

Ash has to give a truck driver all the money that's left in his wallet to get us a ride. But we're not going to Quincy—we're going back to Ryland to get that paperweight.

It's a forty-five-minute drive that feels like forty-five days. The truck driver lets us out at the corner of Jefferson and Van Buren. Every nerve is on edge as we rush to my house, taking the long way so we can avoid the high school. Brandon Lennox, the man who killed

Lily Summerhays, is at the Little Warriors Training Camp at the high school. Principal Duston, the man who must have killed Miss Buckley, is probably there too. Javier Soto, the man who tried to kill Ash and me, could be there as well. Chief Paladino could be anywhere.

We arrive on my street. The house next door to mine is empty. I shudder when I think that I almost declined Mrs. Yost's offer to take Joey camping—he would have been in the plane crash with Ash and me.

Across the street, Keith's curtains are open. He's at the Training Camp along with the rest of the baseball team—and the killers.

We slip inside my house. Joining my head and ribs in misery are my feet and back, from walking miles and miles in my black ballet flats. Ash won't admit that he's in pain, but I can see it on his face. He clutches his bad shoulder with his good arm.

"Sit," I order him, pointing to my couch. I get the first-aid kit from the kitchen and wrap his arm in a sling, one I bought last year just-in-case because it was on sale at Kammer's Pharmacy and I had a coupon. I give him a glass of water and some extra-strength Advil, then take some myself.

"I'll get the paperweight," I say. "But we still need to figure out what to do with it."

"We'll take it to a defense lawyer," he says, leaning his head back and closing his eyes. He's as tired as I am. More than anything, I want to curl up and fall asleep in his arms, right here on the couch, but there's too much to do. "Tell them to get it tested for DNA. Brandon's fingerprints. Lily's blood."

"If there's any evidence left on it, it's eighteen years old. Will it still be viable?"

Ash shrugs, wincing when he moves his shoulder too much. "Doubtful, but testing a new piece of evidence might be enough to postpone my dad's execution. Buy us more time to prove it was Brandon Lennox."

The floor creaks behind us.

Chief Paladino steps out from the hallway. Behind him is Brandon Lennox, his eyes wide, still wearing his Yankees jersey and Warriors hat from the newscast this morning.

The chief rests his hand on the gun at his waist. "I'll take that paperweight."

CHAPTER SIXTY

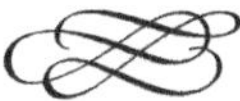

EVER ~ PRESENT DAY

Brandon Lennox is in my house with his hatchet tattoo, and Chief Paladino is in my house with his hatchet tattoo and his gun. I'm frozen. Can't move, can't breathe. Ash scrambles to push me behind him on the couch.

"You two are supposed to be dead," Paladino continues. "Javier Soto's been out looking for your plane since last night, and to finish the job in case you somehow survived."

"Leave her out of this, Paladino," Ash growls. "She didn't do anything. I convinced her to help me."

"We both know that's not true." He strides over and grabs my arm, pulling me off the couch. "My man Lennox and I came here to get rid of any evidence you may have collected, but you can do that for us now. Let's go, Nancy Drew. Get me that paperweight." He tosses his handcuffs to Brandon. "Lock him to the table leg."

Brandon obeys, slowly, like he's stunned. Ash protests and struggles, but with one arm in a sling, he doesn't get much traction. Paladino pulls me away.

"Don't you dare hurt her, you son of a bitch!" Ash shouts after him. "I'll kill you if you hurt her!"

Paladino scoffs. My mind racing, I consider telling him I don't know anything about a paperweight. But he heard Ash and me talking about it, so I have no choice but to get it for him. I lead him to my bedroom. Shaking, I pull open my closet doors. The paperweight is hidden in the back corner at the bottom of a basket of my winter sweaters, wrapped in a pink infinity scarf.

Paladino snatches it from my hand. "How the hell did you know about this?" he demands.

"M-Miss Buckley told me," I say. More believable than the truth. From the family room, Ash shouts. Something breaks.

"Damn that woman," Paladino says, unconcerned by the sounds of struggle. He grabs my arm and hauls me back to the family room. The coffee table is broken, tipped onto a corner. One leg is broken off. Brandon has Ash pinned on his stomach with one foot on his bad shoulder, the arm in its sling pinned underneath him. His other wrist has a handcuff locked to it, the other end swinging free.

Paladino holds up the paperweight in one fist, triumphant. "Got it."

Brandon falters. "What are you gonna do?"

"History is going to repeat itself," Paladino says. "Morrison will bash the girl's head in with the paperweight, just like his dad did to poor Lily Summerhays eighteen years ago. Like father, like son."

"Go to hell, Paladino," Ash says. "There's no way I'll do that and you know it. Kill me if you have to—"

"Ash, no!" I cry.

"—but let her go."

"It doesn't matter if you do it yourself or not," Paladino says. "It's what the police report is going to say. It'll also say that I arrived on the scene while you were still here, but I was too late. She was already dead. But then you tried to attack me, and I had to shoot you in self-defense."

"Fuck you!" Ash shouts.

In response, the chief kicks the coffee table into the bookshelf. Everything goes flying—the glasses of water, the TV remotes, a Griffin University brochure, Joey's Matchbox cars. My mother's romance novels tumble from the shelves.

"I'm sorry you got caught up in this, sweetheart," Paladino tells me, almost sympathetically, as he pushes on my shoulder. "It'll be easier for you if you cooperate. We'll make it quick. Go on. Get on the floor."

"Ever, no!" Ash shouts, struggling to get free. I do *not* cooperate, so Paladino forces me to my knees, then onto my back, holding me down with one foot on my chest. I squirm, kick, hit, reach for something to help me push away, but the only thing my fingers can grab is one of my mom's paperbacks, the new Regency with the woman in the fancy yellow gown on the cover, the one who looks like my mom. Paladino presses his foot on my chest, awakening the pain in my sore ribs. I cry out, and Ash shouts again.

Paladino tosses the paperweight to Brandon, who catches it reflexively in one hand like it's a baseball. "You know what you have to do, Lennox. Get over here."

"Me? But—"

"I've been covering for you for eighteen years," Paladino says. "I did it for you so you could become the success you are today. You owe me your entire career, your entire life. If you fuck this up, we'll both go to prison. *You* will get the needle instead of Vinnie Morrison."

Brandon nods miserably. He straddles me, clutching the paperweight. Ash shouts, but Paladino cocks his gun and aims it at me, and Ash goes rigid.

"Do it, Lennox," Paladino says. "Now."

Brandon's panting, sobs catching in his chest, his eyes red. With shaking hands, he raises the paperweight.

The last words Lily heard, *"You left me no choice,"* echo in my ears.

"Brandon, please, you don't have to do this," I plead from underneath him. "You thought Lily left you no choice back then, but you have a choice now. You don't have to kill me. You *do* have a choice."

He freezes. The pink glass diamond catches a sunbeam and he sits down hard on my stomach. "I didn't want to kill them," he mumbles. "I didn't mean to."

I gasp for air. "Them?"

"Neal. Lily. I didn't mean to..."

Lily was alone when she was killed. The only victim. "Who's Neal?"

"Shut up, Brandon," Paladino says. "Do your job."

In my periphery, Ash is moving, slowly, trying to stand. I need to keep Brandon talking, keep him distracted. "Who's Neal?" I ask again.

"Neal Mallick," Brandon says. "I hit him. With the car. The..." He sighs and hiccups, searching for the word. "The Viper. I didn't mean to. The Yankees gave me the Viper as a bonus, you know, so I'd sign with them and not with the Astros, and so we went driving it, you know, to test it. It was late, and there was no one on the street, so I pushed it as fast as it would go, gunned the engine... and Neal Mallick, he just, he just appeared out of *nowhere,* and—" He groans with agony. "And I hit him. Killed him."

A sob tears from his chest. "My whole career. My whole life. We thought it was over. I was about to play in the majors, and it was over, in an instant, just like that. But we called Paladino and he came and helped us throw Neal's body in the creek, made it look like an accident, like he was walking home after work and slipped off the bridge and drowned."

"Lennox! Shut the fuck up!" the chief shouts. I can't inhale. My ribs hurt; surely they're broken now. My arms are splayed, and I clutch my mom's book as if I'm clutching her hand.

"Everyone believed it," Brandon says, openly weeping. "Even *I* started believing it. We hid the Viper and dismantled it and scattered the parts. We thought it was done. Over. But Lily..." He inhales a jagged breath. "She didn't believe it. She was the only one. She kept digging and digging, and she figured it out, she knew it was me..." He heaves an agonized sob. "I didn't want to do it, but she left me no choice!"

He howls, and with eyes unseeing and furious, he raises the paperweight in both hands. I scream, and with all the strength I have left, fueled by adrenaline and fear and the desire to live, I drive the romance novel right into his neck, edge first, crushing his windpipe.

He gasps a raspy breath and drops the paperweight, and I twist away before it hits me. Pain explodes again in my ribs, but I push him off and scramble away.

Brandon Lennox is *not* going to kill me twice.

CHAPTER SIXTY-ONE

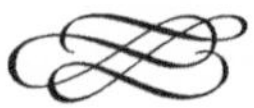

EVER ~ PRESENT DAY

Brandon grasps his throat. Paladino is shouting, swearing, swinging his gun madly between Brandon and me. I can't run, can't breathe. My ribs hurt too much. Ash leaps up, one arm still in the sling, a handcuff swinging freely from his other wrist. He kicks the gun from Paladino's hand and it flies into the wall. They both dive for it, and Ash rises, triumphant, gun in hand.

The house goes silent.

The power has shifted from Paladino to Ash, and they both know it. Ash glares at him, smiles cruelly, and growls, "Get on your knees."

"Don't be ridiculous," Paladino says. "You're not gonna use that gun. I bet you've never even held one before."

"But according to you, I'm a criminal. A vandal, a drug dealer, a thief, a thug. And now you say I've never held a gun?" Ash cocks the trigger. "Knees, asshole. Now."

Shaking, Paladino obeys. He shuffles to his knees and raises his hands. The one Ash kicked is red and swollen, definitely broken.

"You have another set of handcuffs?" Ash asks him. "Give them to me."

Again, Paladino obeys, using his good hand to unhook the cuffs from his belt. "You know you won't get away with this. I have every cop in the county in my pocket. The mayor too."

"If that's the case, I'll be doing them a favor. They'll thank me for getting rid of you." Instead of handcuffing the chief, he tosses the cuffs to me. "Put 'em on Lennox," he says. "Hurry. Before he catches his breath."

My ribs ache and I haven't caught my own breath yet, but I stumble over to Brandon and look down upon the nationally revered professional athlete. This man killed two people. Some guy named Neal Mallick, and Lily Summerhays. Brandon Lennox killed *me.*

It hurts to bend, but I pull his arms behind his back and snap the handcuffs around his wrists. Weeping, he doesn't resist.

Paladino isn't resisting either, but when Ash presses the barrel to his forehead, he begins pleading. "Don't do this, son," he begs. "We can work this out. We can make a deal."

Ash chuckles bitterly. "Now you call me *son*? After you tormented me my entire life? After you hurt my girlfriend? You poisoned her and her little brother with carbon monoxide. You tried to kill us in a *plane crash*." With each sentence, Ash becomes angrier. "My dad spent eighteen years of his life in prison and is days away from execution because of you. Fuck you, Paladino." Ash spits on him, then says over his shoulder. "Ever, how many people are killed by guns in this country every year?"

I clutch my ribs. "Forty thousand."

He glowers down at the trembling chief. "Make that forty thousand and one."

"Ash, no," I cry. "He deserves it, but you don't."

Paladino whimpers, bracing himself.

The front door bursts open. "Stop! Morrison, put down the gun."

It's Principal Duston.

~

Principal Duston puts his hands up and advances slowly. "Put down the gun, Ash."

"Fuck off, Duston," Ash says, not taking his gaze off Paladino. "You killed Miss Buckley."

"No, I didn't. I promise. I have the sheriff and a deputy attorney general with me, Ash. Now put the gun down."

Behind Principal Duston is a dark-haired, brown-skinned woman in a red pantsuit, and pushing past them into my living room is a man in a sheriff's uniform. He has his gun drawn and aimed at Ash, and through my front door I see more police officers in my yard, too many to count. It's like a SWAT team has surrounded my house.

"Ash, do what he says," I plead, but he doesn't move. He stands tall over the trembling police chief, the gun still pressed to his head.

A flash of navy, rushing silently from the kitchen, grabs Ash from behind and pries the gun away from him. The cop is about to wrestle Ash to the floor when Principal Duston stops him. "Not the kid. He was just defending himself and protecting his girlfriend. It's the chief you want."

He turns and looks at me, then to the sobbing sports hero handcuffed at my feet. "And, apparently, Brandon Lennox."

CHAPTER SIXTY-TWO

EVER ~ PRESENT DAY

Chief Paladino and Brandon Lennox are taken away, the former struggling and protesting, the latter meek and sobbing. The blonde reporter who interviewed Brandon for the local newscast this morning is now in front of my house, capturing on camera the disgraced police chief and the fallen baseball hero being placed in the back of two squad cars.

There's also an ambulance, and the EMTs take Ash and me to the emergency room in Eastfield. My second visit in less than a week. Ash and I sit together on a cot. The doctors examine us with difficulty because I won't let go of Ash. He's still shaking. He won't let me go either, and when a doctor looks at my ribs and I cry out in pain, Ash almost punches him.

Finally, my ribs are bandaged and Ash's arm is in a new sling. He has four little butterfly stitches under his lip and it's hard not to kiss them. As we wait to be released, we carefully curl up with each other on the cot, my head on his good shoulder, on my good side. I kiss his neck gently, assuring him that I'm okay, and he's okay, and we're safe, and we're together.

Principal Duston enters our area of the emergency room, followed by that dark-haired woman in the red pantsuit. She's speaking quietly but authoritatively into her phone. Ash jolts upright, stiffening into bodyguard mode again, and my stomach does flipflops. Can we trust them? Principal Duston told me to stop investigating Lily's murder. He told me to do what Paladino said. He called me "*Lily*." The only reason I'm not yelling for help—the only reason I'm willing to *try* to trust him—is because they told the sheriff to arrest Paladino and Brandon, not Ash.

"Ever, Ash," Principal Duston says, "I know I have a lot to explain. But first please know that I'm on your side."

"You've never been on my side," Ash growls.

"I know. I sincerely apologize for that," he says, lowering his head in shame. "I was wrong about you. I was wrong about a lot of things."

"Why are you here?" I ask.

"For the past couple of weeks, I was looking into Lily's murder, just like you were."

"And?" Ash asks, still suspicious.

"I admit that at first I thought you were playing Ever so she'd drop out of the scholarship competition."

Ash snorts and rolls his eyes. "Of course." I pat his arm.

"But Paladino was so *angry* that you were investigating Lily's murder," Duston continues. "He was so defensive about it. He came to the school and asked questions about Ever, one of our best students; Ash, you were arrested; Ever, your house suddenly had carbon monoxide poisoning. Paladino was always involved. I remembered something Lily told me once about him..." He fades off for a moment and moves his toothpick to the other side of his mouth.

"How do we know you're not working with Paladino and Brandon?" Ash says, still suspicious. "I think you're just saying all this to save your own ass."

"I don't blame you for thinking that way," Principal Duston says, genuinely sorrowful. "In the weeks before Lily was murdered, she was trying to prove that a friend of ours named Neal Mallick didn't slip from Railroad Bridge and drown in the creek like the police report said, that he was instead hit by a car. She told me that Paladino was protecting the killer. At first I believed her. I even tried to help her find proof. But we had a falling out and I didn't believe her anymore. I thought she'd lied to me about Neal, about *everything*"—he says, giving me a pointed look—"in order to help her father get my family's land. And then she was killed. Still, I didn't believe her. For eighteen years I didn't believe her—until you two started investigating her murder. Then I realized Lily had told me the truth. I was trying to keep you away from Paladino, to keep you out of it, while I investigated things. I was trying to protect you."

I want to believe him, but Ash's clear suspicion and dislike for the man is making it difficult. Anger is rolling off of Ash in waves.

Principal Duston must realize it too, because he gestures to the woman in the pantsuit, who's still pacing and barking orders into her phone. "The woman with me is Devi Mallick. I looked her up when I became suspicious of Paladino. She's a deputy attorney general for the state of Indiana. At this moment she's making calls to get your father's conviction overturned."

"She can stop the execution?" I ask.

"She's stopping the execution," he confirms.

I slide my hand into Ash's and squeeze, then give his shoulder a kiss. "We did it, Ash," I whisper. He doesn't move, but he swallows hard.

Principal Duston continues, "Devi lived in Ryland as a child. Her brother was Neal Mallick, the boy Brandon Lennox has just confessed to killing with his car. Now that she knows Neal's death wasn't an accident, she wants justice as much as you do. As much as Lily did."

He turns to me, hesitates, then whispers, awestruck. "You're different from Lily in almost every way. She was impulsive, reckless. Always causing trouble."

"I know that now," I say. Lily was not the prim, demure girl her scholarship poster made her out to be.

He regards me again. "You're so different, but you're both fearless."

I suck in a breath, moved almost to tears. I've never been fearless before, but I am now.

Beside me, Ash grunts, not at all convinced of Principal Duston's sincerity. "Brandon Lennox said *we.*"

"What do you mean?" I ask.

"When he was telling us what happened. He was crying and blubbering, but he definitely said '*we went driving.*' Keyword: *we.*"

"There was someone with him when he killed Neal Mallick," I say, realizing it's not over; there's still someone else out there involved in a murder—no, *three* murders: Neal Mallick, Lily Summerhays, and Diana Buckley.

Ash continues, "I think that person was you, Duston."

CHAPTER SIXTY-THREE

EVER ~ PRESENT DAY

"You think I was with Brandon when he killed Neal?" Principal Duston asks.

Ash nods. "I think you were the other person in the car that night, I think you knew Brandon killed Lily, and I also think you pushed Miss Buckley down the stairs when she was about to tell everyone the truth."

"I understand your distrust for me," Duston says. "But I did not kill Neal. Nor did I know that Brandon killed Lily, nor did I push Diana down the stairs." He sighs wearily. "All of them—Neal, Lily, Diana—were my friends. Brandon Lennox and Rick Paladino, too. My God." He rubs his eyes with his hand, masking his emotions.

"If it wasn't you," I ask, "then who was it?" I gasp as I remember something. "Warrior74!"

Principal Duston goes white. "What are you talking about?"

"We found a chat history on Miss Buckley's laptop," I explain.

"Ever, shh," Ash growls.

"He already knows we took the laptop," I say. "And I think he's proven that he's on our side." I rub his arm. "We have to trust *some*one, Ash. I think we can trust him." I stare into Ash's eyes—his beautiful, dark, conflicted eyes—until he softens. He gives me a cautious nod, and I continue.

"Ash and I found a chat history on Miss Buckley's laptop," I tell our principal. "She was chatting with someone named warrior74, telling him that she was going to get a defense attorney and confess. They both knew Vinnie Morrison didn't kill Lily. He warned her not to say anything, and the next day, she was dead."

With each word, Principal Duston looks more and more ill.

"We tried to figure out who warrior74 is," I say, "but the account was deleted. Best I could come up with is it was his old uniform number. I know Brandon's number was 09, but I couldn't find a list of the rest. Maybe it's Javier Soto. What was his uniform number, do you remember?"

Ash watches Principal Duston closely. "It's you, isn't it, Duston," he rumbles. "You're warrior74."

Principal Duston has moved beyond white and is almost green now. "No, but I know who is." He swallows hard. "The 74 isn't a uniform number. It's his daughter's birthday, July 4th. Seven-Four."

"Hey, July 4th is Courtney's birthday," I say. "We're going to Chicago to watch the fireworks at Navy Pier this year to celebrate."

Ash stiffens, and Principal Duston gives me a regretful look. It takes another beat for it to hit me. Do they actually think...

No. Impossible.

I shake my head. "No. It can't be. You're wrong."

"Coach Nolan is warrior74," Principal Duston says. He sinks back in his chair. "If Diana was chatting with him about Lily's real killer, it means he knew it was Brandon."

"Why wouldn't he say anything?" Ash asks angrily. "Why would he keep it a secret all these years and let my father take the blame?"

Duston shrugs. "The same reason Paladino did, probably. The same reason Diana did. To protect Brandon's baseball career."

"Wait. Stop. No. We're talking about *Coach Nolan*," I say. "Courtney's dad. My best friend's father. I *know* him, really really well. There's no way he would have done that."

Principal Duston nods gravely. "I know him well too, Ever. He was my coach too, and now we're coworkers at the school. But it's him. I'm sure of it. Look." He holds up his phone, showing us emails he's received from warrior74. Some are signed Coach, some Dave, and some David Nolan.

"So Coach knew that Brandon killed Lily," I say. "That's bad, yeah, horrible, but it doesn't mean he was in the car that killed that kid Neal or that he pushed Miss Buckley down the stairs."

Devi Mallick stops pacing and ends her phone call. "That was the DA's office. They're interviewing Brandon Lennox right now. He waived his rights and refused a lawyer. He's confessing to everything. He said that his high school baseball coach was in the car with him the night he killed Neal," she tells us with a sigh. "The coach is the one who called Paladino, who came up with the plan to make it look like an accident."

"So that answers that," Principal Duston says. He looks as crushed as I feel.

"They're bringing in the coach for questioning," Devi says. "They picked him up at the Training Camp."

"I *knew* Miss Buckley didn't fall down those stairs. I *knew* she was pushed," I say. "I just can't believe Coach was the one who pushed her. God, poor Courtney." If I feel like I've been kicked in the gut by this news, Courtney's got to be devastated by it.

"The coach didn't push Diana Buckley," Devi says. Her heels click on the linoleum floor as she paces. "We have the security cam footage."

"If you're talking about the footage of Miss Buckley falling down the stairs," Ash says doubtfully, "it's been edited. There are a few seconds missing."

I give the principal a sheepish but defiant shrug, and confess, "We stole the security cam video too."

He gives a little chuckle. "Lily would have done the same thing," he murmurs. Affection laces his voice. Regret, too.

"We have the original, unedited footage," Devi went on. "After Will told me everything that's been happening at your high school—Ash's arrest, Diana Buckley's death—I had some tech guys do a search of the building's security footage. We found no proof of Ash storing cocaine in his locker. When we watched the footage of Diana Buckley's death, we discovered the missing seconds. It took some digging, but this morning they were able to find the original footage in a backup file that's stored off-site."

"And?" I ask, breathless.

"You're correct that someone pushed Diana Buckley down the stairs, Ever, but it wasn't the coach."

I sink back into Ash's arms, relieved. Courtney's dad may have obstructed justice, but at least he's not a killer. "Who was it?"

"If it wasn't the coach, it's got to be Duston," Ash says, growling.

I shake my head. I no longer believe Principal Duston pushed Miss Buckley. "Paladino was at the school that day. It must have been him."

"It's neither of them," the attorney says. "We can only see the arms and hands of the person who pushed Diana, and it's obvious they don't belong to anyone you suspected." She takes an iPad from her case. "Any idea who it could be?"

Frowning, Devi Mallick shows Ash and me the footage on her iPad. We've seen it before: the back stairwell alternating between long stretches of no movement and flooded with students going to their next class between periods. I keep my eye on the time stamp in the corner. At a little after 13:05:29, Miss Buckley appears on camera, climbing the stairs in her pencil skirt and heels, her arms filled with books. At 13:05:32, Mrs. Buckley reaches the second-to-top step. At 13:05:33, she pauses and glances up.

On the version Ash and I have, the video skips to Miss Buckley starting to fall. But on this version, the original unedited version, Miss

Buckley is still on the step, and a pair of arms appear, reaching for her, making contact, and pushing her.

Devi taps the screen to freeze the black-and-white video. With her thumb and index finger, she expands the image, zooming in on the hands that are reaching for Miss Buckley.

The hands aren't those of a man. They're smaller, smoother, feminine. The left one is decorated with an intricate pattern of swirls and dots.

No. That's—That's impossible. I must not be seeing it correctly. It makes no sense. There must be a mistake.

Swirls and dots. I look again and the room narrows. Swirls and dots.

I don't recognize my own voice. I can't believe my own words as they come out of my mouth. "Those are Courtney's hands."

Courtney killed Miss Buckley.

CHAPTER SIXTY-FOUR

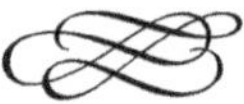

EVER ~ PRESENT DAY

My best friend, Courtney Nolan, is a killer. And Courtney is missing. No one knows where she is. She was last seen at the Little Warriors Training Camp, but she disappeared when her father was arrested. The Training Camp was called off once the news spread about the arrests of Brandon Lennox, Chief Paladino, and then Coach Nolan. Javier Soto turned himself in.

There are cops and reporters all over Ryland. The cops are looking for Courtney. The reporters are looking for Ash and me. A helicopter flies over town, its propellers making a *whup-whup-whup* sound when it's above our house. I don't know if it's a police helicopter or a news helicopter.

Ash and I are hunkered down in my family room with a couple of cops for protection against the reporters outside. Principal Duston and Devi Mallick are here with us as well, conferencing in the kitchen.

Joey's home too. News of Ryland's chief of police and MLB Hall-of-Famer Brandon Lennox being arrested right outside our house had already reached the Yosts at the campground, and concerned and curious, they ended their trip early and came home. Joey's disappointed his camping trip was cut short, but he's too excited by all the commotion to give it much thought.

The family room is a mess: the broken coffee table, the spilled glasses, the scattered books. In the clutter, I spot the romance novel I used to fight off Brandon Lennox. I give a silent thank-you to the woman on the cover who looks like my mom.

I use our landline to call my dad, who's awake and recovering, but still too groggy to talk much. I tell him I got stuck at home, but I'll be there as soon as I can.

Next I call Courtney, not expecting her to answer, and she doesn't. I tell the police that her mother lives in Cleveland, so they alert the search team to look for her on the highways heading there. "I feel so helpless," I tell Ash. My ribs ache. But I'm on pain pills, so maybe the ache is coming from my heart.

Questions spiral around in my mind, but I'm too distressed to organize them into a mental, numbered list. Instead, I ask them aloud to Ash. Why did Courtney push Miss Buckley down the stairs? Did she know all along what her father did all those years ago? Did she know that Vinnie Morrison was innocent—is that why she was trying to stop Ash and me from investigating Lily's murder? Did her father *make* her kill Miss Buckley? Did Paladino? She was so distraught when Miss Buckley died. Was that anguish caused by guilt, or was it all just an act?

Ash doesn't have the answers, but he keeps his good arm around me, stroking me with his thumb. Occasionally, he kisses the top of my head. Joey catches him doing it and giggles.

I shift closer to Ash and brush a kiss on his jaw. His messy dark hair curls around the collar of his dirt-stained T-shirt. He's so gorgeous, even now, with stitches under his lip and his tired, troubled eyes. He gazes at me with those eyes, soulful and dark. "You're so beautiful." He sighs, and I love him so much that I can feel it in every cell of my body.

Principal Duston comes out of the kitchen. Ash pulls me closer but doesn't lash out. I think he's starting to trust him now.

"The guys in the copter spotted someone on the bridge over Deep Creek," Principal Duston says. "They think it's Courtney."

CHAPTER SIXTY-FIVE

EVER ~ PRESENT DAY

It takes us under ten minutes to get to Railroad Bridge. Principal Duston drives, but when we reach the movie theater on Main Street, Ash tells him to pull over. We can get to the bridge faster on foot from here than driving around the long way. I leave Joey with Principal Duston and Devi Mallick, and Ash and I dash as fast as we can, sliding through the hole in the fence, dashing across the pebbled lot and along the tracks through the woods, until we reach the creek.

Courtney is sitting on the bridge, wearing a Little Warriors Training Camp T-shirt, her black hair in braids behind her back.

When she sees us, she scrambles shakily to her feet. "Get back. Stay away." Above us, the helicopter *whup-whup-whups*. On the other side of the creek, a police cruiser's red-and-blue lights flash in the parking lot beyond the field, and a train horn wails in the distance.

"Court," I call. "We can work it out. We can help you."

"It was an accident," she says.

"Of course it was!" I yell to her. "Come back here and tell me what happened."

She shakes her head. "I just... I saw her messages to my dad on his laptop and he told me what he did. I know it was awful, but it was so long ago. He's a good person. It was just one mistake." She speaks through her sobs. "The next day I saw her in the back stairwell. I was just going to talk to her, to make her understand. But I... I don't know what happened. I didn't mean to push her. I didn't mean to kill her."

"It's okay, Courtney!" Ash yells. "We can help you."

Above us, the helicopter hovers, tilting, perhaps looking for a place to land in the field. Across the creek, the cops are getting out of their cruisers. I wave at them to stand back. I don't want them to spook my friend.

The ground rumbles, vibrates. The train is in view now, coming closer. The engine's single headlight is getting bigger, brighter, the horn louder. "Courtney, get off the bridge!" I shout. "Everything will be okay. Come to me. Please."

"Come on, Courtney. You can do it," calls a familiar voice, sweet and young.

"Joey?" I look behind me, and my little brother is walking toward the bridge.

Principal Duston comes running up from the woods. "He ran after you," he says, panting. "I tried to stop him but he's too fast."

"Joey, stop," I say, but he ignores me. He continues walking to Courtney.

"Ever showed me how to cross the bridge," he says. "It's easy. You just have to be very careful and you have to hold someone's hand. Come on." He takes a step closer to Courtney, extending his little hand to her.

"Joey, get back here!" I cry.

The train is coming closer. The horn blows. Startled, Joey looks up and freezes.

I run toward him, but I slip and fall, and this time I know my ribs must be broken. "Court!" I scream. She's closer to Joey than I am. "Get him!"

She's standing in the middle of the bridge; Joey's frozen a few feet away. She's hesitating, looking first at the train, then at Joey, then at the train, coming closer, closer, faster, faster, its horn blowing madly.

"Get him, Courtney!" I scream. "Joey!"

In a flash, Ash runs onto the bridge and scoops up Joey, then drops him onto the bank. Joey cries and runs to me, crushing me, and somewhere in my brain I register the pain in my ribs as he hugs me, but all I can think is he's safe, Ash saved him, but Courtney is still on the bridge and the train is still coming, and Ash is running back onto the bridge, heading for Courtney, heading for the train, and the train is huge and loud and close and it's on the bridge, closer and closer and bigger and bigger, huge, immense, monstrous. The whistle blows, the tracks tremble, the ground shakes, the train is feet away, inches away, and Ash reaches Courtney and pushes her into the creek, but he—

Brakes screech and squeal and scream, horns blow, the train roars by—the longest train in the world; it won't end. Principal Duston grabs me and holds me back, and I scream, scream, screeeeeam, louder than the train whistle, louder than the roar of the wheels on the tracks. "Where's Ash? Where is he?" Courtney's bobbing in the creek, but where's Ash, oh God, oh God, oh God...

Finally, the train passes, getting farther away, and the whistle stops blowing and the ground stops shaking. I yank myself from Principal Duston's grip and run to the bridge, clutching my ribs, not caring about the pain. Two cops are in the creek, pulling out Courtney, but where's Ash? I don't see him. I can't look on the tracks. I don't want to see what's left of him—

"Hey, beautiful," a voice rumbles from behind me.

I turn, and there he is, soaking wet, covered in mud and seaweed. My gorgeous boyfriend. I collapse into him, sobbing with relief. "How—?"

"I jumped into the creek on the other side," he says. "Then I swam to shore and climbed up the embankment. Easy."

"With one arm in a sling?"

He shrugs with his one good shoulder. "That's why it took me so long."

CHAPTER SIXTY-SIX

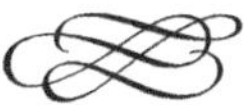

EVER ~ PRESENT DAY

He catches me on the Summerhayses' porch, coming up behind me just as I'm about to knock on the door. "What are you doing here?" he asks in that delicious rumbly voice of his. "It better not be to withdraw yourself from the scholarship."

"What are *you* doing here?" I ask back. "It better not be to withdraw *your*self from the scholarship."

He grins. "Busted." The stitches under his lip are starting to dissolve, leaving a tiny scar that makes me want to kiss it constantly.

"You'll win it anyway," I say. "You deserve it more than I do."

"No, you're going to win," he counters. "You were the one who brought the whole thing to light. If it weren't for you, my dad would have been executed yesterday. Brandon Lennox would still be free, and Paladino would still be running this town."

I sigh. We can add Coach and Courtney to that list too. Unlike Paladino and Brandon, the coach and Courtney were both released on bail and are on house arrest until their trials. Devi Mallick informed us that Coach, as an accessory, will likely get the same sentence as Paladino: life in prison. Courtney, who's just months away from eighteen, will be tried as an adult for voluntary manslaughter. She'll probably get ten years and will be released in five.

Javier Soto was also arrested for his part in sabotaging the Piper. Even though he did it because Paladino threatened his daughter, he'll most likely be convicted of attempted murder in the second degree.

The prosecution team is going to recommend that Brandon Lennox be sentenced to death, just as they recommended Vinnie Morrison be executed. Everyone knows it won't happen—his celebrity status practically guarantees that—but he will most likely spend the rest of his life behind bars. He has enough money and fame that the best defense lawyers in the country are offering to represent him, but he hasn't hired anyone. He confessed that Diana Buckley delivered the first blow to Lily the night of her murder, pushing her into the brick fireplace hearth, and that he finished her off in order to protect both Diana and himself. He and Diana stayed a couple for about a year after graduation, and she even went to Florida with him. But the stress and guilt was too much to handle, so they broke up and she came back home to Ryland. He says his life has been utter hell since the night he killed Neal Mallick and he just wants to go to prison and serve his time.

"The car accident that killed Neal Mallick eighteen years ago destroyed so many families then, and so many families now," I say.

"I know," Ash says. "But how do you think Lily would feel about what you did?"

"She'd be glad I did it." I know this, because *I'm* glad I did it. She is me, and I am her.

"Exactly. You need the scholarship for yourself *and* for Lily. I'm withdrawing." He raises his fist to knock on the door. "You need it. You deserve it."

I pull down his arm. "You need it and deserve it just as much as I do. I won't let you give it up."

"And I won't let *you* give it up." He grins. "We're at an impasse. What should we do?"

I grin back. "Let's let the Summerhayses decide. No interference from either of us."

He considers it, then nods. "No interference. Deal." He puts his arm around me, still a little stiff from his shoulder injury. "Come on. I'll walk you home."

He turns serious as the sun shines down on us. "How's your dad? Settling in okay?"

"He's tired and sore, but he's okay." I took Seth Siegel up on his offer to take Joey and me to get our dad at the hospital in Illinois and bring him home. On the way there, Mr. Siegel said that when he was a teenager, Paladino got him out of some scrapes that he otherwise should have been arrested for. Stupid things like shoplifting, underage drinking, and buying weed from Vinnie Morrison behind the movie theater. But he grew up and cleaned himself up, while Paladino had only become more corrupt.

We got back with Dad yesterday, the same day Ash brought his own father home. Vinnie is living in a small apartment just outside of town, and Ash is helping him get adjusted to the outside world after spending almost two decades behind bars.

"Maybe your dad can get a job at Siegel Freight," I suggest to Ash. "Mr. Siegel is really generous. He's giving my dad a twelve-month paid leave, and when he goes back to work, a job as the office manager. With a pay raise. Mr. Siegel might be able to find something for your father too."

"I'll tell him," Ash says. "But is your dad happy about the office job?"

"I think he's apprehensive about being around Joey all the time," I say, "but I gave him the number of a grief counselor and he took it. So he's trying. When I left to come here, he was watching *SpongeBob* with Joey. It's not much, but it's a start."

Ash and I walk in silence for a while. We're both mourning so many people, so many things: Courtney, Miss Buckley, the years

Vinnie Morrison lost to prison and injustice. But there's also a sense of peace and contentment as we walk. I feel free, liberated, *right*.

We turn onto my driveway. Across the street, Keith is in his own driveway, getting into his car, wearing a Batter's Box polo. I give him a little wave, which he returns with a nod. We haven't spoken since the morning of my birthday, before the plane crash, so there was no formal breakup. But he knows it's over. Even if he hadn't cheated on me, even if I hadn't fallen in love with Ash, it would be over. He wanted to marry his childhood sweetheart, but I'm not that person anymore. He wants who I used to be, not who I am now.

Keith looks at Ash and nods at him too. Then he gets in his car and drives away.

"You know, I did a Google search for Neal Mallick last night," Ash says, smiling a little as we step onto my porch. "Found his obituary. Strangest thing. He died on the exact same day I was born."

"Oh yeah?"

"Same time, too. I was born a few minutes after midnight, and Neal was killed right around that time. Cool coincidence, don't you think?"

I stop, stand on my tiptoes, and kiss his neck on the soft spot under his jaw. "That," I say, "is a *very* cool coincidence."

CHAPTER SIXTY-SEVEN

EVER ~ PRESENT DAY

The Lily Summerhays Memorial Scholarship Announcement Ceremony is a semi-formal affair held in the high school's conference room. Usually the only people who attend are the committee and the finalists and their families, but this year many of our classmates come to watch, and there are several reporters too. It's in the auditorium this year.

I wear a nice dress, a new one, loose to account for the bandages around my ribs. The arrests of several of Ryland's most respected citizens was just two weeks ago, but I'm still too sore to balance in heels, so I have to wear my black ballet flats. Joey pulls at his little red bow tie and scuffs at his new dress shoes. His button-down shirt is already half untucked. Our dad swings in on his crutches, insisting on leaving his wheelchair behind. He's wearing his old suit, but it's fresh from the cleaners, so it looks new.

Ash wears a new sport coat and navy blue tie. The stitches under his lip are barely visible. He comes with his dad, who is wearing a brand new suit and tie, and his mom, who is wearing a pretty floral dress. His parents are not getting back together, but they are cordial to each other. Vinnie gives me a hug, a gentle one because of my ribs, and almost cries when he thanks me for clearing his name. He has a lot of work to do to get reintroduced to life on the outside, he says, but he promises to make Ash and me as proud of him as he is of us.

Principal Duston is here, smiling, and Devi Mallick is with him. They had their first date last night, and now they're holding hands. Twice I catch him kissing her cheek. She blushes, then kisses him back.

Mr. and Mrs. Summerhays arrive last, he in a gray suit and she in a dress and heels. Her auburn hair is down today, the first time I've seen her like that, and it makes her look younger and vulnerable. When they see Ash's dad, they freeze, just for a moment, then acknowledge him a tiny nod. He nods back. They're all victims, but there's too much to say, too many feelings to process, and there hasn't been enough time to heal eighteen years of pain. That will come later.

The Summerhayses ignore the reporters' questions and walk straight to the stage to take their seats with Principal Duston, who shakes Mr. Summerhays's hand and gives Mrs. Summerhays a hug. The scholarship committee is now only three people, two people fewer than a month ago.

The oversized poster of Lily Summerhays is displayed on the stage, the one that shows her smiling demurely, her copper hair hanging straight down her back. That's not the real Lily. The real Lily was wild and fearless and impulsive and reckless. I think each one of my previous incarnations had those same traits. I rarely died in the same place I was born, so I know I traveled a lot. I usually died doing adventurous and heroic things. The impulsiveness and recklessness ended with Lily, driven away by terror when she was so brutally murdered by trusted friends. But the fearlessness survived, hiding itself away in me until now. And now I'm going to set it free.

Ash comes up behind me as I gaze at Lily's poster. He wraps his arms around me and pulls me close.

The Summerhayses are looking at me, and Mrs. Summerhays gives me a small smile. There's something maternal and affectionate in her smile, and I know, my heart soaring and sinking at the same time, that the scholarship is mine.

"Ash." I whirl around in his arms. "You told me once that if you don't get the scholarship, you're going to stay here in Ryland and live down to everyone's expectations of you."

"Yeah..."

"No one has low expectations of you anymore. Especially not me." I grip the lapels of his sport coat. "Promise me that if I get the scholarship, you'll still find a way to go to college and get all those fancy astro-science degrees, and that you'll still go to Mars. I'll help you. Just don't give up, okay? Promise me."

He kisses my cheek. "One condition. If *I* get the scholarship, *you* will still find a way to go to college."

"I promise. But definitely not for accounting."

He chuckles. "Good. What will you study?"

"Aviation," I say, only half-joking. "I've decided that I want to be a pilot. Or a motocross champion. What college degree is that?"

"You'd win every race." He grinned. "But what do you really want to do?"

There are suddenly so many possibilities. I can be anything. I can do anything. "Maybe investigative journalism. Or travel writing. Or archeology. Or anthropology! I want to visit the places I lived in my past lifetimes. Learn about them. Explore. Visit new places too."

"Perfect." He kisses me, then turns serious. "I hope you win. I really do."

I glance again at the Summerhayses and know that he's about to get his wish.

Mrs. Summerhays stands, and the crowd hushes as she walks to the podium. The reporters hold out their microphones and start their cameras. Ash and I take our seats in the front row, surrounded by our families.

This is it.

Mrs. Summerhays is shaking as she unfolds several pieces of paper. She smooths the creases for an unnecessarily long time, taps the edges on the podium to straighten the pages, then taps them again. I don't breathe. I squeeze Ash's hand, and he squeezes back.

She finally finishes smoothing the papers, then she clears her throat, inhales, exhales. "I have a big speech prepared," she says, her voice high and strained, "but I don't think I can get through it." She pauses and wipes a tear.

Mr. Summerhays joins her at the podium, placing his hand on her lower back. "Then skip to the end, darling." He moves the bottom page to the top. She sniffs and gives him a grateful nod.

"Over the past eighteen years, we've had many excellent candidates for Lily's scholarship," she says, struggling. "But this year was the hardest decision we've had to make. It was, at first, an obvious choice. But new circumstances arose in the last month that made our decision an impossible one. Both candidates are..." She looks at Ash and me. "Well, they're both wonderful and they both deserve to win. We're forever grateful to both of them. How could we choose?"

"Maybe you'll both win," Ash's dad whispers to us.

For a moment, my heart lights up. Wouldn't that be perfect, if both of us win?

"We tried to figure out a way to give both candidates the scholarship this year—to double the prize—but because we could no longer accept the annual contribution from our biggest sponsor..." Mrs. Summerhays's face screws up at the shadowed mention of her daughter's killer. "...we didn't have enough money to do that. So in the end, we decided to select the winner based on who we think Lily would pick."

Ash takes my hand, brings it to his lips, and kisses it. "It's you," he whispers. "It has to be."

Mrs. Summerhays lets out a long, long breath. "The winner of the Lily Summerhays Memorial Scholarship is..."

Everyone freezes. *Please, please, please,* I pray.

Mrs. Summerhays wipes her eyes. "Ash Morrison."

"Yes!" I cry, jumping up and hurting my ribs, but I don't care. The crowd hoots and applauds. Vinnie claps Ash on the back.

Mrs. Summerhays catches my gaze and holds it. *I'm sorry,* she mouths. Her gaze flickers to Vinnie and back to me.

I nod at her and smile. I understand. *Thank you,* I mouth back to her. Lily picked the right one.

But Ash remains in his seat, stunned and shaking his head. "I don't want it," he whispers to me. "You should have it."

"Ash Morrison, if you don't get up there right now and get your scholarship, I will never forgive you," I hiss. "You're going to be an astronaut. You're going to live on Mars! Lily would love that. I *know* she would."

"You sure?"

"One hundred percent."

He kisses me, hard. "I love you. I love you so much."

"I love you too." I pull him out of his seat. "Now go get your scholarship."

CHAPTER SIXTY-EIGHT

EVER ~ TEN MONTHS LATER

From my back pocket, my phone rings. I drop my shovel into the dirt, wipe the sweat from my brow with my forearm, use my teeth to pull off my gloves, and answer my phone.

"Hey, beautiful."

I snort. "Trust me, Ash, I am not beautiful right now. I'm covered in dirt and sweat and who knows what else. Bone dust, maybe."

"But you love it."

"I do," I admit. "I love anthropology. And I *love* Greece. I lived here for three lifetimes, you know. All ancient times."

"That's a lot of togas." Ash chuckles. "You also loved Italy last semester. You'll love Spain next semester even more. And Nigeria after that."

"I'm sure I will." I laugh and swipe some dirt from my Carroll-Freywood Global University hoodie. After I lost the Lily Scholarship, the Summerhayses pulled me aside and offered to give me a loan for my tuition at Griffin University. A loan, they said, that I would never have to pay back, as a thank-you for discovering the truth behind Lily's murder. I was moved to tears, but I turned them down. I no longer wanted to be an accountant, and I no longer wanted to go to Griffin.

A few days later, while piecing together Lily's last days with Principal Duston, he mentioned she had told him that she'd found a maroon Warriors hat in the blue Viper and had hidden it somewhere. I knew where: inside her wooden globe. The Summerhayses gave us permission to retrieve it, and I also retrieved the crumpled-up letter that was hidden inside the globe alongside it. An acceptance letter from Carroll-Freywood Global University. *That* was where Lily wanted to go to school, not to Griffin, and I realized with a sudden, fierce certainty that CFGU was the school for me, too.

I applied after the deadline, but Principal Duston made a call, and because of my high grades, they accepted me. And after Mr. and Mrs. Summerhays informed them that I was the girl who solved the Brandon Lennox murders and freed an innocent man from death row, the school gave me a full scholarship. I'm living Lily's dream after all—and mine.

I haven't told the Summerhayses that I was Lily in my most recent past life, but I think they have a feeling. They love me like a daughter in any case. I can see it in their eyes, hear it in their voices, when we FaceTime. I love them too. They gave me Lily's diamond pendant, and I wear it on the chain with my daisy charm.

Leaving Joey was the hardest part. I miss him terribly, but he's loving kindergarten and he's having the time of his life with Dad, who's ready to start back to work soon at Siegel Freight and Transport as the office manager. The Summerhayses have become Joey's surrogate grandparents and they spoil him rotten.

"How's Hidding University today?" I ask Ash. "Are you calling to tell me your professors are sending you to live on Mars already?"

"Not quite yet." He chuckles. "And when I do go to Mars, it's only to visit, not to live. I'm calling to tell you my dad got promoted at

Agri-So today. Assistant shift manager. And he sent me yet another picture of him and Valeri. He loves that cat so much, it's ridiculous."

"That's awesome about the promotion. Tell him I say *congrats*," I say. "Hey, did you get Principal Duston's wedding invitation? They're having it on his new farm. Did you know he and Devi scheduled the wedding for this summer just for us, so we can both be there?"

"He told me that yesterday. Wanna be my date?"

"Of course."

"I mean, wanna be my date *tonight*. Today. Right now."

"Right now?" I say, confused. "But how..."

"I'm a pilot, remember? Turn around."

I turn, and he's standing a few feet away, right here in Greece, his dark eyes deep and soulful, his dark hair curling over his shoulders, and holding a bouquet of daisies. "Hey, beautiful."

ACKNOWLEDGMENTS

This book was a lifetime in the making. Maybe two lifetimes. I've been afraid of falling down the stairs my entire life. I've never actually fallen down the stairs, yet my fear of it is almost phobic. I *always* need one hand free to hold the railing. The sight of a long flight of stairs makes me shiver. The sight of a person standing at the top of the stairs, just chatting casually, is enough to make me grab them and drag them to safety. My friends and family laugh, but the fear is real, you guys. Someone asked me once why I have such an instinctual, visceral fear of falling down the stairs. I didn't have an answer, so I joked, "Maybe it's how I died in a past life." And the idea for *Kill Me Once, Kill Me Twice* was born.

I wrote this book on and off for almost eight years. Eight years! It was a passion project and I wrote it for fun, when I had time—which wasn't often. I'd write a draft, put it away for a few months or years, take it out and rework it, put it away again, until I was finally ready to finish it and share it with *you!*

Many thanks to the dear friends who supported me while I wrote this book, especially Liza Wiemer, Heather Marshall, Lynne Hartzer, Sonali Dev, Melonie Johnson, Melanie Bruce, and all the women of

Aphrodite Writers and #PortlandMidwest. Big hugs to my insightful editor and friend, Amy McNulty, and infinite gratitude to my cherished author co-op, Snowy Wings Publishing, and our fearless leader, Lyssa Chiavari. Special thanks to Alex Rosario, who is a good friend and also my Subject Matter Expert on carbon monoxide. More special thanks to my friends Mike and Mary Kay, who let me use their hamster's name in the book. Eternal love to my husband, Glen, who patiently listened to me ramble about the characters and the plot for the better part of a decade. I hope I didn't spoil the ending for him.

I still love this book as much now that it's a finished product as I did when it was a shiny new idea. Ever, Ash, Lily, and Will have a permanent place in my heart, and now that you've read the book, I hope they have a place in yours, too.

ABOUT THE AUTHOR

CLARA KENSIE, AUTHOR OF DARK FICTION FOR YOUNG ADULTS

...don't forget to breathe...

Clara Kensie grew up near Chicago, reading every book she could find and using her diary to write stories about a girl with psychic powers who solved mysteries. She purposely did not hide her diary, hoping someone would read it and assume she was writing about herself. Since then, she's swapped her diary for a computer and admits her characters are fictional, but otherwise she hasn't changed one bit.

Today Clara is an award-winning author of dark fiction for young adults. Her books include *Deception So Deadly, Deception So Dark, Aftermath,* and *Kill Me Once, Kill Me Twice.*

Her favorite foods are guacamole and cookie dough. But not together. That would be gross.

~

CONNECT WITH ME

Want to know when I have a new book? The best way is to follow me on Amazon, Goodreads, and Bookbub. You can leave reviews at those sites too, please and thank you.

You can also subscribe to my low-volume newsletter (https://www.subscribepage.com/clarakensie), join my Facebook group, The

Insiders (https://www.facebook.com/groups/clarakensieinsiders/), and follow me on Twitter.

- bookbub.com/profile/clara-kensie
- goodreads.com/ClaraKensie
- twitter.com/ClaraKensie
- instagram.com/clarakensie

THE DECEPTION SO SERIES

CLARA KENSIE

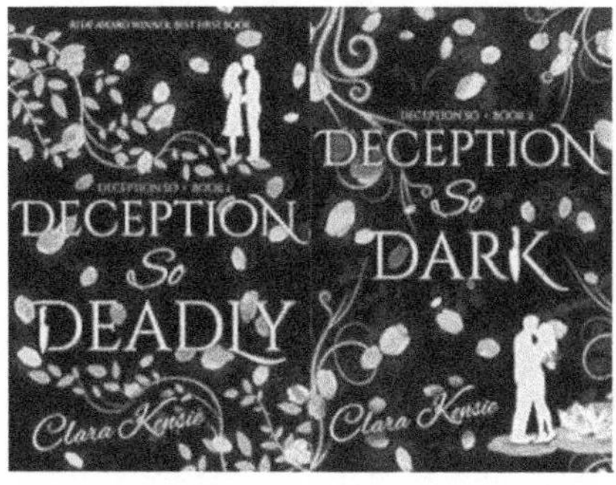

Winner of Romance Writers of America's 2015 RITA© Award for Best First Book

RUN. It's all sixteen-year-old Tessa Carson has ever known. Hunted by a telepathic killer, Tessa and her family have fled home after home, hiding behind aliases to survive. Her scars are more than just physical, and as the only one in her family without a psychic ability, she lives a life of secrets, lies, and fear.

After the Carsons flee to a new hideout and take on new identities yet again, Tessa meets confident, carefree Tristan Walker. Their attraction burns fierce, but she runs from him too, knowing their love can never be true when she can't even tell him her real name.

But Tristan has secrets as well—secrets that will either save Tessa, or destroy her. The only way Tessa can save her family—and uncover the real reason they've been hunted all these years—is to forget everything she's learned from a lifetime of running away, and run straight into danger head-on.

Book One in the YA paranormal thriller Deception So series, Deception So Deadly was originally published as the Run to You serial parts 1 – 3, and is the winner of the prestigious RITA© Award for Best First Book.

"A dark, suspenseful, and romantic ride!" - USA Today

"The perfect blend of mystery, romance, paranormal thrills, and danger." - Mundie Moms

"A well-written YA paranormal read, with welcome dashes of thrills and plot twists, Kensie has written a gripping and engaging series that features great family dynamics and the enormity of first love." - RT Book Reviews

"A thrilling story, packed with twists, secrets, and swoon-worthy romance. I couldn't read it fast enough!" ~Erica O'Rourke, author of the Torn trilogy (Kensington) and the Dissonance series (S&S BFYR)

Read DECEPTION SO DEADLY (Book One) and DECEPTION SO DARK (Book Two) today!

AFTERMATH

CLARA KENSIE

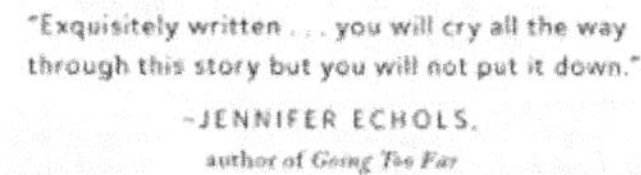

Charlotte survived four long years as a prisoner in the attic of her kidnapper, sustained only by dreams of her loving family. The chance to escape suddenly arrives, and Charlotte fights her way to freedom. But an answered prayer turns into heartbreak. Losing her has torn her family apart. Her parents have divorced: Dad's a glutton for fame, Mom drinks too much, and Charlotte's twin is a zoned-out druggie. Her father wants Charlotte write a book and go on a lecture tour, and her mom wants to keep her safe, a virtual prisoner in her own home. But Charlotte is obsessed with the other girl who was kidnapped, who never got a second chance at life--the girl who nobody but Charlotte believes really existed. Until she can get justice for that girl, even if she has to do it on her own, whatever the danger, Charlotte will never be free.

"For all of us who have watched the chilling news of kidnapped females rescued and thought 'There but for the grace of God' and 'How do they go on?'...here is the answer fully imagined, exquisitely written, ultimately triumphant. You will cry all the way through this story but you will not put it down." ~Jennifer Echols, award-winning author of *Going Too Far*

"Kensie deftly explores what happens after the supposedly happy ending of a nightmare. But nothing is as simple as it seems--not even the truth." ~April Henry, author of *The Girl I Used to Be*; *Girl, Stolen*; and *The Night She Disappeared*

"A captivating story of self-(re)discovery, Clara Kensie's Aftermath introduces us to Charlotte, a sixteen-year-old girl trying hard to reclaim her place in a family decimated by her kidnapping four years earlier. Charlotte wants only to catch up to her twin Alexa and live out all the plans they'd made as children, but finds the journey back to 'normal' is not only hers to take. Charlotte is a heroine to cheer for...with gut-twisting bravery and raw honesty, she takes us through that journey--back to the unspeakable tortures she endured in captivity and forward to how those years scarred her family, leaving us intensely hopeful and confident that she will not merely survive, but triumph." ~Patty Blount, author of *Some Boys*; *Send*; *TMI*; and *Nothing Left to Burn*

"Delving deep into the darkness of abduction and its 'Aftermath,' Kensie takes us on an unflinching journey of healing, courage, and triumph of the human spirit. Heartbreaking, yet stubbornly hopeful." ~Sonali Dev, author of *A Bollywood Affair* and *The Bollywood Bride*

"*Aftermath* is a timely, powerful portrait of hope amid tragedy, strength amid brokenness, and the healing power of forgiveness." ~Erica O'Rourke, award-winning author of the Torn trilogy and the Dissonance series

"Gripping, powerful, deeply moving, *Aftermath* is a book I didn't want to end. It's written with such compassion that it will help readers heal. A must-read." ~Cheryl Rainfield, author of *Scars* and *Stained*

A Children's Book Review pick for one of the Best New Young Adult Books, November 2016

Get your copy of AFTERMATH!

LOOK FOR MORE YA AND NA SPECULATIVE FICTION READS FROM SNOWY WINGS PUBLISHING

Snowy Wings
PUBLISHING

ALL THE TALES WE TELL

ANNIE COSBY

"A darkly romantic beginning to what promises to be

an unusual contemporary YA fantasy series." —USA Today

She's filthy rich. He's not. It'll take patience, an old woman who thinks she's a selkie, and one salty-sweet summer on the beach to make them realize what's between them.

When Cora's mother whisks the family away for the summer, Cora must decide between forging her future in the glimmering world of second homes where her parents belong, or getting lost in the enchanting world of the locals and the mystery surrounding a lonely old woman who claims to be a selkie—and who probably needs Cora more than anyone else.

Through the fantastical tales and anguished memories of the batty Mrs. O'Leary, as well as the company of a particularly gorgeous local boy called Ronan, Cora finds an escape from the reality of planning her life after high school. But will it come at the cost of alienating Cora's mother, who struggles with her own tragic memories?

As the summer wanes, it becomes apparent that Mrs. O'Leary is desperate to leave Oyster Beach. And Ronan just may hold the answer to her tragic past—and Cora's future.

ALL THE TALES WE TELL is a sweet YA contemporary romance with a dash of Celtic magic. If you like classic boy-meets-girl stories and blurring the line between fantasy and reality, then you'll love Annie Cosby's magical tale of first love riddled with mythical mysteries.

Buy ALL THE TALES WE TELL today to start the summer adventure that USA Today calls "darkly romantic"!

WHEN DARKNESS WHISPERS

HEATHER L. REID

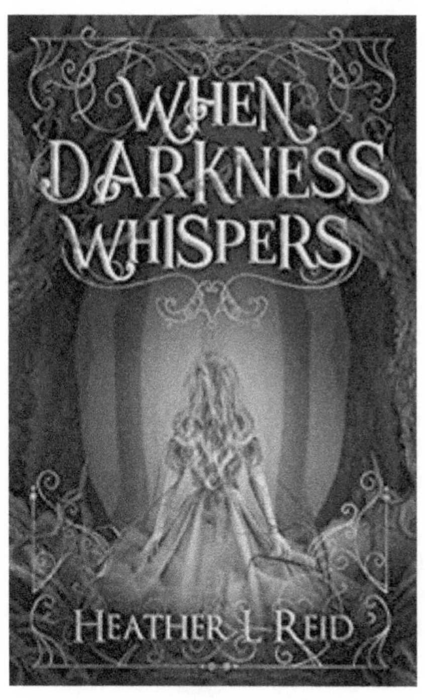

It's time to choose: Love or lies, faith or fear, darkness or destiny.

Quinn Taylor hasn't slept through the night in months. Not since the demons from her dreams began materializing in the school hallway, feeding on her fears, and whispering of her death. Trading in her cheerleading uniform for caffeine drinks to keep the nightmares at bay, Quinn's life is in ruins from the demons' torment until Aaron, an amnesiac with a psychic ability, accidentally enters her dreams. He's the light in her darkness and she's the key to his past, but the last thing the demons want is for them to be together. To keep them apart, the demons must convince Quinn that Aaron will betray her or, worse, confirm her fear that she's crazy. Aaron and Quinn's combined powers could banish the darkness for good, but only if she learns to trust her heart and he recovers the secret locked away in his fragile memory. That is, unless the demons kill them first.

Buy your copy of WHEN DARKNESS WHISPERS today!

ALEXANDRA'S RIDDLE

ELISA KEYSTON

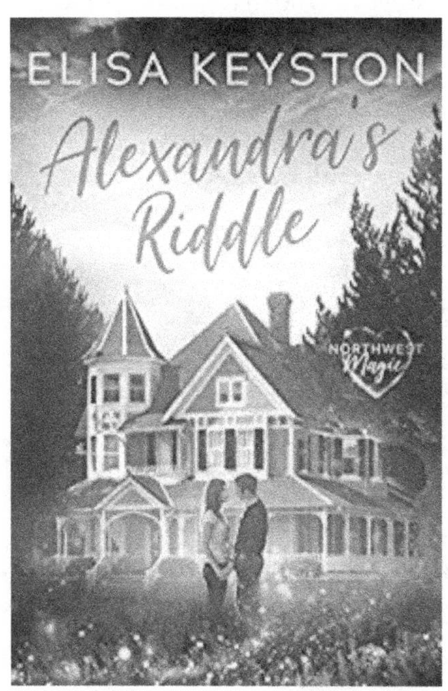

Lose yourself in the magical forests and charming towns of the Pacific Northwest, where picturesque

Victorian homes hide mysteries spanning decades, faeries watch from the trees, and romance awaits... for those bold enough to seek it.

Cass is a drifter. When she inherits an old Queen Anne Victorian in rural Oregon from her great-aunt Alexandra, all she wants is to quickly offload the house and move on to bigger and better things. But the residents of the small town have other plans in mind. Her neighbors are anxious for her to help them thwart the plans of a land developer eager to raze Alexandra's property, while a mysterious girl in the woods needs Cass's help understanding her own confusing, possibly supernatural abilities.

And though little surprises Cass (thanks to her own magical powers of prediction), she never could have anticipated her newfound feelings for the handsome fourth-grade teacher at the local elementary school—feelings that she thought she'd buried long ago. Cass has sworn off love, but Matthew McCarthy is unlike anyone Cass has ever met. If she isn't careful, he could learn her secret. Or worse—he just might thaw her frozen heart.

But falling in love could spell danger for both of them. Because it's not just the human residents of Riddle that have snared Cass in their web. Cass's presence has caught the attention of the fae that dwell in the woods. They know she has the Sight, and they don't want to let her go...

With its unique blend of small-town romance, cozy mystery, and light fantasy, the Northwest Magic series is sure to delight anyone who believes in faery gifts and happily-ever-afters. Read FREE in Kindle Unlimited and get lost in the magic now!